FOR GEMS AND GLORY

For Gems and Glory

ISABELLE M GUERNICA

THE GEMS AND GLORY SERIES
BOOK THREE
For Gems and Glory
By Isabelle M. Guernica

Guernica Publishing LLC.

Cover Art by Barbara J. Kennerly
Edited by Jaime Ryter at The Ryter's Proof

This is a work of fiction. Any similarities between real people, places, or situations is completely coincidental. This book is recommended for readers eighteen and older due to language, depictions of blood, gore, sexually explicit scenes, and other events that may be triggering for some readers.

WARNING

This book contains plenty of violent and sexually explicit scenes. Not to mention, it is a why-choose. Which means the FMC will enter a completely consensual relationship with multiple male love interests.
There is no cheating.
This is a dark fantasy romance. There are mentions of rape, mentions of suicide, depictions of gore, sexually explicit scenes between the FMC and her multiple partners, and finally, monster x female love making.

No. I'm not sorry. If you've made it this far in the series, then you should've expected as much.

Have fun, fellow nightmares.

THE GEMS AND GLORY SERIES
BOOK THREE

For Gems and Glory

Isabelle M. Guernica

For my loyal readers.
Thank you.

IT'S MY IDEA TO CALL IT THE REVERIE.
ATTICUS DOESN'T BELIEVE IN IT, AND ATLAS
IS INDIFFERENT ON THE MATTER.
BIT I THINK IT'LL WORK.
IT'S A WAY TO KEEP US CONNECTED DESPITE
FIGHTING ON DIFFERENT FRONTS. ON
DIFFERENT SIDES OF THE WAR.
I FIGHT FOR THE CELESTIALS, WHILE
ATTICUS HAS SINCE PLEDGED ALLEGIANCE
TO A FEW OTHERS, AND ATLAS REMAINS IN
THE MIDLANDS.

WE BURIED OUR PARENTS THREE WEEKS AGO.
I HAVEN'T SEEN MY BROTHERS SINCE.

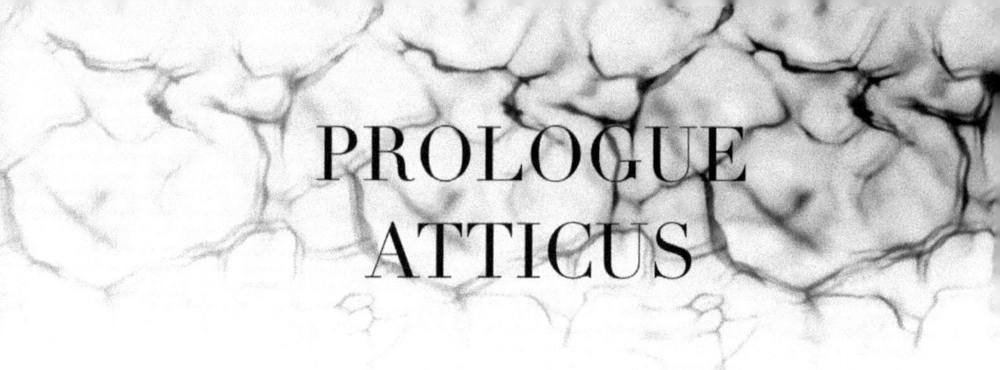

PROLOGUE
ATTICUS

We're surrounded by enemies.

Why does it feel as though we're *always* surrounded by ene-mies?

Apollo, followed by the Apostles that masquerade around in the Zodiacs' bodies, alongside hundreds of angelic foot soldiers, cover us on all sides. For better or worse, though, the foot soldiers are not as powerful as the others, but the sheer number of them definitely has me taking pause.

I'm not much of a gambling man, but even I know the odds are not in our favor.

The atmosphere around us is suffocating, and I nearly choke on the poisonous *evils* and forbidden magic that taint the air. I roar and erupt again, alarmingly mindful of the Falls of Man as they flow upward into the sky, straight into the menacing storm eye that brews above us.

I've lost sight of my brothers, and darkness and miasma cloud my vision as I am forced to a knee, my magic failing me as it is robbed from me.

I fucking hate thieves.

There is only one thief I can tolerate, and thank the stars she isn't here in the middle of all this shit, here to see us fall and struggle so pathetically against vile monsters that seek to harm our spheres and homes. Seek to harm her.

I will not allow it.

I roar again, the darkness suffocating me, forcing its way down my throat to swirl in my chest. Claiming my eyesight and mind and clamping down on my power, and when I erupt again to be rid of the foreign entity, I'm able to clear the haze just in time to meet Alastair's eyes as a *witch* plunges her sword through his chest.

Time stills.

And then I'm running.

Bolting toward my eldest brother as he falls lifelessly to the blood-soaked soil, his heart still in the hand of the witch that bears a striking resemblance to a young, red-headed Lilith.

But that cannot be. For sweet spice killed the crone. Ripped her to pieces when in her feral wolf state back in the Celestial Palace where that winged fuck, Apollo, held her captive.

But nobody has *ever* succeeded in taming Rhesa. She is not one who can be so easily shackled.

I slide through the mud and blood onto my knees, hoisting my brother's lifeless body into my arms as I scream his name. But Alastair's eyes are already glazed over, the silver dull and turning gray.

"*ATTICUS!*" roars Atlas, and I whirl around with Alastair's body still firmly pressed against my chest as I face my other brother's back. His wings are spread wide as he shields me from the witch once more, her sword piercing all the way through his chest and protruding from his back.

He falls forward, and in vain, I try to grab him. Atlas slumps out of my hands, which are slippery with blood, and I roll him onto his back to remove the sword from his chest. But it's no use, because, like Alastair, his heart is already gone.

I sit there on my knees between my fallen brothers, their blood staining my hands as I begin to *vibrate* with rage. My magic crackles across my skin dangerously, splitting the ground beneath me.

And then I hear Rhesamyre's blood-curdling scream.

I snap my head up and bolt toward the wretched sound, eviscerating other angels as I go and nearly forgetting why we were out here in the first place. All that matters is getting to Rhesamyre before that wicked witch kills her, too. And through the suffocating miasma, I spot the crone as she holds Rhesa above the ground by her throat. Her feet dangle and thrash as the witch squeezes the life out of her, her mouth agape as her eyes bulge from her head from the force of the witch's steel grip.

I roar and scream her name, and Rhesa manages to glance at me and spare me a pathetic smile before the witch finishes crushing her throat. Rhesa crumbles to the ground, her head barely attached to her shoulders now that her neck is nothing but a few bloody strands and threads of flesh. I fall to my knees in an attempt to foolishly find her eyes, and I think I'm still screaming, but her eyes are already glazed over like my brothers' and nearly popped out of her skull from the force of being strangled as brutally as she was.

I tip my head back and keep roaring. My wings flare as I scream and explode and eviscerate the rest of the angels that are unfortunate enough to be caught in the blast. Then all goes silent.

I lower my head, my shoulders heavy with my wings and the weight of my rage and grief as I stare at Rhesa's broken body. What was she even *doing* here? Why did she come here?

And how the hell is the witch alive?

I blink away the tears on my lashes, letting them roll over my cheeks and off my chin as I glance around for the crone, but she's nowhere in sight, so I make a move to hold Rhesa again. However, when I grab her, she just . . . *vanishes*. Her skin and bones turn to dust, and the obsidian glitter stains my hands and slips through my fingers like ash. Ahead of me, my brothers' bodies do the same until nothing is left of them. Any sign that they ever existed vanishes from sight, and all I'm left with are the memories of our time together.

Fuck the memories.

I want my family back. I want her back. I WANT—

I whirl around and command a sword to erupt in my hands as I steel myself to defend against whoever the fuck is stupid enough to approach me right now.

The Zodiacs and Apollo stand off behind this new male who approaches me cautiously, as if I'm some cornered, hissing animal gearing up to attack. Though I suppose that is fitting.

The stranger keeps his hands up where I can see them, saying to me slowly, "I mean you no harm, Deity of Chaos and Control."

I snarl and seethe, "I know who you are, *Lucifer*. And you're a bloody liar." I steel myself. "You are no friend of mine."

The strange, battered, and ugly male who wears torn robes and has access to nearly *limitless* wells of power slowly shakes his head. His shaggy, balding hair shifts with the action. "All I want is to coexist here with all of you in peace. The death of the queen of Hell was unnecessarily brutal, and letting her die was never my intention."

I cock my head at him, furrowing my brows. "She banished you once."

He nods. "She did, but I vowed to myself I would do things differently this time. I do not wish you harm, and I apologize that I did not get here in time to save your lover and brothers."

I snarl viciously, getting back on my feet. "Never speak of them."

Lucifer bows his head, bloodshot, black eyes cruel and narrowed. "I won't . . . . Would you please put down the sword and return to Hell with me, Chaos?"

My entire being is *screaming* at me to refuse this male's offer. My instincts and magic hiss within me, violently whispering *liar* as my beast retreats deeper inside of me to get away from him. And maybe it's the grief that compels me to do it, or maybe I just don't give a fuck now that Rhesa and my brothers are dead. Nonetheless, I find myself staring down at my sword, my fist white-knuckling the hilt as I hesitate.

Hesitation is only useful for those who plan to scheme and plot. To decide whether or not this fight is worth it, and if it's one I'll walk away from in the end.

But I don't believe I care about such foolish goals anymore. Living to see the end of the day . . . that was a mated man's dream.

I sheathe my sword and step toward Lucifer.

The self-proclaimed god grins at me with black teeth, then opens a conveyance straight into the throne room of Hell. The Zodiacs—*Apostles*—and Apollo follow us through, keeping their distance from me.

Smart move.

When we arrive, I am taken aback by the sheer amount of carnage that litters the chamber. Another stranger has taken a seat upon the Obsidian Throne, but I don't focus on him for long as I look to the center of the room, where the Horsemen and Seven Deadly Assassins gather around a beaten, bruised, and bloody lump on the floor. They back up, and I meet each of their cold, apathetic gazes before I lower my eyes to spy the woman on the ground, lying in a pool of her own blood.

For a moment, my eyes play tricks on me again, and I could swear I see *Rhesa* crumpled there. However, I hiss when my magic growls, and a migraine causes my head to pulse as though someone has taken a hammer to it, and when I blink again, I find it to be the witch that slayed Rhesamyre and my brothers at the Falls. She bleeds out on the tiles, her breaths labored and eyes closed.

Lucifer certainly works fast.

"The witch will be punished for her crimes," he drawls with a broken grin, prowling toward the woman on the floor, nudging her body with the tip of his boot, regarding her as though she is nothing more than a stain on the bottom of his shoe. "In the meantime, though I know you hate to hear it, Chaos, Hell needs a ruler, which is where my friend, *Abaddon,* comes into the fray."

I slowly peel my eyes away from the witch to gaze up at the Obsidian Throne, where another red-skinned demon sits. He watches me warily, sitting on the edge of the black seat as though he intends to bolt should I take another step toward him.

I cock my head at him, muttering, "You resemble the old Cruel One . . . . You're his son."

Abaddon the Second nods, and I dismiss him for now as I glance around at the Seven and Horsemen again. Their eyes are downcast, scowls firmly in place, bodies rigid. None of them address me nor inquire as to what has happened and what we are to do now, but I find myself not caring at the moment, but I do take note of the fact that Mamba has disappeared, too.

My magic whirrs inside of me, warring with my grief and whispering *we will not stand for this. Avenge them all.*

Burn them all.

I grip the hilt of my sheathed sword and stare at the demon upon *her* throne, and he braces just before I slide my gaze back to Lucifer.

He's already smirking at me. Knowingly, daringly, and I have half a mind to say fuck it and indulge him.

"I would advise against such a careless action, Chaos," he drawls. "You and I may be allies."

"A world where you and I are allies isn't a world worth saving or living in." I draw my weapon, and my magic crackles along my skin and under my boots. "I am not your friend."

Lucifer's smile slowly disappears, and in its place is pure *evil*. A dark, cruel face that doesn't even scowl. He just stares. Assesses. And when I flash forward and strike, he barely manages to evade my steel. I spin and open a conveyance, then clash weapons with *fucking* Apollo when he jumps in front of the self-proclaimed god.

"You're a special breed of motherfucker," I snarl, pressing against him until the floor beneath us *cracks*. "*Fucking bastard. She was your sister!*"

Apollo growls, and I shove him backward before spinning to defend myself against one of the assassins. I'm not even sure which one, but the rest, including the Horsemen, swiftly follow suit.

This is one fight I may not win.

I erupt and take out half the fucking palace with me in the process, and the next conveyance I open is one belonging to that of a coward, and where I land is somewhere isolated and fucking cold.

I lose myself in the bloodshed. For a time, it is
the only place I dare to call home.
Not you two or our allies and friends.
No. I feel most like myself when I am
slaughtering our enemies. Violence has become
a dear friend of mine.
And it scares me. I am afraid of myself.
Alastair? Atticus?
Are you still out there?

CHAPTER ONE
RHESAMYRE

The stone floor is hard beneath my body, and the cold bites into my skin through the thin scraps of clothing I've managed to keep hold of to preserve what is left of my modesty, a concept I have never once bothered with until now. Foul smells of rotten blood, waste, and bodily fluids linger in the stale air of the cells, while a constant *drip, drip* has become the only sound of steady consistency throughout these halls of torment and torture. Whether it's from leaky pipes or from the blood that drips from the bodies that hang upside down in a few of the cells over, I'm not entirely sure.

Pain lingers throughout my body. From my broken toes, shattered kneecaps, bruised and broken ribs, dislocated shoulder, and down to the fractured bones of my wrists and fingers. Everything is purple and angry and infected and inflamed and *crooked*. Dried blood clings to me, and my face has begun to itch from my broken nose and other cuts. My left eye is still partially swollen shut, and my head fucking *hurts*. My horns are heavy, and my hair is tangled and matted, falling around me in messy ringlets down to my waist.

I fought them for hours.

My uncles had been collared by Abaddon and whatever black magic and forbidden curses he had access to thanks to Lucifer, and unfortunately, my family didn't bat an eye when he ordered them to attack me.

So I fought.

I screamed and kicked and punched and commanded alchemy and wielded obsidian with tears in my eyes, but all *eleven* of them at once . . .

I fought as hard as I could for as long as I could stand, but it wasn't enough. And my uncles—*Abaddon*—won. Because in the end, I didn't *want* to hurt my family, and my magic knew that. So I didn't erupt . . . it would have killed them, and I would not have survived that.

I only hope I can survive *this* instead.

I close my eyes, forcing another painful breath into my rattling lungs as I tip my temple to the side so I may rest my head against the bloodstained wall of my cell. I don't know exactly how long I've been here, but they've had enough time to force poison down my throat to keep me from healing. My horns and demonic features remain since I am still in Hell, but my magic hides deep within me, and I'm unable to properly access it. Not to mention, the wards of the cells won't allow it, either.

Not when I am considered a *prisoner*.

Thankfully, I do not share my confines with the others here, but that doesn't keep them from watching me and reaching for me through the bars. I'm curled up in the furthest corner by the wall, and they all coo and curse and spit at me. Demons and monsters and soulless slaves alike. Just watching and lurking and waiting for the minute they'll be given a chance to take a bite out of the *dethroned* queen of Hell herself.

Dirty mongrels, the lot of them. Covered in blood and grime and shit. Many are naked and take advantage of the sight of me when they begin to *pleasure* themselves. Groaning and grunting as they slide their disgusting, lustful gazes up and down my body, their bloodshot eyes snagging on whatever patches of my bruised skin they can find.

I refuse to shift away. I refuse to hide behind my curtain of matted, tangled hair. I just keep my gaze downcast, my jaw locked, committing their faces to memory so I may better plot my revenge *when* I get out of here.

My hit list increases by the hour. With not much else to do but recall how I ended up here, count my regrets and mistakes, and wallow in my pain and grief, I can't think of a better way to pass the time than to scheme the best ways to carve my enemies' bones out of their bodies while they're still alive.

I must not go mad if I am to get out of here and reclaim my crown and throne and kingdom. I *cannot* lose myself here.

Though it is dangerously tempting. As all things in Hell often are.

That is part of the magic worked into the runes and wards of these cells. It slithers and prowls, on the hunt for weak and broken minds to torment, whispering in prisoners' ears how it would be so easy to give up. To give in. That death is a mercy, and the magic of this place craves blood. Swallowing souls and screams alike as it feasts on the last of their hope.

His boots echo down the corridor toward me again, between the screams and shrieks of terror that often punctuate the silence, and I watch in quiet satisfaction as my neighboring prisoners scurry away from the bars of my cell and back into the furthest corners of their own. Many of them start to pray for mercy again, either to stars, angels, or gods, none of which care to listen as they shiver and shake in fear, their bones nearly rattling as their heartbeats pick up.

He whistles as he approaches, jingling his keys and scraping his iron rod across the bars as he prowls toward my cell. And when his shadow falls over me, I watch him through my lashes, his silhouette illuminated menacingly thanks to the dull, enchanted lights of the stone corridors that flicker pathetically.

Warden Bael grins at me, but I keep hold of my scowl.

I will not flinch. I will not yield. I won't let you taste my fear.

"Would you like to play again, little bitch?" he drawls, cocking his ugly head. "I do thoroughly enjoy *playtime* with you."

As to whether or not the warden has fallen under the same spell as the rest of the Hellion militia, I truly cannot tell. He never was that fond of me, but his loyalties to Hell and the obsidian throne kept him civilized enough when dealing with me as both the princess and queen of this kingdom. He was one of many who believed I was the devil's bastard, and therefore undeserving of the crown and claims to rule over Hell.

I suppose it truly doesn't matter to him who's sitting on that throne, though. And the infamous master of torture that oversees Castle Blackstone will certainly not pass up the chance to *play* with me. He believes I have betrayed Hell, after all, as he so *eloquently* explained when breaking my bones and shoving hot iron pokers against my skin.

His keys jingle, and my cell door creaks open noisily. Two of his guards, who resemble a boar and a buck, stride in, and they grab me from underneath my arms to drag me toward the scowling warden. Pain erupts throughout my body as I am jostled and dragged through the halls past other prisoners, but I merely grit my teeth and keep quiet for as long as I can.

I will not give him my screams.

I will not flinch. I will not yield. I won't let you taste my fear, I repeat to myself, and it takes all my willpower and training not to flinch at the sight of the chains that hang from the ceiling of this larger cell. Other torture devices, machines, and workbenches litter the walls, surrounded by more chains, knives, saws, various serrated blades, barbed wires, whips, and then of course, the familiar ingredients and tools needed to shove more poison down my throat to keep my magic *leashed*.

The boar and buck lift my near-useless arms upward to shackle me to the ceiling; my bare, bloody feet barely touch the ground, and they shackle my ankles together to ensure I can't kick their dear warden in the balls *again*.

That act of rebellion is what shattered my kneecaps, but it was fucking worth it, and I'd do it again in a heartbeat to hear his pathetic whimper and see his disgruntled, pain-riddled, and enraged face.

The demons back away from me, and my back arches and strains as I hang; my skin pulls taut, ripping a few of my cuts open again, thanks to the stress of hanging from the fucking ceiling. Warden Bael circles me, and I keep my gaze forward as I feel his fingers trail along my abused skin, pressing into some of the injuries and picking at the few scabs that have formed.

"Such a beauty," he breathes as he trails his nose up the side of my neck, his foul, stale breath mingling with the other scents of these poisonous halls. "You're even prettier hanging from my ceiling, your blood staining my floor due to the pain I have inflicted upon you. It gets me so *fucking hard*."

He *licks* me, then chuckles and backs away with a disgusting grin. When he turns his back to me to survey his tools, I allow myself a single shudder, steeling myself for what is to come.

"Now, then," he drawls, picking up a few different blades of varying styles and sizes, and the black metal gleams in the dim light. "Where did your friends flee to?"

I stay quiet.

"We've already been down this road a few times before, *Rhesamyre*. And we know the lieutenants and a few others fled with beasts such as Mamba in tow. We just want to know *where* they *went*."

Silence is my ally. It will keep my friends safe. What is left of my family, I will protect.

Warden Bael clicks his tongue in disapproval as he finally settles on a menacing, serrated blade. He does a piss-poor job of hiding his excitement as he turns to face me again, and I would almost gamble he *wants me* to keep my secrets to myself, prolong this wicked, torturous game he has going on between us.

He cocks his head at me, pouting dramatically as he draws nearer. "Nothing to say?" he muses. "That smart mouth of yours always seems to be working overtime, yet you've gone quiet these past few days."

I raise my eyes from his chest to meet his wild gaze and murmur something under my breath. Bael raises his brow, then stalks closer and pinches my chin roughly to raise my head.

"Speak up!" he snarls.

I spit at him.

Bael growls and backhands me harshly, and my head whips to the side as his studded rings cut my cheeks. But I force myself to snicker lowly and meet his eyes again. My bloody spittle drips from his cheeks, and he wipes it away with a glower.

I grin, feeling blood pool in my mouth once more as I repeat, *"Get. Fucked."*

Bael roars, then grabs my horns roughly to pull my head back as he slices my shirt away to expose more of my skin to him, *his canvas.* His blade gets to work carving and cutting away pieces of me. Sometimes slowly and deeply, other times swiftly and brutally. I'm proud of myself for keeping my jaw locked for the first many slices as he switches between using different blades, but by the time he adds in the hot poker that burns my flesh away, I'm *screaming*.

....

I don't know when exactly I blacked out or how long I was given a break from him due to me passing out, but when I blink my eyes open again, I find I'm still chained to the ceiling. The room has been dimmed, and only a single enchanted torch flickers upon the wall ahead of me, illuminating his tools. I strain my ears to hear if I am alone, and though my head pounds and I can hardly hear anything over the ringing in my ears, I believe they have left me here to hang in misery.

I try to roll my head and ease some of the tension in my torn shoulders, but it's no use, and everything aches. I can feel blood sliding down my skin and dripping to the floor, a puddle forming beneath me, and I drop my head again and try to close my eyes.

A steady stride echoes into the cell, and I crack my eyes open just enough to find polished boots standing nearby; the tips splash into my blood, and when he crouches to the floor to look up at me, my eyes clash with gold.

Apollo kneels below me, his golden eyes appearing as tortured as I feel as he surveys my form. *The magic of the cells*, I think to myself. Because this version of Apollo . . . this is my *big brother* crouching before me, not the archangel who fraternized and bargained with Lucifer to undermine Hell and use Adriel as a conduit of that forbidden, soul-rendering power to murder Samael.

I do my best to clear my throat, coughing a little as I mutter hoarsely in Enochian, "You're back."

"I told you I would be," he claims softly, his gaze crestfallen as he surveys my broken form. "It pains me to see you like this, little feather."

I close my eyes at the nickname, and when I open them again, Apollo is standing upright, cupping my jaw gently with both hands. His touch is featherlight and warm, and I *almost* believe it to be real. I almost want it to be.

"You're not real," I murmur. "Just a figment of my imagination and the magic of this place playing tricks on me. Attempting to break me by further torturing me with either visions or memories of you . . . I don't know."

"Or it's trying to save you," he replies, his handsome face revealing nothing but anguish. "You're not broken yet, but it's inevitable that you will begin to fade. No matter how strong you are, Bael will have his way with you. Perhaps the wards of these cells still recognize you as the rightful queen of Hell, and are allowing your mind to seek solace by retreating into better memories that you don't acknowledge anymore. Hell is under attack, baby sister. And if you want it back, want your *family* back, then you need to remember why and *how* you fought against Lucifer in the first place."

"You brought him here," I accuse halfheartedly. "Or, at least . . . the real one did."

"Aye. I did, but that's because I forgot, too. Do better than me. *Be better than me*, and don't let anyone forget ever again, Myra."

I huff. "Hate to break it to you, big bro, but I won't be helping anyone anytime soon."

Apollo nods. "Your allies await your commands. They're working tirelessly to free Hell and you, as well as be ready to fight against Lucifer with you, just as we did thousands of years ago. *But the spheres are burning*, Rhesamyre. The magic is enraged and fighting amongst itself and against the foreign spells Lucifer has muttered across the lands, and we want our home back."

"How do you know that?"

"He told you to *never forget that we remember you.*"

I close my eyes, whispering, "*Kure* . . . you're one of *his*. A prophet."

Apollo shakes his head. "You're half right, but I'm not one of Kure's *pets*. The magic within our spheres is *sentient*, little feather. In this very castle, inside of you, and elsewhere. Including the very magic that Lucifer learned to shackle and harness through forbidden soul work, too. *Hell remembers*. And I am here to remind you of that. Here to keep you sane and as safe as possible without alerting Bael and thus Lucifer of what we're up to. You need to stay strong, *Champion*. For we cannot do this without you."

"Why . . . why me?"

Apollo cups my cheeks, rubbing his thumbs over my cheekbones as he all but begs, "*Let me show you.* Please, Rhesamyre. Let me help you remember why it is you. Why it *has* to be you. You denied me once before when I approached you a few days ago . . . but I know you long for an escape."

I go to shake my head no, but his golden eyes bore into mine and make me hesitate. The sincerity there is honest and startlingly real, and I . . . I long for something warmer right now. Perhaps I do need the reminder. Perhaps I do want it.

Slowly, I nod my head, and pure relief washes over Apollo as he kisses my forehead and murmurs in Old Latin, "*Reclaim your memories, Champion. You were robbed of them once, so you must take them back. Because what are you?*"

"*A thief,*" I whisper.

. . . .

I clutch my big brother's tattooed hand tightly as I stand between him and Sammy. 'Pollo said I could join them this time, so long as I promised to stay close and keep quiet while they "play politics."

Whatever the heck that means.

The people we stand before do not bear wings nor power like my brothers clad in white and gray leathers. They smell different, too; they stink of prey and fear, and only a few in this crowd of men and women are actually attractive. At least in angelic terms. Not at all lithe nor muscular like the celestials back home. And they have foul mouths on them, too. Spitting curses I've only heard Sammy and Lux say when they think I'm not close enough to hear them. But I do.

Sammy called them **mortals***. Humans. Creatures that make up the magicless lands of this kingdom and only survive to work and die. Of course, I recall them from my studies with Nihal, but I've never met or seen a mortal before now.*

'Pollo keeps talking in their language. I think he's attempting to settle whatever dispute is causing havoc and bloodshed as a civil war breaks out across this sphere. But I don't really listen as I study the mean-looking forms of these mortals. None of the adults meet my eyes, but I do eventually find the gaze of a little boy about my size. He clutches his mother's hand just as I clutch my brother's, and the boy cocks his head at me curiously. I do the same, then look up at Sammy.

Seeming to sense my gaze, Sammy glances down at me with those kind, dark eyes of his. The metallic color matches his massive wings, and I've always marveled at the size of them.

I hope mine grows to be as big as his one day.

I wave him down toward me in a **come here** *motion, and he raises his brow in amusement as he crouches next to me expectantly, putting us almost at eye level, but he's still a little bigger than me.*

"You see that boy out there?" I ask.

Sammy glances out at the crowd, finding the boy with ease before he looks at me again.

"Can I go play with him?"

Sammy purses his lips, looking ready to deny me before I pout and beg, "Please? I don't ever get to meet anyone my age."

He narrows his eyes, obviously thinking it over before he sighs and gives in. "Okay, but stay nearby where we can see you. Deal?"

He holds out his pinky finger for me, and I giggle as I hook mine with his. "Deal."

Sammy stands upright again, whispering something to Apollo, thus causing my brother to pause his speech, narrow his eyes at the boy in question, and then look down at me. He squeezes my hand once and then lets me go. I grin at him, then hop down the stairs of the outdoor theatre stage and make my way through the crowd of mortals that immediately parts for me.

Their eyes are wary, but I pay them no mind as my wings twitch on my back, enticing me to skip off the ground a little as I bounce up to the boy. He cowers behind his mother's knees, but I cock my head at him and smile as I greet in his language, "Hello!"

He looks up at his mother, but then swallows and says to me with a little wave, "Hi."

"You look like you're my age! I'm Myra!"

He steps out from behind his mother's legs, and she threads her fingers through his hair before pushing him toward me gently.

"I'm Jacob."

I giggle, grabbing his hand. "C'mon, Jacob!"

Jacob follows me through the crowd and up to the nearby tree line of the Forest of Souls, and I meet my brothers' eyes once more before they turn their attention back to the crowd.

Plucking a feather off my dark wings, I hold it in my hands and concentrate really hard to shape it into a small ball.

"Whoa," says Jacob, coming up to me to observe the small, black ball in my hands. "How'd you do that?"

I shrug, backing up and tossing it to him. "Magic is magic. It doesn't always need nor desire an explanation. Only our respect."

At least, that's what my brothers tell me.

Jacob makes a funny face at me, catching the ball before throwing it back to me.

"I wish I could do that," he says.

I scrunch my nose. "I can't do much else. My brothers are the ones with all the cool powers."

"So I've been warned. Your brothers are scary looking."

I giggle. "Yeah, I guess they kind of are. But to me, they're just my brothers. Do you have any siblings?"

"I used to . . . I had an older brother, too. But he died in the last fight we had with the neighboring villages. Your brothers are apparently here to settle the arguments because the adults here can't. Why can't we all just get along?"

"I dunno. I ask my brothers about that, too. But they say not to worry about the matters of foolish adults."

Jacob hums.

"So, what do you do around here for fun?"

"Oh, umm." He lifts his shoulders. "Not much, really. I'm usually busy helping my ma and pa around the house. Sometimes the other village kids and I will run around, but since the attacks have gotten worse these past few weeks, a lot of them have moved away, closer to the capital, where it's safer."

I wrinkle my nose in confusion. "The capital isn't safer. I've heard things are worse there, between all the robberies and crime."

Jacob's eyes bug out of his head. Oops. *I guess I wasn't supposed to share that tidbit.*

Since he's distracted, he accidentally tosses the ball higher into the branches of the nearest tree. We watch as it gets stuck, held captive by the leaves, and I frown at the sight.

"My bad," says Jacob sheepishly. "I'm sorry."

I shake my head at him. "No worries!"

Then I move toward the trunk to run my hands up and down the bark, looking for a foothold. When I find one, I start to climb in my little dress and leggings that Lux picked out for me, and make my way up the tree and toward the branches to shake the ball free.

"Can't you fly?" asks Jacob, stretching his hands out to catch the ball while I attempt to shake it free.

"No," I grunt. "Not yet. They're not big enough."

"Oh . . . when will they be big enough?"

"When I turn eleven or twelve. That's what my brothers tell me."

Finally, I manage to shake the ball free, and Jacob catches it when it falls. He grins up at me, and I smile as I swing off the branch and land on my feet before losing my balance and falling on my clumsy butt.

Jacob laughs at me, and I pout and cross my arms dramatically as I whine, "Don't laugh at me!"

He reaches for me to help me back on my feet, and I take his hand gently. Smiling at him, we laugh together.

And that's how his face looks just before the arrow pierces his throat; his blood splatters across my face and pale dress, and he falls over, our hands still attached, and I don't think to let go of him, so I fall with him, on top of him.

And I scream for my brothers.

In a flash, Samael has his hands around my middle to hoist me up and away from Jacob, and Apollo is there, kneeling next to my bleeding friend.

"Heal him, Apollo!" I scream, sobbing while trying to wipe Jacob's blood off me.

Sammy catches my hands in a single palm, hushing me softly and pressing kisses into my black hair to get me to calm down, but I'm a wreck.

"Where the fuck did that arrow come from!" yells one of the mortal men as he draws closer with a crowd, including Jacob's mother.

She screams and slides to her knees next to her little boy while Apollo removes the arrow and begins to heal him, and all I can do is watch from the safety of Samael's arms. I'm still shaking, and my brother just holds me tighter.

"It's okay, my little feather," he coos. "Look. See? He'll be okay. Apollo's healing him. He's okay."

I sniffle, nodding my head as I turn my gaze toward the direction from which the arrow came, just as a man rushes forward from the woodwork of the forest. He takes in the scene before him before explaining how his friend's arrow missed its mark and went astray. Sammy curses quietly before he turns away to set me against a nearby tree trunk.

"Stay right here. Do. Not. Move, Myra," he commands, and I nod along.

Samael turns away to deal with the aftermath of the accident while Jacob breathes in deeply and sits up in his mother's lap. Completely healed, but sobbing uncontrollably while Apollo stands up to join Sam in getting to the bottom of this, since a few of the men have already begun to exchange punches instead of words.

A strangled, weakened sound reaches my ears, and I glance toward the deeper part of the forest in an attempt to pinpoint it. My brothers seem too busy to notice it, or if they do hear it, they choose to ignore it since they're busy with all this nonsense in front of them. But when I hear the noise of what sounds like a wounded animal again, I can't just ignore it.

So, disobeying Sam, I get up and run off toward the noise deeper in the forest. I can feel it humming with magic and power all around me, but as I near the whines of the wounded creature, the forest's hum almost turns into a menacing growl.

And soon enough, I learn why. For hidden in the woodwork, wounded and bleeding, is a massive stag with eight points and a shimmering, silver coat with faint patterns of angelic and demonic sigils and runes marked across his fur. He twitches and shifts in the dirt while two arrows protrude from his shoulder and between his ribs, and he groans and nearly growls as I approach him.

Cooing softly, I kneel next to him to run my hands through his soft, blood-soaked fur, and then I break and yank on the arrows. He bays in pain, muscles and legs twitching, and once I have the arrows out, I concentrate really, really hard to heal him like my brothers would. But when that doesn't seem to work, I almost panic again before I remember my feathers can heal, too.

So, I pluck two out of my wings, hissing at the sting, before I lay them over his wounds. His blood simmers against my small tufts of black fluff, darkening the fibers even more with his blood. Then a small flash breaks through, and when I blink again, his wounds are completely healed.

He stands up on strong legs, and I've never seen a stag as big and menacing as him. He towers over me, lowering his head to sniff me, and I giggle a little when his breath tickles my neck. His eyes are wondrous and large, appearing as though they're a part of the starry sky when the sun goes down. Dark and glittering and beautiful.

He noses me again, and I hug his face, but then his ears twitch, and he looks over my head and releases a low, territorial growl that sounds odd coming from a stag. I glance back over my shoulder, spotting three other mortals approaching us with bows and arrows drawn and nocked.

"Damn celestial brat," snarls one of them in the strange language of mortals. "Looks like she healed it."

*I turn up to the stag, then push on him gently and whisper, "Go."
He looks down at me, then back at the mortals, and I whisper again
with more urgency in my tone, "Run!"*

*The stag doesn't hesitate again and runs off into the forest, and
the men all curse amongst each other as they watch it go.*

"What the hell are we to do now?" one growls.

*"That would have fed all four of our families for a few weeks at
least," says another. "It was a bigg'en."*

*"Maybe we could . . ." The last one looks at me, and I cock my head
at him. He clears his throat, saying quietly to his friends as though I
won't still hear him. "I hear there are some that'll pay a hefty price for
an angel. Rumor has it their feathers can grant miracles when they're
young like this. We could take a few for ourselves and our families,
then sell her off when she's older. We wouldn't starve again."*

*The men look amongst each other with frowns, but I can tell by
their eyes that they're really considering it.*

*I take a step back, my little foot breaking a twig and catching on
a root, which catches their attention as I tumble backward onto my
bum again.*

"I don't know," drawls one. "I don't like this. She's just a kid."

*"We have children to feed, too, Martin. She's an angel brat. She'll
be fine wherever she goes.* **Our kids** *won't be. And you heard that
scream from the forest's edge. Odds are, Henry's arrow hit someone."
This male steps forward, but he hands his bow and quiver off to his
friend. "Hey there, little girl."*

*I shake my head. My brothers always warned me of strangers, but
just when I ready myself to bolt, the man lunges for me. I scream when
he tackles me, and within a second of the sound penetrating the surrounding forest, Apollo is there, ripping the man off me.*

"You wouldn't dare," he seethes slowly while holding the man up by his throat, and the sound of him making the threat so quietly scares me more than it would if he had yelled it.

Hands grasp me from under my arms again, and Samael sits me on his arm so he can meet my eyes as he reprimands, "What did I tell you, Myra?"

I hide my face in his neck, sniffling. "Stay right where I was and don't move."

He nods, rubbing my back soothingly despite his chest rumbling with a growl as he barks at Apollo, "Rip their bloody, fucking throats out, Apollo."

"Watch your language!" snarls Apollo, and when I glance at him, I find he's still strangling the man in mid-air.

Samael sighs, then glances at me. "Earmuffs, please, little feather."

I do as he commands and press my palms against my ears, and then I marvel at the sight of Sammy's lips moving rapidly as he no doubt curses up a storm at our brother and the mortals. However, when I watch Apollo's hand begin to squeeze tighter, I cry out and remove my hands from my head.

"Apollo! Don't!"

Apollo looks at me, narrowing his eyes. "Little feather—"

"No!" I squirm in Sammy's arms, and he reluctantly places me down so I can run up to Apollo. "Just wipe their memories and be done with it! They didn't mean to shoot Jacob, and they only thought about coming after me so they could provide for their families! They're not bad men! Just desperate!*"*

Apollo surveys my form for another minute and then throws the man to the ground as if he's discarding trash. Then, my brother, clad in gold, crouches in front of me and takes note of the dirt on my dress from my scuffle. Nothing can hurt archangels, but he still frowns at the sight of my torn leggings. Not to mention, I'm still splattered in Jacob's blood, too.

"Myra," he says softly. "They had every intention of hurting you. I cannot allow that to go unpunished."

"They're starving, hunting to survive and feed their families, not to mention **magicless.***" I cross my arms, huffing. "Their whole existence seems like punishment enough."*

Sammy chuckles behind me.

Apollo glares at Sam over my head, then sighs and meets my eyes again. "So then, what would you have me do? Just erase their memories of the event?"

I shrug, wringing my fingers. "I dunno . . . that's adult business . . . I just don't think it's right to kill them, either."

Apollo nods along, then rises to his full height again as he turns back to the mortal men. "You've been spared by her, gentlemen. Don't expect it to happen again. Because this little **misunderstanding** *will* **never** *happen again, correct?"*

"N-Never, Lord Apollo," sputters the man that he strangled, the one that tackled me. "We will never forget your mercy."

"It wasn't **his** *mercy," snarls Sam, stepping forward. He jerks his chin down at me, glowering at the men. "You owe your lives to her. Thank her properly."*

The men fall to their knees and nearly weep as they thank me, and I cock my head at the sight before reaching back to pluck four more feathers out of my wings. Then I stride toward the men and hold out my feathers, and they raise their heads with bloodshot eyes.

"Here," I murmur. "For your children."

They look over my head at my brothers, then carefully take my feathers as they whisper their thanks, marveling at the sight of my feathers in their palms as if they're precious gems.

Apollo picks me up and sets me on his arm, his eyes boring into mine. "You're too pure and generous for these spheres, little feather. I fear one day, they will swallow you whole."

I press my palms to his cheeks, giggling gently. "You won't let that happen."

He presses a kiss to my forehead. "No. I won't."

I DON'T KNOW WHAT ELSE TO DO
ASIDE FROM WRITE IN THIS DAMN
BOOK. WE NEVER SEE EACH OTHER
ANYMORE.
I DON'T EVEN KNOW WHO YOU'VE
DECIDED TO ALLY YOURSELVES WITH
NOW, BUT I KNOW WE'RE ON
DIFFERENT FRONTS AGAIN.
I'M STILL HERE, BROTHERS.
I'M STILL FUCKING HERE.

CHAPTER TWO
RHESAMYRE

I wake with a jolt, still chained to the ceiling, and glance up to find Bael moving about the cell, being unnecessarily loud in order to wake me up, no doubt.

Apollo is gone again, and I feel alone and empty once more.

I had forgotten that happened. That I actually came vis-à-vis with the Eight-Pointed Stag itself. It was a magnificent beast full of wonder and magic. The mortals hadn't known what they wounded; they just saw *dinner*. And then when they saw me, they saw a profit. A potential future that no longer included starving and hunting for every meal.

And I gave them my feathers. I gave them a *miracle*.

"Let's get you healed up a bit more, shall we?" muses Bael, approaching me once more with a vile of clear liquid in hand. "You'll be of no use to me in the mines if you can't even walk properly."

"And whose fault is that?" I snarl under my breath, but Bael hears me.

He grasps my jaw roughly, growling as he forces my mouth open. Uncorking the vile with his teeth, he pours the strange, sweet liquid into my mouth. I gag as it slides down my sore throat, and once Bael has successfully forced it into my body, he drops my head with a force that causes me to swing in my chains. Then, slowly, my body begins to mend itself. Skin stitches itself back together as bones snap back into place, and all that's left is a pounding in my head and horns accompanied by phantom pain as my body aches.

"Little bitch," he seethes, releasing me from my chains.

I crumble to the floor, my knees buckling as my legs give out, and my arms are practically useless since they're stiff from the position I was left in for hours. All of my nerves tingle as if a thousand tiny pins and needles are cutting away at them, and my joints ache as my skin feels raw, while my muscles twitch and cramp painfully.

Bael's trusted guards reach for me, pulling me to my feet, which are still chained together. They release some of the slack so I can walk forward, but running would be nearly impossible. Then, following Bael, we march out of the cells of the castle and into the courtyard, and I have to turn my eyes away from the sun as it blinds me. Once my vision has recovered, I glance around and take in my surroundings.

The body count has tripled in the last few days.

Plenty swing from the archways while others line the walls or sit in cages. Crows pick away at their rotting flesh while chains and ropes dig into their necks and limbs. Some have been dead for days, bloated and beaten beyond recognition, while others still whine and moan in pain as the birds and bugs have their way with them. Plenty are demons and mortals, but as I take notice of the newer bodies, some look more celestial kissed than Hellion.

Heads of other people and monsters and beasts decorate the spikes of the walls, and while the presence of Bael's footmen appears to have doubled, the hellhounds that once patrolled this castle seem to have all but disappeared.

"Soak up the sunshine while you can, Rhesamyre," Bael taunts. "For there's no telling when you'll see it again."

I ignore him, just doing my best to focus on where I'm putting my feet so I don't trip over my chains or step in some dark puddle of suspicious, diseased origins.

Bael and his men march me toward the entrance of the mines where slaves push and pull carts of obsidian in and out of the mountain that Castle Blackstone calls home. As we near the mouth of the glittering cavern, plenty of slaves take notice of me and begin squabbling amongst themselves despite their own chains.

Whips crack through the air as a warning to the slaves, and the murmuring ceases completely. I'm roughly thrown forward, my feet tripping over each other, and I fall to my hands and knees in the mud.

"Soak it in, you maggots!" shouts Bael, drawing everyone to a halt as they watch him circle me. "Let it be known that your beloved *Rhesamyre* has fallen to the mercy of my commands and the rule of our new king, Abaddon, second of his name, our rightful ruler and protector!"

Bael comes to stand behind me, grabbing me by my horns. I hiss and snarl, but he tugs on my horns again and even pulls on my messy hair. I glare at him, then dare to turn my gaze away from his as I meet the eyes of the slaves around me. They're all beaten and dirty like me, wearing nothing but rags and chains. The majority of the males are shirtless, thus showcasing the many open wounds that litter their chests and backs, mostly caused by whiplashes, while the females wear a single, oversized tunic like me, often leaving their legs bare with nothing else to protect them from getting raped should these guards and fellow slaves decide to have their way with them.

I narrow my eyes at a few of the males, noticing how their gazes linger on my bare thighs for far too long. A few of them even have the gall to lick their chapped lips and click at me, and I bare my fangs and snarl viciously at them all. They look equally startled and amused by the sound and disheveled sight of me, and Bael merely chuckles from behind me before releasing my horns and hair roughly to push me forward again.

This time, I'm able to catch myself, and then I get back onto my bare feet and stride forward as instructed, walking past the lines of slaves that sort through the rocks and chunks of raw obsidian that others mine from within the mountain. The darkness is all-consuming as I claim a chipped pickaxe and find a place deeper within the tunnels and mineshafts beside other slaves under the watchful eyes of Bael's guards. However, as I approach an open space riddled with raw obsidian, I find that these males and females keep their heads down as they work. They don't allow their gazes to stray far from their tasks, and the scent of their fear wafts off them to a near-suffocating degree.

And I come to understand with startling clarity that these folks do not belong here.

I have half a mind to claim that these males and females of mixed bloodlines were once free natives of Hell and elsewhere and have since been sentenced to rot and die here in the mines.

But I can't think about that right now. Instead, I put all my focus into doing what Bael *commands*. So I lift my pickax and start mining.

....

Time ceases to matter within the dark confines of the mine. There's only enough enchanted lantern light to reveal where the veins of obsidian ore lie, and the sound of picking and hammering echoes up and down the vast tunnels to the point that I can hardly tell where one entrance begins and another ends. Guards patrol with whips in hand, ready to snap at slaves they claim are *slacking off,* and chains rattle along the floor as slaves move and push heavy carts of black ore out of the darkness and into the courtyard to be sorted.

Further inside the darkness of the mines, the guards become few and far between as they patrol between the lines of slaves that work on either side of the shaft. They often have to divide their attention between the noisier slaves at the mouth of the mine and only venture back to us every once in a while. Thus, the slaves back here, while they are terrified, have taken to murmuring quietly amongst themselves, speaking in all the common languages of the spheres. Explaining to each other where they come from and how they ended up here at Castle Blackstone.

The raids have begun once more. Lucifer is setting fire to the spheres and robbing the people of their freedoms, lives, and souls as a whole.

I close my eyes, forcing myself to take even breaths as pain erupts in my shoulders and head again. I may have been given an elixir to heal my wounds just enough to stay alive, but the poison has yet to leave my veins, thus continuing to rob me of my magic.

The quiet shuffling and clinking of chains draws nearer, and I glance over my shoulder to find the group of older men and women watching me with pained expressions but curious, *albeit frightened*, eyes.

Mortal eyes.

"You're . . . *Rhesamyre*, are you not?" inquires one of the elders in Plebian.

I raise my head, nodding once.

"The dethroned queen of Hell," murmurs one of the males, and another woman hits him gently on the arm as if to say *Don't say that to her!*

I try to offer them a small smile, but they're no fools. They know it to be a painful, pitiful lie.

"We know this isn't your fault," drawls the elderly woman again, her eyes kind. "Under your father's reign, and your own . . . relations with Hell were far better than *this*."

"By a long shot," agrees another woman. "It isn't even worthy of a comparison."

"W-What—" I croak, then clear my throat. I hadn't realized how hoarse it had become. I try again. "I overheard you talking earlier . . . it is my understanding that Lucifer has begun to lay waste to the spheres?"

The elder nods, studying me with a scrutinizing gaze. Though I dare say it isn't judgmental, merely observant.

They're curious to see what has become of the late *dethroned* queen of Hell, and I won't blame them for that. I'm almost curious to know what they see when they look at me, too.

But then again, I am unsure if I truly want the answer to that.

"He's butchering all those who are not pledging fealty to Abaddon and the Zodiacs," she explains, and I nod along, as I already figured as much. "But . . . it's also worse than that. For a few that have succumbed to his false promises and pledged themselves to him . . . he slaughters them, too. He's stealing their souls. Condemning many into slavery and others to death. He spares very few, though we don't know why, while simultaneously freeing many of the slaves that had been shackled under your father's reign. Allowing them to run amuck and rape and pillage."

I swallow thickly. "I wish I had an answer for you, but the magic Lucifer has shackled and now commands is different from what I am accustomed to. He feeds off pain and fear and is most likely savoring the souls as he goes. Saving a few as a later *snack* if you will."

The clusters of nearby slaves that have stopped their mining to listen to us converse shudder and cry quietly, and I survey them all again. Plenty observe me with fear and abhorrence, their limbs shaking as they clutch their pickaxes and tools, while others dare to sneer at me and spit at the ground, but I don't bother to make an example of their blatant disrespect as I survey the eyes of others that appear to *pity* me.

I stand up straighter, my body protesting and aching at the action. "I have failed all of you. I know that. And nothing I do or say right now will make up for my shortcomings, but I am still here. And with every breath I take, I plot and scheme, and I vow to make things right again . . . no matter how long it may take."

A celestial-bred male steps forward, baring his fangs and sneering in Enochian, *"We'll be stuck in here for* centuries, *and I refuse to die next to a useless, dethroned, bastard-bred whore."*

I nod my head, keeping my fangs hidden and voice low. *"This bastard-bred whore is your best and only chance at fighting back against Lucifer."*

"Look around, girl!" snarls another in Butchered Babel. *"There is no* fighting *Lucifer! Only hiding and praying that he'll end you swiftly."*

I cock my head at the Western male, switching to his dialect. *"I'm curious which beings you pray to, because I can assure you. None of them are listening to your pathetic words."* I look around again, speaking in Plebian once more as the majority will understand me. "The gods have forsaken us. *No one* is coming to rescue us. We either die here, or we live long enough to save ourselves. What you choose to do is up to you, but when it comes to Lucifer and his Apostles, there is no such thing as *mercy*. So quit thinking you're special enough to be spared, because you won't be."

"Then," drawls the original elder once more, "what do you suggest we do?"

I meet her brown eyes again, sighing deeply as I shrug as gracefully as I can. "For now . . . keep breathing. Keep your heads down until I . . ." I shake my head to myself. "Until I figure out a way to fix this."

"And why should we trust you?" snarls another mortal woman.

I shrug again. "Do what you want. I'm not expecting you to trust me. In fact, it may be even more foolish if you do, but I lost my home, too. I lost my family and court and crown, and I'm fucking *angry*. So, you don't have to trust *me*, just my wrath. I am the daughter of the Devil, and he was once the Archangel of Retribution. I do not preach hope and prosperity to you. I preach anger and revenge, and I will have Lucifer at my mercy again."

The mortal woman sneers, gripping her pickax harder. I glance down at where her fingers white-knuckle the wooden handle, and carefully, I set my own tool down and meet her livid eyes.

"Okay, then," I drawl. "Let me have it."

She blinks at me, taken aback by my taunt. I lift my stiff shoulders, opening my arms wide beside me.

"This is what you want, is it not?" I inquire. "Well, then. *Come on.*" I bare my teeth. "Let's see how your rage blinds you."

She grits her teeth and then stalks toward me and raises her pickax to strike me. And although I am slower than usual, I still have plenty of time to punch her square in the face. She reels backward, dropping her tool to grasp her broken nose. Then she looks up at me with fury and renewed vigor.

Once again, I shrug at her. "I never said I wouldn't fight back. You want to attack me, I'll welcome it, but you may come to regret it."

With a sniveling battle cry, the woman reclaims her weapon and lunges for me. I sidestep and trip her, her chains rattling as she tumbles onto her hands and knees. Then, sensing another one just in time, I duck and swing my elbow into the celestial male's abdomen. He grunts in pain and swings his pickax at me. I reel backward and trip over my own chains, leaving him to slice my cheek with the edge.

I bring my fingers up to the cut, marveling at the sight of my blood.

Then, I grin.

The sight of my feral smile leaves the male and a few others hesitating to approach me again, but not for very long, as they seem to recall their foolish hostility toward me. A group of six slaves stalks forward, gripping their beloved pickaxes and relying on their pathetic snarls to intimidate me.

I will not flinch. I will not yield. I won't let you taste my fear.

I steel myself as they approach, and when they attack all at once, grabbing me and holding me down to punch and kick and curse and spit, I have to remind myself to pull my punches. I do not have the strength to fight off everyone in here, plus the guards that will surely come running after hearing our scuffle, and then there is Bael to consider, too.

If I want to get out of here with my soul and sanity intact, I have to learn how to take a few more beatings.

Forgive me, Uncle Pride. For this is going to hurt.

I fight off a few of them, breaking a nose or arm or two just to remind myself that I can, but when a few of the larger males grab ahold of my horns and kick my legs out from underneath me, holding my arms behind my back and threatening to break them, I take far too many blows to the head. Blood drips from my nose and temple as my eyes and cheeks swell, and I spit my blood onto their broken toes.

They drop me into the dirt, and pain swirls in my chest as my ribs ache and lungs growl with every breath I force myself to take. And as the group of enraged, mistreated, and misplaced slaves leaves me, I vaguely hear one of them snarl in Enochian, *"Where are your deities now?"*

I will myself not to cry at the inquisition, but the lack of an answer I have is even worse.

I don't know, I want to scream.

But instead, I merely close my eyes.

Alastair, Atlas, Atticus, I chant. *Alastair, Atlas, Atticus.*

None of the other slaves approach me again. Not even the elders who had initially taken to conversing with me in a more civilized manner. Instead, they turn their backs on me and get back to work, picking and chipping away.

The sound of boots crunching in the dirt of the mine heading straight for me forces me to crack open my swollen eyes again, thinking it to be a guard or Bael returning to accuse me of *slacking off* and looking for any excuse to beat the shit out of me some more.

But instead, I find my big brother, Alto, crouching beside me. His gray eyes take in my battered form in a similar manner to how Apollo once did. His black hair is a similar shade to my own and frames his face, and mighty navy blue wings are tucked into his back behind him. He wears light gray leathers, a similar shade to his eyes, and his expression is strained as he reaches for me. His touch is a warm, welcoming caress over my bruised cheek.

"You've certainly seen better days, baby sister," he drawls, but even though I feel as though the tease should warrant a smirk, he doesn't offer me one.

"How observant of you, big brother."

He shakes his head at me, then takes a seat beside me and places his hand over my own, and his thumb rubs over my bloodied knuckles soothingly.

"Punishing yourself over what has happened isn't going to help anyone survive this, little feather."

"I'm not—"

"*Bullshit*," he snarls halfheartedly, then he chuckles, the sound once again devoid of humor. "You've never known when to quit. Always pushing and challenging . . . what was our old adage? The inside joke we all shared?"

Despite the pain in my cheeks, I find myself smiling a little. "When one of you says no, especially Apollo, just go ask Sam. He'll say yes to me just to spite the rest of you."

Finally, he offers me a charming smile. "That's the one, little feather. You always challenged Apollo on his word. Even when you were young. You had such *spirit*. Such fire. And Sam loved nothing more than to stroke it. Feed it. You two . . ." Alto shakes his head, a reminiscent gleam in his eye. "Partners in crime. Even more so than you and Pollux at times, too."

I turn my hand over, under his, so it's resting in my palm, and I squeeze. Then I tease, "Don't be jealous . . . we were pretty good together, too."

"Aye. I recall . . . but do you?"

"Not as well as I should."

He hums. "Then may I remind you?"

I nod. "Please."

Alto offers me a kind smile, then pulls his hand out of mine to rub my temple again softly as he murmurs in Old Latin, *"Sweet dreams, little feather."*

....

"Gods **fucking** *dammit, Samael!" shouts Apollo as he lands near us with Alto in tow.*

I remain on the ground near the cliffside, my limbs trembling as my wings twitch painfully on my back. They're **heavy,** *and I can hardly hold them up after all the exercises Sam had me doing in preparation to finally learn how to fly.*

Standing above me, Sam crosses his arms as he sizes up our brothers as they approach.

"She's never going to learn **anything** *if you keep babying her like you have been," snarls Sam.*

"I told her no for this very reason!" shouts Apollo, glancing down at my trembling form before sneering at Sam again. "But once again, you have undermined my decision and gone behind my back."

"Your decision is not final, brother. She may be the youngest of us, but you and I are the same age. We all came into these spheres at the same time over a century ago, and your word is not final to **me."**

"But it is to **her,"** *snaps Apollo again, pointing at me. His golden eyes scrutinize me as he watches my hands shake as my wings remain lowered and practically useless. He* **almost** *softens his gaze at me, but then seems to recall his irritation and scowls once more when he looks at Sam.*

"She isn't strong enough yet," he accuses.

"Because you won't let her train!" snarls Sam. "Hence why we're out here practicing harder exercises to build up her strength." He narrows his eyes. "Did you think I was going to toss her off the cliff like some fucking newborn bird?"

"With your track record of training and punishing our troops, I wouldn't put it past you! You've tossed our footmen over the edge with their wings **tied** *with the simple instruction of 'get untied before you hit the bottom.'* For. Fun.*"*

Sam snarls, scoffing a little. "I wouldn't do that to her, dammit! But she was getting nowhere with those puny excuses for wing exercises that you had given her!"

"They're all she can handle right now! Her wings are still growing, and putting this much stress on them isn't good for her! Do you wish to rob her of the ability to fly before she even reaches the sky?"

All I can do is sit here and listen to them bicker, and I would love nothing more than to be able to jump off this cliff and fly away. And unbeknownst to them, my gaze drifts toward the cliff's edge as my fantasies of flight take off without me, leaving me here grounded and at the mercy of my overbearing, overprotective brothers.

Knees step into my line of sight, and I look up at Alto as he cocks his head at me. He glances over at our brothers but then extends a tattooed hand down to me. I raise my shaky arm and grasp it gently, and he hauls me to my feet with ridiculous ease before clutching me to his chest and opening a conveyance away from our bickering brothers.

He grasps me by my underarms and places me on a soft surface, and I glance around at the interior of the common den within our manor on the outskirts of Ursa Major. White, gray, and steel furnishings decorate the area, while the walls are mostly made of glass and littered with balconies and open archways that overlook the valleys and farmland beyond the city. We're on the same mountain range as the Celestial Palace, but on a different level of the ridge.

Our home is much higher than the palace, and on a cloudier day, most cannot see our home from down below.

My wings hurt, and my lip begins to quiver as I stare at Alto. He has crouched before me, studying me but not saying a word. I feel a sudden rush of dread sink into my belly at the thought of him, or any of my brothers, being disappointed or mad at me for disobeying a direct order from Apollo.

And I let the waterworks loose.

"I-I'm sorry!" I wail, trying to wipe my eyes with trembling hands. "I just wanted—I just wanted to fly like you guys! To fly with you! I'm sorry I made you angry! Apollo's so mad at me!"

"Shh, shh," coos Alto, sitting beside me and pulling me into his side. "Nobody's mad at you, little feather." He kisses the top of my braided hair. "We were just worried, that's all."

He pulls me back to look at him, then offers me a gentle smile as he cups my cheeks and wipes my tears away with his thumbs. But I'm still sobbing and hiccupping pathetically, and Alto frowns at that.

"Myra, you're fine," he claims. "Breathe in."

I do as he instructs.

"Good. Now, breathe out."

And I do.

"Good girl. You're okay. Your emotions are just all over the place from overexerting yourself. And Apollo definitely didn't help matters by stressing you out when he came barreling down, ready to tear Sam a new one."

I sniffle. "I don't know what that means."

Alto's lips twitch in amusement, and he can barely stifle the grin that overtakes his features. "Ask Pollux. He'll be more than happy to explain it to you." Then he gives me a pointed look. "I know why you did it, Myra. But that doesn't make it okay."

I nod. "I know, but Sam brought up a good point. I don't think it's fair that all of you are so much older than me. Why . . . why is that, Alto?"

He sighs. "To be quite honest, little feather, we don't know. But finding you wrapped up on our doorstep twelve years ago was arguably the best day of our lives. You changed everything for the better, Myra. And we just want to protect you. Never doubt that."

"I don't. I know that, but when one of you tells me to do something, and then another immediately counters it . . . I feel torn. I don't know what to do, but I don't want to disappoint any of you. I just—"

"I know. Sometimes we aren't exactly on the same page when it comes to raising you. And despite all of us big brothers coming into the world at the same time, with established magic and knowledge, Apollo often attempts to claim himself as **our** big brother."

"But he isn't."

"No, he isn't. But he'll try to act like it sometimes. So when you came along, it provided the perfect outlet for his . . . control issues."

I scrunch up my face at that, and Alto chuckles.

"I know how it sounds, but trust me when I say that he loves you unconditionally. He is the one who named you, after all."

I nod along, unsure of what else to say. However, Alto saves me from my dilemma when he sighs again and says, "But, admittedly, Apollo can be rather overbearing. And while Sam enjoys pushing our brother's buttons, he has a point in saying we haven't been letting you explore and train as you should be. That doesn't excuse the fact that he nearly pushed you over the edge today, but I understand what he was trying to accomplish all the same. Even if his methods were a bit bizarre."

I hum. "I asked to keep going. It wasn't his idea."

"But he didn't stop you, either."

"He tried in the beginning, but I didn't let him."

Alto chuckles. "Trust me, little feather. If Samael wanted to stop you, he would've. But I believe he allowed you to keep pushing yourself despite the obvious warning signs. Not that he wanted to see you in pain, but I would wager he was curious."

"Curious?"

"When you came to us, we could tell you were an archangel right away from the sigils and shape of the extra bones on your back that would eventually grow into wings. For they were a mirror image of ours, and no other angels have our type of wings. But even so, we couldn't sense any underlying power. Not to mention, when we came into existence, we were already like this."

"Grown up?"

"Very. We still had much to learn about life, death, and purpose, but we already knew our namesakes and magic. We already knew we were different from the rest and that we were to call each other brother."

"How?"

"That is the way of the Yonder Star and Evergreen Fern. We are to be warriors. Soldiers and protectors. Our magic and names are specified so we may act as a single unit to better the spheres as a whole. Whether that is through war or peace depends upon the times in which we live."

"Then, if you were all put here to be warriors and soldiers, why was I born?"

Alto grasps my cheeks again. "Dare I say you were born to be a gift for us. Someone for us to cherish and protect and love unconditionally, with no strings attached. Our little sister. A light in the darkness."

"That seems like an awfully big responsibility."

Alto laughs, shaking his head with a smile. "It's not. All you have to do is keep being you, Myra. Just be your selfless, caring, strong self. But even if you aren't, we'll always be here for you. Through thick and thin."

I hug him, and Alto embraces me gently.

And then later, he takes me flying. He clutches me to his chest and tucks my wings in tight as he soars through the clouds and night sky, letting me trail my fingers through the clouds and feel the cold wind through my hair.

Eventually, Alto is the one to teach me how to fly on my own. Acting as the perfect combination between tough love and gentle instruction. They all give me pointers along the way, but Alto is there every day to oversee my training.

He doesn't stop me from jumping off the cliff this time.

There were so many bodies. But I turned over every single one to ensure neither of you were buried in the carnage. Our bonds told me you were both alive, but even so, I couldn't shake the feeling.

The thought of "what if" nearly killed my soul and drove me into madness.

Fuck both of you.

Fuck both of you for making me worry.

CHAPTER THREE
RHESAMYRE

Something gently shakes me awake, and I blink my sore eyes open to gaze up at the blurry form of a woman, her silhouette barely illuminated by the dim light of the lantern nearby.

"You need to get up, Rhesa," says a soft, feminine voice in Enochian, and I could swear I've heard her somewhere else before. "C'mon, Your Majesty. Please get up."

I groan in pain as I do as she instructs, and she helps me lean back against the wall of the mine. Then finally, once my vision clears enough, I'm met with the familiar, warm, mortal honey eyes of—

"Juliette?" I croak.

Andrew's late *doll*.

Juliette offers me a kind smile, then holds out a small canteen of water for me. I take it wordlessly, cringing at the poisoned, slimy taste of it, but dehydration is never an ally.

"How—what are you doing here?"

Juliette sighs, then takes a seat next to me. "Same as most here now. After you killed Andrew and disbanded his crews and slave ships, I was freed, but I didn't get much time to enjoy it before Lucifer arrived. Now, here I am. Trying to hide and survive by working in the darkness of the mines, and then the rumors started circling about you." She meets my eyes. "I knew I had to find you."

"And I'm thankful you have, but I'm afraid I can't offer you much sanctuary at the moment. In fact, it might be more dangerous for you should Bael catch wind of our—"

"You misunderstand. I'm not here for your help. I'm here hoping *I* can help *you*."

I blink at her, cocking my head, but before I can inquire as to why, she explains, "You showed me kindness once when no one else did. Let me do the same for you."

"I didn't help you to have you indebted to me."

"I know." She takes a steeling breath. "People are talking a bunch of shit. Saying you betrayed Hell and did all these things to conspire against the people and bring Lucifer here. Bring Abaddon back and put him on the throne. Some even speculate you murdered your own father, but I know that isn't true. Even without you being down here, rotting away like some forsaken sinner, the woman who offered me a simple, kind hand back at the dock house could never be this monster they all speak of. Call me a fool, but I don't believe them. However, I need you to help me find a reason I should believe you."

I go to give her that reason, but then I come up short. She takes note of my hesitancy, then reaches into the pocket of her torn shirt. Pulling out a small bundle of cloth, my mouth nearly begins to water at the sight of the moldy bread in her palm.

"They handed out rations while you were unconscious," she says, offering me a piece while taking a small morsel for herself. "Here. Eat. It's shit, don't get me wrong, but it's better than starving."

I nod, taking a few crumbs at a time and chewing slowly. There is no taste to savor, but my jaw still twinges in pain every time it flexes.

"When a few of those celestials started bragging that they 'beat up the dethroned queen of Hell,' other elders recalled what you had said before they started . . . that you 'preach anger and revenge,' and you'll have Lucifer at your mercy again." She meets my eyes once more. "Why did you say *again?*"

I inhale and exhale carefully, steeling myself for what I'm about to reveal to her.

And when I do, Juliette merely listens, the two of us chewing on the stale, moldy bread and washing it down with poisonous water. Silence is my only answer after I've finished telling her of Myra and the gods and the ten spheres.

Finally, she inquires softly, "And what of your deities?"

I shrug carefully. "I don't know. My brands itch, so I know they're not dead, but so far, when I find the strength to reach out to them, all I'm met with is an eerie silence." I take another breath. "I *know* they're alive, but I fear they have been sent somewhere I cannot follow."

"Meaning the tenth sphere."

I nod. "Presently, I have no way of escaping my current predicament. Nor am I even certain or confident that I can reach the passageway . . . assuming it still exists."

"It would have to, though, if Lucifer is here and drawing power from his altar, right?"

"You would think, but it's like I said before. Lucifer's magic is different from what we command here in our known spheres. He plays by different rules."

"But, luckily for us, you're quite skilled at breaking rules, right?"

I offer her a small, sly smile. "I suppose I can be when provoked."

Juliette matches my grin. "Then how shall I anger you, Your Majesty?"

I can't help the quiet, abrupt laugh that bubbles out of my chest, and I pull Juliette into a side hug. "We'll get out of here, Julie . . . one way or another."

She nods. "I believe you."

. . . .

I don't recognize the ground beneath my feet . . . no . . . these are paws. *And whatever this creature is snorts and growls instead of speaking, and the only thing on its mind is the hunt. He's hungry for blood and death, and this strange sphere I don't recognize seems to bleed nothing but carnage and cruelty, but the beast has simply become one with it.*

And yet, his mind almost feels familiar . . .

But I don't have time to discern what he is or where he is as I'm tugged from his mindscape and placed somewhere else entirely, but at least this one smells more familiar than the last.

The desert is vast and covered in darkness, and the full moon is surrounded by stars that illuminate the sky with brilliant colors of dark blue and violet. But despite the chill, I feel warm, and for once in several days, my body and bones do not ache.

I stand with my toes in the sand, eyes closed as I listen to the quiet of this sphere, which bears a striking resemblance to the one I fled to when Atlas first found me as a wolf.

Little wolf . . .

I twirl, calling his name, and whatever phantom wind connects us, thanks to our shared imprint and brands, causes my voice to echo across the midnight dunes. My heartbeat is loud in my ears as my anticipation and anxiety rise. A foreign emotion, but I need to see him. *I need to feel him. To know he's safe and alive. We'll deal with the* where *later, so long as he's still out there for me to find.*

Ahead of me, a muscular form dressed in blood-splattered, obsidian leathers materializes from the darkness, and his pink eyes glow eerily under starlight. He glances around as though ready to pounce, his sigils and our shared **sarang** *brand faintly illuminated on his skin, and I can still clearly make out the inscription that translates to* **strength** *that rests in the bottom corner of his right eye.*

I take a timid, careful step forward, tears springing to my eyes as I choke on a sob, and he snaps his head toward me so violently I swear a lesser male might've broken his neck trying to look at me.

Atlas tilts his head, brows furrowed as he stares at me with unsure emotions openly playing out on his handsome face. Anguish, confusion, relief, and then wrath.

And then he's running, and I'm swiftly following suit as quickly as I can in my injured state. He wraps his arms around me and buries his face into my neck, and I lift up to wrap my arms around his neck while I lock my legs around his waist. He goes to his knees, and we squeeze each other to the point that we start to shake with the force of our hug. Or maybe that's just me, and his arms band tighter around my form as he starts muttering my name and purring in an attempt to get me to calm down.

"I've got you, little wolf," he mutters, pressing kisses to my matted hair as he nuzzles me. "I've got you. I'm right here."

"But you're not," I mumble, pulling back with tears in my eyes. I cry, and the look of sheer terror and hurt on his face just makes my heart ache. "You're not **here***, Atlas," I sob. "Where are you?"*

I cry harder, unused to it and ashamed that I am, but I can't help it because, fuck it, I'm in so much pain right now, and while he might feel real, this place isn't. When I wake up again, he won't be here. He'll be somewhere far away, and I'll be back in Hell, alone and outnumbered.

"I should've been with you," I snarl between my sobs. *"I should've gone with you. I should've been there."*

"Shh, shh," he coos, and he grasps my jaw in his hands to make me look at him. I can hardly see him through my tears, and he leans forward and kisses my closed eyelids, licking my tears away softly. *"Had you been with us, then you would be in Purgatory with me. And Rhesa . . ."* he hesitates, and I sniffle. *"It's no place for you. It's no place for any of us."*

"Is that where you are?" I ask. *"The tenth sphere? What about your brothers?"*

"Alastair is here with me . . ."

My heart plummets into my stomach. *"And Atticus?"* I whisper, afraid of the answer.

I've never been afraid before. I've never been this fucking scared in my life. But that's what I am right now.

I'm so, so scared.

Atlas shakes his head and growls, *"The fucker's not dead. My brother is far too stubborn for that, but he's not here with us."*

I nod along, hands gripping and rubbing all of him just so I can feel him. I'm desperate for his warmth, and our brands glow and nearly sing as we make contact. All of me shakes, and he grasps both my hands in his and pulls them close to his mouth. He kisses my knuckles and blows hot air onto them, and I finally manage to breathe without breaking down crying again.

"Are you safe?" I ask.

Pink eyes flash dangerously, and this . . . this male is different than the one I've come to love. Atlas has always had an edge to him, but unlike his brothers, he usually manages to keep his range of violent emotions in check. At least in front of me, he has, but looking at him now, I can tell that wherever he's ended up, he's had to resort to old ways. Bloody, violent, wrathful ways that rely on bloodshed and mur-

der, because that's what it takes to survive. It's what he did when he fought and schemed in war and as a leader of the Wild Hunt, and I'm reminded once more that while Atlas may have become a pacifistic vagabond in the desert to escape the memories of his wrath and grief, that doesn't mean he's any less the warrior he once was.

He's the Deity of Sacrifice and Devotion. Forged from bloodstained gems and bred for bloodshed.

And when robbed of options, Atlas is the most dangerous of them all.

He presses his lips against my knuckles again as he mutters, "No, Rhesa. We're not safe."

My heart sinks once more, and all I can do is nod.

His gaze drops as he studies me, and a newfound rage smolders in his pink eyes, turning them redder by the second.

"What have they done to you?" he snarls, and this entire plane shudders. "Who the fuck did this to you?"

I close my eyes, steeling myself.

And I tell him everything.

It doesn't do any good. Just reminds us that we're both powerless at the moment, but despite that, this entire plane created by our imprint begins to crack as Atlas struggles to keep his anger in check. He does his best to keep his hands steady and gentle as he inspects every injury that bruises my skin and tears through my tattoos.

"I'm going to burn them all," he snarls softly.

I grasp his cheeks to make him look at me, and slowly, he does.

"You need to focus on not fucking dying," I order. "Find Alastair. Protect one another, and do what must be done to stay alive until I find you."

He starts to shake his head, but I hold firm, and he growls.

"Atlas," I murmur his name like a prayer. I close my eyes and lean against him, and he takes that as an invitation to kiss my forehead

and nuzzle me once more. "What I need from you now is for you to stay alive. You can't help me right now, but if you give me the peace of mind that you're alive, that'll be enough to get me through this. I have allies here waiting in the wings. You don't. So **please***," I fucking beg him. "Please just stay alive."*

I feel him nod, and a few more tears drip from my eyes as he continues to hold me.

"I love you," he whispers.

....

When I wake again, I'm still crying.

....

The days drag on, and Juliette and I remain in the dark confines of the mines for what feels like an eternity. From the murmurs of various slaves that echo down the mineshafts and from the guards that rotate through their posts, I know a few days have passed. However, chances for rest are few and far between. As are our rations. Julie and I share poisonous water and stale bread while managing to keep our heads down and out of the peripherals of the guards when they're feeling extra antsy and *horny*.

Plenty of others are not so fortunate.

But I do my best to keep the same vow that I made Atlas promise to me.

Stay. Alive.

Screams often echo up and down the mines alongside the sounds of mining tools chipping away at obsidian, but so far, I would claim Julie and I to be among the lucky ones. As to why, though, I haven't quite figured that out yet. Perhaps it is merely a game Bael enjoys playing with us. Allowing us to fall into a routine and a false sense of security. But if that is the way he wants to play, then so be it.

Let them think I have been *domesticated*.

Then I remind myself that I am merely lying in wait. Sharpening my fangs and my claws, steeling myself for the fights to come. Because they will be bloody and brutal, and I will be cruel.

I will not flinch. I will not yield. I won't let you taste my fear.

"You're muttering again," calls Julie softly, still speaking Enochian as she shuffles beside me, attempting to sleep against the walls, the jagged rocks and stone cutting into our backs.

"Sorry," I breathe.

She glances at me, offering a little smile as she shrugs. *"It's okay. I've come to like your motto."*

I spare her a smile. *"I like to believe it's the truth."*

She nods. *"And I believe it. Mind if I use it from time to time?"*

"Not at all. Use it however and whenever you wish, Julie."

She thanks me, and we fall silent once more. However, the tranquil moment doesn't last much longer before guards are shouting throughout the mines for us to get back to work. Julie and I exchange a glance, then reluctantly use the wall for balance as we get back on our feet, retrieve our pickaxes and gear, and then begin mining once more. And it isn't until another hour later that I feel the fine hairs upon my arms rise in warning, and I bristle as I sense *him* drawing nearer.

"Don't flinch," I mutter to Julie, and the only indication she gives that she heard me is her pickax chipping away at the obsidian a little harder.

"Well, now," drawls Bael in a taunting, singsong voice as he prowls toward me. Toward Julie. "What have we here?"

Juliette glances his way, but keeps hold of her frown and focused expression as she ignores his approach. In addition, I don't believe she even knows Babel. Perhaps a few words of Plebian, but she's only ever spoken Enochian to me.

I stop my mining and turn to face Bael with a scowl, and he slowly trails his eyes over my form before scoffing and smirking at whatever he finds. He looks far too cocky for my liking, and I scowl harder.

"Watch the attitude, little bitch," he growls, though his voice is dripping with venomous amusement. "Or I may be more inclined to hurt your friend you're so skillfully trying to hide behind you."

"Don't know her. Don't care," I snarl.

He hums, eyeing Juliette behind me. "We'll see. Grab them both."

I snarl again but don't put up much more of a fight as the boar and buck grab hold of Julie and me. She begins to mutter in Enochian under her breath, her voice trembling in a similar manner to the rest of her limbs as we drop our pickaxes.

"I will not flinch. I will not yield. I won't let you taste my fear."

Bael scoffs ahead of us. "Angelic prayers won't save you now," he spits, then smiles pointedly at me again. "All the archangels have since been imprisoned something fierce. However, their minds remain their own, unlike what is left of the Hellion court . . . as well as the deity."

My stride falters, and I nearly faceplant before the buck hauls me back onto my wobbly knees. I will my heart to stay steady and hope they can't hear it. I also hope that what Kure once told me remains true, too: that my face remains steeled and unreadable despite my stress in the situation that has now been heightened by the revelation of one of my deities being *here*. I knew he was still in our known spheres, but I didn't think he was as close as Hell.

Bael is lying, I think to myself.

He has to be lying.

"You're probably wondering whether I speak the truth," he muses.

Fuck.

He chuckles. "The one of Chaos and Control . . . what is his name again?"

Breathe in. Breathe out. *I will not flinch. I will not—*

"Atticus, isn't it? *Well,* he has since been cozying up to Abaddon and Lucifer. Not doing much to round up slaves and souls for them, but he hasn't tried to stop them, either . . . . He thinks you're dead, I reckon." Bael laughs at my expense once more. "How tragic."

One foot in front of the other, Rhesamyre. Just. Keep. *Walking.*

He's lying. He's lying. He's lying. Because I believe with all my heart, even if Atticus thought me dead, he would never ally himself with the enemy. Not unless he was . . . *collared.*

Fuck.

Bael, seeming unamused by my lack of replies to his taunts, merely sighs dramatically again as he continues to lead us past other slaves and out of the mines.

The sun is startling and blinding when we finally emerge, and I raise my hands to shield my eyes, wincing away from the light and blinking away the sudden shift in my eyesight as I take in my surroundings once more. Plenty of slaves have been rounded up, forced to pay attention to whatever *show* Bael is no doubt about to put on. Juliette is positioned right next to me, and I glance sideways at her before turning my attention back to Bael.

The grin he gives me is nothing short of sadistic and, once again, far too cocky for my liking.

I glare daggers at the male, but he simply turns away from me and gestures to the crowd of guards and slaves. "It has come to my attention that we have a *thief* amongst our ranks!"

His eyes rake over Julie's form again, and she lowers her gaze as she attempts to hide and make herself look smaller.

"You, celestial wench," he growls. "You've stolen something from one of my guards."

"I believe the language barrier will hinder your ability to properly accuse her, *warden*," I snarl.

"Then," he drawls, "care to translate, *Your Highness*?"

I bare my teeth. "What are the accusations?"

"A dagger was stolen off his belt." Bael jerks his chin at the boar demon that holds Julie in place. "And thievery is not tolerated here."

I glance at the boar in question, swiftly finding his sheath to be empty. However, I know Julie didn't take it, as we've been together for the past few days, and the boar demon never came in contact with either of us the entire time we were in the dark. But I have no doubts that Bael knows that and chooses to ignore it.

This isn't about thievery or fairness. This is about instilling fear.

And the barely concealed lump in the boar's tunic is proof enough of that.

"Thievery is rarely tolerated anywhere," I drawl, meeting Bael's gaze again. "But she didn't steal his blade."

"Oh? I thought you didn't *know* her, nor did you *care*."

"I don't. What I care about is the misuse of your power. Because you're a *liar*."

He hums again. "Well, unfortunately, this isn't a misuse, and your actions have consequences. As such, a few dozen lashings upon the post should do the trick in reminding her of why thievery is a *no-no*."

Bael nods at his henchmen, and the boar begins to push Juliette forward. However, she's smart enough to know that whatever is about to go down will not be in her favor and begins to resist quite impressively for someone her size. She whimpers and cries out in Enochian, and I glare at the boar as he drags her forward, before glancing over my shoulder at the buck demon that now holds my arms behind my back.

Moving swiftly despite the aches and pains that still echo throughout my body, I stomp my foot down on the buck's and rip my arms out of his hands. He groans at the unexpected maneuver, and I jerk my elbow back into his gut before spinning and thrusting my knee into his balls. He goes to his knees with a pained growl, and I twirl again to jump on the boar's back. With him thrown off balance, I spin on his shoulders and wrap my legs around his thick neck and bring him to the ground, then grab the "stolen dagger" he had hidden away in his tunic.

Rising to my feet, I look Bael dead in the eye before flinging the dagger at his face. He catches it a hair's breadth away from his nose, but no grin adorns his features as he surveys me and his fallen men that remain on the ground on either side of me, moaning in pain.

"Is that the dagger in question?" I mock.

Bael makes a show of turning it over in his palm, drawling, "I believe it is."

I hum. "Then it would appear as though Juliette is not your thief, after all."

He bares his teeth. "So it would seem." Then he smirks again, clutching the dagger as he places his hands behind his back. "And it would also appear as though the thief I am looking for is *you*. Seeing as how you just disarmed and stole it from my guard and then dared to threaten me with it."

"Seems like you need to get better guards," I seethe.

His gaze is humored again. "I suppose I'm inclined to agree, but all the same, I believe they're perfectly capable of devising an appropriate punishment for your actions. So, if you wouldn't mind. Please, *little bitch*. Step up to the whipping post."

Other guards have stepped forward to seize Juliette, where she stands staring at me with horror-filled, wide eyes, but I don't glance at her again as I lift my head and stride toward the thick post that Bael stands beside. Then, once I am near it, his buck and boar goons grab me again and kick my legs out from underneath me, harshly forcing my hands into the manacles that hang from the top of the post. My shoulders burn as my arms are stretched around the wood, my knees dig into the gravel, and obsidian shards are scattered across the ground beneath me. I press my torso against the post, resting my cheek against the wood as I steel myself for what is to come.

Behind me, Bael shuffles around and tugs at my shirt, slicing it in two and gliding the tip of his dagger down my spine as he goes, tracing the inked masterpiece there.

He scoffs. "More brandings. Which monster did you bargain with to attain such an intricate tattoo?"

I remain quiet, and he snarls lowly. "No matter. I'll peel it from your skin and hang the piece over my office desk. I believe *that* would send quite the message to your loyal subjects when they finally find themselves at my mercy here in the mines."

I hear him unfasten his whip from his belt, and he glides the leather thong over my skin gently, teasingly, before cracking it over my back ruthlessly. My muscles tense, and I toss my head back, gritting my teeth to avoid screaming as tears spring in my eyes. Bael hums appreciatively, and I feel the blood dribble from the first of what will surely be many wounds.

He grabs me by my horn, pulling my head back so he can meet my gaze, and snarls lowly.

"I don't want your submission. I know you won't give it to me yet. So for now, I'll be satisfied with just your screams. This is what we do to thieves."

He shoves my forehead into the post again, then brings the whip down in quick succession. I clench my jaw and shut my eyes tight as the lashings continue, huffing deep breaths as I remind myself to keep breathing.

It's all a bad dream, calls Atlas, a faint, gravelly voice in the back of my head. *It's just a nightmare, little wolf. It's not real. Stay alive.*

I don't reply—I can't bring myself to reply to him as Bael has his way, but as Atlas keeps talking me through it, eventually everything fades into nothingness. The pain numbs, and I go deaf to the sound of the whip, but over time, the sound of Atlas's voice falls quiet, too.

I don't know how long I remain here. My back is no doubt a bloody mess of loose skin and red ribbons, and I've gone completely numb to the pain and burning. My head bows against the post as my muscles ache from the strain of the manacles, and my shirt barely conceals my breasts as it hangs off my arms in tatters. The gravel and soil dig into my knees painfully, but I use it to keep myself grounded as I force myself to breathe evenly despite Bael's *lesson.*

I don't know exactly when he stops and walks away, and slave work resumes all around me as the day drags on. The heat of the sun feels good on my skin after the days spent in that dark, dank mine.

I don't know where they've taken Julie or if I'll ever see her again.

At some point, I close my eyes, and when I open them again, I find nothing but darkness once more. Panic consumes my body for a heartbeat, believing I have found myself back in the mine; however, when I allow my eyes time to focus, I glance upward to find the stars.

Enchanted lantern lights and torches flicker along the walls where guards either sleep or patrol quietly, while other shackled slaves either do their best to find rest or hide from the guards when they go looking for trouble. I shift a little, the torn skin upon my back stretching and stinging again in protest, and I suppress a cry of pain as I attempt to relieve some of the pressure on my aching knees and shoulders.

My magic warms within me, attempting to reawaken and heal me despite the poison in my veins, and a gentle hand comes to rest against my forehead. His palm is soothing and cool as it eases the fever and acts as a cushion between my forehead and the post.

I crack open my eyes again, as they had closed once more without my consent, and am met with the gentle, icy gaze of Castor.

My heart skips a beat, my mind playing tricks on me and almost having me believe it is the real *Pollux* crouching in front of me and not his twin brother. However, Castor's auburn hair is cut closer to his scalp than Pollux's braidable locks, and his angelic tattoos are closer in color to a light blue than that of the white of his wings, which he also shares with his twin.

I lean into his palm. "I was wondering which of you would be next." I try to clear the gravel from my voice, but it doesn't really work. "Hello, Castor."

"Hey there, baby sis," he replies softly, his eyes glancing sideways to take in the state of my back. A muscle in his jaw moves as he clenches his teeth, and he slowly peels his gaze away from the bloody sight.

"How bad?" I inquire.

He shakes his head. "I know when you looked at me a minute ago, you were hoping it would be the real Pollux here to rescue you."

I try to shake my head, but he stops me—good thing, too, because the movement makes everything hurt more. "I'm still happy to see you."

He nods. "I know, but I find myself wishing Pollux was really here to save you, too." He sighs, his frown deepening. "I wish all of us were."

"I know, but at least for now, you can take me away from here. At least for a little while."

He nods, then says in Old Latin, *"I'll take you wherever you want to go, little feather."*

. . . .

Huffing with lungs that burn with every breath I take, I clench my sword and attempt to quiet down as I lean back against a tree, aggravating my wings in the process as I lean on them. I strain my senses and ears to listen to the woods around me. I can hear every bird, insect, and faraway critter that scampers off after no doubt hearing our swords ring throughout the woodwork.

Feathered wings ruffle behind me, and I steady my breathing and steel myself once more as I listen to him land quietly and prowl forward with near-silent steps.

"That was good," calls Castor, hunting me. "Had it been anyone else, it probably would have killed your foe."

I don't reply and instead focus on his footfalls and the sound of his voice drawing nearer.

"Sam will be proud to learn you've taken to that maneuver so well." Castor chuckles. "Of course, he did come up with it just for you and your magicless self."

I want to snarl, but I know he's listening for me, waiting for me to slip up and give in to his taunt.

Think again, brother.

His footfalls falter, and though my lungs want to hitch when I scent him close by, I don't allow myself to crumble under the pressure. Instead, I grip my sword tighter with one hand and reach for another one of my white daggers strapped to the bodice of my training leathers.

Castor prowls closer, and when he's a hair's breadth away from my hiding spot, I whirl around and throw my dagger at his head. Of course, Castor was ready for it, and he catches it with one hand, inches from his nose; however, what he wasn't quite prepared for was for me to follow close behind my dagger, and I raise my sword to strike him. Swiftly, he throws my dagger away and commands a sword to erupt from white flames into his tattooed hands.

Steel clashes with steel once more, and I flutter my wings to give me strength so I may pressure him to his knees. Castor snarls, then pushes back and manages to throw me off balance by overpowering me, and then he swipes my feet out from underneath me. I flap my wings to regain my balance, flipping backward and catching him in the jaw with the heel of my boot as I go. Castor growls, and I immediately go on the offensive as I charge him once more, knocking his sword from his hands and tackling him.

We roll on the ground, and I struggle to get my legs around his throat as I put him in an arm bar hold. He struggles against me before finally relaxing, chuckling, and patting my thigh in surrender. I release him, breathing heavily as I pant on the forest floor.

Castor sits up and pulls my legs down onto his lap as he grins at my disheveled form. He's looking none the worse for wear, handsome as ever; meanwhile, I feel like I got trampled by a horse.

"You did good, little sis. Had I been anything other than an 'indestructible asshole,' as you have so eloquently put it, you probably would have killed me about four different times by now. That's good. Apollo will be happy with the improvement."

I scoff, rolling my eyes as I sit up, pulling my legs off Castor as I cross them underneath me. "Doubtful. He's such a fucking perfectionist."

"Hey! Watch that foul mouth of yours!"

I scowl at him, leveling him with a look that I learned from Sam.

Castor chuckles, shrugging. "I know, I know. You're fifteen and think you know everything, so you can say whatever you fucking want and all that shit," he mocks, grinning. "But seriously, Apollo knows how hard you're working. And he'll acknowledge your improvement, Myra."

I cross my arms, huffing. "Debatable."

Castor rolls his eyes, losing his smile. "Fucking hell, you're so irritable these days. Hormones and puberty and all that shit as if you're some goddamned mortal teenager."

I narrow my eyes at him, rising back onto my feet. "It's not my fault none of you ever had to 'grow up' like a normal creature! You're the weird ones who came into the spheres all big and bad! Yet sometimes you're all so immature! It's infuriating!"

Castor rises to his feet to tower over me, another one of his intimidation tactics. "Don't try to lecture me on immaturity. *Because trust* me, little feather, *you're quite infuriating yourself! You might be pint-sized, but you've got enough attitude stuffed away in that tiny, weak little body of yours for all eight of us* real *archangels!"*

I puff up in a vain attempt to make myself look bigger, but seeing as how I'm fucking tiny compared to him, it doesn't do much but throw my center of gravity off and make me uneasy on my toes. My wings flare for balance, and Castor's eyes roam all over me as he targets my weak spots should he decide to knock me on my ass again.

I jab my finger at his chest. "You're just pissy because I managed to get you on the ground! Because stars forbid anyone *learns that I'm actually capable of bringing a* real *archangel to his knees despite my body growing like a* mortal's*!"*

Castor's icy eyes grow colder by the second, and he seethes through bared teeth, "Ten laps around the perimeter. Now. *Go cool the fuck off, and then we'll move on to the next task. And if I find you flying at all, I'll bind your fucking wings. Got it?"*

I snarl in his face, but he just points his finger over my head and growls. "Now, Myra!"

I throw my hands up in exasperation, growling and huffing in annoyance as I curse Castor's existence under my breath.

"I heard that!" he calls as I turn from him.

I raise my hand and make an obscene gesture at him, then take off running into the woodwork before he can call me back to do torturous balance training or a ridiculous number of exercises that will have me puking my guts out later.

With my wings a heavy reminder upon my back, I keep running. The desire to fly off and leave Castor behind is strong, but I know there's no hiding from him or the rest of my brothers.

They always find me.

Breathing heavily again, I slow to a walk and soon stop to lean against a tree as I sigh and think things over, cooling off *as Castor instructed.*

I fucking hate to admit it, but I know he's right. I am *being overly dramatic and snarky. My attitude toward him was uncalled for, and he didn't deserve the backlash of the unresolved issues I have with Apollo at the moment . . . but it still felt good to yell at him.*

I should probably go apologize before he starts thinking of more ways to sweat the attitude out of me.

Turning on my heel, I jog back toward Castor; however, upon arrival, I find him to be nowhere in sight. Placing my hands on my hips, I snarl to myself and curse aloud, "You've gotta be fucking kidding me."

He left *me here.*

Granted, it's not like I can't find my way home. We're still in the Starry Mountains by Ursa Major, and I've been playing, hunting, and training in these woods all my life. But still, it's a matter of pride and principle now.

Castor's an ass.

Huffing again, I take another look around, but then my eyes snag on where the ground appears roughed up, the soil and leaves disturbed as if there were a scuffle.

Immediately, I'm put on edge as my minimal magic strains to listen to my surroundings. Sensing no immediate danger, I prowl toward the freshly turned-over soil. This isn't where we sparred, and as I crouch to trail my hands through the dirt, I take note of the tracks left behind. Some of the marks and steps match the treads of Castor's boots, but there is another pair here that I don't recognize.

Alarm bells ring in my head, and I take another closer look around at my surroundings. Glancing between the trees and even up into the branches, my eyes finally catch the glint of a white dagger embedded in a high branch between the green leaves. Flapping upward, I perch on the branch and reach for the dagger, noting that the runes and sigils are of Castor's designs.

An archangel cannot be killed or physically harmed by other beings, but there are still forces out there that can challenge us and seek to hurt us through poisons and other dark arts, so perhaps he was weakened and taken. But even then, if he had been taken, to move my brother would require at least another person, but there was only one other set of tracks. And he wasn't dragged, but I don't sense the remnants of a conveyance, either.

So that only leaves one option:

My brother and his assailant are still here. Hiding like fucking cowards.

I sigh, dropping from the branch with his dagger still in hand. Reaching out with what little magic I have access to, I close my eyes and search for ripples in the air around me, looking for disturbances in the runes and wards and magic worked into the forest itself. It isn't nearly as sentient nor wild in nature as the Forest of Souls, but these trees have eyes all the same.

The wind howls. The breeze whispers its secrets, and I flip the dagger in my hand to grasp the tip before whirling around to throw it into the shadows upon another tree trunk.

A hand flashes outward from the darkness to catch the blade, and the handsome stranger steps out of the shadows, adorned in a black, glittering suit and numerous jewels that are of Hellion luxuries. Dark sigils and tattoos of demonic origins crawl across his skin, and his red eyes darken as they focus on me, sizing me up. Black hair is perfectly slicked back away from his face, a few strands are even braided, and not a scar or shadow of facial hair mars his otherworldly face.

I cross my arms. "Where's my brother?"

The demonic stranger smirks, chuckling a little as he drawls in perfect Enochian, "Well hello to you, too, little wing."

I scowl at the nickname, reaching for another one of my daggers. "You've got two seconds."

The demon rolls his eyes and scoffs. "Castor, get out here and leash your **pet**."

"Pet?" I repeat, baring my teeth and growling at the male. "Who the fuck do you—"

"Myra."

I whirl around to face Castor as he steps out of his own shadows, and he comes to stand next to me as he folds his arms and glowers at me. I raise my brows and gesture toward the demon incredulously, and Castor merely sighs before leveling his icy glare on the stranger.

"Hey, don't look at me like that," says the demon, raising his hands in mock surrender. "This was **your** idea."

I glare at Castor again, and he glances at me before doing a double-take as if surprised that I'm still mad at him. Then, just to punctuate my point, I punch him in the arm.

"I thought you were in trouble!" I yell at my imbecile of a big brother.

"I don't know if I should be insulted or flattered by your concern, baby sis," he says while rubbing his arm where I hit him. "I just wanted to see what you would do! Pride agreed to help when he showed up looking for me!"

"Pride?" I repeat with a snarl, looking back at the demon in question.

Said assassin merely shrugs and steps forward, looking amused by the situation as he sizes me up. "Technically, I was looking for your twin. Ya know, the one who usually has useful information to barter? Hell, I would've even settled for Samael at this point."

"They're off on another assignment at the moment," says Castor.

"Leaving you to babysit, I see." Pride glances down at me again, his red eyes studying me, and a corner of his lip turns up into a smirk at the sight of me.

I bare my teeth at him, and the demon has the balls to chuckle as he quips, "She's all but feral."

Castor shrugs, seeming unfazed. "She's been taught stranger danger."

"She *is* right here," I quip. "And thoroughly confused, I might add."

"Right, my bad," drawls my brother, turning to face me and giving me his undivided attention. "After you stormed off—"

"You ordered me to go run and cool off—"

"Pride showed up looking for Pollux. Said he had some things to discuss with our brother of perception, but his informants mistakenly took me for my twin. Honest mistake. Anyway, I wanted to see what you would do if you returned and believed me to be gone. Would you storm off? Look for me? I wasn't sure, so I wanted to check."

I blink at him. "You're an ass."

"I'm aware. And now I'm pleased with the results. Good job, baby sis. You threatened your first assassin and lived to tell the tale."

"I thought we weren't allied with any of the Seven?" I inquire, needing a segue and another explanation for the infamous demon's presence before I tear Castor a new one.

Castor shrugs. "It's a complicated relationship to explain, but we're not enemies with any of the higher-bred demons of Hell . . . we just . . ."

The archangel and assassin lock eyes, and Pride shrugs with impressive grace.

"Don't usually see eye to eye," finishes the demon. Then he softens his gaze and gets on a knee before me to better meet my eyes. His smirk is kinder now, and I narrow my eyes at him. He extends his ring-clad, tattooed hand, and I place mine in his gently to shake hands with the demon. "It's nice to finally meet you, Myra. My brothers and I have heard a great deal about you. I'm glad to formally put a face to the name."

I feel my anger start to deflate, and I offer the demon a small smile as a peace offering. "Likewise, Pride. I'll admit, I've studied a fair number of your assassinations, strategies, and infiltration tactics. You're quite remarkable."

Pride winks and gives me a charming smile. "I'm flattered, little wing. You know, I've met a lot of angels in my time, archangels included. However, none of them hold a candle to you."

"Watch it, Pride," snarls Castor, placing his hands on my shoulders; I let him.

Pride chuckles again, rising back onto his feet in one fluid, graceful motion. "I meant nothing by it, Castor." He glances down at me again. "Keep an eye on your brothers, okay? They're often prone to trouble."

"That's rich, coming from a demon," growls Castor.

Pride rolls his eyes, and I grin, nodding. "I'll do my best, Pride," I tell him.

"Atta girl. And just know that if you're ever in a tight spot, you've got a friend in Hell. You're a skilled little warrior, little wing. Castor told me how capable you are, but seeing you piece together what happened. . ." He shakes his head, chuckling. "Then you threw that fucking dagger at me like it was nothing. You'll be a formidable foe in no time. I'd wager that Greed would bet on you to win in his pits against any demon in a heartbeat."

"Not. Happening," growls Castor again.

Pride rolls his eyes once more. "Not a threat, angel boy. Just an observation. Inform your twin I'm looking for him, will you?"

Pride gives me one last parting smile, then opens a conveyance and disappears.

I step out of Castor's hands, turning around to cross my arms at him. He sighs, then goes to his knee in front of me, just as Pride did.

"I'm sorry if I scared you," he apologizes, his eyes gentle and sincere. "But I needed to gauge your reaction. We may not always be around when you need us, so I want you prepared for anything. I want *you to know how to defend yourself and fight for as long as may be necessary until we find you."*

I nod along, lowering my gaze to the ground between us.

"Myra?" he questions, pinching my chin to tilt my head back up. "Something else is . . . bothering you."

I roll my eyes. "I thought your namesake wasn't **perception?***"*

He huffs a quiet laugh. "It doesn't take a namesake and magic to see what's written all over your face. You're not too good at hiding your emotions yet."

I scowl, then sigh. "I know, and I don't mean to be difficult. I just . . . I don't know! Sometimes I want to cry for no reason, and other times, I just want to scream and fight everyone in sight. I can hardly keep up with my own emotions. I shouldn't expect all of you to navigate my mood swings, too."

Castor frowns, then takes a seat on the ground. I follow suit.

"Listen, I know it's difficult keeping up with us," he admits. "Truthfully, we've all still got a lot to learn when it comes to raising you. And it's not on you to navigate us, either." He chuckles again. "If you haven't noticed already, we're just making this up as we go. There isn't exactly a handbook on raising kids we can follow, and we can't order you around as if you're one of our soldiers, either. Not to mention . . . none of us had parents to learn from. As you know, we just . . . are what we are."

I nod, scooting closer so our knees are almost touching. "Do you remember anything from before you were placed here?"

He shakes his head, tipping his head back to gaze up at the sky and sunlight that bleeds through the leaves. "No. There was no before. There was just us. The eight of us and the spheres and the rest of the beings and beasts. Very few predate our own existence, or have been here as long as we have been."

"Such as Pride and the other high-bred demons, to name a few. The Seven Deadly Assassins and the Four Horsemen."

Castor nods, meeting my eyes again as he leans back on his hands. "Them, yes. As well as creatures like the Obsidian Serpent and the Alpha Brothers . . . hell, even the Sleipnir were here before us. Along with the Eight-Pointed Stag and Three-Eyed Bull."

I nod along. "Why do you think Pride is looking for Pollux?"

Castor shrugs. "He mentioned something along the lines of rumors starting up in the Midlands regarding a new contender entering the fray. Pride had been hired out by a few men who had some run-ins with the new foe, so he was hoping to speak with Pollux on the matter and get some credibility on the threat."

I hum. "Should we be concerned if Pride himself has come looking for answers?"

My brother doesn't look too concerned, and he shrugs and shakes his head again. "Threats come and go, Myra. But we're indestructible. Decades drag on into centuries, and history often repeats itself. The only new thing that has happened as of late has been . . . well . . . you." He grins at me. "You've become our only wild card, little feather."

I roll my eyes again and snicker, but then my smile drops as I inquire, "Do you . . . do you not consider me a real archangel?"

Castor blinks at me, looking alarmed as he asks incredulously, "What? Where the hell did you . . . oh . . ." He winces, rubbing the back of his neck as he leans forward closer to me. "Listen, Myra, I shouldn't have—"

"Please don't give me excuses, Castor." I meet his gaze again. "Just answer the question."

He sighs. "No, Myra. I don't believe you to be any less of an archangel than the rest of us. That was wrong of me to say, and I only did it because you were pushing my buttons. I shouldn't have pushed back like that, and I'll regret it for the rest of my days. You know that's not true, right?"

I shrug, shifting around to hug my knees.

"Myra—"

"I've heard other angels call me that."

He straightens up, cocking his head as he says through clenched teeth, "What? Who the fuck—"

"It doesn't matter."

"Yes, it fucking does. Myra, who's been calling you a hoax archangel?"

"Just some of the footmen. I don't know their names."

"Lie."

"I didn't see their faces!"

"Another lie."

I growl. "I thought you weren't Perception!"

He raises his brow at me. "Pollux is the one who taught you how to lie, which is why you never get away with lying to the rest of us. We know your tells because we were there when he taught you how to get away with sneaking out past your bedtime when you thought Apollo wasn't paying attention. Little did you know that the rest of us were. So. Who. Were. They?"

I keep my mouth shut, and Castor growls at me. "Should I go get Apollo?"

"NO—No! They're in lower leadership . . . out of Apollo's branch."

Castor nods, his eyes of ice and steel.

"Are you . . . mad at me?"

"At you? No. Never, Myra . . . I'm annoyed that you didn't tell me, or at least one of us, sooner, but I'm not mad."

"It's not a big deal. I don't care what they have to say about me."

Castor nods, then rises to his feet and holds his hand out for me. I grasp it, and he hauls me onto my feet again.

"Well, I'm glad to hear that **you** don't care, but the rest of your overprotective brothers do."

"What're you gonna do?"

He chuckles darkly. "Some things, my sweet baby sister, you're still too young to know about."

I make a face at him, but he ignores me, and together, we return home.

Tell you what, brothers.
I'm already growing tired of this.
No. Not tired. Bored.
I'm fucking bored.

Do you remember that hot-ass summer we had
at the cottage a few years back, Atticus? When
we hid all of Alastair's summer wear so he had
to either parade around naked or purchase
new clothes that we could hardly afford?
Let's do the same thing with his armor and
weaponry next time we're together. Then
maybe he won't go charging into battle, lest he
desires death.

CHAPTER FOUR
RHESAMYRE

It's a nightmare, whispers Atlas as his arms disappear from me, and he fades from whatever sanctuary this imprinted mindscape is. *It's not real. Stay alive, little wolf.*

Stay. Alive.

A body thumps next to me, and I jerk in my chains as I snap my eyes open to find the empty, void gaze of Juliette. She lies lifelessly on the ground beside me, her bloody insides spilling from her in a messy heap, and she's naked and covered in bruises and lashings.

I turn my eyes away from her, and Bael stalks over and rips my head back by my horns to have me look up at him.

"Let this be a lesson that you can't save them all, *Rhesamyre,*" he snarls.

I snarl back at him, and he tosses my head into the post while his goons free my wrists from the manacles. My arms are practically useless after being in one position all night, and the ripped skin of my back stretches painfully as they jostle me and force me back onto my bare feet.

They walk me back to Bael's private cell, where he keeps all his tools and devices built to torture me in painful, creative ways, but instead of being chained to the ceiling, I am strapped to one of his wooden worktables. The wood digs into the wounds of my back and irritates the ripped skin even further, and the boar and buck strap my ankles and wrists to the table. Bael comes to lean

over me, surveying my form with a curious gaze that promises
pain and suffering.

"We know that General Haidar fled with your allies, little
bitch," he drawls, pushing off the worktable to retrieve one of
his tools to start carving away at me again. "He took a generous
number of flyers and wranglers with him, too. Meanwhile, we still
have yet to locate the rest of the Hellion beasts that disappeared.
I'm sure you've noticed the lack of hellhound presence here as of
late."

Bael returns, situating himself near my legs, but I can't see
what he's grabbed; I don't believe I want to know.

"Surely you know where they may have gone in search of
sanctuary?" he inquires, trailing the blunt edge of a knife up the
outside of my thigh. "I'll even be nice and discuss the possibili-
ties with you. Even if it's just a guess, I'll ensure you're warm in
your cell tonight. I'll even throw in a proper meal. Whatever you
want."

"If I say I want the blood of my enemies, will you drain yourself dry to satisfy me?" I inquire, glancing over at him.

He smirks, digging the tip of his knife into my thigh, prodding
my muscle gently. "If you wanted a taste, all you had to do was
ask."

I blink at him, and Bael frowns at my lack of reaction. "*Oh, well.*
Have it your way. It doesn't make a difference to me. I prefer it
when you struggle and play hard to get, anyway."

Bael lifts his knife and starts to carve.

··············

I sense a presence in the cell with me again, and I turn my stiff
head and blink my eyes open to find a broad male leaning back
against the worktable. His wings appear more mahogany than red
in the dim light of the enchanted torch upon the wall, while his

pale sigils and runes barely illuminate his ebony skin in the darkness.

"*Orion*," I breathe, my voice quiet and painfully hoarse once more.

Orion whirls around, pink eyes—which are a different shade than Atlas's—settle on me as he kneels next to me. His large hand pets my hair and rubs around my horns softly, and I whimper pathetically. He frowns as he observes me, his eyes nearly glossy at the sight.

"You're being so brave," he whispers. "We're so proud of you, little feather."

I nod a little, tears pricking in the corners of my eyes.

"But you can't keep this up forever, baby sister."

I swallow the painful lump in my throat. "I have to try."

He nods along. "I know. You've always been the one to try. Rarely ever fearing failure." He chuckles a little and presses his forehead against my own gently. "Even despite our own trepidations, you've never been one to back down from a fight. Not as Myra, and not as Rhesamyre."

"But it's tempting, Orion," I admit quietly. "I'm fucking terrified. I'm *tired*."

"You can't be brave without knowing first what fear is, little feather. To tell you the truth, I'm scared shitless all the time, mostly for you and our brothers. But we learn how to control our fear instead of letting it control us, and you've always been skilled at that. You've never allowed anyone to control you."

"Unfortunately, I think your confidence is a little misplaced at the moment. Seeing as how I'm the one strapped to a table behind bars."

Orion shakes his head. "It's not misplaced, but your confidence is wavering," he says aloud, but I know he's saying it more to himself now. "You put on a brave face, and I know you're scared, but you have yet to give that sadist what he wants. You have yet to give up your allies. Your friends."

"And I wish I could say with certainty that I never will . . . but I don't know anymore, Orion." My tears fall freely now, and I release a quiet sob. "I want to go home, Orion. Please, *please* take me home!" I cry.

I fucking sob.

"*Shh, shh,*" he coos softly, leaning over my body as he presses his forehead against my own again. He cups my cheeks and wipes away my tears, a few of his own falling now and wetting my cheeks. *"You're so brave, little feather,"* he says in Old Latin. *"You're being so brave."*

. . . .

"Are you sure you opened the conveyance in the right spot?"

"I'm certain of it. I'm not a fool."

Orion scoffs. "Debatable, brother."

Sam snarls, his wings flaring as he sizes up our brother. "This is the origin of the prayers, brother. *I know how to follow the scent of faith and desperation."*

"Oh, is that what we're calling it now?"

Standing off to the side with my arms crossed, I just roll my eyes at the two of them. All three of us are dressed in gray battle leathers and armed to the teeth, surrounded by the feral flora of the hardwood groves just outside the Sacred Cities.

While the males hash it out about directions, *I allow my gaze to wander over the sentient greenery that thrives all around us. Birches, pines, and oaks are riddled with vines, while wiregrass thrives along the forest floor, and there is a sense of darkness here that is a far cry from home. The breeze has a ferocious, curious taste to it that leaves me to believe that if it could slice me open and taste my blood, it would. However, it refrains from doing so and instead twirls the un-bound tendrils of my hair that have fallen from my braid as if more curious about the dark color and soft texture than the taste of me.*

The feathers of my wings prickle in sync with the fine hairs on my arms, and I stiffen where I stand as I open my senses wider to better pinpoint the threat that has begun to prowl toward me. I draw my daggers, rotating my body and fluttering my wings slightly so I may take flight if necessary. My brothers have also ceased their bickering, and we all go still and silent to heed the warnings of our instincts and magic.

"What are you doing out here, little wing?"

I relax at the sound of the suave, deep voice that reaches my ears, and I lower my daggers as I offer Wrath a kind smile.

"Answering prayers," I reply. "I'm afraid an angel's work is never done."

Wrath chuckles as he steps forward out of the woodwork, thus showcasing his lethal, leather-clad body and dark features. Handsome as ever, he's armed to the teeth just like us, and a corner of his lip curls into a devilish smirk as he sizes me up alongside my brothers.

"I'm afraid then that neither is an assassin's," he drawls, his eyes flickering to my brothers as he crosses his arms. "I've been called in to deal with some folks who have . . . unfortunately *chosen the wrong side, it would seem."*

"Wrong side?" I inquire, and Wrath looks at me again. "Wrong side of what?"

Wrath raises his brow, giving my brothers another pointed look as he inquires, "You haven't told her?"

"Apollo believes the threat shall pass," explains Orion. "He's just another false prophet who's gotten a taste of power. But that's all it is and all it shall remain. A taste.*"*

Wrath hums, seeming unconvinced. "And you believe this, too, Samael? Even after what you've witnessed with us?"

"Jury's still out," drawls Sam deeply, shrugging.

"Still here and awaiting an answer, by the way," I snap, looking between the males.

Sam meets my gaze, his dark eyes steeled and revealing nothing. "Lucifer. The most recent threat that has appeared in the Midlands. Laying waste to a few outlying villages at a time while claiming himself to be a **god**."

I bark a laugh. "Unlikely."

Sam nods. "I agree, though he has proven to be quite the nuisance."

Wrath scoffs. "That's putting it politely."

Sam raises his brow at the demon, seeming unimpressed. "I don't see Hell stepping up to aid the mortals, either. All you're doing is running errands for the highest bidders." My brother grins, the action unhinged and feral as he taunts, "Swallow any good souls lately?"

Wrath bares his teeth, seething, "King Abaddon doesn't meddle in foreign affairs."

I cock my head at the hostility, reviewing Sam's words for a heartbeat before I drawl, "I didn't believe you assassins and Horsemen were beholden to his reign . . . and you didn't answer his question."

Wrath raises his brow, his attention divided between my brothers and me.

"About the swallowing of souls," I clarify.

The assassin does a double take at me, cocking his head and surveying my form once more before he scoffs softly, humming a quiet, "Huh . . . I suppose there is hope for you yet, little wing."

I furrow my brows, still not following their thoughts. I had heard rumors of a new foe rising up in the Midlands and claiming some land out there, but Apollo and the rest of my brothers had reassured me that another tip in the scales was bound to happen eventually. However, while ruling powers rotate and are challenged, and civil wars often follow suit, they claim it's nothing to lose sleep over. Mortals and other beings will pray and bargain if they need assistance in dealing with this new evil, and until they do, we are to stay out of their affairs.

Apollo says we have our own people to look after, and stretching our resources isn't beneficial to celestials. Mortals have nothing to give.

And I . . . I have yet to decide if I agree with him.

"Well," drawls Orion. "Who are you here to murder?"

Wrath narrows his eyes. "That's demon business."

Sam scoffs at that, muttering, "Typical."

I roll my eyes harder, stepping in front of my brothers as I address Wrath. "It's possible our paths will cross while here, and we're following a rogue prayer path. Pollux flagged it as . . . unusual. We're here to investigate."

Wrath reveals nothing as he hums again, but thankfully, he doesn't give me attitude when he replies, "My brothers and I, as well as the Horsemen, have been keeping tabs on a few of the followers that Lucifer has managed to accumulate over the past year. Mortal men desperate for a power fix, mostly . . . though some do stand out as more desperate than others."

"Who are you hunting?"

He smirks a little. "Rephrase that question, little wing."

I raise my brow, even more curious now. "What are you hunting?"

"There's been another wendigo attack. I've been hired to dispatch them."

"That seems a little below your pay grade," quips Sam.

Wrath shrugs gracefully, glancing at my brother over my head before looking down at me again. "Rumor has it, these wendigos have been leashed."

"Leashed?" inquires Orion. "That's not an easy feat by any means. Nor is it a wise one."

Wrath inclines his head. "We know. Hence why I'm here looking into it."

"But you've been hired to dispatch the wendigos," I think aloud. "What about the one leashing them?"

"That will come in time. This is the job first and foremost, but rest assured, consequences will find the one who collared the beasts."

I hum in thought, then glance back at my brothers. "The prayers we're here to answer . . . can you recite one?"

Sam raises his brow at me, but then nods as his eyes and sigils begin to glow; the dark angelic runes that are tattooed and branded across his arms and hands hum to life as he recounts the prayer we're here to answer. "Oh, angels of the heavenly sphere, here our cry when we ask that you aid us in fighting off the rising evils of our sacred sphere. The monsters are real, and they have come for our children."

Wrath raises his brow at us again. "That doesn't sound all that different from the usual pleas and prayers."

Orion dips his chin. "In addition to this, we've also heard whispers of strange happenings that only occur when the magics here are provoked."

"Someone or something has angered this sphere," I add. "Pissed it off quite impressively. We're here to investigate because the magic has grown wilder in just a few days since we received the prayers for help. Yes, it sounds like all the rest, and we try to answer as many as we can, but this one just felt different, and Pollux confirmed as much. It's a rogue prayer because of who it originates from."

"And who might that be?" the assassin asks.

"Lilith. A witch."

Wrath blinks in surprise. "A witch." He narrows his eyes. "Of which side?"

"Witches are loyal to magic, not kings or the duality of men and celestials or demons," says Sam. "The fact that she reached out to us at all speaks for itself, as witches tend to deal with matters themselves, and we stay out of it. For better or worse."

"Lilith is a woodland witch, not a Westerner," I say. "She's in line to assume leadership of her coven."

Wrath hums again. "And where might this witch be now?"

"Home. We were planning to go speak with her."

He nods. "Then let's go."

Orion scoffs. "You're coming along with us?"

"Well," drawls Wrath. "It is as Myra said. Our paths will most likely cross again while we're here. Thus, we might as well search together. Perhaps this witch of yours knows something of the wendigos."

I nod. "Then together it shall be."

I walk onward toward the main square of the Sacred Cities, the males close behind and quiet as we pass the wards and a few outlying cottages scattered amongst the woodwork. Then, as we near the town, the noise of pedestrians, animals, and village life fills the air that smells of bread and herbs.

This square of the Sacred Cities is not littered with higher castles and sky-scraping towers. Instead, homes, shops, and taverns litter the gravel roads in tighter clumps within thin property lines. Wildlife grows freely while fountains litter crossroads and walls, and children of varying breeds run amok as their parents work or mingle on the outskirts of the paths.

The four of us draw plenty of attention as we continue down the road, but I do my best to offer gentle smiles and little waves to the people here. Very few mortals, and mostly off-bred celestials and demons, and even a few angels, too, make up the population here.

The fine hairs on my arms stand on end, and I pause mid-step as the breeze plays with my hair again and draws my curiosity toward another scent of damp but sweet herbs. Then, settling my gaze on the beautiful redhead as she consoles a crying child, I stride forward once more.

"Lilith?" I call in Plebian.

The witch's pensive green eyes snap up to me, and she flicks her gaze all over my form before rising to her feet and nodding.

"The feral magics of my craft whisper your name, lass." She tilts her head at me. "They're fond of you."

I cock my head in return, inquiring softly, "Who is?"

Lilith shrugs. "I do not know. Their names are not to be uttered by our tongues."

I nod carefully, and Sam and Orion appear on either side of me with scowls and steeled forms.

"You're Lilith?" asks Orion.

She bows her head.

"You called," drawls Sam, sounding bored. "We came."

Lilith looks at me again, and I drop my eyes to survey her attire. She's dressed in a casual green dress of soft material paired with black flats, and while her fair skin is kissed by a faint layer of freckles every-where, I don't see any sigils or runes that depict her craft.

"While I am curious to know just how many prayers you truly do answer," she starts, "I know better than to ask you now and risk you turning your back on us."

"Who's us?*" inquires Orion, because Sam looks livid.*

"The people here, as well as the other witches in my coven. We didn't see them coming. They came in the night and stole the babes from their beds. It was strategic. Too planned out for it to be a wild attack."

"What came?" I inquire.

Lilith looks over and locks eyes with Wrath. "I had told my kin not to make deals with devils, but I suppose your presence here means they did sign a contract with you. What was the price?"

"That isn't any of your business," growls Wrath. "Nor should it be a concern of yours now. Where were the wendigos last seen?"

Lilith hums as if displeased, but then points north and gives us the directions necessary to hunt the wicked beasts. The males thank her, then head off. However, I remain behind and keep eye contact with the witch for a minute longer. She offers me a beautiful smile, but it is full of mirth and, dare I say, mockery.

"What magics whisper my name, witch?"

"I cannot say, Myra. I do not know them."

"Would you tell me if you did?"

She shrugs gracefully. "I don't know. I don't know you, but something out there does." She cocks her head, green eyes inquisitive and curious. "Your destiny is not clear to me. Your brothers and the high-bred males of Hell, it is clear who they are and what they have been put here to do, but you are an anomaly of an archangel. Your fate isn't sealed. Your story is unwritten . . . yet you have already attracted the attention of higher powers in your short sixteen years of life. Why do you believe that is?"

"I wish I had an answer for you, as well as myself."

Lilith hums. "Me, too . . . thank you for coming to our aid."

I nod. "We do what we can, but may I ask, why haven't you and your coven gone after them?"

"We tried, but their leashes are tight. And the hand that holds them is a closed fist that we cannot release. A different sort of strength is needed here, and we do not have that power."

I dip my chin. "Understood. We'll see to it that it is done."

"And we thank you for it."

Leaving Lilith in town, I catch up with my brothers and Wrath as we traverse back into the woodlands. Soon enough, Orion and Sam pick up a faint trail, and I walk in the back with Wrath as my brothers lead the way, following the foul stench of evil and wickedness.

"You still haven't answered him," I quip, glancing up at Wrath.

He side-eyes me. "About what?"

"About the soul swallowing thing."

Wrath sighs. "Ah. That. *Yes, well, there aren't exactly any souls left to swallow at the moment."*

I pause mid-step. "What the hell does that mean?"

Wrath stops walking with me and sizes me up again, then inquires quietly, "How much have your brothers told you about Lucifer?"

I cross my arms. "Apollo says it isn't a big deal. The rest seem inclined to agree."

Wrath hums, mirroring my stance. "Yeah, I wondered about that," he mutters. "If you're so curious, ask them again. And this time, mention the fact that you know Lucifer has been stealing souls."

I gawk at the assassin. "What? How? For what purpose could he—"

"We don't know yet. And unfortunately, we don't know much about him at all. We've never encountered anything like Lucifer before."

I start walking again, my gaze low as I contemplate Wrath's words. "I can't imagine Death is too happy about that."

Wrath chuckles lowly, darkly. "No. He's not."

We fall silent once more, thus giving me a chance to better observe my surroundings. Then, soon enough, we're coming across a small camp within one of the clearings. Or, at least, what's left of it.

Blood splatters across every surface, and the few tents are torn and ripped to shreds while supplies litter the site haphazardly. We spread out to survey the mess of blood and claw marks that mar the trunks of trees and the ground, and I step around the many tripping hazards as I survey inside the tents and few belongings. I crouch before one of the few bags still intact, reaching inside as my magic purrs gently.

"Sam," I breathe, and he's beside me in a heartbeat as I grasp the jar of glowing dandelions that dance about.

Peri.

I meet my brother's steeled gaze. "They captured fucking Peri," I snarl.

Sam nods, his dark eyes looking as enraged as I feel, but then he tenses and twirls as a sword erupts from black fire in his hands. He knocks me back further behind him as a snarling, shrieking beast lands on him after leaping from the branches above us, and I scurry backward and cradle the jar of helpless Peri against my chest as a dozen wendigos reveal themselves and drop from the trees.

Wrath and Orion command their magic and weaponry to defend themselves, and Sam roars as he plunges his sword through the massive, vile monster of bone and melted flesh that shrieks and snaps its oversized teeth at my brother. Long limbs, claws, horns, and poisonous barbs, Sam removes the creature of its head before he spins to kill another.

With the Peri still in hand, I roll away and jump to my feet just before another wendigo lands in front of me. Cocking its head and twitching as dark blood and black goo seeps from its flesh and pores, it shrieks and launches for me. I spin and kick outward, drawing my sword and slicing the monster in two while keeping hold of the Peri. Another one snarls in my face, venomous spittle landing on my cheeks, and I wrench myself away from it just as Wrath drives his sword through the monster's skull.

"Defend the Peri, little wing," he growls, standing in front of me protectively as my brothers slaughter monsters all around us. "We'll handle the wendigos."

I would feel more inclined to argue with him if it weren't for the jar of Peri in my hands, so I rise to my booted feet again and back away from the carnage to stay out of their way.

Leaving the Peri unprotected is not an option.

I retreat further into the woodwork, away from the bloodshed and wendigos; however, when I turn to flee and find somewhere safer to release the Peri, I stop in my tracks and size up the approaching wendigo as it removes its camouflage. It had blended in perfectly with the tree, then steps away from the bark as if it and the hardwood were one and the same. Risking a glance upward at the branches, I spy the mutilated bodies of the mortal men who had no doubt attempted to leash the wendigos in the first place, as well as capture the Peri.

Foolish, foolish men. First for believing they could leash wendigos and then for attempting to steal the Peri. They deserve the brutal deaths they got, and from the looks of them, it was indeed bloody.

Their bodies are nothing but bloody strips and ribbons scattered throughout the branches where the wendigos had no doubt been feasting before we stumbled upon the remnants of the campsite.

The wendigo ahead of me cocks its head and twitches oddly like the other one did, then inhales deeply and growls lowly. I clutch the jar of Peri harder, baring my teeth to snarl in warning.

A terrifying monster of nightmares, raw bones, rotten flesh, and venom that can bring even an archangel or high-bred demon to his knees. Claws for hands and lithe appendages with a chest of sharp ribs that protrude forward as if they're teeth.

Evil and mean, with nothing on the mind except its next meal.

And I'm not it. Nor will it get the chance to consume the Peri like candy. Wendigos do not care about cravings, only satisfying their hunger with whatever or whoever may be nearby. Be it a mortal or an angel, or even a bunny, if they feel so inclined to catch one.

The wendigo charges, and a heartbeat before the monster is upon me, I toss the jar of Peri into the air, draw my sword, and drive it through its chest. Then I kick it backward, away from me, and leap forward to catch the Peri again.

"Sorry," I murmur in Old Latin to the little stars. "Just hang tight. I'll get you out of here."

I flap my wings and take flight, launching into the sky to get far away from here and release the Peri elsewhere so I may return and fight alongside my brothers and Wrath.

Finding another clearing a few miles from the fight, I touch down and go to my knees in the grass. The Peri float about in their glass confines, and I break the lid and set the jar down to let them float out on their own.

"You're free now," I continue in Old Latin. "Get far away from here. Go where others cannot follow you. Where they cannot find nor harm you."

The Peri float out of the jar and hover in front of me for a few heartbeats, then proceed upward toward the clear sky and disappear in the breeze. I remain where I am for a second longer, then rise to my feet once more and launch into the sky again, back toward my brothers.

Upon arrival, all the wendigos have been slain, and Wrath, Sam, and Orion stand in the middle of the carnage, covered in blood and gore. I land next to them, and Orion surveys my form as he asks about the Peri.

"Free and gone from here," I reply, crossing my arms as I survey the slaughtered wendigos. "It's scary how well they can hide in plain sight."

Wrath chuckles darkly. "More than you know, little wing."

"We should get going," quips Sam, looking annoyed, as usual. "Things are changing quicker than I would like to admit."

"Agreed," says Orion, looking to Wrath. "And you?"

Wrath studies my brothers for a moment, then looks at me. "We'll be in touch."

I nod in reply, and we burn the bodies before parting ways with the assassin.

Do not preach to me about love and loss or
good and evil.
It's all the same lecture given by different
lords and leaderships all throughout different
points of our history.

I do not care to listen.

Are you listening now, brothers?
Do you hear them when they weep for saviors
and saints?
I don't think we are any different.
We will be martyrs.

CHAPTER FIVE
RHESAMYRE

Bael is ruthless. Relentless.

I'm hanging from the ceiling again, and I can barely see him because my eyes are swollen shut.

However, when he hits me again, I don't have much time to register the pain as it blooms in my head before another's phantom hands are grasping my cheeks. I focus enough to see lilac eyes, and Nihal sweeps my consciousness away from me just before Bael hits me again.

....

The doors to the library open with a quiet creak, and I glance up from my book to survey Nihal as he strides forward in a white celestial suit. He looks exhausted, *no doubt thanks to playing politics all day, and he dramatizes the emotion as he plops down next to me on the sofa with a heavy sigh. I eye him skeptically as he slumps against the cushions and spreads his legs out before him in an ungentlemanly manner, while I remain curled up in the blankets with a book of fantasy in hand.*

Nihal glances at me pointedly with those ever-curious, lilac eyes of his.

"And where have we ventured off to today, little feather?" he inquires, leaning against my shoulder to read part of the page.

Thankfully, it isn't anything inappropriate . . . this time.

"The fantastical world of a faraway kingdom that relies on the earth and elements to fuel their magic. They call their kings and

queens demigods, *not* deities, *as we might if we were more god than man.*"

Nihal hums. "It certainly beats reading over documents and war maps all day."

I snap my fingers in his face, making him raise his brows at me, but he doesn't flinch like I wanted him to. "Hey! You know the rules! No politics when our books of fiction are open!"

Nihal chuckles. "Right, right. My bad."

I grin at him, then bookmark my page and set my book down as I turn to face him.

Time with Nihal is different than time with my other brothers. Usually, we're curled up on the couch together, reading or studying history, art, and languages, with snacks and tea scattered about the tables around pages of literature and notebooks. He's a good teacher. It's almost impossible to ruffle his feathers, and I've only seen him pissed a handful of times. Usually, those times are when someone makes a crude comment about me. Or worse.

Threatens me.

May Hell have mercy on the souls that dare to threaten the youngest of the archangels, because my brothers certainly won't.

"How goes the discussions of allegiances and allies?" I inquire.

Nihal sighs again, rubbing the bridge of his nose as he leans his head back and closes his eyes. "We're fucked."

I laugh abruptly at that. "Damn, okay . . . should I . . .?"

"No." He opens his eyes again and gives me his undivided attention once more. "You've done enough. Let us pull our own weight, Myra."

"I've seen the turmoil this new self-proclaimed god *has begun to stir firsthand, Nihal. You lot can't keep me tucked away in here forever. I* **will** *run out of books eventually. Then what will you do?"*

He chuckles again. "I know . . . but we would like to try at least."

I hum, lowering my gaze in thought. "The Seven and the Four are at least on our side . . . perhaps that will be enough?"

He shrugs gracefully, his violet wings twitching with the motion as he leans back on them. "I suppose we can only hope, at this point in time."

"Or . . . maybe . . ."

"What?"

"We could ask for more help? You know . . . from another?"

He raises his brow at me, looking skeptical. "You want to pray to . . . what?" He huffs a laugh that resembles a scoff. "The Yonder Star and Fern above?"

I scowl. "You make it sound so primitive."

"Because it is. Archangels don't pray, Myra. We **answer** prayers."

"And how well has that been working out as of late?"

He sighs again. "Myra—"

"Don't brush the notion aside so swiftly, Nihal. I'm not saying we get on our knees and fucking beg, but you know just as well as I that magic, at times, tends to have a mind of its own. Magic believes in bargains and good fortune . . . perhaps there is another way to gain its favor and defeat Lucifer."

Nihal shakes his head. "Defeating Lucifer isn't the goal, baby sister. Defending our home is."

"Isn't that one and the same?"

"It's . . . complicated."

I scoff. "Only because you make it so. You said it yourself, Nihal. We are supposed to answer prayers. And I don't know if you've been listening lately, but the prayers have all begun to sound the same. Lucifer and his Apostles are a menace, and they must be dealt with swiftly."

Nihal inhales and exhales again slowly. "I hear you, but threats come and go, Myra. This one is no different. We have been here for *centuries, and we will be here for thousands of centuries more. Long after Lucifer is gone and nothing but a fragment of a memory remains. If you are to put your faith in anything, put your faith in that. Archangels are steel and stone and stars. We are mountains and valleys and shadows and magic.* **Nothing** *can harm us, and we do not fall."*

....

I wake again with a jolt, feeling Bael twist his knife deep into my lower back.

"Ah, good," he drawls, chuckling. "Where did you go? I'm not done with you yet."

I pant as he plays with the knife again and suppress a pained groan as he removes it and lets me bleed. He grabs me by my horn again, twisting my head to the side so I can meet his sadistic gaze. He grins at me, then licks my cheek sloppily, and I'm startled at the fact that I had been *crying.*

"Your tears taste so sweet," he breathes. *"Like fucking prey."*

I snarl at him, but he yanks my head back further and presses his fingers into my newest wound. My snarl turns into a pathetic whimper, and he drops my head, seeming satisfied with the sound.

"Poor little bitch," he muses. "Your growls are growing weaker by the day. It's music to my ears."

If Atticus doesn't do it first, I'm going to skin him alive, growls Atlas in the back of my head.

You mean to say, if I don't do it first, I reply quietly just before he disappears again.

Bael returns to his workbench riddled with tools, and I shudder in my chains and steel myself for whatever else he has planned next. He rarely asks me any questions anymore. All he does is play with me. Torture me, hurt me, torment me with freedoms, shackles, and what may or may not remain of my family.

Not to mention, Atticus is *alive* and here in Hell. At least, that's what Bael says, and a part of me wants to foolishly believe it despite the implications of what his being here actually means.

Bael whistles a nameless tune while he works, sharpening his blades and holding some up so I can no doubt spy them as they glint in the lights.

Hands come into my field of vision and clamp over my eyes gently, and a male whispers lowly in my ear, "Don't look at them, Rhesa*myra*."

I inhale sharply, tensing at his voice as I mutter, "*Adriel*."

"I'm here, baby sister. Though I don't know if that calms your nerves or fuels them, considering what has happened and what I've done."

I shake my head, his hand still over my eyes to keep me from watching Bael. "I don't . . . I don't know anymore . . . I *should* hate you. I *want* to hate you—"

"I know." He sighs. "I know things are convoluted and scary, but you're not alone right now. I am here with you."

I almost choke on a sob but refrain so as not to draw attention to myself and bring Bael closer. "No. You're not. Because I killed you," I whisper.

He doesn't reply. What could he say other than the truth? That he knows I killed him in cold blood because he did the same to Samael?

And I don't regret it.

"I wouldn't expect you to," he says, reading my thoughts. "You did what you thought was right. What was best . . . just as you did back then. And just like back then, you were right. And we were wrong." He curses quietly under his breath, then says in Old

Latin, *"I have failed you more times than I can count, Myra. So please, let me do this for you. Let me take you away from here, at least for a little while."*

I'm helpless to stop him when he does.

················

"You're an ass, Adriel!" I scream.

Adriel snarls as he rushes toward me, a few of us having just returned from a mission and are scattered about the great hall. Samael places a hand on our brother's chest in warning, and Adriel scowls at him with a glare that would force lesser males to their knees, but Sam merely raises his brow in challenge, standing between him and me like a brick wall.

"Turn around," snarls Sam. The sound is soft and quiet, but ultimately sharp and deadly, nonetheless. "And walk away. Go cool off. You approach her like you are, and so help me stars, I will *hurt you."*

Adriel snarls again, glances at me one last time, and then scoffs and stalks off in the opposite direction. However, I'm not through with him yet, and I take a step to go after him. Hands wrap around my middle, and Pollux chuckles lowly.

"Whoa, there," he drawls. "Easy, little feather. While I'm confident you could hold your own, I'm not too sure you truly want to fight that one at the moment."

I snarl in my brother's arms. "How dare he claim the title of loyalty! *He's nothing but a self-serving, conniving, son-of-a—"*

"Fucking hell, Myra," starts Orion, eyes wide with equal parts humor and alarm. "What happened out there? I thought this was a recon op?"

"It was supposed to be," says Sam, studying me as Pollux attempts to calm me down as he would some frenzied, feral beast, but I don't relent. "However, the intel was slightly off."

"How *off?*" inquires Apollo, arms crossed as he eyes me, his stance all business and ruthless archangel.

"By a few **thousand**," I quip. "We weren't surveying and walking into a camp of dozens of slaves that his Apostles rounded up. We walked into a camp of thousands of footmen."

"It was a bloodbath," adds Sam. "We're none the worse for wear, obviously, but I can't say the same for our own footmen who joined. As well as a few other allies that had infiltrated the camp under the Horsemen's instructions."

"And where might they be now?" inquires Apollo, no doubt trying to piece together exactly what went wrong and why I'm so pissed about it.

"Dead," says Pollux. "Out of our men and allies, including the few slaves that were there, too, we're all that remains."

"Because Adriel was a coward and opened a conveyance to flee before we could liberate them all!" I snarl.

"His priority was getting you out of there first and foremost, Myra," says Sam, though he doesn't appear or sound all that happy about it, either. "Any of us would have done the same, too."

"Liar. And what's the point of being fucking indestructible if we don't stay behind to hold the line? Dozens of good lives were lost today! Angelic lives and others!"

"What about the rest of the camp?" inquires Nihal.

"Lucifer's forces there have been dealt with," answers Sam.

Apollo turns his attention back to Pollux. "How did we miss this?"

"I'm working on that as we speak," replies Pollux, and he shifts around so that he's standing in front of me, brows raised. "If I let you go, are you going to do something reckless?"

I debate lying for a heartbeat, and Pollux narrows his eyes at me. I cock my head, sneering, "I just have a few choice words for our dear brother. That's all."

Pollux sighs and shakes his head. "What's done is done, Myra. There is nothing we can do to change it."

I inhale and exhale very carefully, and slowly, Pollux removes his hands from my shoulders.

He nods. "Good. Now, if you'll all excuse me, I have some matters to attend to."

Pollux takes his leave, and Sam sighs. "I, too, should probably go discuss matters with those of Hell. Things are not going exactly as planned."

"You wanna make the stars laugh?" I quip, watching him go.

"Make a plan," he replies as he exits, the doors of the great hall clicking shut behind him.

Apollo shakes his head at me, and he and the rest of my brothers busy themselves with discussing politics and schemes again. So, while they're momentarily distracted, I make myself scarce and go search for Adriel.

It doesn't take me long to track him down, as we all have one thing in common when we need to cool down and get ourselves under control again.

We go to the mats.

The training hall is empty and quiet, save for Adriel in the center. He's shirtless, already having discarded the white leathers that were splattered with blood from the unexpected battle we fought against a few hundred of Lucifer's footmen. Angelic sigils and tattoos litter his torso, and his muscles ripple as he punches the sandbag that hangs in the center of the room.

He's your brother. He's your brother. He's your brother.

Even so, they're all tall and handsome and muscular and littered with tattoos and—

"Get out," snarls Adriel.

Oh, that's right. I'm angry with this fucker.

I cross my arms and stalk forward. "No. And you had no right to grab me mid-battle and haul me back here against my will!"

Adriel punches the bag again, and it goes swinging; the enchanted ropes above us groan with the impact of his fist. He settles his gaze on me, sizing me up, and I bristle at the challenge.

"We were winning that fight," I argue. "And we still had more intel to gather. Especially considering the fact that what we already had was **wrong**.*"*

"Exactly," he spits.

I raise my brow at him. "Excuse me?"

"We. Were. **Wrong**.*"*

I cock my head at him, and he snarls and seethes, "So who's to say we aren't wrong about other things regarding our sphere and species as a whole, too? You're right about one thing, Myra. Lucifer **is** *different than other foes we've faced in the past, and I don't want to find out if those differences also include him being able to harm us . . . harm* **you**.*" He growls to himself again. "It doesn't help that you're already different from us on a fundamental level."*

I snarl at him. "It isn't for you to decide when, where, or how I choose to fight and potentially lay down my life for others if it comes to that. **None** *of* **you** *gets a say in the matter of* **my** *choices!"*

"Then what the hell are we to do as your brothers, huh? Just stand aside and potentially watch you be harmed if Lucifer **can**, *in fact, do so?"*

I clamp my mouth shut.

He scoffs. "Yeah, that's what I fucking thought. You're too young and idealistic for your own good, Myra. And despite you not believing it, I **am** *the Archangel of Loyalty, but my loyalty belongs to you and our brothers first and foremost, and then our home. Allies become a second thought when* **you** *are on the battlefield."*

I blink at him. "How chivalrous of you, but I feel as though I should take a part of that and feel insulted by it." I narrow my eyes at him. "Do you not believe me capable of handling myself, Adriel?"

He growls, taking a step toward me. "That isn't what I said."

"Isn't it, though?"

"No. It isn't.*" He sighs in exasperation, closing his eyes as his wings grow heavy on his back. "Fucking hell, Myra . . . no matter how old or powerful you may one day become, you are still our baby sister.* **My** *baby sister. And I will* **always** *worry. That is my job. I know you're capable of handling yourself and protecting others at the same time, but our first instinct will* **always** *be to* **protect you.** *It is our nature just as much as it is ingrained into our magic."*

I open my mouth to say something, but I find myself coming up short.

What do I do in this situation? Chew him out some more? Apologize? No, fuck that, I'm not apologizing . . . reassurance, then.

I nod to myself, taking a breath to calm the rage in my blood as I approach my brother.

I take his hands in mine, noting the blood still caked underneath both our nails and on our palms. "I'm not going anywhere, Adriel. I am just as much an archangel as the rest of you. I am indestructible. I am a warrior. And I will fight beside all of you when that time comes."

Adriel meets my gaze with those green eyes of his, and though he sees me, hears me . . . I don't know if he believes me.

....

When I wake again, it takes me longer than usual to get my bearings and focus on my surroundings.

Bael, that motherfucker—

He strung me up upside down.

There is a pounding behind my eyes, and my horns ache—*everything aches*—and I can feel all the blood has rushed to my head.

Atlas? I call out to him silently, though it pains me to do so.

Still here, little wolf, he replies. *So long as I'm able, I will stay by your side.*

"There you are," croons Bael, and he crouches beside my head. "You passed out on me again. That's no fun," he *tsks*.

I stare at him.

He frowns at my silence, then pokes his fingers into my stomach and pushes me a little to make me sway in my chains. I clamp my eyes shut to keep the nausea at bay, and Bael laughs at my expense again.

"Anyway, since you're just hanging there, and I seem to have your attention again. I thought you would be pleased to hear that you've been summoned by his majesty, the king."

I open my eyes again, and Bael smirks cruelly.

"Congratulations, little bitch. You're going *home*."

WE HAD FOUND OURSELVES ON THE SAME SIDE AGAIN, BUT NOT FOR LONG BEFORE ATTICUS WAS TAKEN FROM US.
TAKEN BY OUR ENEMIES. THE SAME CELESTIALS HE ONCE CALLED ALLIES.
HIS BODY WAS BROKEN. HIS MIND STILL ACTIVE, BUT DULL. NOT AS SHARP AS IT ONCE WAS. AS IT SHOULD HAVE BEEN.
THEY BEAT HIM. TORTURED HIM. UNTIL ONLY A SHELL OF A MAN WAS LEFT BEHIND.
ATLAS AND I DON'T KNOW WHAT TO DO FOR HIM. HE WON'T LET US HELP HIM. A PART OF ME BELIEVES HE THINKS HE IS BEYOND REPAIR.
HE CERTAINLY LOOKED LIKE IT WHEN WE FOUND HIM. IT TOOK US TWO MONTHS TO FIND HIM.

CHAPTER SIX
ATTICUS

Their moans are quiet and pained, and I step on top of hands and directly onto torsos as I make my way through the carnage I created. I snap my fingers to light the smoke between my lips, and I inhale the cherry and vanilla taste of the cigarette before exhaling slowly and tipping my head back. I still in the middle of the chaos, narrowly avoiding the ceiling as it caves in around me, but I don't flinch as the lit particles of ash singe the corner threads of my leathers and disheveled suit.

The rest of the fire rages onward on all sides, and Lucifer's troops of beasts and monsters scream in agony before snuffing out completely as the camp goes up in flames.

Over one hundred thousand men. Gone in an instant.

Where he keeps getting the bodies to add to his armies remains a mystery to me, one which I'm too miserable to solve at the moment, but at least I'm inconveniencing him in some manner. I'm sure it has something to do with that stupid altar on the other side of the passageway at the Falls of Man, but I haven't quite worked up the courage to venture into the unknown yet.

I unscrew my flask and knock back a shot.

My courage is ever increasing, at least.

I maneuver through the smoky clusterfuck that this camp has become, tossing my smoke away and igniting another portion of the tents in the process just as I grab another cig to chase the first. The foul, singed scent of burnt corpses is thick in the air like miasma, and it taints and clouds a large portion of the Midlands where Lucifer's Apostles have since been laying waste and making camps to shackle their monsters and slaves.

For every three camps I destroy, another pops up in a new area of the sphere, or sometimes in a completely *different* sphere. I have no doubts the same will happen once more as soon as Lucifer and his leaders learn of my handiwork here on the outskirts of Goldfinch, but I'll be long gone by the time they get here.

I take another look at the smoky carnage. Active flames still devour the semi-permanent structures of this camp, and as far as my magic can tell, no one has been spared from the heat of my wrath.

Ah—wait.

My magic flickers, and I command a bow and arrow to erupt from black flames into my palm. I nock and take aim, ignoring the way my cigarette burns my lips as the ash gets too close to my skin, and release my arrow on a fierce wind. It slices through the smoke and settles deep into the foreign monster's eyeball before the tip shoves out the other side at the back of his mangled head, and he drops into the puddles that have begun to form upon the ground, thanks to the blood and other bodily fluids that have drained from the bodies. Other barrels of alcohol and lighter fluid catch fire and explode, and the wood shards fly past my head and cut my cheeks.

I swipe my tongue upward to catch a droplet of blood, and it tastes foreign and foul on my tongue.

I crave Rhesamyre.

My body vibrates as my magic snaps its teeth under my skin, and I growl before roaring toward the sky and erupting once more. I can feel the entire sphere itself crack and splinter, and the ground rumbles beneath my boots and nearly caves in on itself as I destroy everything within a few miles of me.

I grit my teeth as my magic seethes, not at all satisfied with the outburst of force, and I reach for another smoke and light it with a snap of my fingers once more before I open a conveyance and step through it with burning sigils. My brands and tattoos flare and itch, and I resist the urge to take a knife to my skin and carve them out. The one on my ribs—*Rhesa's truculent brand*—is ever inflamed and enraged. Hot to the touch as though it festers with infection and fever.

It's a pain to do so, but I ignore it.

The frigid air of the caps upon the highest peaks of the Starry Mountains smacks me in the face, and I growl as I stalk through the snow to enter the humble cabin I once used during the first wars when my brothers and I had yet to unite with the Four Horsemen and commence the Wild Hunt.

Nobody knew it existed then, and thankfully, no one knows it exists now.

I snatch my half-empty bottle of demonic whiskey off the kitchen table and stalk into the living area where the hearth burns. The cabin itself is pleasantly luxurious and sentient, hence why it has managed to stay upright all these years, unaffected by the elements and uninhabited by strangers or animals, but similarly to back then, I do very little to please it.

Rhesa once told us stories of how she'd feed her blood to her cabin back in Soulton, or she'd read it something smutty.

Yeah. I'm not fucking doing that.

My head aches, and so does my fucking body at the thought of her. My magic itches beneath my skin, and I uncork my whiskey bottle and take a long swig, then tip backward and lounge against my settee with my legs spread and head bowed before I work up the courage to stare up at the wall above the hearth.

Intricate maps of our *nine* living spheres decorate the wall, riddled with notes and dozens of giant *X's* that mark Lucifer's campsites and slaving pits. Another cross-mark covers the original *X* to showcase where I've done my part to slow down his conquering, but at this rate, it's a losing game. I know that the only way to stop him lies with offing his Apostles and destroying the altar, but presently, I have no way of getting to it. And it does no good to murder the Apostles when, A: he can bring them back so long as the altar is active. And B: they reside within the Zodiacs' bodies, where only the Zodiac Blade can touch them.

I light another smoke to chase the taste of my whiskey.

This is exhausting. Fuck my fucking life.

And I would try to end it again if not for—

You don't get to.

I take another swig of my whiskey bottle when that ever-fucking-persistent voice, which almost sounds like Alastair's disappointed tone, breaks through the fog in my head. It fails to provide any sort of clarity or answers as to why I don't get to off myself when everyone I care about is gone, but here we fucking are. Hardly coexisting, but breathing nonetheless, despite my attempts to drown it or smoke it out of my head.

I knock back the rest of the fucking bottle and promptly pass the fuck out before it can judge my poor coping mechanisms.

Because swallowing the whiskey is easier than swallowing the fact that Rhesa and my stupid brothers are dead. And they're never coming home.

··············

The hearth crackles violently, the wood within the fireplace snapping much louder than usual, and I wake with a start when I feel the outlying wards of my small territory snarl in warning.

I stand and slowly advance toward the door, but just as I near it, my magic flares. I whirl around, dagger in hand, and fling it at the approaching figure that has just materialized in the center of the room from a conveyance.

The reaper catches it a hair's breadth away from his neck, and he narrows his ghostly eyes as he scowls at me.

I stand up straighter. "How the fuck did you find me?" I drawl, crossing my arms. "And how'd you get in here?"

Damian shrugs, flinging my dagger back at me, which I promptly catch. "Cabin let me in."

I slam my dagger into the wall of the cabin, and the wood groans at me.

"I wouldn't piss off your house if I were you. It's not like you have anywhere else to live at the moment."

"Fuck off," I snarl. "And you didn't answer my question. How did you find me, boy?"

Damian's scowl is impressively professional. Reaper or not, this kid is a demon.

"The stench of death wafts off you just as much as that smoke from Rhesa's favorite cigarettes does, and reapers have always had a keen nose for it."

"You tracked me here because I *smell*?"

"*Something like that*," he seethes through gritted teeth. "Though you are still one tough fucker to find. Even with all the fireworks you've been setting off out there to piss off the over-lord."

"Maybe that was by design," I drawl, stalking back toward my settee.

"You've certainly been causing a lot of damage. Leaving nothing but singed wastelands in the wake of your warpath."

I hum lowly, plopping back down onto my sofa to light another smoke.

"But the problem is the passageway and the Apostles. We need to take them out, and the rest will fall."

"Looks like you've got it all figured out," I quip. "So how do you suggest we do that, *lieutenant*?"

He remains quiet, and I take a slow drag from my smoke. "That's what I fucking thought. So until you come up with a more permanent solution, I plan on sticking to my meddlesome inconveniencing that is sure to at least give that fucker Lucifer a headache."

"You're a pain in the ass, Atticus."

"That is the goal, boy."

He scoffs. "I didn't want to believe Kure when he said enlisting your help would do no good, but fucking hell, man. You're just . . . wasting away in here . . . all while Rhesa is still being held captive in the—"

My hand is on his throat before he can blink, and I pin him against the wall and slowly exhale the remnants of smoke in my lungs onto his face as I seethe, "*Our queen is dead*. And you'd do well to remember not to speak of her when in the presence of a vengeful, wrathful deity, boy."

Damian blinks at me, alarmed at first, but then he grows confused. He wraps his hand around my wrist in an attempt to break my hold, but I stand firm.

I've got entire *centuries* on this kid. He's a fucking *child* when compared to my wrath and magic.

"Rhesamyre is alive, Atticus," he avows. "*She's alive.*"

I bang his head back against the wall, and he quickly defends, "Why the fuck would I lie about that?" he snarls. "All of us love and miss her just as much as you do, and she's *alive!* And so are your brothers!"

I drop him, stepping back as my magic whirrs and crackles. My brands flare once more. *All of them.* The ones I have with my brothers in arms, my blood brothers, and my mate.

He straightens and pops the collar of his leathers to busy his hands as he glares at me. "Granted, your brothers are lost in the tenth sphere somewhere, but according to Kure, they're still alive." He studies me, brows furrowed. "Why would you think otherwise?"

I bare my teeth. "Because I saw them perish at the Falls. All three of them were slaughtered by the revived crone."

Damian shakes his head. "Lilith is still very much dead, and Rhesa was never at the Falls." And then a realization seems to dawn on him. "Holy fuck, you've been *spelled*, Atticus."

I growl. "I would know if I was under a spell, boy."

He scoffs. "Clearly the fuck not." He shakes his head and runs his hand through his hair. "Kure didn't mention this part," he mutters more so to himself than to me.

"Did he send you here?"

"No. I came of my own free will because we need you if we're to save Rhesa. Though Kure said it wouldn't do any good, and now I see why. Whatever spell you're under, he isn't able to break it on his own at the moment, and I would wager it's something similar to the one the generals and assassins are under, too. Though their leashes appear to be much shorter than yours. And if we brought you in, Lucifer would know where we're . . ."

He watches me with renewed wariness, and I lift my chin in both challenge and understanding.

We need to play this carefully. Even through the fog of whatever *this* is, I can recall my namesake.

Chaos. Control. *Command* and *calculation*.

"You need to stop talking," I order, shaking my head. "If what you claim is true, you need to leave. If I am spelled, he knows where I am, and now he knows you're here, too. I would wager you're with the allies in hiding."

I think about this, and my blood rages and boils my blood as it burns away whatever the fuck is clouding my mind.

Maybe . . . *maybe* that *was* an illusion at the Falls.

Maybe that *was* Rhesa on the throne room floor. Bloody, beaten, and half dead because her court has been placed under similar spells.

I'm seeing fucking red.

"Her location," I demand on a growl. "*Now.*"

Damian shakes his head. "Atticus, I would advise against—"

"Advise all you fucking want, but I don't listen to you. Her location. *Now.*"

He works a muscle in his jaw and bares his teeth. "Last known location was Castle Blackstone."

Everything goes quiet as my rage sharpens into a dagger, and I focus on one name.

"Warden Bael has been making sadistic sport of her, I take it," I drawl lowly.

Damian blinks at the sheer violence in my tone as he nods, and the grin I spare the reaper is something carved from nightmares.

"Then I suppose it's only fair to make good sport of *him*."

"*Atticus*—"

"Get out of here. Don't tell me where you're going. And don't come for me again until that know-it-all fucker Kure commands it, *lieutenant.*" I turn on my heel and arm myself to the teeth, seething under my breath in Old Latin, *"Because I've got a mother-fucking butcher to burn."*

WE ALL HAD OUR OWN TREPIDATIONS IN ACCEPTING THE POWER OF THE GREAT STAR AND FERN, BUT NONE MORE SO THAN ATTICUS.
HE REFUSED IT AT FIRST. CLAIMING THE STAR AND FERN TO BE "GUTLESS COWARDS" THAT ONLY PLAN ON USING US AS CEREMONIAL SACRIFICES FOR OUR ENEMIES AND THEIR SCHEMES.
I MAY HAVE AGREED, BUT I ALSO KNEW WE WOULDN'T BE ABLE TO SUCCEED WITHOUT THE ADDITIONAL POWER.
WE PRAYED FOR A WAY TO END THE BLOODSHED, AND THIS IS OUR ANSWER.
WE MUST FIGHT FOR IT OURSELVES.
BUT AT LEAST THEY WERE COURTEOUS ENOUGH TO ARM US.
ATLAS CLAIMED HIS MAGIC AND NEWFOUND TITLE WITH A RELUCTANT SCOWL, BUT ATTICUS...
ATTICUS IS RESENTFUL.

CHAPTER SEVEN
RHESAMYRE

Bael hauls me forward on my unsteady feet, straight into the throne room through a conveyance, and the first thing that catches my attention is the fact that half the fucking throne room is *missing*. I gape at the large chunk of stone wall that appears as though it was ripped to shreds by some massive monster the same size as the damn tower or something, thus allowing the elements complete access to the room. Wind and rain flood the floor, thanks to the storm outside, and there are massive, spider-web-like cracks in the tile and fixtures, and all of the windows have been blown out, too.

What the hell can do this sort of damage?

And why isn't the magic of this place mending itself?

I glance away from the damage and raise my head high to stare Abaddon directly in the eyes despite the chain and collar around my neck and the few rags I wear for clothing.

I will not flinch. I will not yield. I won't let you taste my fear.

Abaddon looks the same, just as foolish and skittish, and he slouches upon the throne with *my father's* crown haphazardly slumped upon his horned head. I cock my head at the sight, a snarl ripping through my lips, and Abaddon *flinches* in his white leathers. The color is a stark contrast against his tattooed, shimmering red skin and dark, bloodshot eyes.

And despite the rage and pain I feel in my heart and soul, I grin at him, baring my fangs in promise.

I will hurt you.

Bael kicks my legs out from under me, and my knees hit the splintered marble floor and just about shatter all over again. I grit my teeth as hard as I can, then raise my head once more to scan my surroundings and survey what has become of the rest of my palace and court.

They've already replaced the banners and paintings in here to feature Abaddon and his late father as the *rightful heirs*, and a new crest marks the flags and symbols upon the guards' leathers. The demonic footmen of my kingdom appear just as stoic as ever, but I would imagine that they, too, are under the new spells of Lucifer's magic and control. And a crown of fire appears upon every banister and archway.

My uncles stand at attention upon the steps of the dais, thorn collars still firmly wrapped around their throats while their eyes remain steeled and vacant. And then, when I inhale a shaky breath with poisoned lungs, I almost close my eyes when I scent *him*.

Atticus was *here*. It's a faint scent, hardly there, but he *was* here.

Atticus. Atticus. Atticus.

"Do you like it, *Champion*?"

I still at the sound of his voice, and it takes all my willpower not to growl and bare my teeth at the male who should not be here.

Lucifer.

He's dressed in the fine, proper dark threads of Hell, claiming Abaddon's cursed crest over his heart.

Assuming he even has one.

The ugly, deformed male that is Lucifer strides toward me with a subtle, mocking grin, then circles me as he draws nearer. He clicks his tongue in disapproval at whatever he finds, and I force myself to suppress another growl, watching him out of the corner of my eye as he stalks about as if he owns the place.

"I'll admit, you've looked better, Myra," he *tsks*. "Seems as though time with Bael has not been kind to you."

He stops in front of me, grabbing my chin to tilt my head up so I can meet his bloodshot eyes. I allow my gaze to wander all over him, and my eyes snag on the sight of the Zodiac Blade hanging off his hip. Lucifer, of course, notices, and his grin broadens.

"Do you like it?" he inquires, unsheathing the dagger I once created to seal him away. He balances it on the tip of his finger, and I watch while trying to breathe evenly so as not to lash out at him too soon.

In addition, his scent is *foul*. Something rotten and evil and utterly foreign, but at the same time, all too familiar. I know this scent all too well, for once upon a time, as *Myra*, I came vis-à-vis with him too often. It would cling to me after battles against his soulless footmen and Apostles, and I would spend *hours* soaking in the bath and taking showers to scrub away at the smell and blood coating me. And even then, I never felt all that clean afterward.

"That blade," I mutter, meeting his eyes. "It was buried with Samael. As was the crown that now sits atop the usurper's head." I bare my teeth, seething through my fangs in Old Latin, *"You robbed his grave."*

And though my hands are shackled behind my back, I lunge forward and headbutt Lucifer, tackling him to the floor in an attempt to sink my fangs into his throat and bleed him dry. He, of course, doesn't let me get that far, and Bael is immediately upon me, too, hauling me backward by the chain connected to the collar around my throat. He holds me on my knees against his thighs, his fingers curled tightly around my throat as I scream and kick and roar and curse. Lucifer rights himself and straightens his suit, sheathing the blade once more as he scowls at me.

"You're nothing but a ravaged beast nowadays, *little feather*," he mocks.

I spit at him, and the glob of my darkened, poisoned blood lands on his polished shoe with a gentle *splat*.

"Enjoy it while it lasts, Lucifer," I snarl, tasting my own blood on my teeth.

He grins at me, but the smile doesn't quite reach his eyes now. "Believe me, I plan to." He looks pointedly at Bael behind me. "Take her below."

Bael hauls me onto my bruised feet again and drags me away, and I follow wordlessly as we travel downward into the cells and dark halls that reside below the palace. All the guards we pass stand stock still with the same vacancy in their eyes, and we don't pass any other servants or members of the aristocracy, either. Then, outside the windows and grand archways lies a *quiet* Heart of Hell.

The city used to have a heartbeat of its own, fueled by the life and lights of the free demons and people that called this place home. Music and the smells of spices, herbs, and baked goods would waft throughout the streets, along with the scents of Hellion roses, dark lilies, and lilacs that grew wild upon the walls and gargoyles, punctuating the shadows and dark alleyways where sins ran amok.

I look away and force myself to focus on my bare feet again so as not to trip down the winding stairs as Bael leads me to the darkest depths of the palace.

"I thoroughly enjoyed our time together, little bitch," he drawls in a sing-song manner. "If you ever find yourself in need of a *playmate*, I'd be happy to entertain you."

He opens a creaky cell door for me before removing my shackles but leaving my collar—*ever the gentleman*—and I stride inside wordlessly. He slams the bars closed with a loud *clang* behind me, and I almost *flinch*.

I let my eyes wander over the dank space, my nose crinkling at the stench of this place. It doesn't appear as though I have any neighbors. In fact, I don't see many prisoners left down here at all.

I turn around to face Bael, since he remains in the hall, lurking about and watching me with that odd gleam in his eye.

"Where are the rest of the prisoners?" I inquire.

Bael shrugs. "Lonely already, are we?"

I blink at him, and he chuckles darkly, beginning to wander off and call over his shoulder as he goes, "Lucifer doesn't waste much time. He's already freed most and put them to work again. They're laying waste to the spheres as we speak. Happy to rape and pillage and take their fill of whatever remains out there."

I stand in the center of the cell and listen to him whistle away, the sound of his retreating boots echoing off the otherwise quiet walls. Then, once I hear the prison doors shut and lock for good, I allow myself to exhale slowly as I roll my neck and shoulders. I rotate in my cell slowly to survey the space, and the only thing that occupies it is a small cot made of rotten and moldy straw settled below a barred window that is positioned high upon the wall. This cell has bars on either side of it, allowing me to see into the many cells both to the left and right of me.

Most of which are empty. Save for a few dark lumps upon the cots or against the back walls, while some rotten bones litter the floors in others.

All is still. All is quiet . . . and I'm alone again.

I'm with you, avows Atlas. *Always with you through this nightmare, little wolf.*

This isn't real, I mutter to him silently. *It's all a bad dream.*

At least, that is what I tell myself.

I walk up to the locked bars of my cell that face the narrow hall and glide my hands up and down the enchanted metal in an attempt to coax the magic into listening to my commands. However, all I am met with is a subtle burning sensation, and I hiss as I remove my red and weakly blistered palms.

Very well. I suppose Lucifer has all the magic locked down tight here, too.

Backpedaling, I slowly take a seat upon the straw cot and, being mindful of my horns, rest my head back against the stone wall and close my eyes.

I need to contact my allies . . . Atticus . . .

Shuffling comes from the cell to my right, and I glance over to watch out of my peripheral vision.

"I would be lying," he murmurs slowly, "if I said I wasn't at least a little relieved to see you . . . *Your Majesty.* As it stands, you are potentially our only hope now . . . just as you were back then."

I cock my head at his detached, drawled voice, then rotate forward to kneel by the bars and peer further into the dark cell where the scattered bones across the floor begin to rattle and move upon their own accord. The cracked and splintered, enchanted bones reattach themselves to form the familiar skeleton of the necromancer, and he stalks forward and peers down at me with those vacant, void eye sockets that shimmer with a hint of sentient magic.

"*Dante*," I breathe.

He kneels in front of me, leaning into the corner of the bars and wall in a similar manner as me.

A skeletal reflection.

You are not dead, Atlas snarls in my head. *He is not your mirror.*

"Hello, Rhesamyre . . . or is it *Myra* now?" Dante shakes his naked skull. "I can never keep track of all these titles and names nowadays."

I blink at him, furrowing my brows in suspicion, but I'm curious all the same. "Just call me Rhesa . . . I'll admit, I'm just as surprised to see you're still *here*."

He chuckles lowly, darkly. "I have no desire to be shackled by that self-proclaimed god as the rest have been. Being cursed to remain in this form has its advantages."

"You've been down here hiding amongst the *bones*."

He nods. "Ever since you damned me to become a *chew toy* for your hounds, yes."

I hum, glancing all over his skeletal armor to spot the many indentations and marks caused by sharp *teeth*. I meet his vacant eye sockets again. "If you're expecting an apology, you won't be getting one from me."

He chuckles again, leaning back against the wall. "I wouldn't expect one. You've certainly looked better."

I scoff, huffing a quiet laugh at that as I reposition myself against the wall, too. "You've had your sessions, and I've had mine."

He growls. "Warden Bael is a cruel, sadistic son of a bitch." Then he adds quietly as an afterthought. "You're dying, *Rhesa*."

I grin at that, still tasting blood in my mouth. "Then I guess it's a good thing I'm talking to a necromancer."

I see him shake his skull out of my peripheral vision, and I give him my full attention again.

"Just as your magic has been shackled, so has mine. I do not have what I need to bring you back if you were to die here, *so don't*. My connection to my sources in the Umbra Mundi has been severed, and things regarding the dead have not been the same anyway since Lucifer has returned and taken to stealing souls and shackling Death himself."

I hum. "Well, that is unfortunate."

I believe that if he could form proper emotions upon his face, he would spare me something similar to an unamused scowl.

"Were you aware that Abaddon had a son?" I inquire before he can comment on my *lack of commentary* regarding the state of our spheres.

Dante remains silent, and I nod silently.

"You must understand, I was angry and vengeful and—"

"When?" I demand, cutting him off. "And *how*? You managed to scheme and keep secrets from both Samael *and* Pollux, and that is quite an impressive feat."

Dante exhales slowly, and the action rattles his bones. "Abaddon . . . the *Cruel One* bedded many females of various social classes and breeds throughout his monarchy, and kept a harem close by at all times. But bastards did not become taboo in Hell until your—*Samael's* regime, which is ironic, considering many believed *you* to be his bastard for a time.

"So when the females surrounding the Cruel One became with child, he would be rid of them swiftly and quietly, killing both the mother and unborn babe to ensure no one would arrive one day, claiming riches or titles. He did not like to share . . . so much later on when the general and I had our falling out around the same time as the Great Betrayal, Apollo sought me out and read me in on his schemes. And together, we brought Abaddon back long enough to shackle him and . . . breed him to Lilith."

I gape at Dante, and his bones shudder again.

"You. Did. *What*?" I snarl.

"I know," he sighs, the sound full of pained regret and raw anguish. "*I know*."

"But Lilith . . . Lilith only knew of the Reformation Spell. She didn't know of Apollo's contingencies. A few of which she was not even factored into."

Dante dips his skull. "That is correct. When we brought Abaddon back for the short amount of time we needed him, I didn't bring him back *whole*. I didn't need his mind or soul, only his body, blood, and *seed*. Then, we conspired against Draven and stole the necessary ingredients to force a mind into a dream, and Apollo asked Lilith to complete the spell for him, claiming it was for insomnia or some shit like that. And because she was still so blindly in love with him, she was willing to do just about anything if it meant her, Apollo, and Andrew could all be together as a family without ridicule."

He takes a breath. "Then we used that very spell work on Lilith without her knowledge, and had her climb atop the Cruel One's enchanted corpse, thinking it was Apollo, *and we bred the witch*. And once we confirmed she was with child, I disposed of Abaddon once more. Apollo ensured Lilith remained hidden in the dream the entire time she was pregnant. Then when she gave birth, he took the child and hid him away. I'm not sure where."

I'm quiet for many heartbeats, needing the silence to wrap my head around the atrocities committed. The conspiracies that have been in play for near *centuries* now.

"No one would have ever had reason to suspect Apollo capable of breeding the crone to the Cruel One," I think aloud softly. "Pollux would have never known to inquire about such acts. To ask the right questions from his genies . . . no one knew . . . and because the Cruel One's soul was not taken and stuffed back into his body, Uncle Death didn't know, either."

I look at the bones again. "*Why*? What . . . *what* occurred between you and Death that would cause you to betray him as you did? To fraternize with a corrupted archangel and a wicked witch? Why do you hate him?"

Dante chuckles darkly again, shaking his skull. "Even now, they get the stories wrong . . . *I* didn't betray Death . . . *he* betrayed *me*."

I furrow my brows, and the necromancer continues, "As you know, I was his lieutenant once. I'm sure you can recall my original body from your memories as Myra. All of the original lieutenants, for that matter, but what you might not recall is that Death and I were *lovers*."

I'm silent again.

"There is no more passionate a lover than Death. He is perhaps the only guarantee in life. We may claim immortality, but death finds us all eventually. Relieving us of these binding forms and returning us to the stars and light from whence we came, whether it is because we were slain or because the magics of the spheres deem us out of time. Either way, death is certain. Many feared him, but I didn't. I served with him for many years, and lay with him for many more."

"Until?" I prompt.

"Until I found him in bed with another . . . many, *many others*. I had laid down my life for him time and again, but the being that is Death is not capable of reciprocating such love, and he *lied* to me. Over and over again, after he finished with me, he would find others to satisfy his hunger and lust. The entire time I claimed him as mine, and truly thought that he was, he was sleeping with others. Cooing to them in the same manner of voice as he had done hours prior with me.

"And so, I sought to destroy him as he destroyed me, and thought that if perhaps I found another lover to occupy my time, surely Death would become jealous and come after me . . . but he never did. And I truly fell in love with this new man, and he was devoted to me and only me, but as all good things, it didn't last, and he grew ill. When he perished, I begged Death to let him live. To bring him back, but he refused . . . so I did it myself. And when Death learned of what I had done, of how I had bent and broken the rules of magic and laws of nature, he destroyed my creation and cursed me to remain in this form for all eternity, *alone*."

I'm quiet again for another few heartbeats, and then I think aloud, "It was for love."

He barks a sudden, harsh laugh. "*Yes*, Rhesamyre . . . it was for *love* . . . it's *always* for *love*." I can feel his gaze on me, and after a moment, he says, "You know one of yours is still here in the spheres, right?"

I nod. "Atticus."

He hums. "The one of Chaos and Control, but you don't know what became of the other two?"

I shake my head because I'm not about to tell him that Atlas has been conversing with me through the magic of our imprint and taking up a semi-permanent residence in my head.

He hums again, and then the bones shift around until he is better positioned against the wall to sleep. I stay as I am, allowing my mind to wander and quiet as I attempt to rest. Nothing but the distant sounds of guards patrolling outside fill the silence.

It certainly beats the screams.

....

Something stirs awake inside of me, and I blink my eyes open to find a dark silhouette of a winged male just starting to kneel in front of me. He raises his hands to cup my face, and I close my eyes again as I hum gently, nuzzling into his warm palms.

"*Sam*," I breathe.

He grins. "Don't feel like calling me *Daddy* anymore, baby girl?"

I laugh softly at that, but it swiftly turns into a quiet cough as I choke on both a sob and the blood that has been pooling in my mouth, sliding back down my throat as I attempt to sleep. I'm curled up on my side upon the cot now, my arms wrapped around my legs and tucked tight against my chest in an attempt to keep warm.

Samael's obsidian eyes are soft, but the rest of him is stony and steeled as he surveys my form just as the rest of our brothers did as they visited me one by one.

"I wish I could hold you," he all but snarls, the sound quiet and almost synonymous with a prayer's tone. "I wish I could make it all better for you. Make all the pain and suffering go away. Return you to where you're supposed to be."

His hands slip away from my cheeks again, and I shiver as I am once again reminded of the cold, dank air that weighs down on my body and mind as I remain in these cells.

"Where am I supposed to be?" I croak, my eyes slipping closed again.

"Upon the Obsidian Throne, with three deities and the entirety of Hell to guard you."

I hum, then slip my hand out from around my thighs and reach out to him, my pinky poised for a promise. A bargain.

Sam's pinky finger engulfs mine.

"You promise it'll all be mine again one day?"

His next breath is almost a sob, too. "I promise, baby girl."

I nod, and my hand slips from his as he disappears.

I can't help the quiet sobs that begin to wrack my body alongside the shivers, and I tremble where I lie curled up in a ball.

I can feel Atlas watching me from the back of my mind.

The Wild Hunt is a peculiar thing. How the lines blur between friend and foe. Lovers and enemies.

Alastair and Atlas are blood, but the rest of our brothers in arms are more than that.

We are all warriors and sinners and saints and shadows.

Leaders. Lords. And kings.

Wings and horns and hooves.

Death is a dear friend of mine.

CHAPTER EIGHT
ATTICUS

Shadow Alchemy has always come so second nature to my brothers and me that we often never needed to define it as such. We can move silently and swiftly between the dark spaces so that we are practically one with the shadows themselves.

And Castle Blackstone is nothing but shadows.

Rhesa's scent is all over this godforsaken place. The smell of her *blood* is everywhere. And I crave it just as much as I crave Bael's life force to be drained from his fat face and rancid body.

I grin at the thought of getting to drain him dry while peeling his skin back from his bones, and I lie in wait within his sleeping quarters. The shadows are my friends, and he's none the wiser as he comes waltzing in with a whore whilst whistling a nameless tune. She's collared and unwilling, as far as I can tell, and he kisses her in a slobbery manner as he grabs her and throws her onto his bed. She bounces and squeaks, and he lunges for her and sinks his teeth into her throat while pawing at her breasts. She's already nude, and while she winces and braces for whatever the fuck he's about to do to her, she doesn't try to resist.

His bare ass is to me, and I stalk forward from the shadows. She spots me first, and she screams bloody murder as I unsheathe my sword from the same darkness I call home. The obsidian steel glitters in the dim lights of the enchanted candles throughout his room, and Bael whirls around with a wild gaze before he snarls at me.

A ruthless, sadistic grin curls to life on his pig face, and he extends his hands outward from his engorged, hairy belly as he chuckles.

"Hello, *Your Majesty*," he taunts. Then grabs his whore by her collar and holds her in front of himself as a human shield. She whimpers and cries, and I remain a stoic front of professional indifference. "Would you like a bite? She's accustomed to pleasing a number of clientele, after all."

I raise my sword and snarl. "Where's Rhesamyre?"

His smile widens. "I'm afraid you just missed her. She's gone back home."

I approach him, but he *tsks* and lifts the whore off her feet to literally dangle her in front of me.

"I wouldn't," he quips with a pathetic growl. "You're not one to waste innocent lives. You and your brothers always did your best to avoid needless casualties and—"

I slice the whore's head clean off, and then I plunge my sword through his shoulder and shove him into the back wall. He sputters and hiccups in outrage, and I twist my blade deeper into his muscles, scraping it across the bones there as I press him into the wall and leave him hanging.

"There goes your shield, you fucking coward," I snarl in his face, spitting in his eye. "Now. *Where's Rhesamyre?*"

"I already told you!" he shouts, and I flex my hand to make my sword hitch upward, and he croaks and pants. "She's back at the Obsidian Palace with Lucifer!"

His other hand is helpless at his side, that arm already broken, thanks to my swift movements. My magic craves violence just as much as I do, and took to breaking something else while I was otherwise occupied with my sword.

I bare my teeth and rip his ear clean off with my fangs before spitting it onto the floor in front of him, and he wails like a fucking pussy.

"She's *where*?" I demand once more through gritted teeth.

"The palace!" he cries. "She's back at the palace!"

I back up, leaving him pinned there against the wall with my sword as I go. Working a muscle in my jaw, I glower at him as I reach out for her, but nothing but pain and grief greets me in return. She's cold, angry, depressed, and above all, *terrified*.

I don't believe I've ever felt her fear like this before.

"Alive?" I demand.

He nods. "Yes! Down beneath the structure, in the cells."

I dip my chin, then command another sword to erupt from the shadows as I approach him once more. Slowly, I dig the blade into his opposite shoulder to completely pin him against the wall, and then I gag him and move to bind his feet.

But kneeling at eye level with his floppy cock is not going to fucking happen.

So I cut it off.

He screams through his gag, and I shove his head back with the tip of my dagger as I meet his pained gaze.

"I know what you're capable of, *Warden*," I spit, beginning to carve away the flesh of his face. "I know what techniques you prefer and which ones you alternate between to get what you want."

The blue skin of his face sluffs right off as I peel it away, revealing the red and bloody meshing of sensitive tendons and muscles beneath.

"I know," I continue, getting close to the ear that remains. "*Because I fucking invented them.*"

He moans in pain and alarm behind his gag when I go for his horns, and I saw them off despite his cries of protest.

I peel off every inch of blue skin from his body, and then I carve into the next layer and saw all ten of his fingers and toes off after popping his kneecaps. He's gone quiet and limp with shock by the time I slice off his other ear, and I grab a smoke and light it, then take a satisfying puff before putting the cigarette out directly in his eye.

That makes him scream again, and I grin.

"There you are," I purr. "Thought I'd let you off that easy?" I click my tongue and *tsk* at him. "I doubt you showed my queen such mercy."

I remove his gag, and he sobs pathetically.

"*Please*," he cries. As though I'm going to show him *any* mercy after what he did to Rhesa. Fucking imbecile. "What do you want from me?"

"What I want," I drawl, "you have proven you cannot give." I lean in close to whisper, "You took my heart, so now I'm going to take yours."

I lengthen my claws and then stab through his pectoral and rip out the beating muscle.

I leave his body there to rot and hang as I drop his heart onto the floor, soaked in his blood, then step over the beheaded whore's body as I make my way outside. Smoke wafts from my footfalls, and sparks fall from my fingertips as I scour the entirety of the grounds, destroying the foundation of this mountain and castle as I prowl in search of my mate. And everywhere she *isn't*, I destroy and roar and erupt in a tantrum because sweet spice isn't here, and that fucker Bael was telling the truth.

He gave her back to Lucifer. *And I was too late again.*

A large chunk of Castle Blackstone implodes on itself as the realization dawns on me, and I fall to my knees when they buckle with the weight of my unhinged magic. I'm going to get her back, but first, I need to break some shit and remind myself that *I am in control.*

Another part of the castle wall bursts into flames, and around me, screams from slavers and slaves alike echo throughout the space as several conveyances open in tandem. The footfalls of multiple armed soldiers make themselves known, and I raise my head to spot the Horsemen, Seven, and Apollo all standing guard near Lucifer.

The self-proclaimed god snarls at me. "You're more trouble than you're worth, deity," he drawls. "If I had the means of killing you off permanently, I would." He sighs, and I twitch at that little slip.

We *can* be killed . . . *at least* . . . I *thought* we could be. We've certainly been wounded and come close to death, that's for damn sure, but now that I think about it . . .

No. I've never full-blown fucking *died.* Obviously. But I know if I had, my brothers would have bargained to bring me back, just as I would have for them, despite our endless bickering and threats against one another.

We've never once meant any of it.

"But alas," Lucifer continues, "you're something *other,* even when compared to the higher beasts of these spheres and myself. The only spells I've managed to forge that work against the likes of you are that of memory-altering *shackles.*"

I get back on my feet, but faster than I can move, the miasma that *leaks* out of Lucifer prowls toward me and forms the massive maw of some beast not of our spheres, and despite my best efforts, I'm locked in place, and it devours me whole. I erupt and flash my daggers and swords and roar in anguish and outrage, but the monster has its jaws wrapped around my entire being, and I feel it *tug* on my fucking *soul.*

In the darkness, the weight and grief gnaw at my mind and chew on my soul, and when I'm released, I'm not myself anymore. And none of it fucking matters.

Because Rhesa and my brothers are dead.

Do you regret the lives we've taken and ruined?
I don't, but I remember their names.
I remember all of them.
What about you, brothers?
I'm sure they remember us, too.

CHAPTER NINE
RHESAMYRE

I stand next to Sam in identical dark leathers amongst the Four Horsemen and Seven Deadly Assassins. We surround a war table that displays the terrains, territories, forts, villages, and palaces of the Living Spheres within the war room of the Celestial Palace. The rest of my brothers are out in the field, leading their warfronts alongside the Twelve Zodiacs; the celestial beings have since morphed into the incarnations of their namesakes in order to better fight Lucifer and his Apostles.

"We've rallied all the beasts," says Sam, leaning forward with his fists on the table. "Mamba, the Alpha Brothers, the Three-eyed Bull. Hell, even the fucking Stag *itself answered Myra's call to arms. But even still, we lack the necessary means to fucking defeat him! And we are still no closer to learning why!"*

"The Lords of Exile have assisted where they can, as well," I add, ignoring my brother's outrage. "But the Wise Men are no-shows."

Pride chuckles darkly. "No surprise there, little wing. They're fickle politicians, not soldiers."

"Though," drawls War, "speaking of soldiers, at least we have managed to rally most of the sell-swords. And plenty of mortals have sided with us, though a fair number are hiding within our walls. Women, children, and the elderly, alongside the others *who cannot fight, too."*

"Or refuse to," quips Dante bitterly, the handsome male of other *origins standing at attention beside General Death.*

"They're afraid, brother," says Nile, War's lieutenant.

Gale stands next to Famine, and Tyler remains by Conquest's side in silence, knowing better than to add to Dante's unnecessary commentary regarding some beings refusing to fight despite being capable of doing so.

I shake my head at their bickering. "We need to house and protect even the ones that are a pain in the ass. If we don't, and Lucifer gets a hold of them, they'll just be another soulless body we'll have to butcher later. Cutting his strings to their limbs is tedious work, and we've wasted enough time already. We need to focus all our efforts on developing ways to permanently dispose of his creations, as well as the Apostles and self-proclaimed god himself."

"Any suggestions then, little wing?" inquires Wrath, and Sam narrows his eyes at the continued use of the nickname.

I shake my head, sighing. "Unfortunately, no, I don't . . . my apologies."

Sam wraps his arm around my shoulders above my wings in silent comfort, and Wrath nods quietly before turning to speak to his brothers in Babel.

"Walk with me for a moment?" asks Sam softly, directly into my ear, and I incline my head.

Sam steers me away from our allies and the confines of the war room as a whole, and we proceed toward one of the balconies before flapping up onto the roof to sit amongst the stars. Ursa Major glitters ahead of us, housing more than just rich celestials now, as we have opened our walls to refugees fleeing Lucifer's terror.

"You're doing all you can and more, Myra," he lectures.

I sigh, rolling my eyes. "All of us are, but it still isn't enough."

Sam shrugs. "Maybe not at the moment, but at some point, something will give. We'll find a way to defeat him."

"What happens if we're the first to give?"

"Then . . . we'll flee."

I whip my head around to meet his eyes, but he keeps his gaze trained on the flickering stars above us. The little lights shimmer in the black pools of his own eyes like a mirror.

Shooting stars and falling angels, I swear it.

"We can't just **flee***," I repeat.*

He shrugs. "Sure, we can. When we've done all we can to fight back, but there is nothing else to be done. I am not above throwing you over my shoulder and fleeing with our brothers and a few select friends in tow to somewhere so far away that it'll take thousands of centuries before Lucifer reaches us."

Sam meets my gaze now, and he cups my cheek gently. "I dare say we're all already on the same page as far as that is concerned, little feather. If push comes to shove, I will have no regrets abandoning this place if it means keeping our family safe."

I start to shake my head, but he keeps a firm hold of me as he continues. "You've done your damn best to save as many as you can. Because of you, we have stood against Lucifer for as long as we have. Countless lives have been saved because you made us accountable for our actions, and we opened our home to those in need . . . but in the end, Myra, if the monsters get in, we're getting out of here. And we will live on for another day. Away from the bloodshed and carnage and betrayals. Away from the evil that is Lucifer."

He holds up his pinky finger to me, and I study his tattooed hand for a heartbeat before curling my smaller finger around his.

"Just promise me you won't do anything stupid in the meantime," he quips.

With a shaky breath, I nod. "Then you have to promise the same, big brother."

Sam nods, then pulls me in for a hug.

We stay up on the rooftop for a long while just watching the stars, until eventually, Sam is called back to reality to return to war games.

I remain where I am, staring up at the twinkling stars. And when the middle of the night falls across the land and all is still and quiet, I don't pray.

I don't beg. I don't weep.

I make threats.

And something in the magic of the stars finally stirs awake in answer.

• • • • • • • • • •

"*—myre!*"

Who . . . ?

"*Rhe—myre* . . . RHESAMYRE!"

I startle awake when Dante's bony hand grasps mine and shakes it through the bars of our neighboring cells, and I shift just enough to look up at him from where I am curled in on myself upon the rotten cot.

His bones rattle as if he's breathing frantically, and he releases a heavy sigh when he meets my eyes.

"You went so still in your sleep," he says quietly, shaking his skull while continuing to squeeze my hand through the bars. "I wasn't sure if . . . I couldn't hear you breathing, and I . . ."

"I'm okay," I croak, curling back into myself, but I leave my hand in his . . . for whatever reason.

"*No,*" he growls. "You're fucking not. You. Are. *Dying*, Rhesa . . . . . You can't die, Your Majesty. *We need you.*"

For once, I agree with the bones, drawls Atlas in the back of my mind. He growls, and the sound warms my heart and core. *Your breaths were labored. You weren't answering me, either, little wolf.*

I hum, wanting to laugh at the desperation in their voices, but I can't muster up the strength to do anything else aside from focus on my breathing.

Dante's strange, bony fingers rub circles on the back of my hand, keeping me grounded, and I finally gather up the strength and courage to inquire, "What were you hoping to accomplish when you conspired against . . . *everyone* . . . to create the son of Abaddon?"

Dante releases another quiet sigh, but he still doesn't let my hand go. "You must recall that it was after Alastair erupted and his brothers disappeared. I was already angry at Death and those who sided with him, but the Great Betrayal made the wounds fester. Samael had claimed Hell and, in turn, Death, as a part of his court alongside the rest I once called allies. So when Apollo later came to recall Lucifer and *you*, he wanted a different way to write the story. A second chance at history, one that could potentially benefit him and his newfound second family if he played his cards right. And I, so consumed by all things evil and cruel, agreed."

"I bet you didn't expect this outcome, though, did you?"

He squeezes my hand again, but not quite in warning. Just to remind me to stay awake, I think.

"No," he agrees. "No, I didn't quite predict things would end this poorly, though I suppose I should have." He growls at himself. "The *minute* Apollo approached me with the recollection of Lucifer, I should have disappeared. Should have run away and hid and anonymously tipped you and the others off from far, far away . . . but I didn't . . . because I also recalled what Death and I once were when you were alive back then, too. He and I had our falling out after Lucifer was banished and you died, but it rekindled the flame of hatred I thought I had buried, and so I agreed to aid Apollo in his foolish schemes. Both to breed Lilith, and then later to bring Adam and Evelyn back from the dead behind Death's back."

He sighs again. "I regret many things in my existence, Rhe-samyre. And this . . . *this* will remain my biggest failure."

I hum. "I guess that's why you're so hellbent on keeping me awake and alive now, huh? You're attempting to right old wrongs. Make up for past mistakes."

He chuckles lowly. "Yes . . . yes, I suppose I am."

I hum again. "Then, how do you suggest we keep me alive long enough for me to save the spheres? Because currently, I'm broken, poisoned, starving, and dehydrated to a nearly irreparable degree."

Stop that, growls Atlas, but I ignore him.

"I . . . I suspect there is one thing that might work," drawls Dante. "It will be a temporary solution, of course, but it might just give us enough time to get out of here and contact your allies."

"Borrowed time." I huff a quiet laugh, then groan as pain flares throughout odd points of my body as I sit up to lean against the wall to face him. "I suppose I am out of options by this point. What do you have in mind?"

"A bargain."

I raise my brow at him, sparing him an incredulous look.

Exhausted as I may be, it's easy to read the *what the fuck* in my eyes.

This fucker better not be playing tricks, snarls the deity in my head again.

"A bargain in which you borrow what remains of the magic I have stored in my bones," explains Dante. "It is what gives me the ability to keep hold of this form and walk around as though I am still alive. In theory, it should be enough to kickstart your own magic into replenishing itself to keep you alive, too."

"I guess it's certainly better than nothing."

"I agree."

"Well then, fuck it. I've bargained with worse beings than you."

He stares at me a beat, then sighs and relinquishes, "If you still have the strength to sass me, Your Majesty, then there is hope for us yet."

Unfortunately, I think I agree with him . . . again, mutters Atlas begrudgingly.

I grin, then reposition my right hand in Dante's as his bones begin to rattle in place. Shimmering, white lines and sigils trace the indentations of his skeleton, and warm, raw magic begins to flow into me, coursing through my veins and heating my blood. And in the magic's wake, dark lines begin to trace the bones that make up my own hand, marking the skeleton beneath my skin while thorns and hellion mandala patterns act as the veins and tendons between the bones, too, wrapping around my fingers and wrist and intertwining with the first few letters of my *trouvaille* brand.

Dante's bones quake one last time and then drop to the ground as he loses the ability to hold his shape.

I blink at the sight, a little amused by it despite the situation. "Holy shit, are you okay?"

"I am fine," replies the skull. "How are you feeling?"

"Better." I nod my head, rotating my shoulders and neck a little. "The aches are still there, but it's manageable at least."

"Good." The skull exhales through his teeth. "That's good."

I reach through the bars to pull his skull into my own cell, then pull my legs up and balance him on my knees while I sit against the wall.

"My uncles," I start. "The Horsemen and Seven. How do I free them? What sort of spell is it?"

"One of Lucifer's favorites. Something he perfected long ago to ensure complete loyalty from his soulless creations and Apostles. I'm sure you can recall naming it the Caged Bird Spell."

I curse angel names under my breath. *"Of course, it's that one.* Then the thorn collars are merely upon them as collateral. Used for the secondary black magic, most likely related to and leftover from Lilith's more recent spell work. Either way, I only recall us being able to successfully surpass the CB Spell once, and I needed Kure and Draven to do it."

"And where might they be?"

I narrow my eyes at the skull resting casually upon my knees.

"If I could shrug in nonchalance to appease you, I would," he deadpans. "Need I remind you, I didn't *have* to save you. But I recognize the consequences that would have come my way had I not . . . . Rumor has it, the Lords of Exile and some others fled together, though their trail went cold once they disappeared from Hell."

I nod along. "They're somewhere safe for now, waiting for me, though I don't exactly have a way to get word to them yet." I steel myself before I inquire, "And what of Atticus? Bael informed me that he is currently here and under Abaddon's rule, but I didn't see him up top."

"From the few whispers I've heard, I believe Chaos has gone rogue. He thinks you're dead and has been laying waste to all he can in outrage. Though I don't exactly get a daily news report down here."

I hum, not liking the sound of that, but there's nothing I can do about it at the moment.

Atticus was, and forever will be, a loose cannon, growls Atlas.

It's one of his many charms, I suppose, I muse.

"Speaking of which," I drawl to the skull. "How often do the guards patrol down here? I haven't seen . . . well . . . *any*."

"All of the high-profile prisoners are gone now. You are all that remain. And they don't seem to deem you as a *threat* anymore. Not since you were hauled down here, looking no better than a corpse."

I scoff. "Rude."

"And it's perhaps your greatest and only weapon, seeing as how we aren't exactly armed with much else at the moment."

I hum. "I believe I'm inclined to agree with you there, and the magic of these cells do not currently recognize me as the rightful queen of Hell, either."

"It would stand to reason that Lucifer's CB Spell is sphere-wide. What of your brothers' fates? The archangels, where are they?"

"Bael mentioned something about them being locked down tight in the Celestial Cities. I don't believe they'll provide much aid at the moment, either."

Dante is quiet for a beat. "You've muttered in your sleep a few times. I considered it delirium, but the magic stirred around us. I have never heard or felt it . . . *wake up* like this before. Not in such a way that would imply it is *self-aware*."

"What did it feel like?"

"A *heartbeat*."

"A heartbeat," I repeat, nodding as a distant memory flickers to life. I can barely recall it as it was so long ago, and so much has happened since, but I suppose that has been the purpose behind my brothers visiting me.

They've been escorting me down memory lane.

"I suppose that would mean it truly is sentient," I muse, thinking it aloud for Dante's sake.

"Perhaps you are delirious, and I am swiftly drifting into madness after you."

I scowl at the skull. "Trust me, I had my doubts in the beginning, too . . . but I've *felt* it. I've been kissed by the Peri all my life, and blessed by the Yonder Star and Evergreen Fern. In fact, for a time, Yonder used me as a vessel. It's how we finally learned of a way to Lucifer's weakness."

"And why weren't you made aware of this supposed *weakness* beforehand?"

"Because Yonder *half-assed* the creation of her Champion."

I swear, the skull doesn't seem all that impressed with the poor excuse for our misery.

"Are you upset?" I tease, grinning. "Because I can't quite tell, with the lack of facial muscles."

The black voids shimmer, and the skull clacks its teeth together a few times. "I think I liked you better delirious and nearly dead."

"Don't be rude."

I set the skull beside me on the cot, then crisscross my legs.

"What are you doing?" he inquires.

"Quiet. I'm concentrating."

"On what?"

I shrug gracefully. "Summoning a friend, I suppose. We'll see how far I get before you start calling me delirious again."

"My creativity knows no bounds. I know more words in several languages."

"Then ponder them in *silence*."

Dante clacks his teeth again and then goes quiet as requested.

The silence drags on for what feels like hours; the low hum of the magic that lies within the cells gradually grows louder as I attempt to call upon my own power. Then, all at once, the sound ceases completely, and I open my eyes to find a vision of Pollux standing before me.

He grins at me. "You called, little feather?"

I cock my head at him. "You claim different forms, but you're all the same creature. You said you weren't one of Kure's, so what are you?"

Pollux's grin broadens, and he kneels in front of me while tilting his head. Icy eyes glitter with unbridled, sentient magic—*uncaged magic* that does not answer to celestials or devils or even *Lucifer*, much to the self-proclaimed god's dismay.

"You once approached the Yonder Star and Evergreen Fern above. Just as you are approaching me now. And just like back then, you're surprised to receive an answer."

Never lie. "I am."

"We don't take kindly to many."

"I know."

Pollux hums. "Then do you remember now, Champion? Can you recall my name?"

I nod, tears lining my eyes. "You guided me to speak with Yonder and Evergreen once. Our unique creators, but you were far more intimate with them. You were their first, and you called them *Mother* and *Father*. And when we spoke, I wasn't presented to them as a potential savior or champion. Not at first. Instead, you called me your *fiancée*."

Pollux shifts from the handsome male of white wings and angel feathers I am so familiar with into the form of another gorgeous male I once claimed as *mine.*

He stands at about the same height, with a warrior's build, his skin bronze and covered in shimmering silver and gold tattoos, brands, and sigils belonging to *all* the spheres and languages. Scriptures, wicked mandalas, creatures, and constellations of both holier attributes and the Devil's work. While mighty, silver wings of fire claim a permanent home upon his back.

Black hair sits intricately braided over his left shoulder while the right side remains closely cut to his scalp; mandalas are shaved into the dark fuzz, and his silver eyes gleam like the flames that are his feathers. Pearly white facial markings trace his high cheekbones and brow like a mockery of a halo, and the delicate patterns of Old Latin roughly translate to *devoted creature of vengeance and chaos, bringer of sacrificial concord.*

He's dressed in dark battle leathers and armed with obsidian weaponry, but emerald siphons punctuate his chest plates, hands, and shoulders, in addition to the hilts of his larger daggers and white swords, too.

The gorgeous male I once called a friend, and later a lover, smiles beautifully at me as he leans forward to press a gentle kiss to my forehead.

"Hello again, little love," he murmurs in Old Latin.

I close my eyes. *"Astraeus,"* I breathe.

A tear falls, and he licks it away, kissing my cheek gently.

"I thought I'd never see you again," I whimper. "I was told I never would . . . that is what your *mother* said."

Astraeus growls, then pulls me into him as he sits and hauls me onto his lap. I wrap my legs around him, but refrain from burying my face in his neck. Instead, I keep eye contact with the firstborn son of Yonder and Evergreen. The First and One True King. The Sun of our Spheres.

"I fought tooth and nail to bring you back to me, Myra," he claims, his eyes skittering all over my face as he studies me. "*I wanted you back so badly,* but she was relentless and vengeful and cruel, and no matter what magic I am or what I claim to be, she is still a god. A being of existence that can rewrite the rules on a whim. And she did and she has . . . that is perhaps the only consistent thing about her."

I nod along, whispering, "*I know.*"

He smiles softly at me, though the action is melancholic and strained at best, weighted with the knowledge that we were robbed and betrayed by one he thought we could trust. Thus leaving our time together to feel more like a dream, but I knew it wasn't. Because he still visited me every night. Every chance he could, he would find me on a battlefield or float into my bedroom through the open window I left unlatched just for him.

The Peri have always been fond of me.

I huff a quiet laugh, fiddling with the collar of his leathers. "I feel as though every time I call upon you, it is when I need help. I'm taking advantage of you again."

"You can do whatever you want with me, little love," he replies smoothly, nuzzling into my hair to inhale my scent deeply.

I'm reminded then that I haven't had a proper bath in ages, and I attempt to push him away from me. However, my hands are met with a solid brick wall of muscle, and his chest rumbles beneath his leathers as he growls deeply, feral and fierce and ancient.

As if sensing where my thoughts drifted, he husks, "I have never once cared about such trivial matters. I want all of you, just as you have all of me. My body and the pieces of my soul and mind are yours. All I am, will be, and ever have been, all belongs to you, little love."

I shudder in his arms. "We've been here before . . . history always repeats itself."

"It reincarnates, baby. You and I are nothing but scattered stardust attempting to feel whole again, and the shadows fill our voids in the meantime." He sighs, and it seems to take him an impressive amount of strength and restraint to pull away from me in order to meet my eyes properly, and not just keep me clutched to him like he so obviously desires. "But just as I did back then, I know what has befallen these spheres. I know you need assistance in contacting your allies."

I nod. "Is that something you can accomplish? Can you meddle in such a manner that Yonder will not know?"

Astraeus nods. "My mother will keep out of it. Gods are arrogant and often stagnant in their mindsets of life and death, but every so often, when a being like you is born *or created*, it rattles their cores. Your existence has challenged theirs, and she took it as a threat. Never mind the fact that her firstborn son fell in love with her little creation. You were not supposed to be anything but a little sister to arrogant archangels. A toy. Their light, yes, but powerless in the face of her magic and wrath. Yet you have become everything but."

The grin I share with him is nothing short of feral and triumphant, and he chuckles.

Hell below . . . he sounds like Alastair when he laughs like that.

"I will do what I can for you," he vows. "Just as I always have." He presses his forehead against my own, breathing me in deeply again. "I have loved you from afar for so very long, and I will continue to do so for all of eternity. For as long as *they* live, I will love you alongside them."

His touch soon becomes featherlight, and he shifts me off his body as his whole being begins to fade into the spherical and dandelion-seed orbs of raw magic that love to dance amongst the stars.

"You always have a friend in the Peri," Astraeus mutters in Old Latin, his body overcome with light and magic as he becomes the Peri once more.

The dainty Peri brushes past me and kiss along my cheekbones, floating out of the cell through the barred opening that sits high upon the perimeter wall. I inhale deeply, allowing another tear to slip down my cheek before I wipe it away and steel myself once again.

"What was . . . *who the fuck did you just speak with*?" inquires Dante.

I turn around to face the skull once more, then return to the cot and resume the position we had prior to Astraeus's arrival, acutely aware of Atlas's silence in my head.

"Astraeus," I start to explain to the skull settled upon my knees. "The first male I ever kissed and fell in love with. The ancestral soul of my deities. Yonder had attempted to separate us once, but all she did was succeed in giving him back to me in the form of the Three Kings."

Dante is silent for many heartbeats, and I do not speak again until he inquires about the whole story from start to finish.

And I give it to him. Slowly and quietly, I finish my trek down memory lane with the recollection of how I once loved Yonder's son.

"He was perhaps Yonder's greatest secret. Her firstborn son. Her first attempt at creating something with Evergreen in a more intimate way. Often times, Evergreen created beasts, while she created beings like the archangels or Horsemen and Seven Sins. However, as Astraeus was her first success, she was overbearing and overprotective. Claiming that if he wanted to visit the spheres he protected from afar, he could only do so as disembodied magic. He did not exist as you and I do now. He was a free soul. He is the Peri. The very sun in the sky and the magic around us.

"As a child and later a teenager, the Peri had always been fond of me in innocent but curious ways. I had always believed I was an enigma to them, and so they followed me around from time to time. And then Lucifer appeared, and chaos ensued. We needed help, but I was tired of praying for it. So I wept and screamed and threatened and demanded aid from whatever stars and celestial beings would listen. And I received a startling answer.

"He quite literally swept me off my feet. I was *taken*. Stolen off the rooftop of the Celestial Palace. I had angered the Peri with my demands, but I didn't care. I wanted answers, and we needed help. When I came to, I wasn't anywhere tangible at first. There was darkness, and there was just the Peri. And then I *heard* him. He spoke to me, and something feral and magical inside me shuddered at the sound. Wanting to submit and please this being of raw magic and stars, but I refused to yield.

"He asked me a single question at first. *What do you want?*

"I honestly didn't know how to reply. I wasn't sure what sort of being I was speaking with, but I knew better than to lie. So I steeled myself and answered in the most truthful way possible.

"'*Power*,' I said. '*I want power.*'

"'*That is not what you want*,' he replied. '*That is what you believe you need, but what do you want?*'

"I was silenced by that at first. I thought power was what I wanted *and* needed, but evidently, that wasn't the case. And I knew better than to say something foolish and shallow like paradise or eternal peace or some shit like that. So finally, I said, '*Closure. I want the bloodshed and the war to end, be it either because we found a way to kill Lucifer, or found a way to kill ourselves. Mark me a coward, but I want the conflicts to end. Either because I am no longer there to witness them, or because we found a way to defeat him.*'

"After a few heartbeats of silence, in which I could only hear my own breathing, the Peri shifted as he hummed lowly, and then Astraeus revealed himself.

"I was intimidated, to say the least, but still plenty angry at the gods and spheres as a whole. So perhaps that is why I was able to keep my wits about me, for I had wrath on my side, boiling my blood and feasting off my rage. Astraeus took it upon himself to show me what happens if an archangel dies. We do not go to the heavens like the rest. Instead, we return to the Great Star herself. Where she had once taken a kernel to create us, we later return to fuel her entire being, and she feasts on our life force and the knowledge we gathered throughout our existence, and then dishes it out to her sons and the other distant spheres to make them *better*.

"Where we have had to learn on our own, and bleed to make ourselves better, the spherical systems Yonder and Evergreen have gone on to create after us are simply born with the knowledge and power we fought for. And the sons they have borne after Astraeus are considerably—according to Yonder—more suited to walk amongst the beings they oversee and protect.

"But the archangels in our ten spheres could not be slain at the time of this interaction, and when I questioned Astraeus about this, he claimed that *the stars always find a way to reclaim what was once borrowed.* Thus, whether I created the Zodiac Blade or not, it was inevitable that one day, someone else would, or my brothers and I would turn on each other and spill our own blood in a different kind of war. One that no one would recover from.

"Either way, the revelation was both enlightening and soul-crushing at the same time, and Astraeus took advantage of my stunned, silent state to explain that he is one of Yonder and Evergreen's sons. The very sun of the spheres, and the very magic we command, worship, and abuse. He is the firstborn, and our ten spheres are his domain. His plane. While his brothers claim others elsewhere. Some bloody and different, and some all too similar.

"We don't know of them and cannot access them, nor can we pronounce their names in our languages. Only a few have the Sight to see glimpses of these other lands, such as Kure, but those countless suns up there are Yonder's sons. The sons of gods that create, destroy, and oversee the existence of these foreign spaces. And Astraeus serves our spheres as the First and One True King . . . though he was and still is not permitted to walk amongst his mother's creations. If he wants to visit and observe up close, he can only do so as the Peri.

"I . . . I spent *decades* with him in a faraway dream. Another odd plane of existence where he could move between spheres freely, but with a real, tangible body instead of the magical, shapeless one he claims here. I fascinated him, I suppose, and so he chose to keep me close. He showed me glimpses of other planes, spheres, and cultures while telling me stories of his brothers and parents. I met a few of them, too. And in turn, I told him stories of my own family and friends. He knew of them all, of course, though he was never supposed to get too close, but he favored me. Loved me.

"So finally, when it came time to inquire if he could keep me as his *queen*, Yonder was furious. She was jealous and insulted that she wasn't enough for her son, and above all, she was enraged by the possibility of having to share her crown and place within the stars. So she offered me what I initially thought I wanted. *Power*. And I . . . I was told that if I didn't return from whence I came, she would devour me whole, right in front of Astraeus.

"I couldn't have that, just as I couldn't leave Astraeus any more than I could leave my brothers for any longer than I already had. So I took her offer, took the limited power and information she offered me, and I returned home. And when I did, I found that no time had passed. Not a second had been wasted. I felt as though I had aged fifty years, yet all I did was blink in my own sphere. But I had what I initially bargained for: the power to defeat Lucifer . . . or so I had thought.

"*But Yonder cheated.* All she wanted to do was get rid of me, and she succeeded because I was foolish enough to steal what I could and bolt. She sent me back with a kernel of her magic in tow under the ruse that it was for my benefit, but the manipulative bitch just wanted to get me away from her son. She never cared about saving us or defeating Lucifer, hence why I was never told of the altar. She *wanted* me dead, and I swear, she had salivated at the thought of finally getting to devour me."

I grin at the memory.

"But what she didn't count on was that when I died and sacrificed myself, Astraeus had planned to claim my soul before she could. He stole and hid me away, and we were able to pick up where we had left off. The spheres were safe for a while, and no one could remember me, so I felt no guilt or shame in staying with him. But then Yonder found us again. He still had duties to uphold for our spheres, after all, and Yonder took advantage of that fact. One day, he left, and then he never returned.

"She entrapped her own son in a wicked spell, then divided his soul into four pieces in order to hide him from me. One remained with the sun so that life and magic would remain, and he could also continue to traverse his spheres every so often under the ruse of the Peri. While the other three pieces of him were stuffed inside the forming bodies of three unborn brothers who would later go on to repeat history and make a name for themselves as kings and deities. I had scoured the spheres and a few of the other planes to find him, and once I learned what Yonder had done, I began to scheme. Just as Astraeus taught me, I learned how to watch the spheres from afar as something else."

I laugh to myself again, the memories tumbling back into my mind at an alarming rate as I voice them to Dante.

I had forgotten so, *so much*.

"I was a starry-eyed wolf, and I saw *everything*. I watched Astraeus orchestrate the Great Betrayal. I couldn't do anything from my estranged space in the spheres, not quite dead, but not alive, either, but I was angry and disappointed in him for whispering in Adam and Eve's ears about the Tree of Creation and the Forbidden Fruit that grew with my—*Yonder's*—power. I knew what would happen if the tree was tampered with, for the spell holding back Lucifer would be damaged and weakened, and he could possibly return one day with renewed vigor and vengeance . . . but at the same time, the thought of being able to return to the Spheres of the Living to be with the deities—the carriers of Astraeus's incomplete soul that I loved and cherished—*was oh-so-tempting.*

"And Astraeus was counting on it. He told me as much in passing when he could manage to communicate as the Peri. So the *minute* Eve became with child, I seized the opportunity to clamber inside the unborn babe's body and claim it as my own, as well as claim the power from the forbidden fruit. My soul was reincarnated in the process, but of course, in doing so, I had forgotten about everything. My memories were lost to the shadows and stars until now."

I stare into the deep, dark pools that are Dante's eye sockets. The darkness there shimmers with raw emotions and magic, but he remains silent.

"The deities are *him*. His soul may be split and tethered to three different bodies, but they are no less *mine*. And Yonder . . . Yonder didn't *give* them their magic. She simply showed them how to access what was already inside of them. For they are the physical incarnations of her firstborn son, and though it enrages her to no end, there is no keeping them from me. Nor I, from them. Such devotion has been proven once already, and dare I say, the god has grown bored of interfering with us.

"So maybe . . . *just maybe* . . . that is one thing Yonder has done right by us. By choosing to ignore what we do, she has *allowed* us to be together. And coming from her, that is as close to a blessing as I am ever going to receive."

I bare my teeth. "And I will burn everything and everyone that stands in my way. I will get all three of them back. Potentially all four, if I have anything to say about it."

Dante remains quiet. Meanwhile, my heart beats loudly in my ears. My magic and adrenaline attempt to rise with the declaration of war, but my power remains shackled.

"If you do anything reckless again," he drawls, "I will be incapable of healing you. You'll be half dead again soon enough, and I have no magic left."

"Your bedside manner could use some work, Bones."

He clacks his teeth once. "So then, what are we to do now?"

"Just . . . give me a minute to think."

That minute lasts an eternity, and I eventually succumb to sleep.

. . . .

The shivering wakes me up first, and I realize with a start that I'm *freezing*. I was able to recognize that my body was cold, thanks to the fever coursing through my veins, but this is different. The temperature is noticeably below the freezing point, and when I open my eyes, my ragged breath fogs up before me.

I uncurl my sore and frozen limbs, scanning my cell that now glimmers with the beginnings of frost upon the walls and metal bars, and I breathe deeply again to watch as my breath fogs once more; my lungs and ribs ache and rattle with the action, which used to come so naturally before I was broken so thoroughly.

A fact that never fails to piss me off.

Carefully, I rise onto my shaky and unsteady legs, and I shuffle backward until I can just barely glimpse what lies beyond the bars that sit high upon the back wall.

"What is it?" inquires the skull.

"It's cold," I murmur, blinking away the pounding in my head so I can focus on what lies outside.

"Is it?"

"It's . . . *snowing.*"

"*What*? That— that's *impossible.*"

"I agree. It *should* be."

I reach for Dante, then hold him up as high as I can so he can see what I do outside.

White.

Shimmering, glittering *white* blankets what I can see of the outside world, the wet mush falling from the sky like ash.

I lower Dante again, then reclaim my place upon the cot and settle him on my knees once more.

"This Hell isn't my home . . . not anymore," I mutter. "My kingdom sits frozen in time. My people enslaved by my enemies and often slaughtered in their sleep like sheep. And my crown—Samael's crown—now sits atop a usurper's head."

It might be the fever; it could be the poison, but it's probably the cold again.

But my body begins to *quake*.

My bones rattle as my teeth chatter, and magic growls and reawakens, pushing on the restraints of the spells of these cells, as well as the poison in my bloodstream.

"You're angry," states Dante. "As is Hell."

"*No shit*," I snarl, teeth chattering.

Dante clacks his teeth again. "*Good*."

I feel as though if he could grin, he would.

Call me a coward. Go ahead. But at least I am brave enough to admit when I am scared.

I'm fucking terrified.

I miss you both. I'm scared I'll never see you again.

CHAPTER TEN
ATTICUS

Smoke rises into the darkened sky from the ruins of Goldfinch.

What remains of the mortal kingdom's capital is nothing but a tragic, rotten wasteland that reeks of burnt flesh and betrayal. The stench is thick in the miasmic air.

With crossed arms, I watch as rows of shackled slaves move in and out of conveyances, either to or from these ruins under the command of Wrath and War. The males are stoic and steeled as they give their orders to the few mortals that remain, all hand-picked by Lucifer's Apostles to undergo extensive training to become prized pets and slaves of Lucifer and his ever-loyal followers. The majority of the older folks have been dispatched, while the younger males have been selected for manual labor, and the prettiest females were selected for breeding and pleasure.

The prisoners that Lucifer released from Hell's cells stand guard with whips and collars at the ready; many of whom are *others* or demons once condemned for heinous, vile acts, and they are all too quick to slip back into their old ways when given the opportunity to do so.

I turn a blind eye to it, uncaring of how the spheres fare now. But as I listen to the women's screams as the demons and goblins have their way with them right here in the street for all to witness . . . something in me hears *Rhesamyre* again. Her screams. Her pleas. Her begging for them to stop as they abuse and fuck her body ruthlessly.

"We should stop them," I mutter to Wrath.

With slow, unfocused eyes, Wrath finds the group of gang bangers and rapists, but then he shrugs and goes back to watching the lines of slaves enter conveyances into the work camps and prisons that have multiplied since Lucifer's arrival.

"It isn't our place to interfere," drawls Wrath.

I snarl. "*She* wouldn't want this," I remind him.

"*She* is *dead* . . . and you would do well to never mention her or the rest of them again. Move on, Atticus . . . we have a new god now."

I snarl again, but Wrath ignores me; the hellfire in his steeled gaze has been snuffed out with the news of Rhesamyre's death.

They—*we*—have all been complacent. Quiet.

The Hellion Court calls a stranger *king* and another, *god*.

Pain flares behind my eyes as I dare to think of our predicament too deeply, and I'm struck with exhaustion again. My hands shake, and I tighten them into fists in an attempt to hide the tremors that plague my body.

I focus on the lines of slaves again, then dare to glance at the group of rapists once more as they pull away from the female, leaving her lifeless body in the dirt, discarded as though she is worthless scum.

The demons and goblins chuckle amongst each other, returning to their posts so they may surely choose another female of their liking later on.

I won't be around to watch them rape again.

"I'm returning to the palace," I claim, turning to open my own conveyance.

Neither Wrath nor War stops me or utters another word, and I step through my portal straight into the estranged halls of the Obsidian Palace.

And I *shiver*.

Glancing outward at the silent capital, nothing but glittering snow greets me. An eerie, cold quiet has settled over the land. Snow falls in wet clumps from the sky as ice and frost cover the walls, and a shiver races down my spine again, but this time I dare say it is closer to that in nature of a growl as my magic hums in warning.

The witch is here.

My magic and mind are unsettled with thoughts of her being so close. She's just below my feet in the cells of the palace, rotting away like the scum she is, while I remain in torturous luxury, surrounded by the fleeting scents of Rhesamyre.

Her chambers have begun to lack the usually sweet smoke and spice scents that once occupied her belongings: jewels, gowns, pampering supplies, and even the multiple daggers hidden throughout the space. Such as within her panties or upon her nightstand. I haven't let them claim her things, nor have I let them take what little is left that belongs to my brothers, either.

My magic growls within me again, at war with my mind and the memories of their deaths that plague me every time I close my eyes. I can hear their screams. I can hear *her* screams.

Rhesa, Rhesa, Rhesa . . .

I fiddle with the pack of smokes I also found hidden amongst her belongings as I finally make my way to her chambers and stride through her room to sit against the railing of her balcony, my back to the quiet city that still mourns the loss of its queen. Then, with a flicker of my magic, I light the smoke and inhale the sweet vanilla and cherry taste.

It tastes like her kisses. It tastes like her sweet cunt that often dripped for my brothers and me. Her moans soft and sultry, and obsidian eyes full of lust and challenge.

Fuck . . . fuck-fuck-fuck-FUCK—I loved that female.

I miss my brothers. Dammit, *I miss my brothers.*

But I fucking loved Rhesamyre.

I inhale the last of this smoke, then immediately light another one. However, the foggy veil that has clouded my head and made my magic heavy with grief refuses to leave me be. It is ever persistent and riled up, hissing and coiling tight inside of me as if I have any say in the matter of her and my brothers' deaths.

But I failed them. I let them die.

My magic growls and hisses inside of me again, and another stabbing pain reverberates behind my eyes. I groan quietly, attempting to suppress the pain by closing my eyes and breathing in deep, even breaths. But it's no use. It's no fucking use.

They're dead. They're dead. *She's dead!*

And now, here I am, wasting away within the Obsidian Palace. Watching the spheres burn from the safety of a balcony like some fucking coward. Lucifer and Abaddon have chosen to leave me be, and the Hellion court remains eerily quiet, too.

Though something is amiss . . . Mamba is gone. As are the lieutenants and their little females, along with Rhesa's wolves and the rest of the hellhounds.

My body grows heavy again with even the *thought* of attempting to figure it out . . . . The answer is just out of reach, but I'm so tired. Exhausted.

So I opt to ignore it once more, allowing myself to believe I'll deal with it tomorrow.

And I light another smoke before eventually washing the taste down with some of Rhesa's favorite Hellion whiskey.

It still tastes like her. Smells like her. Something sweet and bitter and lingering and addictive.

. . . .

"Get up."

My head pounds again, this time with the lingering remnants of a hangover, I think.

"Get. Up."

Fuck off.

My magic stirs and hisses beneath my skin again, and my tattoos and sigils are all itchy as they burn, and all I want to do is rip them from my bones. Rip myself apart and be done with this shit.

I open my eyes, blinking away the crusty shit that lines my lashes in the process, and I glance out at the snowcapped, dark, eerie, and ever silent Heart of Hell again. I've slumped over on my side upon the balcony, the bottle of whiskey and pack of smokes now empty.

The bottle is shattered, and the cigarette buds sit littered amongst the glass shards.

"Go to her."

I growl, and my magic vibrates deep within me in answer, rattling my bones as the war between my memories, mind, and magic continues. And that insistent voice that I've been hearing as of late . . . I ignored it at first, then proceeded to tell it to fuck off. But just like the weight that drapes over my shoulders like an obnoxious wet towel, the lingering presence remains.

If I didn't know any better, I'd say the voice almost sounds like Atlas. Other times, it sounds like Alastair.

Sometimes, it sounds like me.

"She's alive. She's here. Go. To. Her," it snarls again in Old Latin.

"She isn't," I mutter aloud, uncaring of my slow descent into madness by this point. "The one I love is dead."

"She's not. She's here. She's alive. Find her. NOW!"

I snarl, baring my teeth at the disembodied voice . . . but then I'm moving. I'm moving, albeit slowly and sluggishly, but I prowl out of Rhesa's chambers and further down the dark, quiet halls where too few guards are left to patrol. I don't even recognize these halls now, as the banners have been replaced with Abaddon's crest. The wicked, beautiful art of the Hellion court and Samael and Rhesamyre have been removed, too. To where, I don't know. I don't think I care, by this point.

But as I proceed toward the halls that will lead me below the palace into the cells, I look around with a touch more clarity.

And before they can hear me, I hear *them*, whispering and scheming in the shadows as they proceed together as though they're lovers or some shit. And fuck it, it wouldn't surprise me if they are.

"She seems tame enough now," says Abaddon.

"Don't be a fool, boy," replies Lucifer. "She is still a wild beast. Though if we are indeed to keep her shackled close, perhaps Siren is best suited to test her skills in the bedroom before we gift her back to our new warden at Blackstone."

"You know, *I* could always—"

"She shall get no closer to your throne, my king. Only when she is begging on her knees shall she be permitted to approach you. Ready to please us all as our court's *whore*. She's used to multiple cocks, after all."

Abaddon goes quiet, I suppose in agreement with Lucifer, but I don't stick around to find out.

Soon enough, I'm deep below the luxuries of Hell, in the belly of the beast, staring into one of the few occupied cells at the slumbering form of the redheaded witch that, for a moment, I swear is Rhesamyre again.

The cot is thin and rotted, and the woman upon it stirs slowly before blinking over at me. She cocks her head, then sits up slowly as if she doesn't believe what she's seeing. Her eyes are bloodshot and wide with dark bags beneath them, and I lower my gaze from hers to better observe her body.

She's covered in dried blood and grime, and bruises litter her skin in varying stages of healing. Black and blue, mostly, but some have turned to a sicker shade of green and yellow. While scrapes and cuts scab over on her arms and legs, but some are clearly infected and have been left to fester. Obviously, she's been put through quite the ordeal, and a fair amount of poison must still be pumping in her blood if she has been left alone and trusted to rot down here unguarded. Her wounds are slow to heal, and her magic is inaccessible.

"*Atticus?*" she croaks, and dammit if it her voice doesn't sound like Rhesa again.

I close my eyes, inhaling deeply to keep my magic under wraps. However, strangely enough, it has settled inside of me again. Content and quiet. The weight of my grief is still there, but the incessant growling has gone silent. And I would be lying if I said I didn't relish it.

The witch rises on unsteady legs—legs that have been broken once or twice before—while using the wall to balance as she breathes in deep, her lungs rattling quietly with the force it takes to inhale without coughing. Then she slowly approaches and stands before me, careful not to touch the bars as she observes me with tears lining her eyes.

"You're really here," she mumbles, but then she furrows her brows at whatever she sees on my face and in my body language. "What have they done to you?"

I snarl, baring my teeth, and before she can react, I whip my arm through the bars and grasp her throat in a steel vise. She inhales sharply and chokes, and I squeeze her little neck harder as her fingers curl into pathetic claws as she attempts to remove my hand.

"At-Atticus," she croaks again, whining pathetically as her tears drop, leaving dirty streaks down her cheeks.

"Do *not* speak my name, you filthy crone," I hiss.

Her eyes close, and her body shudders, and when she opens her green eyes again, they flicker with obsidian and hellfire for a heartbeat.

"You don't recognize me," she mutters, and I squeeze her throat again.

"On the contrary, I know who you are. You are the wicked witch who slayed my brothers. You murdered the one I love!" I roar in her face.

"What-What if I were to tell you that *I* am the one you love?"

I snarl again. "*Lies.*"

"It's not!" she cries, snarling and sniveling now. "They put a collar around your fucking neck, Atticus! I'm still here! I'm alive!"

I roar again, then squeeze her neck and pull her forward against the bars. She snarls and curses as the bars burn her cheeks from the imprisonment magic imbedded here, and then I throw her backward with enough force that she trips and falls on her ass again. Her entire body buckles beneath her, and she whimpers in pain and winces from the fall.

I growl to myself, then back up and hit the bars of another empty cell, and I slide against them until I am seated on the floor.

"Why . . . why would you venture down here if you believe I am indeed the witch?" she inquires, her eyes full of fire and rage as she looks at me through the tendrils of her dirty, matted hair.

"My magic demands retribution and insisted I come vis-à-vis with the crone responsible," I growl. "Though . . . I will admit . . . it has gone silent now that I am before you. Sated and still, though I don't know why, because all I want to do is slaughter you."

"Then why don't you?" she prompts, rearranging herself to sit more comfortably on the stone floor.

It doesn't look comfortable by any means.

"Lucifer and Abaddon have plans for you, and it is not my place to interfere."

"The fuck it isn't!" she screams. "Do you know what they're doing out there? How many innocent lives they've taken and sold and raped? Everything we fought for has all been for not, Atticus!"

I bare my teeth. "I find that I no longer care."

She scoffs, shaking her head. "Fucking hell . . . out of them all, I didn't think you'd succumb to it so easily."

I cock my head at her. "What do you speak of, witch?"

Hellfire eyes flash in place of the green again. "Are you not the least bit curious as to why your magic is settled when near me? Perhaps it knows something you refuse to acknowledge. It knows who I am. Your magic has always known!"

I growl again. "And what? Am I supposed to believe you are, in fact, *my* Rhesamyre? The queen of Hell and Myra come back to life?"

"*Yes!* Lucifer's hold on you is strong, Atticus. But you are stronger. *Fight it.* Fight him. *Look at me.*"

I watch as she shifts and raises her scrappy shirt to reveal a part of her bruised hip bone, and she strokes her damaged skin softly.

Fire ignites and flares as my magic pulses, and I hiss as I feel my *truculent* brand awaken and simmer as though Rhesa is . . .

I look at the witch again, and her expression is steeled as she gazes at me. Her eyes reveal nothing, and her busted lips are set in a tight line.

"That collar of thorns around your neck is not strong enough to withstand what you and I share, Atticus," she whispers. "No black magic could ever compare to the magic of soul bonds. We share brands. We share magic. Your brothers are *alive*, and they need our help, Atticus, *please*." Her eyes close as she ducks her head, beginning to sob quietly again. "Please see me. Please hear me and recognize me again. *I need you*."

I jump to my feet once more, successfully startling her as she whips her head up to look at me.

My magic is angry and simmering and bloodthirsty and wild again. Warring beneath my skin and rattling my bones as my *truculent* brand itches uncomfortably as that voice returns to whisper *Believe her, believe her, believe her!*

I shake my head in a vain attempt to get the voice out, and I growl loudly. The sound reverberates off the walls and echoes throughout the cavern of cells, rattling and splintering the ground beneath my boots.

The distant sound of another door creaking open and shutting softly cracks through my skull painfully, and Lucifer's voice echoes through the halls as he approaches us, successfully splitting my brain in half again. The pain nearly brings me to my knees, and though it makes me dizzy and nauseous, I remain upright.

"Let him go!" snarls the witch from within her cell, getting close to the bars again despite the magic humming in warning at her proximity. "You don't need him! You can't use him! I'll fucking tear you apart limb from limb, Lucifer! I swear to the stars above, I will slaughter you until nothing remains of your body or soul! I'll devour you whole!" she screams, then continues to curse and threaten him in Enochian and Old Latin and all the languages she can possibly think of to get her point across.

Some of which I don't even recognize in my pained state.

I glance over at Lucifer while my skin continues to burn like a festering wound hot with fever and full of maggots and worms, and the self-proclaimed god merely regards the witch with a scowl. Then he proceeds to unlock her cell, and the witch sets her shoulders and snarls at the male in warning and protest. He ignores her feral sounds, though, and quicker than she can retreat in her wounded state, grabs hold of her face and slams her into the back wall.

He snarls lowly, and I'm unable to process his words over the ringing and buzzing in my ears. And then, all I bother to do is watch as he beats the ever-loving *shit* out of her. Smashing her face into the wall, breaking her fingers, snapping her elbow, and dislocating her shoulder while he pounds his fist into other vital organs, surely cracking a rib or two in the process.

Then he leaves her there, limp and broken, as he straightens his suit and struts out of the cell as though he didn't just beat her senseless.

"Atticus," he calls, and his voice grates on every single one of my nerves, irritating me to my core.

I meet his eyes, my scowl firmly in place again despite the war in my head.

He smiles tightly at me, though the action doesn't quite reach his eyes as he gestures toward the exit, where two of his guards prowl forward and into the cell to grab her while he stares at me.

"She's a bloody liar and a manipulator," he claims. "You would do wise to avoid her altogether. She will be dealt with accordingly, my friend. So please, rest easy. There is much work to be done elsewhere."

I scowl, and everything is numb and empty and heavy again as I step forward.

I don't bother to waste another glance at the witch as they haul her to her feet and drag her out of the cell.

THE SHADOWS ARE SENTIENT.
THEY LISTEN TO OUR SECRETS AND SPELLS,
COUNTING OUR PRAYERS AND STARS.
I TELL THEM EVERYTHING. THEY KNOW ALL.
PERHAPS THEY KNOW ME EVEN BETTER THAN
I KNOW MYSELF.
SOMETIMES I FORGET WHO I AM AND WHAT
I'M DOING HERE, BUT AT LEAST THE STARS
REMEMBER.

CHAPTER ELEVEN
RHESAMYRE

They are mine, Lucifer claimed. *Their minds, bodies, souls, and magic are shackled. Collared. And I hold the leash. Be patient*, little feather, *for your time shall soon arrive.*

And Atticus . . . Atticus just stood there and watched.

But he's here. *He's alive.* Collared by black magic and thorns and looking paler than a corpse, but *alive.*

I'm trying to reach him, snarls Atlas in the back of my head. *But whatever spell has him caged is smothering our brands. He can't see you, Rhesa. And he can't hear me.*

Atticus strides forward just ahead of us as Lucifer's goblins drag me onward like a sack of potatoes, and no one speaks as we proceed through the halls toward the throne room, where Abaddon and my family are no doubt waiting. I glance to the side, getting lightheaded again, but I have just enough wherewithal left to survey what remains of my capital.

The entirety of the Heart of Hell sits encapsulated in a blanket of glittering snow.

"Even Hell itself knows this is wrong," I mutter. "If you still think what Lucifer and Abaddon are doing is *right*—"

"I've *never* thought that," Atticus snarls under his breath.

"Then why—"

"Because everyone I love is gone . . . what do I have left to fight for? Why should I still care about what happens to the spheres when no one I care about still calls them home?"

"Because . . . because I would tell you that their memories are just as important, but we're not just memories, Atticus. *Not yet.* I am here with you, even if you don't believe me and can't see me. I need you to have faith in me. *In us.*"

Atticus's steps falter for half a heartbeat, but we're already entering the throne room, and I'm brought to the center and set down on my knees before the Hellion court and Abaddon. Snow piles into the room since half the fucking wall is still gone, and Atticus steps off to the side. From behind, Lucifer enters and stalks toward us slowly.

He dumps Dante's skull and bones in a pile next to me, and the necromancer clacks his teeth and curses up a storm in various languages.

"I believe we have this traitorous menace to thank for that new ink upon your hand," snarls Lucifer as he takes his place near Abaddon and the throne. "Perhaps in some way, you truly were the Devil's daughter. Bargains litter your body like scars on a slave, but I suppose that is a fitting description for you by now."

I glance over at Atticus, but he looks . . . *distant* again. As do the rest of my uncles as they stand at attention upon the dais.

"Don't bother," quips Lucifer, and I slowly meet his gaze again. "They hear what I want them to hear. See what I want them to see. I told you. They. Are. Mine."

Lucifer sweeps his gaze down to Dante beside me, and the skull clacks his teeth again.

"Well, then. As for that one, I believe there is only one way to get rid of him for good."

Like a dog summoned by his master, Death begins his trek toward us while the rest of my uncles remain still, and I mutter to Dante, "*I'm sorry.*"

"You are not the one who needs to apologize here, My Queen," replies the skull smoothly without a lick of fear. "We have failed you more than once. So let this be the end of it so that I may not fail you anymore."

I bow my head, and it takes all my willpower to hold back my tears as Death stalks closer and kicks Dante's bones into a tighter pile. Then, once my estranged uncle is satisfied, he ignites his magic, and the bones go up in flames.

It's just a nightmare, whispers Atlas in my head. *Just a bad dream, little wolf.*

The skull shrieks, and I turn my gaze again to look Atticus straight in the eyes this time.

His eyes flicker to mine for half a heartbeat before he focuses on the burning bones before us. Then, not soon enough, the shrieking stops, and Dante's bones are nothing but ash and dust.

Lucifer smirks at me. "Seeing as how Bael's sessions didn't quite exude the desired reactions, I believe it is time for a new curriculum of *conditioning.*"

The throne room doors open again, and a steady, confident stride heads straight for me, but I don't dare turn my head as the scent of sexy musk and sweet pheromones reach my nose.

Fuck. It was diluted and almost nonexistent when I met him as *Rhesamyre* this time around, but then again, that was also Atticus playing *dress-up.* However, I remember plenty about the sexy, gorgeous male from my time as Myra, too.

I have just enough warning to shut my eyes before fingers pinch my chin to turn my head toward, who I know to be, a handsome male that would no doubt have me on my knees, begging him to put a thorn collar around my neck with a leather leash to match.

"*Rhesamyre*," purrs Siren deeply—the real one this time. "I'm hurt, pet. It has been so very long since we've seen each other. So why don't you open your eyes and greet me properly?"

I growl at the male with my eyes sealed shut. "Get your fucking filthy hands off me, you fucking traitor."

Siren chuckles beautifully, his fingers rubbing along my chin and jawline gently, soothingly, and soft tingles follow in the wake of his fingers as he rubs the ache in my jaw away as if he's—

Hell below.

"Come on, pet," he coaxes, his warm breath by my ear as his other hand begins to roam further down my body, gently pressing and prodding at my injuries before slowly pushing magic into me to help me heal, albeit slowly, but I'm sure that is by design.

Lucifer must not know.

"Let me tempt you, precious," he coos. "Let me *keep* you."

This place is meant to tempt you, Queen of Hell. Kure's words echo in my head immediately, whispering that things will be okay. I am not alone. *But it is not strong enough to keep you here.*

I inhale a slow, shuddering breath, then open my eyes to meet the deep green of Siren's.

The handsome male offers me a soft, sultry smile, then murmurs, "There you are."

His sensual pull on me is there, but it coaxes me to relax more than it demands I worship the ground he walks on, and I steel myself in order to keep the relief off my face.

His pearly white smile broadens, and he pets my hair and rubs around my horns as if I truly am a pet in need of reassurance. Though everywhere his hands explore, his fingers and magic seek to heal, not invade or harass in search of sexual gratification.

"Good girl," he purrs again as he moves to stand behind me, brushing his fingers along my neck as he grabs a gentle fistful of my hair to hold me against his thighs as I kneel on the floor.

"I will get you what you want," drawls Siren, his voice hardened since he now addresses an amused-looking and aroused Lucifer.

I'm going to be sick, but Siren keeps rubbing my head, so I do my best to keep it together.

Siren is a ballsy fucker, snarls Atlas. *But I do believe he's on your side. And Lucifer's death can't come soon enough.*

"Our new warden of Castle Blackstone, Gulliver, will be in your debt," says Lucifer.

Gulliver? What the fuck happened to Bael in the short amount of time since I left him?

I would suspect Atticus happened . . . before he was caught in Lucifer's snare once more, says Atlas. *My brother did his best, Rhesa.*

I know, I murmur.

"As will I, if you can indeed tame that beast," continues Lucifer. "Make it so that even if we decide to remove her collar, she doesn't run off and cause trouble. Such a headache, that one is."

My blood runs cold in my veins again.

Lucifer intends to give me to this new warden as a gift, I realize. As his new sex slave. And he has enlisted Siren to see it through.

Scheme, scheme, scheme . . . I don't know if Siren is truly on my side or not, and despite what he said earlier, it could very well be that he somehow came upon the right words to say in order to gain my trust. But that is once again a risk I am not willing to take. I *can't* take any chances with loyalty. Not now. Not *ever.*

Right now, the only one I can truly count on is myself.

I love you, I tell Atlas.

Siren shrugs. "Very well. I will have my way with her, and then you can—"

"*Master*?"

Siren's fingers still in my hair for a heartbeat, and then he replies, "What is it, pet?"

I look up at him, nuzzling into his thigh for the sake of dramatics, and Siren narrows his eyes at me.

"I do not wish to suffer any longer," I whimper. "Please . . . please. I will behave. Please do not shackle me with more chains. I cannot bear it any longer . . . but maybe a ring would do. I can be loyal and honest. I would make a good wife."

I turn my gaze toward Lucifer, and then I look to Abaddon, who, as always, looks awkward and insecure upon the throne.

He knows it is not his, and I intend to help him better understand that concept.

But that is not the game right now. For right now, I need to channel Siren and Lust and use all that I am and have to give in order to get back what I want and what is mine.

It will all be mine again.

Yes, it will be, avows Atlas.

And if I must swallow my pride to ensure it, then so be it. If I must endure the horrors of another warden once more. Then. So. Be. It.

And I will be with you, my deity vows once more.

So I slip into the role of a seductive demon, and I lick my lips with hooded eyes as I gaze at Abaddon, forcing my eyes to rake up and down his body as if I am impressed and aroused. As if I want to devour him because he is the most delicious thing I have ever set my eyes on, and I'm starving.

Pretending he is Atticus or one of my other deities makes it a hell of a lot easier, but my stomach still churns in protest despite my best efforts to keep my nausea under control.

Lucifer chuckles. "You cannot have this one yet, little feather. Though I'm sure Gulliver will be ecstatic to learn you wish to take him as a husband."

Biting my tongue, I whimper, "If it means I may be warm and fed well, then so be it . . . my god."

Lucifer raises his brow again, the corner of his mouth curling into a twisted smirk as he drawls to Siren, "Well, that was easy enough. You truly do have a way with unruly females. Though I do believe it is cheating if you resort to magic to pleasure and train them."

Siren chuckles darkly, though, dare I say, it isn't as sensual as usual. "My gifts are certainly one of a kind. When may I take her?"

"You may take her back to Blackstone now, and I shall inform Gulliver of his newest whore. *Oh*—pardon me. I meant *wife*."

I close my eyes so that Lucifer is incapable of seeing the rage brewing in them, and then give all my attention to Siren as he tugs on my hair and pulls me to my feet gently. I don't even bother to glance at Atticus again, but I do feel his eyes on us as we take our leave.

Siren leads me right outside the throne room, then opens a conveyance straight into the courtyard of Castle Blackstone. I glance around at the space dusted with a layer of frost, gaping at the sight of it in *ruins*. Similarly to the throne room, large portions of the castle have been removed, leaving nothing but large caverns and gaping holes behind, and the actual stone structures themselves appear as though they've *melted*.

Siren tugs me gently, and I walk with him as he leads me up the steps toward the nicer accommodations and suites that lie above the rotten cells and dank caves.

"Your deity's handiwork," Siren mutters. "He's been lighting fires in your name, pet."

"He's been shackled."

"*Now* he has been, yes. But that's a newer inconvenience. You can thank him for Bael's sudden departure from the spheres of the living, too."

Atlas chuckles menacingly in my head.

I stay quiet since soldiers patrol just as they did when I stayed here, but I feel as though there are even fewer slaves now. Not nearly as many are shackled to the walls nor hanging off the bars of their cages, and there are fewer bodies just lying around in waste, too.

But then there are plenty of burnt corpses. Fried until nothing but lumps of flaky flesh remain scattered across the yard. Slaves and soldiers, I realize.

Atticus fucking erupted.

I dare not utter a word to Siren regarding my observations, and instead focus on putting one foot in front of the other. Finally, we're entering one of the en suites of the castle, and Siren leads me to the center of the lavish chamber fitted with obsidian weaponry and décor. The soft carpet beneath me is comforting on my sore feet, but I don't get long to enjoy the silence and warmth before the door to the bathing chamber opens to reveal this new warden, Gulliver.

He bears a striking resemblance to Bael, and I suppose I never cared to learn that the sadist had a brother.

He was rarely around, explains Atlas. *Often drunk and deep into his cups. Never one to actively associate himself with Bael's acts.*

Seems like times have changed, since he's been promoted, I snarl.

The monster that is Gulliver grins at me, but I remain steadfast and stoic as Siren drawls, "I would suggest you let her bathe first."

"Of course, of course. She is quite filthy, isn't she?"

No thanks to your kin, fucker, growls Atlas.

"Quite, yes," replies Siren tersely.

Gulliver hums. "Well then, I suppose we shall leave the lady to bathe properly. I'll need her scrubbed clean and well-polished before this evening. The men are quite excited to get a glimpse of my new *wife* and their new fuck toy."

Gulliver prowls toward me, then grabs me by my jaw and tips my head back. His foul breath assaults my nose as he says, "I plan on wedding you before the masses tonight, bitch. And once I'm done fucking you bloody, I'll let my men and every other beast and goblin in this castle have a turn ripping that sweet cunt of yours to shreds. I'd be impressed to see if you even survive our wedding night."

It takes all of my self-control not to spit in his face, and instead, I keep my eyelids heavy and gaze downcast. He grins, then leans downward and presses his lips against mine. His tongue invades my mouth harshly, and he groans as he nips at my lips and draws blood, continuing to suck on the wound and drawing out as much as he can.

I remember to breathe through my nose, and Siren's hand in my hair is the only thing grounding me, along with Atlas's subtle growls in the back of my head.

Gulliver rips his mouth away from mine and breathes heavily as he stares at me with wild eyes.

"I can still taste poison on your lips, bitch," he growls, grabbing me by my neck as he licks the seam of my closed lips. "Your blood is tainted."

"Unfortunately," drawls Siren, sounding bored. "Unless you desire her to call upon her magic, she will have to remain *tasting of poison*. My own wells of power are grand, but until she submits wholly to you, she is still a threat and thus must be shackled properly."

Gulliver hums, then removes his hand from my neck.

"Unfortunately, I agree," he admits. "I trust you will keep an eye on her while she cleans up?"

"It would be my pleasure."

Gulliver chuckles. "Yeah, I bet it would be. No matter, you're welcome to use her if you so wish to. Just ensure that she is ready to be presented before tonight. In the meantime, I must prepare for the feast of a lifetime, before we feast on *her*."

Gulliver licks his lips, then takes his leave.

Siren sighs deeply once the door closes behind us, and then he releases my hair and pushes me forward gently toward the bathing chamber. Inside are two slave girls positioned by the tub, which steams with hot water full of bubbles and rose petals, and with a detached voice, Siren orders me to *strip*.

There isn't much left to strip out of, and I pull the torn scrap of a shirt over my horns before stepping into the steaming tub.

I haven't had a proper bath in ages, but I cannot bring myself to enjoy this one since these female servants work with a strange haze over their eyes as they prepare me for Gulliver and his men, like some concubine. They wash my hair and scrub me with harsh hands, not being mindful of my injuries or bruises, then swiftly dress me in obsidian jewelry and a revealing *white* gown that only has sheer fabric and lace over my breasts and intimate parts.

All of me is on display. Every brand, cut, bruise, and battered piece of skin and infected flap of flesh that has yet to heal.

The female I see staring back at me in the mirror is a skinny little thing with an unhealthy complexion and bags under her eyes.

You're still beautiful to me, little wolf, whispers Atlas, though he sounds pained.

"That's enough," commands Siren from the corner, where he watches with crossed arms and pensive eyes.

The slaves step away from me and bow their heads, and I meet Siren's gaze through the mirror. He stalks toward me, surveying all of my body, but his eyes are not lustful.

No. While no one is here to witness it, the Lord of Temptation reveals his inner rage at the sight of me. At the state of me.

"Fix your face," I mutter just loud enough for him to hear, and he schools his features back into cool calculation and quiet confidence, exuding swagger and sex.

He grips me by my shoulders and gently turns me around, then grasps my chin with one hand while he places a finger over his lips with the other. Then he opens his hand to reveal the writing on his palm, which reveals itself just long enough for me to read it.

We await your commands. Kure sends his regards.

I blink, and he lowers his hand again to press it into my lower back, guiding me out of the bathing chamber and bedroom and through the halls of Castle Blackstone toward the great hall. The hallways are alight with enchanted candelabras and torches, and as we move closer to the disaster ahead, the noise of Gulliver's loyal men and monsters only grows louder. The mess of males drink and eat away at the tables as Gulliver sits at the head of the room as though *he* is a king.

I stand in the doorway, and Gulliver doesn't bother to rise from his seat as he spies me. He smirks, then gestures for his men to quiet themselves as Siren presses me onward, into the den of monsters. I feel his magic wash over me, and I inhale his pheromones deeply to help calm my racing, raging magic and heartbeat so I may get through this and see our plans through. Siren doesn't drown me in his magic, but he does allow just enough to seep through to make the show believable.

We make our way down the center aisle between the tables of gawking goblins and lustful prisoners-turned-guards, and all of them guzzle their drinks as they drunkenly lick their lips and stare openly at me as if I am to be their next meal.

And according to Gulliver, I will be.

They can try, quips Atlas lowly.

I step right up to the new warden, and he grins at me before sliding his chair backward and patting his thigh.

And like a good little soon-to-be wife and whore, I take a seat right on his lap as though it is to be the only throne I will ever have again.

Gulliver laughs noisily behind me, his entire chest rumbling and moving with the action as he keeps me seated on his lap with a meaty arm slung around my middle. He chuckles along with his men at some story Siren tells them of a whorehouse he founded in Ursa Major under Apollo's nose.

I don't care to listen, too busy doing my best to ignore the bulge that presses against my ass.

Gulliver is rock-hard and *drunk*.

Cut it off, little wolf, orders Atlas.

I almost smirk.

The rest of the men ahead of us have continued to indulge in their drunkenness and debauchery to the fullest. Fucking the many girls and boys that wear nothing but collars, and the monsters and goblins are all too happy to play *fuck around the table.* Sometimes even with each other, and I know Siren is to thank for their complete descent into the maddening haze of lust and pleasure. Sex weighs heavily in the air, dulling their senses on top of the alcohol they consume. And all that is heard is laughter and moans and growls and groans and skin slapping against skin as everyone fucks each other.

Gulliver shifts forward and inhales my scent deeply, then licks the nape of my neck.

"Would you like to join them, pretty bitch?" he inquires gruffly, and I want nothing more than to gag.

But I manage to refrain and keep my wits about me, then spare him a sultry smile as I glance back at him over my shoulder teasingly, leaning against his chest as I nuzzle the underside of his jaw.

"Only if you'll join me, master," I prompt.

Gulliver grins, then grabs my jaw roughly and smashes his lips against mine, forcing my lips open so he can stick his tongue down my throat. It's suffocating, and his spit tastes like cheap alcohol and smells of a rotting corpse and stale cigarettes.

There is nothing kind or passionate about the action; it is merely a show of dominance, and not in the way I have come to adore. For Gulliver is no alpha. He is no king, no leader, and certainly not my *master*. He is simply another traitor who has come to stand between me and my throne.

I will do away with them all.

I thread my hand through his hair, and he groans pathetically and bucks his hips upward, into my core. I lower my other hand and grab him by the balls, and he gasps and pulls his mouth away from my own, excitement now evident in his gaze as I massage his pathetic little cock through his slacks.

I'm honestly surprised he even chose to wear clothes, seeing as how the rest of his men were nearly naked before I even arrived.

I gaze at him with the loveliest, lovesick, most innocent look I can muster as I mutter in a faraway foreign tongue, *"Behead them all."*

Gulliver's head explodes.

Blood splatters all over me as pieces of his brain land in the chicken on his plate, and I gaze outward with a steeled expression as heads *pop* dozens at a time. The shackled whores scream as they are splattered with blood, and the remaining men of Gulliver's guard look amongst the carnage and claim their weapons as though they will be able to stop the enemy they cannot even see.

It's futile, and I rise from Gulliver's lap and stride forward through the bloodshed as the rest of the men at his personal table are decapitated and butchered in a similar manner to the way the Forest of Souls claims its victims. Blood and gore fly across the room as heads explode. Bodies thump into the red puddles as screaming whores make their escapes to get away from me, and although I am no threat to them, I suppose they aren't quite in their right minds at the moment to hear me out.

No matter. I don't believe I have much patience to explain everything, anyway.

Blood nearly rains down from the ceiling since some of the heads exploded so violently, and the white I once wore is now stained red in a similar fashion to the feast that dots the tables.

I step around the main table and take a seat upon the flat surface, crossing my legs and pouring myself a drink to watch the bloodbath commence. Gulliver had a little over a hundred men packed in here for the orgy, nearly what was left of the entire castle, I would wager. Which just makes murdering them all so much easier, and bodies continue to drop across the floor and tables as chunks of their heads decorate the chandeliers. The sound of wet crunches as skulls are crushed and brains are turned to mush is simply music to my ears.

Then, finally, it all ceases as the few in the back who attempted to flee are finally slaughtered.

You're exquisite, snarls Atlas. *I love you so goddamned much.*

I take another slow sip from my drink, then lower my cup to wipe my nose of the blood that has begun to seep from my own head; my body is still not quite ready to handle such magical spells despite Siren's best efforts to heal me.

Shoes splash through the puddles, and I glance over at the lord as he approaches me warily. He is splattered with blood, too, though I would wager he doesn't wear it as war paint like I do.

"Dare I ask?" he inquires slowly, cautiously.

He sounds like he's afraid of me, but I don't even grin at him; I can't find the strength to at the moment.

"It was an impressive feat of magic derived by a sorcerer from a foreign sphere far, far away from here," I explain. "He was actually a king, albeit a cruel one, but powerful, nonetheless. He called it the Guillotine Spell, and he used it to butcher the masses by the hundreds when rebels would rally before his gates. It is designed to only slaughter those guilty of treason, but if overused and abused, one might find his own head *popping* off instead. Such as the very king who created the spell when the magic itself revolted against his tyranny. The son of that spherical system was evidently not amused by the continued misuse of his magic."

Siren cocks his head a little. "All magic comes at a price, it would seem. No matter the sphere."

I nod. "Astraeus and I visited many spheres together, and I learned much from each one. Though I'll admit, I never thought I would have to resort to this spell. Satisfying and efficient as it may be, if the majority of those you claim to be traitors are in fact not so, the spell will seek *your* head instead. However, it doesn't take much to utter the spell and activate the magic that craves the blood of *rats*. It feeds off itself once it is let loose, but first, I still needed enough of my own magic to bring it to life. Thus, I would not have been able to pull this off had you not healed me as minimally as you did. So I thank you, Lord of Temptation."

Siren dips his head. "Of course, Your Majesty. It was both my pleasure and my duty."

"And seeing as how the spell did not come for your head, I suppose I can trust you wholeheartedly, after all. That is certainly some good news after all the shit I've been put through as of late."

Siren chuckles awkwardly. "I am here for you, my queen. Then, now, and always."

I hum, nodding along. "Very well. Then let us finish what Atticus started, and burn this fucking castle to the ground, shall we?"

He grins for real now, but I don't bother to match it.

Instead, I slip off the table in a bloodstained wedding dress and stride through the slaughterhouse, into the remaining hallways of the castle. Siren follows a pace behind me as I trail my hand across the wall and mutter the commands for another foreign Siphon Spell. This one draws magic from the castle itself, stealing and borrowing the magic that belongs to the enchanted candelabras, runes, torches, and wards of this place.

Lights flicker and snuff out completely as I siphon their power, and windows crack and shatter as I stride outside, murdering more guards and ex-prisoners as I go. Leaving nothing and no one behind as staircases crumble to dust once I descend them.

I will ensure nothing of this retched castle remains. The little magic Siren used to heal me managed to burn away just enough of the poison in my blood so I may command lesser magic; the spells I mutter are foreign to this land and thus not beholden to Astraeus's regime and rules, nor Lucifer's shackles.

But it's not like my old lover would stop me anyway.

I know I wouldn't, avows Atlas.

I almost smirk at that.

Shackles that remain around slaves shatter with a snap of my fingers, and they flee without a second glance as Castle Blackstone goes up in flames. The magic I siphon from this property burns away the last of the poison in my bloodstream, and the rest of the injuries and cuts across my body are finally given a fighting chance to heal properly and completely.

Siren stands at attention a step behind me as the flames devour the castle, and I breathe in the scent of cursed smoke and burning corpses as the red-stained wedding dress falls away from my curves and is replaced with my battle leathers. The nearly endless pools of my magic swirl and snarl deep within me, all too happy to be free of our shackles as I command it to do the simplest of tasks, such as equip me with my weapons and obsidian attire.

"Where are the rest?" I inquire.

"Awaiting your commands within the sands of the West."

I hum. "And what of my brothers?"

"Still imprisoned in Ursa Major, under Apollo's watch."

The last of the flames lick at the stone and wood of the castle lazily, and I turn to face Siren.

"I still have unfinished business elsewhere, and we cannot reclaim Hell until the matter is settled."

Siren nods. "Very well . . . may I inquire as to what sort of business?"

Finally, I smirk a little, though Siren almost looks more alarmed than relieved at the sight of it. "Summon your neighbors, Lord of Temptation. I believe I will have use for all four of you within the confines of the Hollow."

I don't know what I would change if given the chance to go
back. To start over and do it all again.
There are too many things I've done wrong in this life, and
I am unsure of how to go about fixing it all.
We're distant again.
We've forgotten once more.
Brothers… what have we become?
Kings?
Some days, I'm not always so sure.
I think we were once.
I think we were so much more.

CHAPTER TWELVE
ATTICUS

I'm disoriented, to say the least. Uncertain and confused, and I'm still not completely certain that the witch kneeling before Siren is my Rhesamyre, but after hearing what she said, as well as what Hell itself has become . . .

The more I question what reality is. As well as what it isn't.

Not to mention, my magic is *boiling*. It raged when I had her in my grasp, my eyes playing tricks on me again as I *swore* I gazed at Rhesa, and then it was angered once more when Lucifer struck her. My magic demanded that I soothe some of her worries and eviscerate the male.

But I didn't. I just stood there like a coward.

And now here she is again, kneeling before the Lord of Temptation, about to be sold off and wed to Gulliver, the younger brother of that sadist Bael, while Lucifer and Abaddon watch from the Obsidian Throne that once belonged to me and mine.

I turn away. I cannot watch this. I will not watch this.

I am a coward . . . and I need answers.

Siren glances my way as I step back into the shadows to take my leave. Lucifer and Abaddon are too focused on the witch to notice me slipping away, so I open a conveyance and find myself outside the palace in the dark gardens, where the stone art and flora have been removed or destroyed.

Fucking hell, it's *freezing*.

Snow caps the entirety of the capital, and my breath fogs up in front of me as though I am in the frozen Midlands.

For Hell does not freeze.

I glance around again at the snowcapped garden, glad to be anywhere but inside that throne room; however, as I continue my sweep, my eyes snag on one of the decorative mirrors that is held in the maw of a massive obsidian hellhound. The mirror is shattered, but the hellhound is mostly intact. The majority of the statues out here that did not survive Abaddon's initial ascent to the throne are those of Rhesa and the original court, but a few of the beasts were spared, although not very many.

My reflection flickers ahead of me, and I go still.

For ahead of me is not . . . *me*, but the male in the mirror looks eerily similar to my late brothers in some odd light. As I cock my head, so does he, and when I bare my teeth, he mimics that action, too.

I step closer, peering around the mirror and surveying the hellhound statue itself for tricks and spells, but my magic doesn't warn me of anything. So I meet the stranger's silver gaze again, the molten steel flickering like the metallic flames of his feathered wings.

And then the all-too familiar reflection *grins* at me of his own accord, snapping his hand forward and through the shattered glass of the mirror, cracking it further and making it ripple oddly as he wraps his tattooed hand around my throat.

I reel backward, snarling and growling while summoning my magic to shatter the mirror completely, but I halt when the male smirks and holds up a black, thorned collar in his hand before he crushes it as though it were nothing.

It all comes rushing back to me; the spell is broken.

I stumble backward, forced to a knee as the weight of everything presses on my shoulders.

The truth of what occurred at the Falls invades my mind. *My brothers are alive somewhere.* And I was fucking around, messing with Lucifer's troops, and then Damian found me, *and Rhesa is alive!* I tortured and murdered Bael, and that's when Lucifer shackled me, but Rhesa is alive and injured and hurt and alone and—

"Get her brothers out of Ursa Major."

I snap my gaze forward and surge toward the mirror, clasping the sides of it as I growl and hiss at the male within.

He's not amused and simply narrows his eyes at my show of aggression.

"I cannot just leave her there—"

"Our queen has her own games to play. The one called Siren is with her and will not allow any more harm to befall her, but you must retrieve the archangels. You will need them to subdue the Hellion court and reclaim Heart first, if all is to be righted."

I snarl at him again. "And why should I trust you? Who the *fuck* do you think you are to give *me* orders?"

The stranger who resembles my brothers tilts his head and then reaches through the mirror again to grasp me by the back of my neck. He pulls me in close until our foreheads are nearly touching, and he says in Old Latin, *"Because I am you, and you are me. Your brothers share a soul with us, too. And Myra was mine before Rhesa was yours."*

And then my magic and mind are flooded with the memories that belong to this male, yet they fit perfectly within me, too. It feels right to know what he knows. To feel what he once felt.

To love both Myra and Rhesamyre back then and now. Altogether as one.

Memories of Yonder and Evergreen and distant brothers and sons and stars and shadows and bargains and pleas and promises and all that lies in between. But above all, there is Myra. Rhesamyre. Our soul-bonded mate and lover and *queen*.

The One True Queen.

And Three Kings.

A Champion and her deities.

Astraeus removes his hand from the nape of my neck and pulls away from me, and I straighten as my magic boils deep inside my chest with the revelation of feeling *whole* again.

"Why did you wait this long?" I inquire.

Astraeus sighs. "It's not like I fucking *wanted* to, but maneuvering behind both my mother's and Lucifer's backs takes time. I am not supposed to interact with the spheres in this manner, and as I once explained to Myra, I may be what I am, but my mother is still a *god*. A hypocritical one at that, and I must gauge her moods before I make a move to either defy her or attempt to please her, for the temperamental goddess has nothing but time on her hands."

"Your family dynamics sound worse than my own."

He chuckles lowly, sounding like Alastair. "Our family dynamics are certainly troubling, yes. Though I will say, just as your brothers come to your aid in your most dire times of need, as have mine."

"The other sons . . . they have revolted against your mother, haven't they?"

"They have . . . *expressed* their displeasure with her, *yes* . . . Myra and Rhesamyre have yet to realize the impact they have upon the distant lives and spherical systems as a whole. They have both made friends everywhere. Allies in the strangest of places. And my brothers recognize that many of the problems in their own spheres would not have been solved if not for Myra.

There is a debt to be paid, and this is how they have sought to pay it."

"By demanding that Yonder stand down."

Astraeus nods.

I narrow my eyes at the son. "Though . . . that is not all, is it?"

He chuckles a little, the sound conniving and similar in nature to Atlas now. "I suppose I have done enough damage on my own to warrant her participation, though threatening to erupt and take my surrounding brothers out with me, alongside their spheres, did more to piss off our father than it did our mother, and he finally stepped in to rein her in. Truly, he remains the only one that really can. Evergreen and Yonder are not the same as us. They are gods. Celestial beings whom we cannot compete with. There are no fair battles to be won against them, as they can change the rules on a whim."

"So we must cheat."

Astraeus stares at me a moment, and I get the sense he doesn't want to dignify that with a response, though he knows I'm right.

"Lucifer has been allowed to grow more powerful in a forbidden way," he segues. "And thus, even I must be careful about when and where I appear. Even as the Peri, he once managed to set a trap for me. I believe he knows of my existence outside of the magic, and a part of his long-term plan is to come after me next. But Myra never let him get that far, and neither will Rhesa, with your help."

I shake my head, and although everything is clearer than it was, now that Lucifer's spell work is gone, I'm still sorting through the information and memories I have been gifted by this male who claims my soul was cut from his.

Sliced into four separate pieces by his very own mother.

Astraeus has been working tirelessly behind the scenes to send messages to Rhesa's allies, ensuring that Lucifer does not catch on in the process, and when I fled the throne room like a coward, Astraeus seized the opportunity to approach me.

I inhale slowly, hold my breath, and then exhale, mind made up.

"Their rules do not matter," I say, steeling myself as the last of his memories settle into place. "We will prevail and do what must be done. If they want to fight for a crown they have no chance of keeping, then to war we shall go."

. . . .

The lower halls and cells of the Celestial Palace are dark and dimly lit with just a few enchanted torches upon the walls, and angelic foot soldiers are scarce in their patrols of the towers and winding stairwells.

No matter, for even if there were dozens, they would be no match for me.

I am darkness, and darkness is me, and nothing will keep me from serving my queen.

So when I approach the heavily spelled cells that hold suspended archangels inside each of them, I do not falter. Instead, I merely flick my wrists and shatter the entirety of the barred doors themselves. The imprisonment magic within the bars hisses and snarls at me, but I growl back in warning, suppressing the magic into submission.

And it obeys.

So *this* is the power of a *son*.

I am magic, and magic is me.

The archangels within are awake and aware, though they are spelled by wicked chains and collars, suspended by their bound wings above the ground while their limbs are stretched outward.

I snap my fingers, and their chains snap next.

I approach Pollux first, extending my hand to him, which he grasps in order to haul himself back onto his feet. He stretches his limbs and wings, groaning as he rolls his neck and flexes his fingers into fists to regain feeling there again after being locked up for weeks.

"Took you long enough," he huffs, narrowing his eyes as he surveys my form. "You seem . . . *different.*"

"Perceptive as ever, Pollux."

Pollux cocks his head, then bares his teeth in a feral, shit-eating grin. "You've finally reconnected with your original soul, haven't you?" He chuckles. "That damned Spell of Silence was implemented by Yonder to keep us away from the origins of Lucifer and the altar, but it appears as though Astraeus has done his work to ensure she steps aside."

I nod, glancing over the rest of the archangels as they near us. "And how much do you know?"

"I know enough. Though to take action too soon without the ability to properly explain *why* would have been a fool's errand. I needed Astraeus and Myra back first."

"Speaking of our sister," drawls Nihal, arms folded. "Why is she not with you?"

"Unfortunately, she is still imprisoned in Hell, though I have reason to believe that will not be the case for much longer."

"And what of the others?" inquires Castor.

"The Hellion court is still shackled by Lucifer, but Rhesa's allies lie in wait."

Alto hums. "We don't yet have a way to subdue or cage Lucifer. I am not sure how successful we will be in storming Hell if he is there and able to summon his Apostles for aid."

"Then we get rid of the Apostles here and now," snarls Orion.

Nihal looks between Pollux and me. "Do we have the necessary information and spell work to be rid of them and free the Zodiacs? Because, though I have faith in us to see it through, I am less than keen to repeat history in a few centuries should we fail again."

"I can recall the commands," says Pollux, then he side-eyes me. "And we have since acquired the means to access the magic necessary to do it, though the only being within our spheres that can ensure the souls are never misused again is Death. If we are to seal them properly without fear of Lucifer stealing them back, we'll need the Grim Reaper on our side. However, breaking the Caged Bird Spell isn't so simple either. Similarly to Myra back in the day, we'll need the Lords of Exile."

"Can we not at least capture and hold the Apostles until we free Death and the others?" inquires Alto. "Like we also did back then?"

I look at him. "You remember?"

The archangels look at each other, and it finally dawns on me to count how many of them are left.

Five.

Six, including Apollo, when once upon a time, there were technically *nine.*

"For better or worse," drawls Pollux, his voice heavy with the weight of his grief and knowledge, no doubt. "During our time imprisoned here, we were plagued with memories of a better time in the past, when Myra was young. And that, in turn, includes when Lucifer first appeared and wreaked havoc, tearing our spheres apart and later claiming our sister's life and memory."

"Our memories of before are still foggy in places," admits Castor. "Though we know enough of what happened and how we defeated a few back in the day. If we are to be completely rid of the Apostles this time, Death must devour them. Not escort them to the bottomless pits of Hell or Purgatory or elsewhere, or shackle them somewhere Lucifer will surely find them again. He must swallow their souls and be done with it. Ensure they can never reincarnate or return by way of possession, lest we desire another repeat of necromancy."

"Dante is dead," I deadpan.

Their eyes flicker to me, expecting an explanation.

"He aided Rhesa down in the cells and thus paid the price. Death burned his bones."

Pollux curses demon names under his breath. "Damn those bones . . . always a surprise, that one."

"He's responsible for half the shit we're dealing with now," I growl.

"Agreed," says Orion. "Though, dare I say, I believe we grieve the man we once knew. The one loyal to Myra and Death. Seems as though he sought to make amends in the end."

"No matter, the bones are of no use to us now," I remind them. "We don't have much time before either Lucifer or the Apostles realize you're free. Where is Apollo?"

"He's not under any sort of spell work," says Pollux.

"I figured not."

"The damned traitor is waltzing around with the Zodiac Blade upon his own accord poised to follow Lucifer's every command," growls Castor. "I say we dispatch him along with the rest."

Alto nods along. "While it pains me to say it, I do believe you're right. It is clear that Apollo is not the brother we once knew and loved."

"Power, greed, and time have corrupted him," quips Orion. "I don't believe there is much we can do for him now."

"Let him fucking rot," snarls Nihal. "He's betrayed us. Betrayed Myra and her memory, and gone ahead and hurt Rhesamyre, too. I will not risk him being around our sister again. Or any of us, for that matter. Not after what he did to Sam . . . and Adriel, if we're honest with ourselves."

Pollux nods along, looking grim but more pissed off than anything else. "As unfortunate as it may be, I find myself inclined to agree. Apollo has chosen his side, and thus, he will burn for it."

The archangels come to the conclusion swiftly enough, and while I am thankful for that, I know that once upon a time, I had made choices that harmed my brothers when we decided to fight on opposite sides before coming to our senses. My brothers could very well have come to the same conclusion to let me burn, too. But with Rhesa's life on the line, I'm not about to go pointing that out.

"We should get moving, then," I say, ending the discussion. "Time is of the essence now if we are to get back to Rhesa without alerting Lucifer—"

My magic flares in warning, hissing and growling with raised hackles, and I whirl around and command a white sword to erupt from flames so I may defend myself against this winged foe.

Speak of the fucking Devil.

I bare my teeth and grin at Apollo. "We were just discussing the best way to kill you. How kind of you to find us first and save us the trouble of hunting you down."

The golden archangel snarls and presses his sword further against mine, and the metal shrieks and echoes throughout the halls, but with his brothers surrounding us, he remains outmatched. All of them steel themselves and command their own weapons to appear, and Apollo glances around at his kin before settling those bloodshot, golden eyes onto me again.

"For what it's worth," he growls lowly, "I regret almost everything."

Pollux snarls. "True as it may be, that won't save you now, brother."

Apollo nods. "I know . . . but if you think I'll lie down quietly, you've got another thing coming."

"We aren't so foolish," quips Orion.

Apollo grins at that. "Debatable, brother." He loses his smile, steeling himself but looking more somber now. "Tell Myra I'm sorry . . . for all of it."

And then Apollo reels backward and positions himself to strike with steel and magic, but his brothers don't allow him to get far. A flash of blinding, holy light erupts as the archangels slay their brother, and Apollo's body collapses to the ground.

And then, just for good measure, I disarm him of the Zodiac Blade and proceed to plunge it through his skull all the way into the stone floor below, splitting his head and the ground in the process.

I look around at the archangels again, making it clear that I regret nothing.

Neither do they, it would seem.

Apollo made his bed, and now, as a corpse, he will lie in it.

"Traitor or not," drawls Castor quietly, "he's still an archangel and must be buried properly, lest we want vultures to come after the magic still active in his blood."

"Then you and I will do it swiftly," says Orion, then he looks to the rest of us. "Start clearing out the palace and Ursa Major of those who are willingly under Lucifer's regime. We'll catch up soon enough and secure our home first, then we'll ready ourselves to either face the Apostles or storm Hell. Whichever comes first."

"Then I'll send word to Rhesa's allies," says Pollux. "They lie in wait for their next orders."

"And what of Rhesamyre?" inquires Nihal.

"She is doing what must be done to break the Caged Bird Spell once and for all," I claim. "As well as remind the spheres of who is in charge around here. So let's go make sure the spheres are properly reminded of the powers that be."

I take a step forward, ready to be done with it, but Alto stops me when he inquires, "Do you not wish to go to her?"

I grin back at him, the baring of my teeth nothing but a show of feral rage. "What a stupid fucking question. *Of course, I do.* More than anything, but she doesn't need me by her side at the moment. She needs me—*us*—to roll out her red carpet, stained with the blood of her enemies, and ensure the Obsidian Throne is still there for her to ascend."

The archangels glance at each other, then Castor and Orion grab Apollo and haul him off to seal him away in a proper tomb, while the rest of us proceed toward the armory, steeling ourselves as we claim our weapons and gear, suiting up into black or gray battle leathers.

Armed to the teeth, we hunt.

Atticus.

I stall at the sound of Atlas's voice ringing in my head, and I blink, then reach back quietly, *Brother?*

I can almost hear the smile in his voice as he replies, *There you are, fucker. It's about time.*

I grin. *Good to hear your voice again, big bro.*

Atlas remains a steady presence in the back of my head, thanks to our brands, and when I reach out for Rhesa, my *truculent* band smolders with renewed interest and loyalty. I can feel her rage and aggression, but above all, I can feel her renewed vigor and magic.

My queen is out for blood, and I plan on adding to her body count.

PEACE IS HERE, BUT THE RAGE IS ALL-CONSUMING.
WE HAVE FORGOTTEN SOMETHING IMPORTANT.
I CAN FEEL IT IN MY BONES.
MY MAGIC IS NOT SATISFIED HERE.

I AM NOT SATISFIED HERE.

CHAPTER THIRTEEN
RHESAMYRE

I've never interacted with the Seven Wise Men of the Hollow. Not as Myra nor as Rhesamyre. We once exchanged letters back when Lucifer first arrived, when I was naïve enough to think they would aid us. Though seeing as how they told me they *do not meddle in foreign affairs*, we never did meet vis-à-vis.

What a load of bullshit.

All they've *ever* done is *meddle in foreign affairs*. Far and wide, across many of the spherical systems as a whole. It is the point of their entire existence, after all. To safeguard and keep the *Hollow* safe.

Though in doing so, they have remained complicit in both Yonder's and Lucifer's schemes. Once before and now again that our enemies have come back to haunt us.

No more. Never again. I will not allow it.

A conveyance ripples to life beside Siren and me, where we crouch upon one of the mighty branches of a redwood, and we glance over to face Kure, Wicker, and Draven as they step forward.

"You're lucky I know better than to accuse you of the same treasons I am about to slay them for, Kure," I say, rising from my crouch.

Draven, Wicker, and Siren at least have half a mind to look startled, but Kure doesn't waver. Instead, the three-eyed minotaur simply inclines his head, then glances over to survey the seven white castles that sit clustered amongst each other in a similar manner to how the lords' towers are all connected.

Kure meets my eyes again. "I suppose I am lucky to serve such a benevolent queen who knows when matters are out of my control."

"Out of yours, perhaps," I quip. "But not theirs. They knew, and they *chose* to stay quiet. The rest of you were silenced quite impressively, but the Wise Men never forgot."

"May I inquire," drawls Draven, "what you are going to do?"

"What I should have done a long time ago, though I didn't quite know it at the time. Back then, I simply acquired the help of you two in order to break the Caged Bird Spell, and for lack of a better phrase, I deadheaded the problem, believing that was the solution. But this time, we're going to completely nip it in the bud. We're going to break and eradicate the Caged Bird Spell, as well as the rest of the spells that have silenced and erased half our history and culture. And by doing so, we will ensure that it will never happen again. The spheres will remember what I want them to, and in order to ensure victory and loyalty, I will have them all."

"*And,*" drawls Wicker, "you plan to do this, how?"

"By slaughtering the Wise Men and dividing their responsibilities and powers between you four and myself."

Kure, once again, seems unfazed, but the other three look at each other as though I just said I was going to slaughter *them*.

How comical.

Very. Considering the blood on their own hands, muses Atlas.

"With all due respect, my queen," begins Siren, "I don't quite understand how that is going to work, nor can I say with confidence that I actually want the extra claims and titles."

"The Seven Wise Men exist as they do to ensure balance," argues Draven. "They are the protectors of the Hollow and all that lies within. To tamper with such magic is—"

"What?" I prompt. "*Treason*?" I can't help but laugh, stepping toward him. "Against *whom*, exactly? Because it is my understanding that as the beloved *queen* to the One True King of our spheres, I have every right to reshape these spheres and make them into whatever I see fit with whomever and whatever I may desire."

I stand chest to chest with Draven, and he is braced to defend himself as my magic coils tight and slightly cracks the wood beneath our boots.

"If you don't want it," I snarl lowly, teeth gritted, "then I'll take it all back."

He remains silent for a heartbeat, then ever so carefully shakes his head and mutters, "I will do as you wish, my queen."

I step out of his personal space, then make eye contact with the others as I regain my composure.

"I understand this is a lot to ask of you," I begin, my voice softer. "A lot to demand of you, but I realize that I must surround myself with those who are wholeheartedly loyal to me if we are to reclaim our rights and freedoms. I will not be unnecessarily cruel, nor will I abuse my power and later be called a tyrant. I would rather die than have that happen. But make no mistake, I will not allow those who have harmed us or stood idly by while we fought tooth and nail to survive to live on in luxury. And the Wise Men have done just that, and though they are fickle assholes who believe themselves superior because they know the names of gods and sons, they are not above taking bribes from beings such as Yonder and Lucifer."

"*What*?" snarls Wicker.

"She speaks the truth," says Kure, looking between his neighbors. "Though silenced, even your baku knew of it, too, Draven. However, unlike the majority of beasts, monsters, and *others*, your baku were able to keep their voices, so long as they did not speak of certain schemes."

"The Wise Men have always claimed to never meddle with the likes of us," growls Siren. "Yet they took bribes from that self-proclaimed god? And then the very god that selfishly plays with our lives as though we're her dolls?"

I nod, quirking a brow. "You now understand my wrath, yes? And why we must dispatch them?"

Wicker grumbles under his breath. "Yes, yes, it all makes sense now . . . *sort of.*" He sighs. "Though it may not matter, may I inquire as to what they were given?"

"Naturally. You may always ask. It is what keeps me honest. And it is my understanding that Yonder first approached them to offer luxury and power in exchange for their continued silence, while Lucifer later offered them immunity and the promise that no harm shall come to them if they safeguard his schemes and keep his spells a secret." I look to Kure. "That about sum it up?"

He nods. "I would say so. Maneuvering around the Spells of Silence has always been a bitch of a parlor trick, though I would claim that many of their rules do not apply to the likes of me. A being who can move between planes and spheres."

"Spells of Silence," mutters Siren, chuckling. "It was never a *vow.*"

I shake my head. "Often not, no . . . . Will you stand with me to take control of the situation?"

"You have my word, my queen," vows Kure. "Now and always."

The three others follow suit swiftly enough, echoing Kure's words, and I grin at them as I turn around to face the white castles.

"Even your uncles could not break in," says Draven beside me, surveying the land with me. "So how do we expect to?"

"By uttering the name of our sun, and waltzing right through their front doors."

He glances at me. "You know such a name?"

"The original, as well as the three others he now claims. Though the first shall suffice."

I command a conveyance to appear before us, and as I stride through, the males mutter amongst themselves behind me.

"She seems . . . *different*," quips Wicker.

"We've watched her grow up two separate times now, friends," drawls Kure. "No more *little feathers* or *champions* and princesses here . . . what you are witnessing now is the ascent of a queen turned conqueror."

They grow quiet after that, and I feel them at my back as I stand before the daunting walls of the white castles. No windows nor doors are visible from the outside, but this does not stop me as I step forward and press my palm against the stone and mutter *Astraeus.*

The castles shudder as the ground quakes, and the stone ripples to life and makes way for a grand staircase and archway that homes solid gates of obsidian and gold. We ascend the stairs, and as we approach the gates, two of the Wise Men approach us from the other side. They are almost identical to that of the Zodiacs, in which they do not have solid forms, but instead appear as sentient silhouettes made entirely of bound magic and knowledge. The one on the left glitters like gold as scripture shifts and swirls all across his chest and arms, while the other appears as though he has an entire galaxy and ever-changing star map within him.

The Poet and the Astronomer.

"History has said in the past that you often inquire about names first and foremost," says the Poet. "So sorry to say, but we do not have such names that will satisfy your curiosity."

"Your names are not what I seek," I drawl. "I've come for your heads."

The Astronomer chuckles. "Unfortunately, detaching our heads from our bodies will not be as simple as removing Gulliver's empty noggin. We are energy and magic, not blood and bones."

"You will not succeed here, foolish girl," laughs the Poet. "We see and know all, and you do not stand a chance."

"And your inflated egos shall be the death of you," drawls Kure quietly. "Arrogance is an assassin."

I grin, then in the blink of an eye, I am behind the gates with my hands through both of their chests.

I lean forward between their heads, whispering, "You cannot keep me out when I already hold the key to your gates." Then I mutter in another foreign language that I once learned with Astraeus, *"Bend the knee and free your energy. Belong to me for all eternity."*

Their bodies explode, their magical energy splattering against the walls and ground before rising again to swirl and conform into two crystal daggers. One of galaxies and the other etched with opal scriptures.

The rest of the spell work that allowed these two males to hold their shapes simply dissipates, and the gates behind me creak open as the Lords of Exile step forward and survey the slight mess I have made in the dull courtyard.

When I get a hold of you, you're not going to be able to walk properly for a week, growls Atlas.

Promise? I taunt.

Atlas growls in my head, and I grin.

I reach my hands out, gesturing for Siren to claim the Poet's dagger, and Draven to claim the Astronomer's; they do so warily, but it is Wicker who drawls quietly from beside Draven, "Your eyes . . ."

"It's Astraeus," I answer. "I assume they're silver?"

Kure nods. "Seems as though he got that trait from his mother."

"I try not to think about it too much."

"I will admit," drawls Siren as he weighs the dagger on the tip of his finger, "I didn't expect . . . *any of that.* I assume that was another spell you picked up from somewhere far away again?"

"It belonged to a witch whose pastime involved trapping trespassers in various objects. Similar to that of Lilith and how she fooled around with curses and genies for a time."

"*Ah,* but your eyes didn't do that last time."

"Astraeus's magic and name weren't needed to slaughter Gulliver and his men, but while this place may appear as a luxurious castle, it is far from tame. And the beings that reside here are similar in nature to those of the Zodiacs. Pure, raw energy bound into single forms. I simply reshaped that form and took away their ability to be as self-aware as they once were."

"*Fascinating,*" beams Wicker, staring down at the Astronomer's dagger in Draven's open palm.

I can't help but smile a little and then glance back over my shoulder to survey the structures behind me once more.

"Wait here," I command, and then I'm gone again.

Moving in and out of shadows and conveyances, I twirl with spells and commands dancing on my tongue and off my fingers to hunt and destroy the remaining Wise Men, not meeting much resistance since they have never bothered with additional security. Castles quake as cracks splinter across walls and floors while chandeliers shatter, and I mutter more spells to siphon the rest of the magic out of this labyrinth so I can hunt the Wise Men with utmost efficiency.

They don't even try to fight me head-on. All they do is flee and hide, then scream bloody murder when I find them, siphoning and stealing their magic right out of them, their energy splattering across the walls as though it is blood.

I arm myself with their daggers.

"They'll overthrow you!" exclaims the Politician, backing himself into a corner.

I stalk forward, raw magic floating around my hands like stardust. His form is nearly black, and no other sigils or silhouettes that may better help identify him dance across his smoky form; he is just dark and corrupt.

How fitting.

"You'll become a tyrant!" he tries again. "It's only inevitable that with this much power, you'll be corrupted, and they'll all come to loathe you eventually!"

"Hence why I am not taking it all for myself," I drawl.

I grab him by his head, squeezing his cheeks as I place my hand over his mouth, coming nose to nose with him. "I'll make it swift, though you don't deserve it."

He screams against my palm as I steal his magic, his entire form exploding like the others as it remolds and becomes another dagger.

"My brothers were always weak," drawls the last one, the Alchemist.

I turn around to face him, and he appears like a silhouette of flames.

"I'm surprised you waited this long," I quip. "I thought perhaps you would have aided your brothers, yet you hid alongside them."

The being of fire shrugs. "It was inevitable you would eventually come for us. We all saw the signs, yet chose to ignore them. In addition, Lucifer once promised us we'd be safe if you ever found out. Yet here you are, covered in the residue magic that could be equated to my brothers' organs."

"You didn't interfere. Their blood is as much on your hands as it is mine."

The being hums. "Perhaps . . . then so be it."

A wall of fire alchemy bursts to life right in front of me, and I shift to the side and step through another conveyance to get behind the Alchemist. He commands another one to open, too, but I tackle him before he can flee. Spells and commands fly off his tongue in rapid succession, and I snarl when he plunges a dagger between my ribs.

I press my hands against the sides of his head and plunge my thumbs into the empty sockets where his eyeballs should be, and he screeches as the magical vessels there *pop* like grapes. Then, in other languages, as well as Old Latin, I spew off a few more commands to immobilize him so I may steal his namesake, this time for myself, just as I claimed the Historian and the Politician.

His magic forms an orb of silver and obsidian first, but I shift its shape in order to create a dagger adorned with an obsidian hilt and crystal blade, the blade a near twin to the one I once crafted from the Zodiacs' light.

I stand on my feet, wobbling slightly as I pull the dagger from my ribs so the wound can close, then summon the lords to my side.

"Holy *fuck*," drawls Wicker, narrowing his eyes at me. "*What* is *that*?"

I shrug, glancing down at my battle leathers that now shimmer with an odd, slimy residue. "*Umm* . . . some sort of magical ecto-plasm, I suspect?"

"It's *disgusting*," the Boogeyman deadpans.

I scowl, then rummage into my pocket and toss him the Trea-surer's dagger, and I hand the Mathematician's dagger to Kure.

"At least your eyes are back to normal," says Siren. "Now, what of the other three? Are you to keep them?"

"For now, though I wouldn't be surprised if down the line I gave them to my uncles or even the deities."

Kure nods along. "That might be the wisest option." He cocks his head. "In order to avoid your body giving out on you first."

I narrow my eyes at him in challenge, but then raise my hand to wipe away the blood that has begun to drip from my nose.

Stay alive, Atlas reminds me.

"I'm fine," I say, both to him and Kure as I turn away. "Besides, we're not finished here yet."

The males follow after me down the hallway that breaks and chips away as we head toward the center courtyard of the castles, and as we draw nearer, the magic that hums to life in this place only grows louder and more prominent. It rings in our ears insis-tently and makes me want to shake my head and twitch, but I refrain from doing so as we come upon one of the internal bal-conies that overlooks the giant pit of smoldering, explosive, raw magic that lies in the center of the castles.

The Hollow.

The very pool of informative magic that many only believe to exist in legend and very few have ever ventured inside of and lived to tell the tale. Oftentimes, the only breeds that can survive simply even glancing inside are the genies and seers, or select others cursed with the Sight.

"You're not . . . planning to dive in there and go fucking *swimming* . . . are you?" inquires Draven, staring at me with accusatory, raised brows.

I nod. "Yep. That's exactly what I'm about to do."

Siren and Wicker gape at me, then look at Kure as though he has all the answers and will stop me, but the bull just shrugs.

"She knows what must be done," he drawls gruffly. "And so long as we are here to pull her out, all will be fine."

"*Wait, wait, wait,*" sputters Wicker. "Am I really going to have to be the one to point out how fucking *insane* this is?"

I scowl. "Says the guy that had me walk off his tower's balcony."

Atlas grunts in agreement in the back of my head.

Wicker points his finger at me, and I have half a mind to bite it off. "*That* was different. I knew what would happen, but *this*." He shakes his head, throwing his hands up in exasperation. "Nope. I'm out. This is a bad *fucking* idea, and you've had a few, but I must say, this really takes the cake."

"It's not like I'm asking you to *go swimming* with me. You three will be staying here, where it's safe and dry."

"That does not make us feel better," Draven deadpans.

I whirl on him. "And *you* had me drink some weird *star tea* so I would dream about Alastair and get answers as to why we were connected!"

"*Again*. Controlled environment. *This*"—he gestures to the smoldering pit of magic behind me—"is anything *but* controlled."

I gape at them, then turn around and throw my hands up. "Fucking hell below—I can't." I take a breath, then turn around to face them again, pointing my finger at their faces. "Look, you guys. This is the *only way* to get the jump on Lucifer, and we're already wasting time. We *have* to get rid of the Caged Bird Spell. *For good*, this time. In addition . . . there's something else in there that I need. Something that only the Hollow itself can provide."

Siren, Draven, and Wicker all glance at one another, and I look to Kure for aid. However, the minotaur's gaze has drifted off, and he stares openly at a wall as though he can see through it.

"Kure?" I inquire, my hackles raised.

He snaps his three eyes to me. "It's started."

Sobering up, Siren steps forward and inquires, "They've begun already? I thought we had more time?"

"Chaos has since moved up our timeline."

I feel my heart skip a beat, and I step forward. "Atticus?"

He's back to his old self, says Atlas. *Annoying and cunning as always.*

Kure nods. "He's woken up, and he's gathered your brothers to free Ursa Major. The Apostles and then Hell are their next targets, whether we're ready to aid them or not. Atticus is . . . *different.*"

"It's probably Astraeus again," I mutter. Then, I look at three of the four lords. "You three, I need you to aid our allies and help lead the charge. I'm hoping it won't take us long to sever the CB Spell, and when we do, the siege must commence immediately. My brothers and Atticus are mighty and nearly indestructible, but so is the Hellion court and Lucifer. We need to tip the scales back in our favor."

"Fuck no!" exclaims Wicker, and Draven cuts in immediately, "With all due respect, Your Majesty. We're not leaving you here to face that monstrosity behind you alone."

"She's not alone," quips Kure, smoke pouring from his pierced nostrils as he huffs indignantly. He meets my eyes. "Not this time."

Never again, agrees Atlas.

I smile gently at him, at Atlas's vows, then look to the other three once more. "I appreciate the loyalty. Truly, I do. But where I need you all the most is not here. You have served your purpose and are now the holders of the Wise Men's magic, just as I wanted you to be. Kure is more versed in the ways of endless knowledge and differing planes and spheres, so he is best suited to remain here with me. But your fights are elsewhere."

"You sound as if you also expect us to use our newfound magic to fight, too," quips Siren.

I nod. "I do. Despite the Wise Men growing comfortable and negligent toward the end, their magic is mighty *if* used correctly. It is capable of more than you might think."

"We're running out of time, Myra," says Kure, glancing off into the distance again, almost reaching for his battleaxe that is strapped to his back.

I look at the lords again, then turn and dive into the estranged, enchanted waters of the Hollow.

CHAPTER FOURTEEN
RHESAMYRE

The waters of the Hollow do not feel like that of the cursed river that runs through the ruins of the Garden.

While the estranged current within the Forbidden Cities sought to steal my magic, this one instead seeks to give me more.

Too much. Far, *far* too much.

The raw magic that makes up this gaping hole in our spherical system is curious and chaotic, seeking to inform me of all it knows, whether I inquire of it or not. And in turn, it desires to know everything of me, too.

The magic attaches itself to me like a thousand glowing leeches, weighing me down while I struggle not to sink as it whispers *what, when, where, why, how, and who* over and over again. Getting louder and louder and heavier until I can hardly hear my own rapid heartbeat as I struggle to *swim*.

I refuse to drown.

I snarl at the little leeches, erupting in place to force them off me. They squeak and swim away almost immediately, returning to their hiding places within the odd shadows and darkness that surround me on all sides.

Stars flicker and blink in the darkness . . . no, not stars. *Eyes.*

Billions of reflective eyes blink and watch from afar in the darkness, making up galaxies upon galaxies as blues and violets come to light up the odd sphere that is the Hollow.

"Why is she here?"

"She searches for answers. For him again."

"Myra, Myra, Myra."

The voices whisper-shout to each other softly in Old Latin and other languages, sounding almost like children.

I touch down on whatever ground respects the magic of gravity, and it ripples like a puddle beneath my boots; however, the reflection beneath me is not *me*, but instead a wolf.

The wolf I once became when I grieved Samael.

"Little wolf?"

I whirl around, daggers in hand.

"Atlas?" I call, and the eyes blink at me. "Atlas!"

I growl in irritation, then call out for Kure next . . . though I receive no answer.

Sighing, I look down at the obsidian dire wolf once more, and she cocks her head at me.

"Well," I prompt, "are you just going to stay down there? Or are you going to make yourself useful and help me out up here?"

She *barks* at me, and the shadows and puddle ripple as she jumps through the reflection and lands next to me, bounding around my legs as though she is a lovesick puppy, and I can only hope I wasn't this obnoxious when I was in her paws.

I crouch, and she slows her pacing and comes to sit before me as though she is waiting patiently for her next commands. I rub her ears, and she makes odd purring sounds of approval as she leans into my hands.

"Can you track him?" I ask, though I don't really expect an answer. "We need to find Kure if we are to succeed in this place, though I seem to have misplaced my guide."

She looks at me pointedly and then bounds out of my hands and trots forward with her nose to the ground. I stand up to follow, taking notice that both her reflection and my own are gone.

We walk onward, the wolf a few paces ahead of me, and the magic here seems to gather its courage once more and slowly approach me. Most of the initial, inquisitive leeches decide to keep their distance, but others float closer in the form of dragonflies, fireflies, and even butterflies. Their wings are bright and colorful, depicting foreign sigils, constellations, or even abstract faces and eyes.

I hold out my hand, coming to a halt as an iridescent swallowtail flaps closer and insists upon resting in my palm. Its blue wings look like eyes that stare straight through me and into my soul, harboring my secrets and holding them close.

The wolf barks gently, and I glance up to watch as she jumps upward and snaps her jaws at the dragonflies that have begun to pester her. She fails in catching them, of course, and the action is more playful than hostile. The dragonflies insist upon buzzing around her ears and landing on her nose, and the wolf snarls.

I snap my fingers at her with the hand that is not preoccupied with the butterfly, and she pricks her ears at me while cocking her head like a pup.

"Play nice. That means don't *eat* anyone."

The wolf stares at me, but then her attention is ultimately drawn to another dragonfly as it takes refuge on her snout. I shake my head at the odd sight, glancing down at the butterfly in my palm again.

The eyes on its wings blink up at me.

I raise my brow at the creature in my palm, tilting my head. "Perhaps you'll be more willing to talk?"

The butterfly flaps away, and I track its movements as it disappears once more.

"Or not," I deadpan.

"She's going to die at this rate, Death."

I whirl around again. "Sam?"

Samael's form materializes ahead of me, and he marches onward as though he is walking and talking with someone else—Uncle Death, I presume.

"We know," replies the unseen Horseman. *"But the only solution at present is to have the magic removed."*

"And leave her defenseless?"

"She won't be defenseless, Sam. She'll have you and us. She'll have Hell."

Sam seems to ponder this, walking right past me as though *I* am the mirage in this situation.

I look at the wolf again, and she just cocks her head at me, our magical friends now gone once more.

"This must be when Sam first saved me as a babe . . . as Rhesamyre," I think aloud, turning back to survey Sam once more as he paces alone, a lonely baby girl's cries echoing onward from the distance.

The shadows ripple again, and Sam's form shifts until he is evidently elsewhere in the memory, and he goes to a knee with a bundle tightly clutched in his arms. I walk closer, peering over his shoulder to survey . . . *me*. Nothing but a chubby lump of flesh with a tuft of black hair on my head. A defenseless and clueless babe.

"Your assistance is required, Mamba," says Sam, his head still bowed. *"She is not built to withstand the power erupting inside her, but it must be kept safe and hidden close by. Thus, I request your aid. A bargain."*

Low hissing is his only answer, and the waters below us ripple as the Obsidian Serpent slithers forward. Mamba lowers his head to sniff Samael, and then at the babe bundled up in his arms.

Ever so carefully, Sam better unveils my cherub face to show the snake, and Mamba cocks his head at the sight of me.

"Help me protect her," pleads Sam, meeting the snake's glittering eyes. *"And you will forever have a home in Hell wrapped around the Obsidian Throne."*

I back away when Mamba slithers closer once more to curl around Sam, and then I turn my gaze toward the all-seeing eyes of this sphere.

"Show me everything, Astraeus," I command in Old Latin.

The eyes open all at once, and then I'm blinded by white.

·················

The original lieutenants were born of other *origins. The term is often used when one's bloodline is questionable, like that of a bastard's, but powerful, capable of becoming a warrior. Some are blessed, others cursed, but magic calls to us all in ways we have yet to comprehend, and perhaps never will.*

Nile belonged to War, just as Tyler belonged to Conquest and Gale belonged to Famine, while Dante was loyal to Death.

They all commanded armies and led battalions under the orders of their generals when Myra called them to arms. Prior to Lucifer's arrival, the Horsemen existed as isolated but wise beings with just a few servants to look after their households.

The lieutenants back then merely existed to serve.

But the Horsemen were capable of great catastrophes. The apocalypse would ensue should the brothers take up arms, but it was already here, thanks to the arrival of Lucifer.

Myra needed them to counteract his chaos, and so they answered her call to arms.

But it was another great folly on the Cruel One's part decades later that led to the deaths of three of the four lieutenants. For Abaddon, in his late paranoia, believed to have heard whispers of a coup, and knowing better than to attack the Horsemen outright when they were at the beck and call of the Three Kings, who had won the more recent Wild Hunt, he sought to attack their lieutenants instead. Vowing that he would not be overthrown so easily.

But Abaddon failed to slaughter Dante, and Death would never let him succeed.

At the risk of losing his lover, Death bargained and conspired with various others *to make use of their eyes. The price:*

His bedchamber.

The best spies at this time were Siren's underlings. The Lord of Temptation's succubus and incubus knew best what Abaddon had in store for Hell and the surrounding spheres, for they lay with him often.

To learn of the Cruel One's secrets and schemes, Death, too, had to lie with the fiends.

But it was at this time that Dante learned of his lover and general's late-night activities, and thus began the beginning of the end.

When Death was called a cheater, *and later, Dante a* necro-mancer.

. . . .

"We owe her, Astraeus, and we do not leave debts unpaid. Let us bargain just this once and ensure our mother can never again meddle in our spheres."

Khronos.

Myra had met him once, a long, long time ago.

She and Astraeus had visited his neighboring thirteen spheres full of different creatures and cultures, but there had been a recent uproar amongst the peoples when their tyrant and cunt of a king sought to behead them all.

Rebels rallied together, and Myra, unable to sit still in peace for extended amounts of time, fought alongside the people. Learning their languages and songs and stories, many of which were eventually said to be about her.

Khronos intervened when Myra warned him that these other *ruthless beings, when not reined in, grow into monstrous, catastrophic evils incapable of being slain while being able to swallow souls.*

The second coming of Lucifer would not come to fruition. Not on her watch.

....

King Jaxon and Queen Ann Marie were none the wiser.

Their bodies were stolen in the middle of the night, and they were robbed of their minds as foreign souls were shoved down their throats.

The crone and bones' spell work ensured that Adam and Evelyn would have complete control over the mortal royals, and their two sons would serve as secondary bodies should it come to that.

"But there was another," I declare, watching the story unfold, the Historian's dagger poised in my hand, ready to slice and reshape what happened back then.

I will have them all, I vowed.

History shall be rewritten, and it shall never repeat.

"It wasn't just two sons," I state, and the story changes with my commands. "There was a younger daughter, but she was stolen as a babe. The entire mortal kingdom mourned the loss of their princess, and everyone searched for *Althea*, but she remained missing for eighteen years. Hidden away in a small village in the outskirts of the Forest of Souls, far away from the capital and the carnage that later followed.

"And Althea, with her kindness, bravery, and beauty, managed to befriend the princess of Hell and rightful heir to the Obsidian Throne. The two remain allies, and Althea's bloodline will forever have a place in the Hellion court as a friend of the queen's. The kingdom of Hell and the Midlands will stand united for further generations to come, for Althea is the rightful heir to the Golden Throne."

The story changes ever so slightly, and as I sheath the Historian's dagger once more, all has been altered.

"Forgive me, Astraeus," I mumble in Old Latin. *"But I am taking more than I was initially promised. For our vows to one another are no longer enough to sustain these spheres . . . I trust that in time, you will come to accept my apologies."*

"No apologies will be necessary, Myra."

I turn around to face Kure, and he strides forward to stand next to me, surveying the multiple doorways and visions that depict our spheres and peoples as a whole.

"You know as well as I," drawls Kure, side-eying me, "that he will stand by whatever decisions you make. Whether that'd be to save these spheres or let them burn."

I hum, looking up at the three-eyed minotaur. "And you, Kure?"

Kure goes to a knee and bows his head. "All I ask is one thing of you, my queen."

"Speak your mind."

He meets my eyes again. "Reclaim your wings."

I raise my brows in surprise, though I suppose I shouldn't be. For even now, the Lord of Sanity still calls me *Myra*.

"I have not borne their weight in so very long, Kure. And I must admit, I believe I may have forgotten how."

"They are no heavier than your crown, Your Majesty. And you bear the weight of your kingdoms without fail."

I can't help but huff a small laugh under my breath, nodding my head as he rises to his hooved feet once more.

"Then I suppose there is only one thing left to do here," I avow.

"A horned angel with raven wings even darker than that of the Devil's," he muses. "Hellfire eyes and a thirst for vengeance and craving for blood. But with a heart of gold that is holier than any monster of heaven bearing a halo."

I grab his hand, squeezing once in thanks as I command, "Escort your queen home, Lord of Sanity. For she has a war to win."

He nods stoically. "As you wish, my queen."

CHAPTER FIFTEEN
ATTICUS

The Celestial Palace has been painted red.

The walls *bleed*.

I slice my sword through the air, cleaning it of the blood that stains it by flinging it toward the floor where dozens of bodies lie: angelic foot soldiers, goblins, demons, and monsters alike.

Whether they were willingly following the Apostles' commands—and therefore Lucifer's—or under the influence of his spell work, is the least of my concerns at the moment.

I will slaughter them all.

Freed pegasus and angels fly in the sky, clashing with our enemies in the streets while the archangels and I clear the palace halls, searching for the Zodiacs that have since been possessed by the Apostles.

"We're about ready to divert our forces," says Pollux, returning to my side while sheathing his own blood-soaked sword.

Both of us are armed to the teeth with obsidian and white steel, but dressed in similar battle leathers of Hellion origins.

"All but Taurus and Sagittarius have been freed," finishes Perception.

"And we've managed to confine the Apostles' souls properly?" I inquire.

Pollux nods. "Once Death is free, he can devour and dispose of them to ensure we never see their kind again."

I nod once. "Good. I only wish it worked on Lucifer, too."

"That evil incarnation has no soul to take."

"So I've learned."

My magic flares, and Pollux seems to be warned of the same threat as we whirl around together to face the other end of the hall, where a giant, celestial bull materializes into existence.

Pollux bares his teeth into a reckless grin, snarling lowly, "There you are, you fucking bull. We've been looking for you."

The Apostles have since forced the Zodiacs into their truer forms since the battles began, calling upon the incarnations of the celestials' namesakes and magic.

Taurus's bull form is larger than that of any common cow, and he erupts with raw energy as he roars and strikes the ground; stars dot his luminescent body in a graceful but dangerous manner, nearly winking at us in challenge as though to taunt *I dare you.*

The bull charges, bowing his head to ram us with his horns, and I brace once he gets close. Then I grab him by the horns and toss him over my shoulder in one fluid motion, and Pollux is quick to summon another sword and stab it straight through the bull's heart.

He mutters off a few commands in Old Latin, and then Taurus's body convulses before a foreign entity lifts out of him. The strange, ghostly monster shrieks and attempts to flee, but Pollux has a firm hold of it, forcing it into an awaiting jar that one would use to catch fireflies. Though this jar, once sealed tight, becomes covered in sigils and runes that glow with enchantments.

I watch as the strange phantom bounces around and rams itself straight into the glass, but the glass doesn't crack.

"The urge to shake it is strong," I quip. "I want to hear the bastard's soul *rattle.*"

Pollux glances down at the jar, then shakes it for good measure, thoroughly pissing off the disembodied Apostle within.

"This will hold him long enough," says Pollux. "At least until we retrieve Death."

I nod. "Then I trust you can handle Sagittarius while I proceed onward to Hell?"

"Yes. We'll be right behind you soon enough. And the others are already there. The lieutenants and Lords of Exile lead the troops to storm Hell as we speak."

The urge to inquire about Rhesamyre is strong, but I tamp it down, knowing she needs me to remain with her allies and keep my wits about me. So I simply dip my chin, then open a conveyance and walk right into the chaos that is the Heart of Hell.

My breath fogs up when I enter the lands still frozen in time, all thanks to the usurper who claims a seat upon her throne.

The Obsidian Palace mirrors that of the celestial hallways in regard to the blood and gore that paint the walls. Bodies lie across the foyers while soldiers bearing Rhesamyre's coat of arms filter through various conveyances at a time; the entirety of the palace shudders in place with the rush of power coursing through it.

Hell craves blood and retribution just as much as the rest of us do. Perhaps even more so.

It always has.

This kingdom and land have always been hot-blooded, often demanding chaos, loyalty, and above all, *vengeance.*

No wonder my brothers and I fell in love with its queen.

Deep, deep in love, says Atlas in my head.

We're fucked, I agree. *And I like it that way.*

The war cries and shrieks of wyverns and rhayvens echo throughout the skies, and the howls of dire wolves and hellhounds reverberate through the streets below as plenty more conveyances litter the entirety of the capital's streets.

Steel swords ring, cannons fire, and Hellion hooves pound against cobblestone while murderous neighs fill the limited heartbeats of silence. Magic vibrates throughout the air in a near-sentient manner, devouring those that do not belong here and seek to do harm.

I stalk my way toward the throne room, exterminating pests as I go with a simple wave of my hand, and as I grow closer, the power wafting from the throne room can only be described as *suffocating*.

The Hellion court is laying waste to the wrong enemy.

Kicking the doors off their hinges as I enter, I immediately shift between the shadows to avoid Pride as he throws a barrage of daggers at me. The assassin snarls, and I return right behind him to kick his knees out from underneath him. However, he's quick and shifts away from me just as I did him, and we go to blows. Blocking, kicking, dodging, punching, and stabbing with daggers and swords alike.

The lieutenants are here. As is Siren, Wicker, and Draven. Their underlings fight alongside us in the hopes of at least slowing down the highly skilled court of demons, but it doesn't seem to be enough.

The baku are fierce and ferocious, as are the nightmarish creatures made completely of glittering shadows that belong to Wicker, while Siren's sex dolls are actually well-equipped in the art of murder, impressively enough.

A crystal dagger gleams in Siren's hand, and he slices through Envy's shields while whispering strange commands in a foreign tongue. Whatever he says seems to do the trick, and Envy is blasted backward into the wall, successfully cracking it something fierce.

"What the fuck is that?" I inquire while in the middle of a fist-fight with Wrath.

"A gift from the queen," replies the lord, glancing at me.

Wrath snarls at me, and an obsidian sword erupts from hellfire in his hands as he attempts to disembowel me. I spin away from him, commanding my own sword to appear when he strikes at me again, the ringing of our steel nearly visible as the surrounding magic reverberates and shatters the windows and chandeliers above us.

"Where has the usurper run off to?" I inquire, forcing Wrath backward with my magic just as Siren did Envy, though the assassins do not stay down for long, and rise again with renewed vigor.

I have to remind myself not to kill them, though it would be so easy to accomplish.

A mere *snap* of my fingers.

But that would make Rhesa sad, and then ultimately angry, and nobody wants that.

She's been through enough as it is, and I will not be responsible for her tears any longer.

"Dunno," replies Wicker, clashing daggers with Sloth. "He and Lucifer were already gone when we arrived."

I growl at that, then shift through a conveyance to land on the other side of Conquest since he has backed Gage into a corner.

Conquest whirls on me, and I grab him by the neck and slam the Horseman straight into the bloodstained marble floor beneath our boots. He growls, his magic rising to the surface as though he is going to erupt . . . and then he goes eerily still.

My magic *shudders*, and I am almost forced to a knee, and the rest of the Hellion court—both shackled and allied—seem to experience the same phenomenon.

Rhesamyre.

Thunder and lightning crackle across the dark sky outside, and I shift through a conveyance to hang off the balcony and observe what has arrived. Luminescent storm clouds cover the horizon, and the clouds rumble forward and almost look like—

"*Holy fuck*," I mutter.

The thunderous sound that echoes across the land belongs to that of galloping hooves, and the clouds themselves roll onward with the multiple legs and muscular, powerful bodies that belong to the *Sleipnir*. Their wicked neighs echo across the sky in a familiar war cry, and the hundreds of wyverns, rhayvens, hounds, and horses all answer with their own howls and shrieks in unison.

In addition, thousands of more wild wyverns and rhayvens appear with the storm of Sleipnir, and other predators and wolves of every sphere fill the streets to tackle our enemies by the hundreds. The Alpha Brothers arrive at last, burning through the streets and wiping out dozens of foot soldiers at a time.

Other conveyances finally open, revealing the archangels that bring forth their soldiers and winged horses to join the fray, and I hear the familiar slithering of scales behind me.

I whirl around to watch as Mamba slides into the throne room with his jaw unhinged and poised to devour the shackled demons whole if that's what it takes to free them. However, the assassins and Horsemen remain still for a heartbeat longer, and then their thorn collars snap in two and clatter to the floor, smoldering and melting into black mush before disappearing completely. The odd veil over their minds lifts as the spell breaks, and their eyes refocus as they take in their surroundings.

And that's when I notice it.

The palace is *mending* itself.

The magic works overtime to fix the chaos of shattered windows and splintered or missing walls, while banners flying Rhesamyre's coat of arms materialize into existence and hang from the walls and archways. Chandeliers return to their glittering forms while the paintings and statues that once depicted Rhesa, Samael, and the Hellion court as a whole all return to their rightful spaces.

But not only that, *Myra* returns.

The history of the Champion and all she once did to save these spheres engraves itself upon the ceilings and walls, while runes and wards are branded into the pillars that roughly translate to *protection* and *remembrance*.

"CHAOS!"

I whirl around, finding Lucifer standing atop one of the higher buildings in Heart. He raises his sword, pointing it straight at me.

The self-proclaimed god snarls. "I will have this piece of your soul, *Astraeus*!"

I command a sword to erupt from dark flames into my palm again, then I dig my heels into the floor and launch myself at the monster.

"If you want it so bad," I growl, "then come and fucking rip it from my body!"

Disregarding the multiple warnings from the recently awakened Horsemen and assassins, I call upon my wings and take flight, spearing toward Lucifer before my words even finish reaching his ears.

We clash swords, and our magics erupt together, nearly blowing half of this tower and the surrounding buildings in Heart away in the process. Miasma and smoke surround us like a hurricane, and the eye of the storm circles above us. Lucifer snarls in my face, his features contorting into something wicked and unsightly, and I bare my teeth at him as our swords cross. He laughs maniacally as though this is all some joke to him, and I shove him backward with my weapon before allowing my magic to consume him. His bones shatter under his cracked skin, and his joints pop out of place as my magic shrieks and eats him alive.

However, the self-proclaimed god just keeps laughing, and when I blink again, he has already regenerated and *consumed* my magic. He rushes me, crowding my space, and I shift through a conveyance to avoid his lengthened claws. He's there at every turn, so I move faster than he can keep up, disemboweling him in the process. His innards lash outward as though they're sentient *tentacles*, and I slice through them, too. He chokes on his own blood as his skin cracks and smolders, strange runes rebranding him as we fight, and foreign commands roll off my tongue as I use spells not native to these spheres.

His body snaps in two, blood and gore spraying outward as his physical form melts and unravels as though whatever cursed threads that hold him together finally split or fray as the binding comes undone. He shrieks and curses in his native tongue, writhing on the ground in two separate pieces as though he has the intention to reattach himself like some fucking worm. I don't give him the chance, though, and keep hacking away. I chop him into tiny pieces, and then I slice those pieces again and again. I decapitate him and stomp his face in, smashing his brain and skull to bits until nothing but a bloody, chunky mess is left behind.

When I'm satisfied with the gore, I step back, breathing heavily as my blood boils and my brands simmer while my sigils smolder with adrenaline and rage.

And then his laugh echoes between the sounds of war.

I brace, raising my sword when the gore ahead of me *shudders* and quakes. Tendons reattach as bones regenerate from the cursed magic that courses through the air, and everything *slithers*.

He rises back onto his feet, backward and broken, rearranging himself and twisting until everything is facing the correct way, and he cracks his neck and turns his head all the way around like a deranged owl. His grin is malicious, feral, and foul, and when I roar at him, his answering shriek is nothing but the lullaby of a nightmare.

We meet in the middle, and I duck under his incoming fist and tackle him to the ground. The entire tower groans and shakes beneath us, threatening to cave in as the flat roof splinters. I gouge out his eyes and slice my whole arms through his abdomen, and the *teeth* that are his ribs puncture my leathers. I snarl and rip my arms out of him, and physical magic seeps out of my wounds as he attempts to devour me.

He grabs a hold of me, headbutting me, and I see stars before I'm hollering in pain and outrage when his teeth lengthen into fangs, and he digs his mouth into my jugular. I rip myself away from him, partially erupting in order to put some distance between us, and I flip away from him.

A flash of blinding-white light slices through the miasma before I even touch the ground again, and Lucifer roars when a double-sided battleaxe swings and decapitates him in one movement.

"Insanity!" Lucifer's head shrieks, laughing, and the three-eyed minotaur roars in his face.

Lucifer's body erupts in a spray of blood and poison before collapsing into mush once more, and Kure stomps on his head just like I did, dislodging cartilage from tissues and bone.

"The fucker regenerates!" I shout, spitting my blood when it pools in my mouth.

"Not this time," he seethes, lifting his axe that glows with runes and convoluted spell work.

Kure starts muttering something in another dialect, pulling a celestial-kissed artifact from his robes. Lucifer's bloodshot eyes flash with mirth, and when Kure holds that mirror up, a delicate, bony hand snaps outward and grabs Lucifer by his ratty hair. The head screeches bloody murder, and once he's hauled through the mirror, Kure sets the rest of the monster's body aflame.

I stride forward, snatching the Mirror of Candor from Kure to peer inside it. The minotaur doesn't stop me, and the disheveled head of Lucifer stares back at me, cursing up a storm as he bashes his forehead against the glass in an attempt to break it.

"What is this?" I inquire, glowering at Kure.

Kure sheathes his battleaxe on his back, then folds his arms. "The mirror wasn't one of Myra's creations. It's one of mine. The looking glass reveals truths, and if one knows the right spells to mutter, sometimes is can show us other spheres, but it can also serve as a prison."

"Why didn't you use it the first time?"

"Because we didn't have it back then. We didn't have a lot of things back then."

I hum lowly, handing it back to him. "Will it hold?"

"For now. At least until you destroy the altar, it will do."

"Where's Rhesa?"

Just as I ask this, the entirety of the Hellion sphere *shivers*, and all at once, the miasma and snow disperse. The Heart of Hell mends itself while warm magic flows through the streets, glowing faintly and smelling of sweet smoke and spice.

"Where she belongs," drawls Kure, a knowing gleam in his eyes.

I don't give him time to elaborate, and I open a conveyance back into the throne room.

CHAPTER SIXTEEN
RHESAMYRE

I drag Abaddon through the palace halls by his horns with one hand, wielding magic in the other. A trail of blood is left in our wake since I cut off his legs, and his arms sit tightly bound against his chest. His mouth is gagged, but he hasn't stopped squirming and screaming, and it's getting really fucking obnoxious.

I jostle him by the horns, seething, "You should have known better than to come after my thrown and crown, boy. This is *my* kingdom." I lower myself, spitting in his face while baring my teeth. "*Mine.*"

He shrieks, and I stride through the throne room doors, covered in blood and gore. The room itself doesn't fare much better, and my court dispatches the last of Lucifer's followers as I make my way toward the dais. I drop Abaddon in the center of it, allowing Mamba to slither closer and eat the usurper alive. The serpent makes quick work of the false heir, and as Abaddon's screams are swallowed by the snake, I ascend the stairs, spin, and take a graceful seat on my throne.

I feel the entirety of the nine spheres shudder as the grounds of Hell growl. Enchanted torches and flames burst and burn brighter as the air pulses with immediate heat and overwhelming, magical power, successfully melting the snow and ice completely from my capital. All the enemies left alive in the streets burst from the inside out like infected blisters, leaving nothing but wet, red, or black residues behind.

The Seven Deadly Assassins, the Four Horsemen, their lieutenants, and three of the four Lords of Exile stand at attention ahead of me, their expressions steeled, faces and bodies rigid and covered in blood splatters, and I know I don't fare much better. I had to fight through dozens of Abaddon's so-called *guards* to get ahold of him, but none of them stood a fucking chance.

The archangels—*my brothers*—filter into the room, and through a separate conveyance, Kure and Atticus step forward.

My breath hitches in my throat at the sight of my deity, and it takes all my willpower not to leap off this throne and land in his arms.

His nostrils flare as he takes me in, scenting and scanning me from head to toe with a wild gaze that promises *when I get you alone, I'm going to devour you.* I raise my chin, meeting his challenge, and he growls while stepping forward. I flash my magic in warning, and he halts with narrowed eyes.

The weight of my horns on my head is comforting, but while the weight rising at my back is still foreign, I will not deny myself the pleasure that comes with bearing wings once more. They are no longer a constant presence; instead, I can summon them at will, much like the deities. However, the sight of them still makes my court take pause, and Pollux is the first to smirk. The rest of my brothers watch me skeptically, blinking a few times as though to ensure I'm really here, but I spare none of them a second glance as I survey my allies. Outside, the battles come to an end, and the creatures and monsters I summoned to fight on my behalf holler in triumph, and the soldiers are quick to follow suit, banging their weapons on their shields as they shout my name and yell to the stars, *Long live Queen Rhesamyre!*

I settle my gaze on Kure at last. "Do you have him in custody?"

Kure inclines his head. "I do not trust it to hold forever."

"We don't need forever." I rise once more, looking to my uncle Death. "And the Apostles?"

"Thoroughly devoured, my queen," he replies, bowing his head.

"I hope they were tasty." I descend the dais, and Mamba slithers closer. I pet his scales when he nuzzles me, eyes flashing to Atticus in the process.

His chest heaves, and raw magic crackles over his skin where his tattoos burn. He bares his teeth. "Are you looking to make me jealous over a snake, sweet spice?"

I lift my head, then glance at Pollux. "Status report?"

"Only a few loose ends to tie up, but the spheres are safe at the moment," replies my brother. "We'll be instigating eminent domain for the time being until the threats are permanently neutralized, but as of right now, Hell and the Celestial Cities are secure."

"Hell shall remain with the Seven Deadly Assassins and the Four Horsemen. And the archangels and Zodiacs, once they've recovered, will regain control of the Celestial Cities. The Wise Men are no more. Their magics have been distributed between me and the Lords of Exile, thus the Hollow shall remain under their protection, though I don't suspect the magic there will need shepherds. The free deserts of the West will fall to the Hussars without further interference unless requested, and the Golden Throne of the mortal kingdom is to be ascended by the rightful heir, Althea. And should he want it, Gage is to be her king consort."

Pollux tilts his head, smirking. "I thought I sensed a rewrite."

"The mortal kingdom will not be commanded by a faulty bloodline. Althea is the rightful heir, and the people will respect and understand as much when they recall the name of their lost princess, who is also a part of the Hellion court, thus ensuring our two kingdoms remain allies for centuries to come." I take another step forward, away from Mamba, as I make eye contact with the males surrounding me. "Are my orders clear?"

"*Crystal*, my queen," drawls Uncle Pride, eyes narrowed. "However, why does it sound as though these might be your *last* orders?"

"Because in the event that another sacrifice is needed, then they will be. And I want to ensure these spheres do not fall again in my absence." I raise my hand, and Kure tosses the mirror to me. I catch it effortlessly, ignoring the flare of magic that pulses every time Lucifer bangs his head against the glass on the inside. He roars at me, and I pocket him in my leathers for safekeeping. "There is no time to waste. We're heading to the passageway to find Atlas and Alastair, and we're going to destroy the altar."

"Who's *we*," snarls Atticus.

I look at him, then extend my hand. "Who do you think?'

He glances at my outstretched hand, then prowls forward and claims it with a bruising grip. He hauls me against his chest, his magic nearly erupting when we make contact, and I can feel him vibrating. He embraces me, nearly suffocating me with how hard he's holding me, and I lift my arms and wrap them around his neck while locking my legs around his waist. He almost buckles from the relief of having me in his arms, and slowly, he goes to his knees with me in his arms. He growls lowly, the sound nothing but a primal and possessive noise, and he buries his nose into my messy hair. He inhales deeply, and I shudder against him.

"I thought I lost you," he murmurs, arms like steel bands around me.

"I know. But you didn't. I'm here, and I love you."

And despite our audience, he reels back before surging forward again to smash his lips against mine. It's all teeth and tongue, and he dives the muscle into my mouth as though to devour me from the inside out, and I moan against him when he presses his knee between my legs.

A throat clears, and Atticus growls, tugging me against his chest and turning as though to hide me from the eyes around us.

"I understand this is your palace," drawls Orion. "And you can do whatever the fuck you want. However, if I may request it of you. Please get a room."

I almost laugh at how uncomfortable everyone looks. Except for Lust and Siren, who seem quite intrigued.

I pat Atticus's chest and lean away from him, standing back up, but his arms only tighten on me once more. I tilt back a little, then grasp his cheeks and force him to look at me again. He's still kneeling and doesn't seem to give a fuck about who's here to witness the action.

"I love you," I avow. "But we need to go. Your brothers—my *mates*—are still out there, and I will not delay in finding them or destroying that fucking altar."

Atticus leans into my palms, gliding his hands down my arms to cup my bloody knuckles as he stands back up.

"I just got you back," he snarls, still sounding more beast than man at the moment. "I can't lose you again, Rhesamyre. I'm not fucking strong enough for that shit."

I nod. "You won't lose me again, Atticus. Because wherever we go, we're going together."

He presses his forehead against mine. "You promise, sweet spice?"

I grin, pecking his lips. "I promise. No matter what happens, we stay together."

"*Rhesa*," breathes Damian, stepping forward.

I turn in Atticus's embrace but keep his arms wrapped around me, his hands on my hips. I glance over my family, both chosen and blood related, and they all look at me in the same manner that I survey them, too.

Like this will be the last time we ever see each other.

"I owe everything I am and once was to every single one of you," I tell them. "Because without you, I would not be who I am today. Both back then and now, you've been a part of my life, and even now, I don't regret any of it. So no matter what happens next . . ." I swallow thickly, almost choking on a sob, but I keep it down. Atticus remains a steady force at my back, and I tuck my wings in so I can lean against him without trouble. "Know that I love and trust every single one of you, and I thank you." I meet the eyes of the court, and then my blood brothers. "I'm sorry it has to happen this way, but I won't apologize for doing what must be done."

Pollux steps forward, grasping my cheek with a pained smile. "We know," he whispers. "And we love you, too."

I nuzzle his palm, then glance at Kure.

"Fastest route?" I inquire, my voice sharp and cutting once more.

"The passageway will split you up, but it remains the *only* route. That old spell work keeps even me from opening reckless conveyances. Not to mention, there are still monsters on that side that we mustn't allow to reach us. And once the altar is destroyed, in the event that you're still alive, you'll have limited time to return to the passageway before it seals shut again."

Atticus growls and mutters curses under his breath. "*Fucking fantastic.*"

I take a breath, then turn around to face him. He glances down at me, and I spare him a lopsided smile. "Now or never."

He breathes in deeply like I do, eyes flicking all over my face as though to commit my features to memory.

And then we're shifting through a glittering conveyance.

The Falls of Man are restless and rapid, veering upward into the sky that crackles with thunder and ominous lightning. Raw magic buzzes in the air, making the fine hairs upon my arms stand on end. Atticus keeps a firm hold of my hand, and we prowl toward the water's edge to survey the jump. We won't fall for very long before we're lifted into the sky, deposited only stars know where once we cross the threshold.

Atticus exhales slowly, then lifts our hands and presses a kiss to my knuckles.

"I'll see you on the other side," he vows.

I bow my head.

And then we jump.

CHAPTER SEVENTEEN
RHESAMYRE

I'm falling, flailing my limbs for purchase, and I catch on what feel like massive leaves and thick tree limbs. The air is knocked from my lungs, and I manage to twist and catch myself on a branch before it snaps and leaves me tumbling toward the forest floor once more. I shout in surprise, thumping unceremoniously and, regrettably, quite ungracefully, straight into a pit of bubbling black goo. I land on my side, and the sticky substance adheres to my body while I scramble to get my bearings. But it's no use, I'm *stuck*.

"*Fucking pathetic*," I snarl at myself, taking a moment to glance around at my surroundings.

Massive, jungle-like trees surround me with gray or violet bark and red leaves the color of blood. The ground itself is lush with dark greenery full of thick roots and briar patches, as well as the odd pit of bubbling goo or what almost looks like poisoned swamp water lying stagnant in a shallow spring. The air is at least warm, but it smells of stale blood and weeks-old corpses, and I scrunch my nose up in distaste.

Atticus is nowhere in sight.

I take a breath, having already prepared for this to happen, but it doesn't make it any easier to accept. I'm alone again in a foreign sphere surrounded by unknowns, and odds are, everything here is going to be unfriendly and bloodthirsty in nature. If such a sphere can breed a monster such as Lucifer, then I'm in for quite a trek through the fucking wilderness.

I glance down at my awkward position, tugging on my arm and leg that remain stuck in the goop, but nothing budges. The sludge threatens to rip my skin from my bones, so I stop struggling and look around again. I need leverage, but none of the branches or vines are low enough to grab.

Fantastic.

Twigs snap, and I freeze. I scent the air, but there isn't much need since a creature bearing huge tusks and horns stomps through the woodwork with its strange, elongated nose pressed against the ground. It's almost like a trunk, and the monster itself is covered in black fur and is larger than any wyvern or rhayven I've ever seen back home. With six eyes in total, three on each side of its bony head, there is no fur on its face, only a unique skull riddled with barbs, horns that twist backward, and tusks that curl forward around the dark flesh of its trunk. Its four legs are muscular and long, and its clawed toes flex into the dirt, crushing everything it comes across with its weight.

I stay completely still, and the creature draws closer until stopping right in front of me. Beady black eyes blink within open sockets, and it kneels closer, lifting its trunk to smell me. Hot air blows in my face, and I slowly lift my hand to grab hold of the tusk it offers me. It pulls backward, hauling me out of the goop, and though my skin stings, my magic is quick to heal me.

I touch down on solid ground, letting go of the monster's tusk, since it stomps forward and nearly walks *over* me. I twist out of the way, pressing my back into a nearby tree trunk as I watch in mild awe and disgust as the animal starts *eating* the goop.

"They're called tar-eaters, foreign girl."

I whirl around, dagger in hand, as I back away from the tree trunk that now morphs into a humanoid face. It speaks like a woman, with an accent I've never heard before, but at least I can understand the Old Latin dialect.

"They're not carnivores, but they will attack when threatened," explains the tree. "They seek the mineral nutrients the tar provides when the pits devour ones like you."

I sheath my dagger, approaching the face once more. "And what are you?"

"A humble bystander. Not much can be done when creatures stumble into the pits." The bark narrows its makeshift eyes. "Or when they stumble into spheres which are not their own."

"What do you know of such matters?"

"Bodies decompose into the soil, girl. My roots take nutrients from the soil, and thus I learn a great deal. Most of which, some argue, I have no business knowing."

I hum. "Well, did any of the bodies you devour happen to have information regarding others like me that ended up here? Males, covered in powerful magical symbols? They should look alike, too. Silver, green, or pink eyes. Dark hair and armed to the teeth."

"No one of those descriptions has passed through my neck of the woods."

"All right. Then how might you advise I go searching for them without getting myself killed?"

The tree hums inquisitively. "Most do not *ask* for my help. They merely threaten to cut me down if I don't tell them how to get out. Needless to say, I don't speak to them much. I just let the pits have their fill."

I cross my arms. "You'll find I'm full of surprises."

"So we shall see."

I spare the tree a look. "Please, I'm looking for my mates. Two of them landed here . . . I'm actually not sure how long ago in your time. But I came here with another, and we got separated."

"And why did they land here in the first place? Our lands are not usually a destination. Well, not a *purposeful* one, at least."

"We're . . . looking for something."

"You want my help, you better answer what I ask of you, girl."

"I lack the information to understand if you'll be enraged with my truths."

"I will know if you lie."

"*You folks always do*," I mutter. "I'm looking for what we call the altar, though I don't actually know what it looks like or where in this sphere I should start looking for it."

The bark shifts again. "You seek to destroy *that* creature."

"*What* creature?"

"The one responsible for making this place *worse*." The tree chuckles. "He had to start devouring souls somewhere, after all."

"You know of Lucifer."

"We all do, and he is no more a friend than any of the others like him are."

"There are *others*?"

"There are always *others*. The beings here move and breed just as the ones in your spheres do. It is possible to survive here, but that doesn't mean you should *want* to."

"What does that mean?"

"Creatures here are not kind, and death is often a mercy, though it is rarely quick enough."

"So what does that make you?"

The tree grins. "A distraction."

The trees around me shriek and roar as odd vultures flap into the sky as something stampedes through the woodwork, and I brace, hands loose at my sides so I can grab my daggers.

"I would start running if I were you," drawls the fucking tree.

I give it a pointed look, then summon my wings. The tree gives no indication of its intrigue, and I launch into the air. Flipping and flapping between the branches, I reach the canopies and soar into the open gray sky. Black thunderheads rumble in the distance over a barren wasteland littered with corpses and skeletons ranging in various states of disarray and decomposition. Massive caverns split the earth, and scavengers race across the land, fighting amongst the scraps, looking like oversized, mutated *rats*. Behind me, the forest looms on for miles before the trees grow larger, covered in gaping hollows that are riddled with *teeth*.

This place is a fucking nightmare, and I need to find Atticus.

Lowering myself to a high branch so I'm not right out in the open air, I reach within my leathers and stroke my *truculent* tattoo. And though it may be faint, my body shivers in the wake of the touch, like a whisper or a long-range shout that is barely audible. Which tells me he's at least alive and aware of himself, but he's nowhere nearby at the moment.

Atlas, I call, but after a few heartbeats, I'm only met with silence.

Fuck. Of all the times to go quiet, now is not fucking it, dammit.

I roll my eyes and grab one of my daggers to slice my palm, muttering the foreign commands necessary for a locator spell. Then, in a moment, my blood forms the shape of a miniature hound, and it floats through the air, barking and growling as though ecstatic to go hunting. I smile at the creature, cupping my hands so he can return to sit. The bloodhound does so, and it presses its nose against mine with a quiet whine.

"Okay, little friend," I coo. "I need you to find the closest deity. Can you do that for me?"

I jerk my chin toward my *trouvaille* brand that Alastair and I share, and then my *sarang* tattoo that I share with Atlas. The bloodhound sniffs both, then sniffs my *truculent* brand that is connected to Atticus. With a huff, he sniffs the *sarang* marking once more, and then floats above me and starts sniffing the air before trotting forward on a phantom wind. I maneuver through the tree branches after him, often leaping from limb to limb or flying the greater distances. We travel well into the night, where faint stars litter the navy sky. It isn't bright here after dark like it would be back home. Everything remains dim and eerie, and throughout our trek, strange noises punctuate the silence.

My bloodhound halts ahead of me, and I land on a tree branch to peer down at the quiet hut nestled amongst the limbs like a treehouse. No candlelight flickers in the small windows, and no smoke puffs from the tight chimney, either. The hut looks vacant, made entirely of wood and built *into* the tree itself. I glance around to search for signs of life or even security measures, but then come up short when nothing buzzes.

I stroke my *sarang* brand, and as though that summoned him, I'm immediately tackled to the forest floor with a feral Atlas on top of me. He snarls in my face, baring his fangs, and I've never seen him so unhinged before now. His pink eyes are nearly red and are the brightest things in this forest, glowing in outrage, and his jaw is much fuzzier than the last time I saw it, too. The Old Latin inscription that translates to *strength* still rests in the bottom corner of his right eye. And his leathers have been torn and mended with foreign materials numerous times, but his sword is still in tip-top shape as he presses it against my throat.

"What have I fucking told you about wearing her skin, *huh*?" he growls, spitting in my face while nearly cutting my neck. I can feel my blood beading to the surface, and I thrash underneath him.

"Atlas! It's me!" I snarl back in his face.

"*Yeah*, like I haven't heard that one before!" He scoffs. "You think I'm that fucking stupid?"

"You *are* stupid!" I shout in outrage, kicking him off me.

He reels backward, clutching his abdomen, and when he looks at me again with those enraged eyes of his, I make it a point to hold up my left arm and *stroke*.

It's me, I tell him through our bond. *I'm here, Atlas. I'm finally here.*

His entire resolve falters, and his sword clatters to the ground as though it's become too heavy to hold, and he stares at me warily, disbelieving that I'm actually here and alive.

He furrows his brows, whispering, "*Little wolf*?"

I grin at him, tears lining my eyes as I take a cautious step toward him, but Atlas beats me to it. He launches at me, engulfing me in a powerful hug that knocks us to the ground. He buries his face in my neck, inhaling deeply while keeping one arm wrapped around my back and the other fisted in my hair around my horns.

"*Rhesa*," he mutters, nuzzling me. "My little wolf. You made it."

I grasp his shoulders, pushing him away so I can see his face. I cup his cheeks, running my thumbs under his eyes to catch the unshed tears there, and he nuzzles into my palms.

"I thought I'd never see you again," he whispers, his voice cracked and utterly broken. "We communicated, but *fuck*, Rhesa—"

I lean forward to kiss him, molding my lips against his. His entire body shivers, and he lets me touch him and feel him however I choose, just relishing in the fact that I'm here to embrace him again.

"I'm here," I tell him, pulling away. "Atticus and I are both here, though I'm not sure where he ended up when we landed."

Atlas nods along in understanding, moving in to nuzzle me once more. I let him hug me, and when he grabs me under my knees and back to haul me against his chest, I don't protest.

"Let's get you inside. It's not safe out here."

He flexes his back muscles, and his wings appear. He flies upward, muttering a few commands so the hut will shift and allow him access. The inside is just about what I expected of a treehouse in the middle of a predatory forest. Most of the space is riddled with weapons and supplies. Makeshift tables and shelves are made out of branches that sprout from the trunk in the very center, and upon the walls, various maps made out of animal skins hang and reveal what Atlas has explored during his time here.

He lets me down to start lighting a few candles, and I spy the netted hammock that swings from the higher branches of this hut before my eyes snag on the *hundreds* of tally marks.

"Atlas," I drawl, turning to face him. "How much time has passed here?"

He sighs deeply, eyes roaming all over me for a heartbeat before he finishes lighting the last lantern in the space.

"A few years," he admits quietly. "I . . . I quit counting a while ago. It wasn't until a few months ago that you and I made contact."

I approach him, drawing him in for another hug, and we melt to the floor again. He presses his cheek against my hair between my horns, wrapping both his arms and legs around me to keep me caged, but it's not like I'll be going anywhere, anyway.

"Where's Alastair?" I ask.

"He's alive."

"*Atlas.*"

"It's complicated."

I pull away from him so I can meet his eyes. "*Everything* is complicated, Atlas. So where is he?"

"A few miles north of here, holed up in a cave."

"And why aren't you together if you know where he is?"

"Because he isn't exactly *Alastair* at the moment, little wolf. He's been consumed by this place and has resorted to old ways and old names in order to survive."

"Then why haven't you become something different?"

He looks at me, and I think somewhere deep down, I realize he *has* become something different to survive and *stay alive.*

"Because I've never been prone to eruptions like he has, and the beast that is *Grief* has a habit of appearing when Alastair's out of options. When we landed, Alastair got the short end of the stick. Where I landed here in a semi-tame environment, or at least a manageable one, Alastair landed deep in the wastelands, where the ground splits. You caught a glimpse of it, did you not?"

"*Fuck,*" I mutter. "He landed out *there*?"

Atlas nods grimly. "He did, and it took him *years* to fight his way out. By the time I found him, he had already succumbed. I've been keeping tabs on him, but communication isn't exactly a luxury we have here."

I press my forehead against his chest, and Atlas's arms tighten around me.

"Dammit," I growl.

Gentle whining draws my attention, and I glance over to find my bloodhound waiting patiently.

"Find Atticus and bring him here," I command.

The bloodhound barks, then takes off, phasing through the walls of Atlas's hut in the process.

Atlas holds up my right hand, spying the intricate skeleton design amongst the mandalas that Dante gave me.

"Despite what he did," drawls Atlas, "I'm glad he was there in the end to save you when I couldn't."

I nod along. "You helped me stay sane, Atlas. Without you, I think I would've . . ."

"*Shh*," he coos quietly. "You stayed alive. That's all that matters."

I hum, then furrow my brows. "Why didn't you think I was real earlier?"

Atlas growls in annoyance. "This place has a habit of playing tricks on everything and everyone that will fall for them. And the trees are the greatest tricksters of all, often conjuring shapeshifters and woodland folk that like to play dress-up."

"But how would they know what I look like?"

"Many that you've slain before were sent here and later devoured by the soil and roots—some more recent than others—and that knowledge is invaluable to stationary creatures. They have no other way to pass time, so they resort to *jokes*."

"And I happen to think our jokes are quite hilarious!"

I blink, then slide my gaze toward the center trunk, which sprouts a face, this one more manly than the one I met in the woods.

Atlas sighs. "Rhesa, meet Woody, my roommate."

I cut him a glance, raising my brow. "*Woody*?"

Atlas shrugs. "Original, I know. But it kinda suits him."

I roll my eyes, then unfold myself from Atlas's limbs and stand to approach the talking tree.

"Why are you two friends if everything in the forest intends to kill you?" I ask.

I feel Atlas brush against my back as he comes closer. "Woody and I have come to somewhat of an understanding. I tell him stories of where I come from, and in exchange, he protects this place and doesn't rat me out to the neighbors."

I hum. "I suppose making deals with creatures that would rather eat your face is a specialty of yours."

Atlas chuckles. "You have no idea, *little wolf*."

"Ah! So you're the one Atlas pleasures himself to!" exclaims Woody. "It's a *pleasure* to meet you, Rhesamyre!"

I shoot Atlas another look, and he glances away, lips pursed.

I shake my head, snickering a little as I face the sentient trunk once more. "Hello, Woody."

"What a lady!"

"Thank you for not killing my mate."

"It's been my pleasure! He's been better company than others in the past."

Atlas crosses his arms. "Well, I'm glad to hear our time together hasn't been all bad. Personally, I think I'm a fantastic storyteller."

I grin at my deity, and he almost returns the look before he goes rigid, eyes cutting to the wall as though he can see through it.

I'm put on edge once more. "What is it?"

"Outlying wards have been activated. We're about to have company."

Atlas turns toward the makeshift door, stepping out onto the wide branch that serves as a short balcony in front of the hut. And there amongst the limbs ahead of us stands Atticus, with my bloodhound bouncing around him like a puppy. His chest heaves as though he just flew a great distance at an even greater speed to get here, and when he crouches a little, I take a step back into the hut.

Atticus barrels into his brother and tackles him into the house, then stops their momentum short and holds Atlas against him with steeled arms. Atlas is no different, and he embraces his brother with the same strength he used to hug me with.

Atticus leans back, cupping Atlas by the nape of his neck.

Atlas grins. "Hello, little brother."

I roll my eyes. *Younger*, maybe, but certainly not *little*. I fold my arms and clear my throat, and the two males look at me.

I open my arms, and they tackle me to the floor.

CHAPTER EIGHTEEN
RHESAMYRE

Sitting amongst candles and fuzzy animal pelts on the floor, I lean against Atlas's chest with my legs in Atticus's lap, and we recount all that has happened back home. Atticus didn't even know parts of my story, either. In turn, Atticus shares his warpath, while Atlas explains what this sphere is like and how far he has traversed in search of Alastair, the altar, and a way back home.

"Kure made it sound like there's another version of the passageway here," I think aloud. "I mean, there *has* to be. Lucifer marched his armies through a conveyance when he first arrived back then. No one just *fell from the sky*."

"It's reckless, but we could always *ask* the bastard," drawls Atticus.

I spare him a look, the weight of the Mirror of Candor heavy in my leathers at the mention of Lucifer. Atticus shrugs, hands on my calves, and I roll my eyes, then glance sideways up at Atlas.

He drops his gaze to meet mine. "I did find the altar, but I haven't found anything remotely similar to the Falls of Man or otherwise."

I glance at Woody. "Would you know?"

The tree scrunches his face. "Nope."

"Well, *you're* helpful," I snark. Then I look over at the maps Atlas has hand-drawn and assembled. I stand, padding over to them and leaving the males where they are. "You've been busy."

I glance back over my shoulder. "You wager this is everything? *Everywhere*?"

Atlas leans back on his hands. "It's as much as I've found."

I trail my fingers along the sketches, taking note of the vast wasteland that homes blood and corpses, the forests and hills, as well as the large watering holes and what almost look like small huts dotted along a few of the tree lines and near the lakes.

"The tree I spoke to when I arrived," I start. "She said there are others like Lucifer."

Atlas nods. "A few have clustered together, and yes, they're just as vile. Bastards born in blood or whatever the fuck Yonder calls them. They have similar bloodlusts, but their ability to band together and complete what Lucifer accomplished remains elusive to them."

"For now," snarks Atticus from behind us.

Atlas meets his brother's emerald gaze. "They won't be a problem."

Atticus tilts his head, then grins. "What'd you do to 'em, big bro?"

I look at Atlas, and he glances at me before scowling at Atticus, who only continues to grin like a madman.

"I went around the villages and slaughtered them all," says Atlas, eyes on me again. "Is that what you want to hear?"

I cock my head. "Were they like Lucifer?"

"Born in blood and cut from the same cloth, they were too similar and clustered together. And I thought that maybe, if I started dropping bodies, then Lucifer would leave our home to come deal with me here instead. But alas, he didn't bat an eye, and I just . . . couldn't stop killing them. *I didn't want to stop*," he admits softly.

"Were they innocent?" I demand.

Atticus growls. "*Hardly*. They bred with one another, incest and inbreeding through means of rape. So no, they weren't innocent. Both males and females were guilty of it, and took to slaughtering one another on top of robbing and impregnating each other, too."

I hum. "Then you have nothing to feel sorry for."

"I don't," he vows.

I incline my head. *And for the record, this feral side of you is very hot,* I tell him silently.

He growls at me, and Atticus makes a face before rolling his eyes and sparing us both a shit-eating grin.

I snort. "And the altar?"

Atlas stands, then brushes my side as he surveys his map before pointing to a clearing in the very center of the wasteland marked with an *X*.

"Of course, it's in the middle of a fucking bloodbath," quips Atticus again.

"And Alastair?" I ask.

Atlas points to the hills. "There are cave systems under the knolls. Alastair lives amongst the beasts."

"The beasts here are, naturally, different from the ones back home." I face Atlas again. "The tar-eater was fascinating to observe."

He blinks at me. "You came vis-à-vis with a *tar-eater*?"

I cock my head, furrowing my brows. "Um, yes?"

He gapes at me, then looks over at Woody. The tree also gapes at me, and I glance at Atticus and shrug.

"I mean, I figured they were not harmless. Nothing here is. But I was under the impression it isn't carnivorous. It helped me out of the tar pit."

Atlas grasps my shoulders. "Nothing here is kind, and everything wants to kill you. Whether or not it *eats* you is a different conversation, but they're certainly not *helpful*."

I cross my arms. "*Well*, this one was."

A muscle flutters in Atlas's jaw, and behind him, Woody hums.

"*What*?" grates out Atticus, standing to size up the fucking tree.

"You mentioned she is the bride of the son?" inquires Woody, his teasing demeanor gone, and I peer around Atlas to survey the tree. He all but scowls, and his bark-eyes are leveled on me, unrelenting. I would take the look as a threat if I weren't so concerned with the fact that he knows of Astraeus, too.

"How do you know such a thing?" I demand.

"Because I told him," drawls Atlas, and I look at him again. "The memories started resurfacing on top of what I learned when you and I started conversing again. I know—well, *everything*."

"And you told your *roommate*?" growls Atticus.

Atlas levels a dangerous look on his brother, and I have half a mind to think that look often leads to a brawl.

"Stories in exchange for safety," drawls Atlas. "Keep that in mind, brother. This sphere is nothing you've ever faced before, so remind yourself of that before you start swinging. Because odds are, whatever you punch will fucking punch back."

Atticus lifts his chin, shoulders set back. "Does that include you, *brother*?"

Atlas gets a little bigger. "Damn straight."

"Oh, for fuck's sake!" I snap, stepping between them. "Will you two knock it off already? Fucking hell, you're both so irritable."

The brothers blink at me, and I snarl at them both before turning my gaze back to Woody. "What does my being the bride of the son have anything to do with the beasts here?"

Woody's bark shifts as he watches me. "The beasts here are still of Evergreen's making, and he is the father. Your relationship with the son has rippled across time and dislodged a few stars from the sky. Most of the greater beasts here, while feral, can sense you are *different*."

"To sum it up, attacking you would bring forth a greater wrath than they can handle," explains Atlas. "And though I suspected as much, I wasn't looking to test the theory."

I furrow my brows. "But that tree was ready to watch me get eaten by something else if not the tar-eater."

"I never said they *all* heeded the warning."

I hum. "Well, maybe this can come in handy later on. If some of the beasts are reluctant to attack me, maybe I can convince them to help us."

"Mind you, I *am* the son, and most, if not all, still tried to claw my eyes out."

I frown at him. "Did you ask them *nicely*?"

"*Rhesa.*"

I grin. "Just had to ask."

Atlas inhales very slowly. "You know I love you, and while plenty of these creatures might think twice about attacking you, some will not. And most of the others will take exception to conversing. Favors and kindness do not exist here. It's eat or be eaten, kill or be killed. And if you mange to get away, you better run fast and far, because whatever you pissed off is most likely faster."

I incline my head. "I hear you."

He sighs. "Good."

I take his hand in mine, getting the sense he needs to feel me. He squeezes my tattooed fingers in thanks, then leans down and kisses my forehead gently.

The gesture is such an *Atlas* thing.

"How soon can we go after Alastair?" I ask, segueing.

"It would be wiser to wait till morning," replies Atlas, and I lead him back to the animal pelts so we can sit with Atticus again. I want them both near me, and they seem to understand that because they sit far closer than they had been before. "Travelling at night never ends well. The monsters are more active, and it's easy to get lost. However, if it looks like a storm is brewing, we'll need to remain near a secure shelter."

Atticus furrows his brows, lying down to rest his head in my lap, and I tickle his scalp.

"Why?" he asks.

"The rain here is highly acidic," says Atlas, keeping me tucked against his chest. "Even the storms are bloodthirsty, and unless you're well-equipped to protect yourself, the rain here will melt your skin and devour your bones. It's extremely toxic to unsuspecting travelers."

"That's disturbing," I mutter.

I don't dare ask how he came to learn this information. I think I already know, and my heart can't take any more torture at the moment.

Atlas dips his chin, then nuzzles against my hair. "The bright side is, storms are few and far between when you're not out in the middle of the wastelands, and most animals born here are well-equipped to combat the acid. Their fur repels it, and I happen to have a few cloaks we can use, but it's not a permanent solution by any means."

I nod. "Okay, then we'll search for Alastair in the morning."

Atlas tilts my head toward him, then presses his mouth to mine. "We'll get him back," he mutters against my lips. "I always knew you'd find us eventually, but all I could do in the meantime was ensure we stayed alive."

"I'm sorry it took so long," I whisper.

He shakes his head. "Don't be, little wolf. You're here now, and that's all that matters." He takes a breath, pink eyes boring into mine. "I tried to destroy the altar when I found it."

I lean back a little, and Atticus sits up. "Brother, you couldn't have accomplished that on your own," he says.

Atlas bows his head. "But I had to try."

I cup his cheek. "What happened?"

He folds his hand over mine, kissing my palm. "*Nothing.*"

I furrow my brows, glancing at Atticus.

"It didn't budge. It didn't try to devour me. *Nothing fucking happened.*" Atlas bares his teeth. "It regarded me as nothing more than an obnoxious gnat. Not even worthy of its time."

"Is it truly sentient?" asks Atticus.

"Sentient enough." Atlas meets his brother's eyes. "It can feed itself, but it's still tethered to Lucifer. Anything or any*one* that gets close to it often becomes a meal."

I grasp both his cheeks now, making him look at me. "There's nothing more you could have done, and until we have Alastair back, there's nothing more *we* can do, either. We'll deal with it soon. It can fucking wait." I lean forward and kiss him again. "Make love to me. *Fuck me.* I need to feel you." I lean into Atticus, then lick his parted lips. "Both of you."

Atticus shuffles closer, but Atlas's gaze cuts to Woody. He's awake and aware, but quiet.

I grab my mate's jaw, turning his head back to face me. "*Let him watch,*" I breathe against his mouth.

Atlas doesn't have to be told twice, and his hands shift on my body. He pushes me into his brother, and Atticus grasps my jaw and tilts my head to the side, then assaults my mouth with his tongue. He runs it over my own and along my teeth, poking into my cheeks while squeezing my neck with his hand, and he growls when I nip him, drawing blood.

Atlas's hands make slow work of removing my leathers, allowing his fingers to trail across my skin and scrape until he draws blood. I'm left completely bare and open to the two of them, and Atticus's other hand slides across my front and grasps a breast, rolling and pinching my nipple while Atlas sucks on the other. They move in tandem, massaging and touching me everywhere, and when Atlas travels south, Atticus moves his sucking kisses to my neck so he can peer down at his brother while he toys with me.

Atlas latches onto my clit, and I arch my back and whine. He chuckles, licking and lapping through my folds that get wetter with every flick of his tongue, and he swirls it over my clit again before diving lower to pierce my entrance. I moan, and Atticus is there again to swallow the sound.

"*Fuck*, I missed you so goddamned much," growls Atlas, flexing his hands around my hips to lift my core closer to his face.

He devours me, opening his mouth wide to scrape his fangs against my sensitive skin, and I cry out again when he plunges two fingers in at once. He strokes my inner walls while he chews on my clit, and I meet his gaze when Atticus releases my mouth to suck on my neck and nipples again in a sloppy manner.

"C'mon, my little wolf," Atlas husks, blowing on my clit. "Give me what I fucking want."

I pant, and Atticus twists and nibbles on my nipples at the same time Atlas adds a third finger, stroking that delicate spot inside of me that has my back arching again. I come undone, shattering and shivering while stars dot my vision. Atlas laps at me greedily, sucking and swallowing everything he can while I'm left twitching and convulsing, my heat still flexing around his fingers while he slowly pulls them out.

"Good girl," growls Atticus, and then he flips me onto my hands and knees. "Look at you following orders. Giving my dear brother what he wants."

Atticus kneels in front of me, the tip of his hard, throbbing length poised close to my lips, and I dart my tongue out to lick the pre-cum off his head. He snarls lowly, grasping my horns as he shoves his length inside my mouth. I growl at him, but the sound comes out strangled and gurgled since his head hits the back of my throat. His groans, his entire body shuddering as he settles deep in my mouth, his balls against my chin. I flatten my tongue to stroke the veins on the underside of his cock, and his fists tighten on my horns.

"*Careful, sweet spice,*" he warns on a breathless moan. "Wait for him. You want us both, then you're fucking going to get us both."

I moan around his cock, loving the raw, primal promise in his tone. Atticus strokes my jaw gently in a loving caress, and I flutter my eyelashes at him. He chuckles, rotating his hips a little.

Behind me, Atlas shuffles and settles his tip against my core, and I wiggle my ass. His fingers flex on my hips again, leaving bruises, and I fucking *love* it. Much slower than Atticus, he slides inside me, letting me relish the stretch and every inch of his veiny cock that rubs my sensitive walls just the way I love and need. I exhale through my nose, whining again around Atticus's length, and when Atlas is settled all the way to the hilt, he leans over me and bites my shoulder with a groan. He licks away the blood, then trails his tongue down the inscriptions and brands of my spine once left by Mamba.

"I needed this," he grunts, pulling back and thrusting once. I can feel him hit the end of me, and I whimper. "I fucking missed you," he snarls, punctuating his point with another brutal thrust. "*Fuck*, I love you so much it hurts."

I'm rocked forward onto Atticus's cock, and he growls. Then, with the two of them settled inside and nestled balls deep, they pull back and slam back in. Sometimes in tandem, other times on alternate motions, and I'm left at their glorious mercy; rocking between them like a fuck doll. Our snarls and moans and growls and groans and their muttered curses echo throughout the space, and everything sounds so *wet*. My arousal drips down my thighs as Atlas pounds into me, and drool has started to seep out of the corners of my mouth and down my chin as Atticus uses me for his pleasure. They slow their paces when they feel close, their cocks swelling, and they edge themselves repeatedly until my limbs start to shake. My throat is numb and rubbed raw, and my wet core is nothing but a swollen, sensitive mess.

Finally, Atlas moves one of his hands to my mound, and he rubs my clit harshly as they pick up their paces again. I thrash and whimper, snarling at them to *hurry the fuck up*, and they both chuckle darkly before pounding into me ruthlessly, mercilessly, and my breath hitches as another climax crashes into me. Everything flutters and shakes, and Atlas comes with a roar, his cock swelling deep inside of me. My muscles flex around him, milking him of everything he has to give, and he shudders and pumps his hips a few times to spill his seed deep inside of me. Atticus comes right after him, and warmth spreads throughout my mouth and slithers down my throat as he stills in my mouth. I swallow around him, drawing more cum out of him, and his tattooed thighs visibly shake with the effort it takes to stay upright.

They pull out of me, and I cry pathetically at the emptiness. I cough on all fours, breathing heavily, but I don't spit a damn thing out. Atlas's seed spills out of me and slides down my thighs, and with a casual hand, he gathers it with his fingers and fucks it back into me.

"Keep this here," he orders. "It's pretty fucking hot."

I laugh breathlessly, and he pulls me upward onto my knees and draws me into a hug. He buries his face into my neck, and Atticus prowls closer and kisses me, uncaring of his taste on my tongue. In fact, that might turn him on more since he growls and sucks on the muscle as though he's sucking on my clit.

"Fuck everything else," he growls against my lips. "All that matters is you. *Us.* I don't care where we end up so long as we stay together."

I grin, lifting my arms until one is wrapped around his shoulders, the other bent around Atlas's head. "We get Alastair back and finish our business here. I don't care what happens after that." I nuzzle them both. "The four of us. Until the stars die."

Atlas kisses my neck. "*Until the stars die.*"

CHAPTER NINETEEN
RHESAMYRE

I watch Atlas shuffle through his animal pelt cloaks while Atticus finishes rebraiding my hair for me. It's become a tangled mess again with all the nonstop movement and fighting. Atticus's thick braids are in a similar state of disarray, too. We're all looking a little rough around the edges, but there isn't much we can do about it at the moment. Luxuries and baths will have to wait until our enemies are gone and devoured.

I look forward to soaking in the scented waters of Hell for hours once all this shit is finished.

Assuming we make it back home, that is.

Atlas seems satisfied with whatever he's assembled, and he turns toward me once more and throws a furry, hooded cloak over my shoulders and horns. I lift my chin, allowing him access to my neck so he can tie the ropes into snug bows. Curiously, I lift my arm and sniff the fur, then reel backward with a scrunched nose. It smells of dried, aged blood and odd, rotten earthy smells.

This whole fucking sphere is rotten. It stinks something fierce.

Atlas chuckles, stepping back. "Yeah, I know. It isn't pleasant. It took me a while to get used to it. I'm fairly certain I lost my ability to smell correctly." He furrows his brows in thought. "Until I smelled you, anyway."

I almost smile, and he winks at me while handing Atticus a cloak.

"What sort of animal did you butcher to get hold of these?" he asks.

"Wolf-rats," replies Atlas, shrugging on his own furs.

"Wolf-*rats*," I repeat. "As in those giant rat-looking creatures I saw roaming the wastelands?"

"Those are the ones."

I wrinkle my nose again. "Gross."

"I know, but they live in the wastelands full-time. Meaning they're the best equipped to combat the acid rain."

"It makes sense, but it's still kinda gross."

"I don't disagree."

"You said storms weren't as common when not in the wastelands," notes Atticus.

"They're not," agrees the middle brother. "But getting caught off guard or cornered when that rain starts to fall will be a nightmare. Trust me, immortal healing or not, it won't be pretty."

I steel my expression into something unreadable, and Atlas catches my eye before turning to Woody with clenched teeth.

"Mind the hut, will you?" he quips.

"Terrible jokes must run in the family," snaps the tree.

Atticus grins, and Atlas rolls his eyes as we stride toward the spelled door of the hut. The walls shift once Atlas mutters a few commands, and we find ourselves standing upon the branch's edge, facing the forest that slowly brightens as the sun rises. Rays of sunshine bleed through the blood-soaked leaves, and distant animals hoot and holler as the sphere blinks, waking up to devour unsuspecting creatures another day.

"It's a short flight," starts Atlas, flexing his back muscles, and his wings ruffle into existence. "Alastair, though more beast than man at the moment, still has routines. He'll be leaving the knolls to go hunting soon."

Atticus stretches his neck, cracking the bones there as his wings appear in a similar fashion to his brother's. "Dealing with Grief is such a pain in the ass. All reason ceases to exist."

I cross my arms, glancing between the two of them. "I've dealt with Alastair's mood swings before. Is Grief really all that different?"

"Night and day, sweet spice," says Atticus. "I have yet to face something that even compares to Alastair when he's unhinged, unchecked, and unreasonable."

I almost laugh. "That sounds like Alastair on a good day." And then I recall Atlas's description of their eldest brother. "When you say he's *more beast than man*, are you being facetious, or are you serious?"

"Unfortunately, I'm being serious," Atlas drawls. "He lost his humanity and has slowly begun to transition into something monstrous. Last I checked, he was at least humanoid, but wolfish features have begun to surface."

"*Fantastic*," I snark.

Atlas inclines his head in agreement, and Atticus smirks.

I hum, then summon my wings, and they almost smack my mates in the face. Atticus bats my feathers away with a humored scowl, but Atlas trails his fingers across the faint sigils that decorate my black wings, and the action makes me shiver.

"That tickles," I growl.

He pulls his hand back with a subtle smirk. "Sorry."

"No, you're not."

He grins, and he looks like Atticus when he smiles like that. "I'm not." Then he leans in closer, husking against the shell of my ear, "Will you let my brother bind them to the bed so I can tickle them some more, little wolf?"

I swallow thickly, and Atlas kisses my temple before pulling away. Mirth dances in his pink eyes, and I huff before gesturing toward the great outdoors. "Shall we?" I quip.

Atticus bumps his brother, muttering, "I didn't hear a *no*."

I spin on my heel, ignoring them. They follow me, and we glide through the branches of the violent trees, leaping between limbs and flapping through the leaves with an assassin's silence until we reach the outlying tree line that neighbors the hills. We land on the last branches to survey the knolls riddled with cave mouths, and while there is grass here, it's a strange brown color, dead and dry. The few pockets of water flow in streams like poisoned veins between the caves and over the knolls, *uphill*.

I stroke my *trouvaille* tattoo, and it prickles and itches in retaliation.

"He's close," I say. "I can feel him."

Atlas looks at me. "He's a territorial bastard. The tunnels are his, and he'll know we're here as soon as we touch down."

Atticus pounds his fist against the palm of his hand. "I could use a good brawl." He bares his teeth. "So, how should we provoke a monster?"

Atlas is still looking at me, and I do a double-take. Crossing my arms, I narrow my eyes. "What?" I demand.

"He's not in his right mind, but when you're involved, our center of gravity shifts. He'll attack Atticus and me without a second thought, but you might make him hesitate."

Atticus snarls. "You want to send her in there *alone*?"

I level him with a look, and he growls at me.

"I'm hardly unprepared," I bite. "I know how to appeal to beasts, remember?"

"No."

I scoff. "*No*?"

"Did I stutter?"

"This isn't up for fucking debate, Atticus. Beast or not, Alastair is in there, and I can handle myself."

He shakes his head, then grabs my waist and hauls me against his hard body. "I'm not sending you in there to face him or whatever else might be in there *alone*." He studies me with an intense ferocity he often reserves for our enemies when he's about to slaughter them, and then his eyes flick above my head to glower at Atlas. "You and I know better than anyone what our brother is capable of when he's like this. He'll rip her to fucking shreds."

"He won't," I snap again.

"*He will*," Atticus snarls in my face.

"So, what would you have me do instead, huh? Because unless you have a better idea, I'm going down there. You're not changing my mind. We've come this far, and I will not allow *you* or anyone else to get in my way!"

Atticus glares at me, emerald eyes ablaze while a muscle works overtime in his jaw, and I tilt my head in challenge. Smoke practically pours from his nostrils with how hard he exhales, and I grin in triumph.

"And I thought you were supposed to be the tactician," I quip.

Atlas sighs, and I spin out of his brother's hands to face him, but he remains a wall of calculated indifference. Even so, I can see the unease in his gaze.

I'm with you, he says silently through our bond. *Always.*

I take his hands in mine, then stand on my toes to kiss the corner of his mouth. When I pull away, he tugs me back up and claims my mouth properly, stroking his tongue against mine in a gentle caress that feels more like a goodbye than a greeting.

Do not underestimate Grief, he says.

You would all do well to remember not to underestimate me, Atlas.

I face Atticus again, and he sucks on his teeth while that muscle still flexes in his jaw. His shoulders and wings are tense, but when I reach for his hand, he doesn't pull away.

"I love you," I tell him. "You know that. And because I love you, let me do this for you. Let me get your brother back."

Atticus looks at me, then cups my cheek. "I'd sacrifice both my brothers if it meant saving you, and they would gladly let me."

"You don't mean that."

But he does. He absolutely means it, and he levels me with a pointed look that says he knows I know that, too.

"Even so," he drawls. "Don't do this for me. Do it for you."

"I'll do it for all of us, Atticus."

He dips his chin, and I glance at them both before reaching back into my leathers. I pull out the Mirror of Candor, where we keep Lucifer contained, the looking glass covered with black cloth, and I hand it to Atlas. He takes it wordlessly, tucking it away into the safety of his cloak, and before either of them can change their minds, I'm leaping from the trees and gliding toward the knolls.

The mouths of the caves litter the hills, and I land before one on silent feet. Prowling inside the dank area, I scent the air for fellow predators, but come up with nothing but the wet and rot of the rocks. Bones litter the ground at the base of the walls, and above me, condensation drips from the spikes of the stalagmite formations. The water—or whatever the fuck that is—is a bright, luminescent pink that pools along the ground. I avoid the puddles, and continue down the tunnel with my hands poised near my daggers and my hood drawn down and off my horns.

Ahead of me, the tunnel opens up to reveal a spacious cavern littered with weaponry, pelts, bones, curing meats, and even a few slaughtered animals that hang upside down, draining of blood. I don't pay them much mind, though; my attention locked on the wall murals ahead of me where Atticus, Atlas, Hell, other places back home, and myself are all painted with the blood of monsters, black tar, and other mediums no doubt created from the leaves, rocks, and nature of this world.

I approach the wall to observe the art, staring up at the portraits and dimensions layered together to create an abstract and complicated piece. The Forest of Souls and the Sacred Cities flank the farmlands of Hell and Heart, while the Obsidian Palace glitters at the base, and above the spires are portraits of the two youngest deities with me between them. Atticus and Atlas have been painted as though their bodies are shifted toward me, with Atlas's eyes brighter than Atticus's, though Atticus wears a smirk as though he knows something I don't. I stand between them, my crown and horns on display with my thick, black hair uplifted around me like a mock halo, and my eyes sparkle like the gems painted around my neck and arms. My hands clasp a dagger, and behind me is a lilac and amber sky littered with clouds shaped like the Sleipnir.

I raise my hand to stroke the dried materials used to paint this beauty, and that's when the cavern rumbles. I whirl around, daggers already in hand as the darkness ripples, and from the shadows, an actual *beast* materializes. There's nothing fucking *human* about him. His face is wolfish and set into a snarl as he locks his silver eyes on me. A white line strikes downward over his right eye in a mockery of his *faith* tattoo, and horns rip from his head and curl forward from matted, black fur near fluffy wolf ears, and he stands on his hind legs that are still more monster than man. His arms, legs, shoulders, and back are covered in black fur, but his chest is gray and riddled with silver sigils and tattoos. Claws erupt from his humanoid hands, same with his feet, and a long tail that looks more snake-like than wolfish swishes behind him.

His growl is one of warning, and it reverberates off the walls and shakes the stalagmites. I glance upward to mind the spikes, then level my gaze back on the beast as he lowers himself to the ground as though to prowl and pounce.

I bare my teeth, cocking my head. "Hello, my love," I purr.

Alastair roars, then leaps and charges straight for me. I jump and roll away just as he makes a move to grab me, and then I shift through a conveyance to avoid his claws. He swipes and snarls at me, gnashing his teeth dangerously close to my limbs and neck. Despite his size, he's quick, and this is his territory. My magic is slower here, as though the literal sphere itself is revolting against my spells, and my conveyances are not fast enough to evade him despite using them in rapid succession.

His claws curl around the tail end of my braid, and he yanks me backward. I flip and roll between his legs, and he thrashes his tail and seizes my torso. I growl and curse him, my claws digging into the ground as he hauls me into him, and he roars and throws me over his shoulder. My lungs seize when my back hits the rocks with a resounding force, and blood pools in my mouth at the impact. My fucking bones rattled with that one, and I spit in his face.

His face scrunches up as his nostrils flare, scenting me, while his long tongue darts out and licks his cheek where my blood landed. His eyes flash brighter, and he squeezes me in his coiled snake tail. He lifts me higher off the ground, his claws landing on my shoulders as he brings his face closer, pressing his short snout into my neck. I headbutt him, and he reels backward with another primal noise rumbling deep in his chest. His tail loosens just enough so I can get my arms free, and I grasp his horns to make him look at me.

"ALASTAIR!" I scream, and he roars back, fangs flashing in my face. "You wanna fucking eat me? Then go ahead! But you better look me in the eye when you do it, you fucking coward!"

He slams me back on the ground, monstrous snout open around my throat, ready to tear out my jugular, and I scream and dig my claws into the sides of his head. His hands slam into the ground on either side of me, back feet digging into the rocks as I grab his horns and push with all my strength, but the damn fucker doesn't budge. He snarls, his jaws closing in, and I feel his fangs graze my skin.

I inhale one last time, and then I stroke my *trouvaille* tattoo right above his head.

"*Alastair*," I whisper. "It's okay."

He growls, lapping over the small puncture wounds he's created, and I wrap my arms around his neck.

"It's okay," I tell him again, stroking the fur around his ears and horns. "You can have all of me if you want. I've always been yours to devour."

He slowly pulls back, and I move my hands to cup his fuzzy cheeks. His eyes flash again, and something almost *human* bleeds into his gaze. I smile, rubbing my thumbs under his eyes, and he closes them and moves closer. He sniffs me, hot air puffing around my hair and horns, and he growls before ripping Atlas's cloak from my body. It tears and stings when it runs across my neck, but I ignore the pinch when Alastair's tongue darts out again to lick my cheek before moving to lap at my blood again.

I exhale slowly, tears pricking at my eyes, and I lift his head again.

"Look at me," I demand. "I'm here, my love."

Something akin to a whine ripples out of his snout as his nose whistles, and I almost want to laugh at the pitiful sound. He licks my tears away, and I nuzzle his fuzzy cheek as he brings it closer. He's terrifying in this monstrous form, but this is *Alastair*. My deity. A piece of my original lover. And he will always be beautiful to me, no matter what form he takes. He will always be *mine*.

"You don't scare me," I avow. "Well, maybe a little. But I love you anyway." He meets my eyes again. "I love you. And I always will, Alastair."

A low rumble vibrates his chest once more, and while this one is lower and less threatening, it still sounds like a promise. Primal and raw, and as Alastair lowers his snout to my mouth, I understand what he needs, loud and clear.

I press my lips against him, and his tongue lashes outward to lick the seam of my lips. I open my mouth for him, and he wastes no time in driving it straight into my mouth. It's larger and wetter in this form, slippery, and he takes me by surprise when he rolls it around in my mouth as though to taste every part of it before diving straight down my throat. My back arches at the intrusion as his tongue slithers and slides down my throat, his jaws open around my cheeks to allow him complete access. I choke on the muscle, but it doesn't feel *wrong*. There is pleasure here, and once I relax in his embrace and allow him to have all of me, he feels it, and he growls in delight again.

His tail loosens and slithers around my body while his claws snap the buckles and buttons of my leathers, and when the cool air of the cavern hits my bare skin, I shiver as my nipples pebble. He presses his body against mine, his chest practically purring by this point, and he shifts his tongue inside my mouth as he positions his hands to cup my breasts. I release a harsh breath through my nose, and he kneads them almost painfully, and when he pinches my nipples, I bite his tongue and clench my thighs together.

He snarls, ripping his tongue out of my mouth while scraping it along my fangs in the process, and the taste of him explodes on my tongue and makes me moan in content. Alastair cocks his head at the sound, and I whimper pathetically when I feel the tip of his tail slither up my leg and settle between my thighs. He lowers his head again, leaning over my body to press his snout between my legs, and he inhales so deeply I'm sure he might pass out. He groans, then tears the remaining leathers off my thighs with his teeth and claws before sinking his snout into the folds of my bare heat. His wet nose trails through my lower lips, sniffing and huffing on the sensitive flesh there as though to get high off my scent, and pleasure races throughout my body, making me shiver again.

I whisper his name like a prayer, and his tongue slides outward and laps at my core. He licks me everywhere. Flat and thick and wet right over my clit, through my slit, and then down to my ass where he takes extra care to learn what makes me squirm and pant the most before slowly lapping upward once more. His claws dig into my hips as he pulls my lower half upward and therefore closer to his face and that damned invasive, wicked tongue. Which, of course, proceeds to dive straight into my entrance once he deems it safe to do so.

The thickness of it provides an incredible pressure that is similar to his and his brothers' cocks, but the sensation and texture is an all-new experience. The friction is fucking marvelous, and he flicks it, twirls, twists, and slides it against my inner walls as though he wants to taste the origins of my climaxes and imprint on me from the inside, claim me in ways he's never been able to before.

It curls and rolls deep inside of me, warm and slippery, licking places that have never been touched, and rocks bite into my palms as I clutch the ground for support. One of his hands lowers to stroke the sensitive and overstimulated bundle of nerves at the apex of my thighs, and I choke on a sound, either a whimper or a curse, I'm not sure, and the beast purrs again. His sharp thumb rubs over my clit, and my climax rises and crashes into me in a rocking, dizzying manner. Alastair growls, clutching me closer as he devours and sucks the arousal right out of me, and I slump back against the dirt as my chest heaves. My breasts are swollen and heavy, and I'm just short of begging him to touch them. To roll that tongue over my nipples as though to milk them, and *fuck me,* the thought just makes me wetter.

Slowly, he pulls his tongue out of me, and I whine quietly at the loss of him. He licks his chops in satisfaction, silver eyes flashing with feral need, and before I know it, I'm flipped around onto all fours. My hands and knees dig into the harsh ground, and one hand wraps around my waist while the other palms my ass. He runs a finger up and down my soaking core, prodding my entrance before adding another claw, and I moan a little when he removes his hand and something much larger prods at my folds. My focus shifts, and I glance back over my shoulder to spot the monster cock that reveals itself from the safety of the furs and skin around his groin. It's black and veiny, not to mention fucking *massive*, and my body shivers in anticipation of taking something that large.

He catches my eye, then growls and grasps the nape of my neck to turn my head forward once more. Claws grasp my jaw from behind, and he rubs the swollen head of his length through my folds, coating it in my arousal before sliding inside. I gasp at the stretch, my mouth flying open as I flex against the intrusion, and he snarls and snaps his hips forward, sinking all the way to the hilt in one fluid motion. It makes a wet, squelching sound, and my entire body heats when I feel his balls slap against my clit.

The fingers grasping my jaw slide inside my mouth, and I suck on his claws as he starts thrusting. He leans over me, slapping his other hand against the ground for balance as his chest brushes against my back as he moves, and his tail rises in front of my face to take the place of his fingers. It slides inside my mouth and over my tongue, the scales surprisingly soft, and I choke again as it thrusts against the back of my throat as his cock pounds me from behind. He snarls deeply, both hands braced beside me as he rotates his hips and hits the end of me with each snap of his hips.

His cock strokes my inner walls, and I feel another climax fast approaching. I clench around him, and he roars and shakes the cave, tossing his head and body backward as he clutches my hips and holds me on his cock. I cry, arms giving out as my climax crashes into me, and my inner walls flutter and start milking him just as his cum shoots into my heat. All of him twitches and convulses, and his cock swells deep inside as I shiver. His tail slips from my mouth, and I gasp and breathe in great mouthfuls of air to fill my lungs. His climax seems never-ending, and warm ribbons of his seed coat my insides to the point that I think my belly might start to swell. Once he finishes, he flips me onto my back once more, and my hands fly forward to catch his horns just as he dives his tongue back into my entrance despite his cum leaking out of me.

He laps at our mixed arousals and breathes in our tangled, tainted scents, and my vision blurs when his tongue strokes my overstimulated clit and inner walls. He groans deeply at our joined taste, claws flexed on my thighs to keep them open despite my weak protests, and when he sucks a slow, third climax out of me, I promptly pass out.

CHAPTER TWENTY
RHESAMYRE

Hot skin is pressed against my own, and as I slowly rouse to take inventory of myself, I register that I'm still naked and *sticky*. I inhale deeply, and his scent envelops me, nearly suffocating me as relief floods my system. What feels like *human* arms tighten on my body, and he nuzzles his face into the nape of my neck and my hair.

"She awake?" someone asks quietly.

"Just about," snarls another. "Though Alastair still has a good grip on her. Possessive bastard."

The chest I lean against rumbles with a growl, and I hum when the pleasant vibration warms me up. His arms flex, and someone else chuckles.

"Seems like she's fine with that," muses the original voice.

A breathy exhale flutters the few loose tendrils of my hair, and he presses a kiss against my temple. "Good morning, love," he husks, his voice low and full of gravel.

Alastair?

He's with you, answers Atlas, and while I didn't mean for him to hear me, I'm glad he did. *We're all with you, and he's okay. We're okay.*

I open my eyes, blinking away the sleep from them as I focus on Atlas and Atticus first. They sit across from me on the ground of the cavern, and Atlas offers me a gentle smile while Atticus scowls, but his gaze isn't locked on me; it's locked on the one behind me, the one that holds me instead of him.

The tears come so fast I can't stop them, and I shift to look up at Alastair. He's human again, handsome as ever, with longer hair and a thicker beard, but his silver gaze is clear. His *faith* tattoo is stark on his tanned skin, and the rest of his ink is on full display, too. He lifts a hand to cup my cheek, and when he smiles so gently and beautifully, I fucking lose it. I leap forward, wrapping my arms around his neck with my legs around his waist despite our nudity, and I bury my face into his neck as I sob.

Alastair nuzzles me as he holds me captive in his embrace, and he coos and shushes me gently.

"I'm here, my love," he avows. "I'm right here with you."

I can't stop crying, and I shake against him, sobbing uncontrollably.

I need all of you, I tell Atlas. *Right fucking now. I just need to feel you.*

He doesn't waste any time, and I hear him and Atticus shuffle around before I feel the heat of their bodies closing in. I inhale deeply, filling my lungs with all three of their scents, and the four of us pile in close and make skin-to-skin contact. I lean back from Alastair and cup his cheeks, pressing into Atticus's chest in the process, but I know the youngest deity doesn't mind. Atlas presses his forehead against the side of my head, and Alastair's eyes shine in the corners where tears threaten to fall.

He looks at all three of us, and something in his resolve fucking shatters at the sight.

"You're as beautiful as ever, love," he whispers. "I dreamt of you." He makes eye contact with his brothers. "All of you."

I sniffle and offer him a pathetic smile, then glance at his artwork. "I know."

"Despite losing your humanity," drawls Atticus quietly, "it seems like you at least had enough sense not to kill her. So thanks for that."

Alastair winces, and I smack Atticus on the arm. In retaliation, his hand wraps around my throat, but he doesn't squeeze. It merely serves as a warning and a promise.

"Be nice," I snarl.

"I *am* being *nice*," he retorts, flexing the hand on my throat once before stroking my pulse points gently.

I huff, rolling my eyes, and Atlas wipes my tears away. "How did you know to come when you did?" I ask.

Atticus snorts, so I smack him again.

"We could . . ." Atlas purses his lips. "*Feel* what was going on."

I blink. "Through our bonds?"

"*Yes*," snarls Atticus. "I could feel you coming on his cock. And while it was hot, it was obnoxious."

"Because it wasn't your cock?" drawls Alastair with a smirk.

Atticus growls.

"And you weren't exactly quiet at times," adds Atlas, ignoring his brothers. "You yelled some pretty explicit but humorous things down the bond."

"Fuck." I look at Alastair. "I know better than to ask if you were in control, but do you remember any of it?"

He studies me. "What would you prefer my answer to be?"

"The truth."

"I remember all of it."

"*Fan-fucking-tastic.*"

He chuckles, then leans forward and kisses my forehead.

"I love you," he husks again. "*So goddamned much*, Rhesa."

I peck my lips against his. "I missed you." I glance around. "All of you."

Atticus loosens his hand, lowering it to clutch my middle. "I can't wait to get you home. You're not going to be able to walk for days. I hope you know that. I'm going to thoroughly fuck you, pamper you, and then fuck you some more."

I laugh, and all three males beam at me. Their smiles are so honest and gentle, and my heart nearly melts despite our impending doom.

"We have to *get* home before that can happen," I quip softly.

Alastair sighs. "I'm afraid I won't be much help in that regard."

Atlas places his hand on his older brother's shoulder and squeezes. "Fret not, brother. Luckily, one of us was able to do something productive around here."

Alastair huffs a humorless laugh. "Thanks, little brother."

"We know where the altar is located," drawls Atticus. "But we have yet to locate whatever is akin to the Falls of Man around here." He furrows his brows, then makes eye contact with me. "Where's your bloodhound?"

"The spell probably dissolved since it was no longer in use," I say, looking around for a dagger. "I'll have to make another."

My leathers and weapons are scattered every which way; I guess it's a good thing I handed the mirror off to Atlas when I did, for Grief would have surely smashed the fucker, and that would have been yet another problem on our plate of never-ending shit we have to deal with.

I reach for one of Atlas's daggers, and he swiftly wraps his hand around my wrist faster than my eyes can track him.

It's a rarer phenomenon compared to his brothers, but Atlas is no less a warrior and fucking *nightmare* to behold when pissed off.

He grabs the dagger from me, and I let him. "You're done fucking cutting yourself for our sakes," he drawls lowly, a warning if I've ever heard one. "And we have a bigger problem."

"We always do," Atticus muses cryptically.

Atlas rolls his eyes, exhaling very slowly. "We still need to figure out how to destroy the altar itself. Without a means of sacrifice to be rid of Lucifer himself, we're not going anywhere fast."

The males fall silent, and I chew on my bottom lip.

"The sphere," says Atticus quietly, and we look at him. He meets our gazes. "We sacrifice this entire fucking sphere in exchange for the altar's destruction."

Atlas raises his brows, and Alastair looks at me as though I might have a better idea.

"Is that even possible?" he asks.

I lift my shoulders. "To be honest, I have no idea. I don't even know of a spell powerful enough to accomplish such a feat. Besides, if we sacrifice this sphere while we're still *in it* . . ." I trail off.

Atticus hums. "Then I suppose we'll just have to toss you through the passageway and ensure you're far away from here when everything implodes."

"Fat chance in Hell," I snarl.

"I'm joking."

"That wasn't funny, Atticus!"

"And you sure as shit weren't joking," drawls Alastair, brows furrowed. He looks at me again. "Though he does have a good point."

I slowly look at the eldest deity. "Try it, and I'll castrate all three of you."

Atlas lifts his hands in confusion. "What the fuck did I do?"

"You're complacent!" I snap.

He opens his mouth to argue, then thinks better of it and bows his head.

I growl under my breath, then unravel myself from their tangled limbs and stand up in search of whatever remains of my clothes. I could just summon more with a Wardrobe Spell, but I need a moment to breathe and think. Stars know I adore them, and would commit great atrocities in the name of that love, but *fucking hell,* they're such overbearing mother hens. I swear, they're *worse* than Astraeus.

I pause, a dagger poised in my hand as I straighten and turn to face them. The memories of my time with Astraeus are mostly fuzzy nowadays, but some things stand out more than others if I can recall them in the correct light.

They halt their bickering where they had been listing off various sacrificial spells, both of our known spheres and plenty further across the stars, and they furrow their brows as they study me. Their gazes are lustful and appreciative, as well as inquisitive.

"When Astraeus and Myra traversed the spheres after Lucifer's first tour in our spheres, they visited numerous planes in search of peace, luxury, pleasure, and problems they could help solve in their intermediate boredom. One of these spherical systems was suffering from a mass plague that was ripping through their spheres, leaving nothing but carnage and wastelands behind. It was the type of spell that eventually developed sentient habits and devoured all it could on its own accord, no longer leashed to the witch that created it when she was wronged.

"Her goal was to bring misfortune to the village that cursed her existence, and drought, sickness, and barren harvests arrived *before* the beast did. These misfortunes served as an omen, and when it arrived, no one was fast enough. There was nowhere to run because the spell devoured *everything*. Entire *spheres* winked out of existence because this force was that powerful, and it devoured them whole. And then, of course, it became too powerful and *hungry*, so it started laying waste to the neighboring spheres that were innocent. Taking on a shadowy form they called *Ragnarök*.

"The son there, Despereaux, had heard of Astraeus's and my deeds, so he sought our help to stop Ragnarök before it finished off the last of his spheres. We created a version of Lucifer's complex Caged Bird Spell and sought to contain the beast within the dark confines of space, between the stars and neighboring spherical systems. His own plane of existence, where only Astraeus, Despereaux, and I know he still exists."

The males look alarmed and impressed, and Atlas drawls carefully, "So you want to change the runes of the CB Spell again and use it on Lucifer and this sphere instead?"

I purse my lips. "Not exactly. The version of the CB Spell we used implied that the beast is contained, but still alive. It's a force of raw magic, much like the altar, and cannot be killed once it grows this big and powerful. Thankfully, Ragnarök never developed the ability to think cognitively. It is an animal with hefty cravings, but when it devours, it does not retain knowledge. His hunger is never satisfied, and all he wants to do is *eat*. Lucifer, on the other hand, has ulterior motives and bears the means to scheme, bargain, and create. I fear that even if we do something similar to a banishment spell on him and the altar, he will break it in a few centuries, and we'll have to do this shit all over again."

Slowly, Atticus spares me a shit-eating grin. "So instead, you're suggesting we alter the spells concocted to contain Ragnarök and fucking summon the beast to devour this sphere and everything in it."

I incline my head. "But *only this* sphere. We let it have its fill, taking out both Lucifer and the altar, and then we recapture it. Nothing will remain of the Tenth Sphere."

"And how do we plan on ensuring it doesn't get loose?" asks Alastair.

I lift my shoulders. "We do what we do best. We *bargain*."

Alastair shakes his head. "*Rhesa*—"

"Do we have a better option?" I ask softly, looking between them. "I'm open to ideas, but I'm under the impression we don't have any."

Atlas dips his chin. "And how do we get home?"

I grit my teeth. "That's the tricky part that I'm not so sure of." I exhale through my nose slowly. "It could very well be that we don't. We end this here, ensuring we don't release another monster on our spheres in the process of destroying the last."

"You wanna fight fire with fire, love?" inquires Alastair, and he stands up with a grin, a cloak wrapped around his waist.

He approaches me, and I tip my head back to keep eye contact with him. He grasps my cheeks, then kisses me deeply. His human tongue feels strange in my mouth after feeling his monstrous tongue and tail, but I won't lie and say I'm not relieved he's back to normal.

I won't lie and say I don't miss that monstrous tongue, though, either.

Alastair pulls away, eyes boring into mine, and I smile at him.

"I'm with you," he husks.

I nod. "I know you are." I look at his brothers, and they're already drawing closer. "I know you both are, too."

Atticus grins. "Always, sweet spice."

I look at Atlas, and he offers me the gentlest smile of all three of them. "You don't need me to tell you," he says aloud. *Because you already know*, he finishes through our bond.

I do, I reply in the same manner. Then I take another steeling breath, setting my shoulders at the same time. "Then lets go summon a fucking monster."

CHAPTER TWENTY ONE
RHESAMYRE

I step forward, and the strange, starry ground beneath my feet ripples with the action. This space almost reminds me of the Hollow, since stars blink and spherical systems sit amongst clusters of colors and stars to create galaxies, but it's colder here. My breath fogs up in front of my face, swirling and shimmering oddly before curling into the air to disappear. If I didn't know any better, I would say it's almost *sentient* here. I may not be speaking, but the space seeks to devour my breath and secrets all the same.

It is a cheap price to pay to walk amongst stardust, and my body is nearly translucent and silver in color, shimmering with holy light that I have not wielded in thousands of centuries.

"You're as reckless as ever, little love."

I grin, then slow my pace as the stars gleam and flicker, glowing brighter to approach me while morphing into Astraeus.

"Walking the path of a son," he continues, crossing his arms as he smirks at me. He looks like Atticus when he does that. Cocky and so sure of himself. Arrogance is an assassin, but fuck me if he isn't hot.

I fold my arms and tilt my head at him. "Do you think Despereaux will mind if I borrow our *pet*?"

Astraeus narrows his eyes playfully. "So long as you keep him *leashed*, it shouldn't be an issue. But therein lies the problem."

"Keeping him leashed," I muse, bobbing my head. "Is the beast capable of bargaining?"

"If he were, he wouldn't be chained here. His inability to communicate works in our favor. He isn't a creature of natural occurrence. He lacks my father's touch."

"Which I suppose is a blessing in disguise, but I've never been good at counting my lucky stars. So, how would you advise I keep him collared?"

"When we created this space, we did so with the intention of never letting Ragnarök see the light of the spheres again. This pocket of a plane is riddled with our magic and sigils, as well as our blood runes. Our scents, if you will, as well as the imprint we leave on the stars when we walk amongst them. He has been shackled here for an eternity, surrounded by the scents of stars. Of *you*."

"Thus, I am no stranger. But does he remember I am the one who put him here?"

"That part remains elusive to me, for after rampaging in the cage for centuries, he eventually sought to slumber."

"Dreamless?"

Astraeus cocks his head. "I'm not sure of that, either."

The plan forms instantaneously, and I scheme. "How much time do you have left here?"

"Not long."

"Do you have enough time to contact the Lord of Dreams back home? Draven? Can you connect us so we can communicate? Possibly even bring him here?"

Astraeus blinks at my rapid-fire questions. "It's risky. If Yonder catches wind of the ripple in space, she'll throw a tantrum and release Ragnarök just to teach us a lesson, trapping us here in the meantime so we're forced to *watch*."

I furrow my brows. "Atticus mentioned when you spoke that your brothers and Evergreen had stepped in to intercept her."

"They have, but I do not wish to push our luck on the matter."

I nod. "I hear you. We'll be quick."

He sighs, grinning a little. "You're lucky I love you."

I laugh. "Yes, I am. At least I can count you as a lucky star, Astraeus."

He winks like Alastair, then bursts into the Peri to travel between the spheres in search of Draven. In the meantime, I keep walking amongst the stars, admiring the beauty here despite the darkness overshadowing us. But this plane is vibrant and violet, with yellow and white stars that shine within clusters of various blues, ambers, purples, and pinks, all scattered across an obsidian canvas. I would be blind not to find beauty here. There is rarely much of it elsewhere.

But even so, a cage is a cage.

The stars ripple again, and Astraeus materializes ahead of me, with Draven in tow. He glances around with wide, violet eyes, but his body glows as though he were made for a plane of stars such as this one. His white hair has burst from its braid and floats around him in silver light, and his monochrome tattoos of spherical systems and baku are tinged with glitter and stardust, glowing and shifting as though the ink is alive on his skin. Then, once he finishes his sweep of the space, he spots me, and a grin splits his handsome face.

He starts toward me, and I meet him in the middle.

"Fuck me if you aren't a pretty sight to behold," he muses, pulling me in for a hug.

I laugh, returning his hug.

"You're all right?" he asks, placing his hands on my shoulders. "We're not dead, right?"

"Not yet."

"And the deities?"

"Safe and awaiting my orders."

He chuckles. "Aren't we all?"

I roll my eyes, sneaking a glance at Astraeus when I see him bob his head out of my peripheral vision.

I roll my eyes even *harder*. "I need your help again, old friend," I prompt.

"Name it, my queen," replies the Sandman. "Whatever you need, it's yours."

I snicker. "Well, as much as I appreciate the sentiment, let's see what we're dealing with first."

He furrows his brows, and I interlock my arm with his and Astraeus's as we continue through the stars.

"I need you to create a dream," I explain. "One that is similar to the one you made for me when I was a wolf, except this one doesn't end in a nightmare."

"Okay, but may I ask what sort of creature we're dealing with?"

I jerk my chin forward. "*That.*"

Draven halts, and I unlink my elbow from his and stand with Astraeus as we take in the massive, slumbering form of Ragnarök in his truest form. He's like a silhouette or mirror of the very galaxies around us. Shadowy, obsidian, violet, and sprinkled with starlight, he bears a striking resemblance to our wyverns. However, he's much larger and riddled with more spikes and horns, as well as equipped with four legs and separate wings.

Despereaux had called him a *dragon*.

"What the actual *fuck*, Rhesamyre?" inquires Draven, gaping at me. He points at the slumbering beast of chaos. "What is that?"

I grin. "My new pet. So, can you help me ensure he stays loyal and doesn't *eat* anyone?"

Draven blinks at me, then glances over my head at Astraeus.

"Is she joking?"

"Afraid not," drawls my original mate, and I elbow him in the ribs.

Astraeus grunts, and Draven sighs before observing the dragon once more.

"All right," he deadpans. "What do you have in mind?"

"His name is Ragnarök, and the origins of his creation will have to be a story for another time. But essentially, he caused a lot of harm, so we imprisoned him here. When he wakes up, I'm not sure how he's going to react to me. I don't know what he remembers or if he's even self-aware, but I need him leashed. He's too feral and dangerous to be left free in the spheres, but I want him to look at me positively. Not as a potential meal."

"Okay, so you wish to be his master?"

"Well, *actually*, I was thinking that if it's possible, I would like to be his *mother*."

Astraeus whips his head down to look at me, but I keep my gaze solely trained on Draven.

Draven sighs, chuckling. "Figures, but in the manner of gods and sons, I don't see much of a difference between masters and mothers."

"I am no god, Draven."

"Aren't you, though?"

I remain silent, unwilling to dignify that with a response. Draven gets the gist, then inclines his head and prowls toward the sleeping dragon. On his way, he reaches upward and plucks a star from the sky, and I furrow my brows at the sheer ease of such an action that I feel should be taboo. And maybe it is, but I suppose we don't have much of a choice at the moment.

"I had thought you would need more ingredients?" I ask him.

Draven crushes the star in his palm, then blows the dust right into the dragon's nostril, which is larger than Draven. It's a fucking tunnel.

"When we made your concoction, it was mixed with Wicker's properties. Thus, I used more ingredients to balance the spell. Here, however, all that is needed is stardust."

I hum, intrigued, and Astraeus and I watch on from afar with crossed arms and similar stances.

"Once I take him back, I fear I will not be able to return again for a little while," he says softly.

I incline my head. "I had a feeling, but thank you for coming this far."

He curls a finger under my chin, tilting my head back, and I meet his silver gaze.

"I will love you through them," he promises, cupping my cheek.

I nuzzle his palm before kissing it. "I will love you through them," I repeat.

The stars rattle as the space roars, and Draven slowly backs away as the mighty eye of Ragnarök opens to reveal a void of white starlight. The dragon shifts and stretches, and I grin when it bares its teeth at us.

. . . .

I open my eyes, and a foreign landscape is there to greet me. My legs are crisscrossed, my hands braced against my knees, and Purgatory continues to thrive ahead of me while I sit atop the knoll.

A tattooed hand extends in front of me, and I grasp it tightly. Alastair hauls me onto my booted feet, and I stand between him and his brothers to survey the land just as the sky is *ripped* open by a giant, cosmic claw. It's as though the threads and stitching that tie this sphere together are snapped and torn apart, and Ragnarök roars into the sphere like a child would scream into a broken snow globe.

Atticus whistles. "You never cease to amaze me, sweet spice."

I smirk, my gaze trained on the shadowy dragon kissed by starlight as he rips his way into the sphere, devouring all he can in the process. He *eats* the sky, revealing the darkness and stars above us that belong to the starlit spaces between spheres. Teeth and claws gleam as he clambers his way inside, and when he lands, the entire sphere rumbles. Distant animals caw and scatter, drawing the dragon's attention, and he unhinges his jaw and inhales deeply before breathing a mouthful of blue flames across the wasteland and forest. His throat lights up with the action, and his entire scaled body ripples as he flares his wings and thrashes the clubbed end of his tail, which is littered with spikes and barbs.

"We don't have much time before we're caught in the crossfire," I tell the deities. "This sphere is about to fall apart, so let's ensure the altar and Lucifer go with it."

The males nod, and then we're stepping through Atlas's conveyance, which deposits us at the location of the altar. I take pause when I see it in the flesh for the first time, for not only is it an archway of grand proportions, but it's also a *well*. It's made of stone, the color of dried blood, and the five archways crisscross one another, leaving the gaping hole in the center of the pattern. It bubbles like boiling water, but it looks more like a tar pit than anything holy or otherwise. Behind us, Ragnarök carries on, and around us, the ground cracks and splits to reveal massive trenches of sputtering magma and tar. Bodies old and new drop into those pits, and the wolf-rats and other monsters flee in a vain attempt to get away from the chaos they so often thrive in.

"Give him to me," I order, holding out my open palm to Atlas.

He hands over the Mirror of Candor, and I unravel the black cloth to reveal the head of Lucifer. He snarls and bares his cracked, rotten teeth at me, then bangs his forehead against the glass in outrage. I hold up the mirror away from me, allowing him to see the destruction and chaos I have brought forth upon his sphere.

"What have you done?" he snarls.

I turn the mirror around again. "What was necessary."

"You'll kill us all!"

I shake my head. "No. just you."

I hand the mirror to Alastair, then twirl and place my index finger and thumb in my mouth to whistle loudly across the wasteland. Ragnarök swivels his massive head around, and within a few short leaps, he's before me and hunkering down to be at better eye level with me. I smile, approaching him to hug what I can reach of his nose. He huffs gently, scenting me, and I rub his scales.

"Be calm, my child," I coo in Old Latin. *"We'll go home soon. I just need you to do one more thing for me."*

I turn again, a fucking dragon at my back as I order, "Drop him in the well."

Alastair smirks, then grins pointedly at Lucifer before prowling forward to drop the entirety of the mirror into the boiling substance.

"I hope you suffer in the meantime, fucker," growls Alastair.

Lucifer screeches and curses at us the whole way down, and the well flashes with raw magic as the mirror melts into nothingness, taking Lucifer with it. I look at my dragon, stroking his scales once more.

"Devour it all," I tell him.

Ragnarök shifts and rears his head back, and the deities come closer to stand with me as the dragon breathes sparkling blue fire on the altar. Trapped souls and raw magic screech in retaliation as the stone melts, and Ragnarok roars before clamping his jaws around whatever he can to swallow it all whole. His body shifts above us, protecting the four of us from whatever flies outward as he eats, and I grasp Atlas's and Atticus's hands while leaning back into Alastair's chest.

"We're going home," I avow, and they look at me. "We're not dying here. *We're going home.*"

"How?" asks Atlas, seemingly stunned as he stares at me as though I might be lying.

I spare him another smirk. "Ragnarök has the ability to shift through stars and space. We're going to jump spheres and enter our system through the Hollow."

Alastair kisses the top of my head between my horns. "Ingenious as always, my love."

I smile, and Atticus kisses my temple and runs his thumb over my knuckles as we stand within Ragnarök's protections, watching the chaos continue to unfold. The dragon devours *everything*; the forests burn, the wastelands are torn to shreds, the knolls and caves are trampled and destroyed, and the sky is eaten until nothing but empty space remains. Ragnarök releases a mighty roar in satisfaction, his wings flaring as he glows and grows bigger with all he has eaten here today. I stroke the underbelly of his scales, and he curls his head underneath himself to look at me.

"You ready to take us home, handsome boy?"

The growl he releases sounds more like a purr, and I smile at the overgrown puppy riddled with scales and teeth. He turns around, mindful not to crush us, then lowers himself until he's lying down again. I kiss the tip of his nose, and his tail swishes as though he's wagging it, and the very tip of his tongue pops out to lick me. I laugh, then flex my back and pulse my magic to summon my wings. His eyes flash at the sight of them, and he watches me flap upward and settle on his back.

Alastair, Atlas, and Atticus are quick to follow suit, and we grasp whatever spikes we can find as Ragnarök lifts up and leaps forward. His mighty wings flap on either side of us, destroying the remaining particles of the sphere even more as he kicks up dust and raw magic. The entire sphere burns, and as we fly further away, into the darkness and stars, it simmers before imploding completely.

I shield my eyes from the blinding light, and when I open them again, nothing but scattered stardust and glitter remains. The raw magic that bound that sphere together now floats between the rest of the spheres, and I plan on leaving it there.

Facing forward once more, I grip Ragnarök's spikes even harder when he dives straight down. The magic burns my skin right through my leathers, and Ragnarök roars as he tears through the protective runes and shields that keep foreign entities out of the Hollow.

It happens in a blink, and then we're darting upward through the Hollow and surrounding castles that once belonged to the Wise Men. I feel the familiar magics and sunshine of this sphere caress my skin, and I let go of Ragnarök's scales with closed eyes. I free-fall, the warm wind like a kiss on my cheeks, and though I could open my wings and fly, I don't bother.

Gentle arms catch me when I get closer to the ground, and I open my eyes to find the stern, silver gaze of Alastair.

"I could have stopped myself," I admonish, crossing my arms while he carries me.

He chuckles. "I have no doubts about that, love. I just wanted an excuse to carry you."

I laugh, and we touch down on one of the larger hills that overlook the castles. Atlas and Atticus are quick to arrive on either side of us, and I watch in awe as Ragnarök twirls and flips through the sky like a young wyvern learning to fly. He's a magnificent, regal creature, and above all, *dangerous*, but I suppose that only makes him all the more beautiful. To me, at least, for I know others may not think so, but what many will never know is that he saved us, and I will reward him with as much freedom as I can.

"What are you going to do with him?" Atticus inquires.

I lift my shoulders. "Let him live here. He'll be able to take nutrients from the Hollow, like drinking out of a puddle, and I trust he'll stick around and behave."

"You're not worried he'll devour this sphere like he did Purgatory?" asks Atlas.

I shake my head. "As far as he's concerned, the spheres that remain are his *home*. What he remembers may not be the truth of how and why he was created, but all he understands now is that this place and our remaining living spheres smell like *me*. He trusts me, and he's quickly growing on me, too. So he'll stay for as long as he can." I meet the eyes of all three deities. "As long as I wear the crowns of these spheres, then Ragnarök shall remain under my control, too."

Atticus smirks. "The return of a queen, and the arrival of a conqueror," he muses. He inclines his head. "You're fucking gorgeous, sweet spice."

I tug him closer by the belt loops of his leathers, and he growls as I cheese at him before kissing him playfully.

"You're not too shabby yourself," I tease, and I hug him, my head turned sideways on his chest so I can face Atlas and Alastair. "Let's go home."

CHAPTER TWENTY TWO
RHESAMYRE

I inhale sharply, the nightmare of Bael's whip swiftly receding, and I sigh and burrow my face into the white fur of Embrace as he acts as the little spoon for me, and I serve as the little spoon for Atticus at my back. His arms tighten around my middle, but otherwise, he doesn't stir, and I sit up a little to survey the dim room barely lit by the rising sun. Alastair sleeps on Embrace's other side, allowing the wolf to sleep on him despite his attempts at implementing a *no dogs on the bed rule.*

I threatened to turn into a wolf again, and he swiftly retracted his statement. Meanwhile, Atticus, in all his wisdom, threatened to leave me outside if I dared to shift.

I threatened to throw him outside anyway.

Atlas sleeps near the cracked balcony doors on a very comfortable-looking chair, and all I hear is the collective snoring of my mates sleeping peacefully. Exhausted and sexually satisfied, they crashed in here after a long day of recounting affairs to the Hellion court and dealing with the final aftermath of Lucifer. A few months had already passed by the time we made it back, and thankfully, nearly everything had been set right again.

Althea's coronation is tomorrow.

So with that knowledge, my mates and I locked ourselves in my rooms and pampered one another for hours on end, with thorough baths and long soaks in scented water. I made my rounds on my knees, worshiping them and loving them by wrapping my hands and mouth around their cocks. I've swallowed and taken so much of their cum in the past few hours, I'm surprised my belly hasn't fucking swelled, but even now, despite the thorough cleaning and worshiping of my own cunt afterwards—in which they practically used their tongues to clean every inch of me—I can still feel their collective seed dripping out of me.

I nearly scowl in irritation since my thighs stick together, and I shift and crawl away from Atticus despite his sleepy growl of protest.

Cute.

But I don't want my deities right at this particular moment.

I want my dog. And my horse.

Maybe my newfound dragon, too.

"*Embrace*," I whisper-shout, and he snorts mid-snore and sits up to face me with sleepy eyes.

I wave him over, and he steps on Alastair's chest and jumps off the bed. I wince for Alastair's sake when he grunts in his sleep before rolling over, and I shuffle into my closet and slip on one of my simpler gowns before padding out of the room barefoot with a wolf on my heels.

We meander toward the stables, and I slide the doors open as quietly as I can before wandering toward Orpheus. The lieutenants managed to grab him along with their own steeds when they fled to my buried manor in the West, and according to them, Orpheus was quite despondent and just about killed Dexter when he went to feed my beast of a hell-horse.

"Orpheus," I call softly at the front of the stall, and he spins around from where he had been sleeping upright in the corner, facing away from me.

He nickers at me, his nostrils flaring as he scents me and rubs his forehead against my chest, and I rub his neck in comfort before opening the stall door and slipping inside to hug him properly. He curls his neck to rub his jaw on my back as I hug his neck and shoulders, and I squeeze my eyes shut as I grasp him like a lifeline.

I let my tears slip when I found my deities, and I let the waterworks show when my uncles and brothers embraced me when we got back, too. But even those little sobs were nothing more than a sniffle and a tear or two.

I fucking *bawl* against Orpheus, and he soaks it all up and stands steady to let me lean against him. In a moment, he shifts and goes to his knees to lie down, and I go with him and curl up against his legs and lean over his back to keep crying. Embrace whines and rests his chin on my shoulder, and I let him lick my tears away as I scream in silence.

I've cried a lot throughout my life, but never like this. Never as violent due to a rush of overwhelming emotions that feel like fear, relief, anger, and above all, worry that this isn't real. That somehow or for some reason, it's all an illusion. A spell, and none of what happened *did*.

But it is real. We did win.

So I cry out of triumph. I cry because I'm overwhelmed with what I remember and what happened to all of us, not just me. I cry because I finally have the freedom to.

Orpheus takes it all, and so does Embrace. And while the wolf's and my relationship is a newer one, there's an unwavering loyalty settled between us as though we've known each other for years.

And then there's Orpheus, the mount I've had since I was a little girl. Sam gifted him to me when he was just a young, fresh colt, and I often loved running around in the fields with him on foot before I learned to ride him.

I sniffle, my cries quieting down, and I lean back to stroke his face.

"Care for a short ride, handsome?" I ask.

I stand back up, with Embrace next to me, and Orpheus does the same. We wander out of his stall, and without any tack, I swing up onto his back and jog out of the palace yards to explore the quiet capital that has yet to completely wake up with the sun. Embrace trots along beside us, and we wander and walk between dark streets without a true destination. I'm happy to find that, for the most part, all the old taverns and shops have recovered from the battle with Lucifer. The population of the spheres has impressively lessened, but I have no doubts that in a few short years, everyone will have recovered and flourished, and the spheres will be densely populated once more.

Hellion flora blooms along the walls, and string lights are tied between the buildings of downtown Heart, and I inhale the scents of roses and wisteria that waft between the smells of freshly baked bread and spices and herbs.

Orpheus walks along the quiet streets, the only sound that of his hooves *clip-clopping* on the cobblestone or the insistent sniffing of Embrace as he explores the closed vendors that dot the wide streets.

I tip my head back to watch the sky change colors as the sun rises, and the obsidian canvas sprinkled with a thick layer of stardust and glitter begins to morph into that of lilacs, navy, and ambers as the sun breaches the horizon past the mountains.

I inhale, feeling whole, and I allow Orpheus to take me back to the palace once more.

....

Breakfast is just as chaotic and rambunctious as usual, and I sip on my glass of blood at the center of the table, admiring my family and laughing with them as we all fall back into a sense of normalcy and peace. Althea, Tally, Trix, and Fern all sit with their respective mates and feed table scraps to their wolves when they think their males are not looking, and I smirk behind my chalice when Damian catches Fern in the act.

A hand grasps mine under the table, and I glance down just as Atticus slips the Ring of Rubies back onto my right hand.

"I thought I'd lost it for good," I muse softly, admiring the red ring entwined with silver and obsidian and littered with scriptures.

"Pride found it," Atticus replies softly, and then he reaches into his pocket and pulls out the engagement ring they once gifted me. "Found this one, too."

I purse my lips, then let him take my left hand so he can slip it back into place on my ring finger.

"Thank you," I whisper, and he kisses one ring after another, my hands firmly grasped in his.

"You're welcome, sweet spice." Then he hesitates. "If I may ask, where did you go this morning?"

"I hadn't seen Orpheus since we got back." I shrug. "Went for a ride with him and Embrace."

Atticus chuckles. "Should've known."

I match his gentle smile, then slip my hands out of his and reach for my glass of blood once more. I meet Pride's eyes over the rim, and I nod at him in thanks. He inclines his head and winks at me, a small smile gracing his lips, and *finally*, everything feels like it's supposed to.

. . . .

I sit with Trix underneath the shade of the large oak in the Hellion gardens, the two of us leaning against our hell-horses, Orpheus and Rhombus, as they munch on volcanic coals and those cinnamon apple treats Althea loves to bake for them. Embrace lies on my lap in a similar manner to how Barter lies on the witch's legs, and I smile gently as I watch Tally play fetch with Dolor from the back of her hell-horse, Hesperia.

"Those three rarely let you out of their sight nowadays," muses Trix, and I glance at her before following her line of sight up to the balcony, where my deities pretend to drink and play cards. She shrugs, glancing at me. "Though, considering what's happened, I don't think I blame them."

I mimic her shrug, humming as I pet Embrace, my gaze wandering to the skies above us where Fern flies with her rhayven, Branwen, and Thea flies alongside her on the wyvern, Edana. Both of their dire wolves, Veto and Vex, sit in the middle of the gardens with their heads tipped back to watch them.

"Have you set a date for your wedding yet?" I ask Trix, dodging her initial observation regarding the deities and me.

She stares at me for a heartbeat, and then hums, lifting a shoulder as she turns her attention to the lieutenants who play board games, cards, and spar across the lawn in the sunshine.

"To be honest, I think I'd rather elope," she says. "We have to support Thea during her wedding and coronation tomorrow, and that's going to involve a shit-ton of socializing. Plus, Tally says she wants a *huge* wedding, so I think I'll scratch whatever itch I might have to be a proper bride while I'm helping her scheme and decorate. Fern said she wouldn't mind a small gathering, but like me, she just wants it done so we can steal them away from their posts for a little while."

I laugh gently. "I hear you. Well, whatever you choose, you have my support and complete access to the funds affiliated with my crown."

She grins. "Appreciate it, my friend. But thankfully, I think Mal's salary has it covered. You've been quite generous already as far as that's concerned."

"It's the least I can do for all they've done for me." I nudge her shoulder. "That includes you, too."

She looks at me. "I haven't done anything."

I wrap my arm around her. "Before you four, I never had any girlfriends to gossip with. I've been surrounded by males my entire life, both as Myra and as Rhesa. And while Envy, Pride, and Gluttony are plenty skilled in fashion and gossip, they sometimes lack a woman's touch."

She giggles. "Naturally."

I smile at her. "But not only are you my friend, Trix." I jerk my head at Malcolm, where he laughs with Dexter, Damian, Silas, and Gage. "You make him happy. You're his, which makes you a part of what's mine. My family. My court. And finally, I have *sisters*."

Trix's face shifts as she gapes at me, and tears suddenly spring to life in her golden eyes.

"I-I'm honored, Rhesa," she whispers.

"I know you are," I tell her. "What's the point of being queen if I can't make my friends and family happy? If there's anything you ever need, never hesitate to ask. I'll do everything in my power to make it happen."

She smiles and bobs her head. "I know, my queen."

CHAPTER TWENTY THREE
RHESAMYRE

The entirety of the mortal kingdom piles into the capital, Goldfinch, and it *reeks* of *men*. I'll admit, the palace and capital are pretty in a modest, mortal sort of way, but I wouldn't trade my crown or throne for this one, even if my life depended on it. It's too bright here, for starters, and there are too many whites and golds and nosy aristocrats that smell of fear. I think I'd rather gouge my eyes out than rub elbows with them for more than a day.

I'm only here for one reason: to watch Althea ascend that dais with Gage on her arm and claim their places on the velvet thrones wearing crowns of gold.

"And to think," mutters Alastair, leaning down close to me to ensure the wrong ears don't hear us, "last time you and I were here, we were bleeding out and murdering the late royals."

"Technically, *I* didn't murder anyone." I furrow my brows. "At least, I don't think I did."

He chuckles, then straightens once more and resets his scowl. Atticus and Atlas stand on my other side, and all three deities are dressed to the nines and armed to the teeth in obsidian leathers and fine threads. I stand amongst them and the rest of the well-dressed Hellion court, archangels, and even the Zodiacs, who have since recovered from being possessed by the Apostles, while Feronia, Bellatrix, and Tallulah all stand with their rightful mates on the other side of my uncles, their wolves quiet and on guard at their feet.

Leadership belonging to the Mortal Suns, Hussars, and the Artemis stand on the other side of the white carpet aisle, closer to the human court, and I feel multiple pairs of eyes on me and the other members of our spheres, especially since the Lords of Exile have decided to grace the mortals with their presence, too. The quartet stands on the other side of Alastair, looking like their namesakes, and while it surprises me that they're here, I suppose I shouldn't be. We're all here to witness the same thing: the web of lies I spun for the sake of our spheres when I wielded the Historian's dagger in the Hollow.

And I regret nothing.

My crown weighs heavily on my head near my horns, and while my dress is more modest than the usual designs I prefer, it is no less luxurious and expensive. My wedding ring sits on my left hand where it belongs, and the Ring of Rubies occupies my right. The rest of the jewels I wear are emeralds, rubies, diamonds, and of course, obsidian, all in ode to my mates and kingdom. Embrace sits at my feet, just as the other wolves do near the girls, and Ragnarök, in all his miniature glory, curls around my shoulders and nuzzles my neck and cheek softly. I managed to spell the massive dragon into a smaller version of himself. Pocket-sized, as Alastair so kindly put it, while Atticus called him *bite-sized.*

Atlas was smart enough to keep his mouth shut, as usual.

A few days have passed since we made it back home, but I've already warned those who are important to me. When all this pomp and circumstance is over, and the spheres are self-sustaining once more, we'll be taking a long vacation somewhere far away from here. I think the four of us have deserved one for a while now, and a honeymoon is well overdue, anyway.

One of the advisors of the human court steps toward the dais, where a servant boy holds a velvet pillow with two crowns, and when the throne room doors open, everyone's attention is directed that way. Vex, Thea's dire wolf, which I gifted her, trots forward with a gold chain collar clasped loosely around his neck, and I smirk at the sight of him striding up the steps of the dais as though *he* is the one being crowned ruler today. Though instead of taking a seat on one of the thrones, he chooses to sit between them, and I turn my eyes back toward the doors just as Gage prowls forward in a gray suit with Althea on his arm.

She's beautiful, dressed in a white gown adorned with silver, obsidian, and golden accents and threads that accentuate her curves in all the right places. The train is long and trails behind her quite impressively, layered with mandalas and floral patterns that look almost more Hellion than human, and my heart swells at the sight of her.

Gage, while he hides it well, looks tense on her arm, and continues to scan the area with his wolfish eyes as though looking for threats or an escape route. He's gotten dressed up for parties and formal occasions before, but even this is a new look for him, one I'm unsure he actually likes. He loves Althea, that much is clear, but I know this is going to be a serious adjustment period for him—for all of us, for that matter.

The pair reaches the crowns, and they kneel before the man who offers them as he goes on about heirs and destiny and responsibilities. To safeguard the kingdom and see to the safety and prosperity of the people, and I'm reminded once again of the oath I once took when I claimed Samael's throne.

Who would've thought that everyone was wrong about me being his bastard because, in actuality, I was his sister.

Fuck, I miss him. Perhaps even more so now because I remember what it was like when he was *just* my big brother . . . him and Apollo. And Adriel . . . and Lilith, too, for that matter. I grieve who they each used to be before the betrayals occurred. Before our hands were forced and we chose other paths over each other.

The man ahead of us finishes his speech, and he places the crowns atop Gage's and Althea's heads before they rise and ascend the dais to claim their thrones. Althea as the mortal queen, with Gage as her king consort, and I almost want to laugh. Who would've thought the day would ever arrive that the street mutt I picked up in Hell and turned into a lieutenant would now wear the crown of a king that belongs to a kingdom riddled with humans?

I grin at the thought and at the sight, and when the room erupts in chants to praise the king and queen, and long may they reign, I'm right there with them, my hand over my heart.

....

I mingle with a glass of wine in hand, often switching from one deity to another as I make my rounds throughout the great hall, weaving between humans who often give me a wide berth. I speak with my uncles and the leaders of the sell-swords, as well as the Zodiacs, who have taken to apologizing profusely for all that has happened. I don't blame them for any of it, and I've made sure they know that, too; however, Taurus is mortified over the whole *horn* comment from a while back. I thought it was fucking hilarious despite the circumstances, but as it turns out, they were aware of everything, but trapped inside their own bodies, unable to speak or break free.

I apologized to them, too. Because I'm sorry none of us noticed in time.

My brothers are a different story, and while Pollux and I are as close as ever, the rest are slow to approach me throughout the night as the coronation party commences through the streets of Goldfinch. In some cases, I seek them out first, making it clear there are no hard feelings, and I don't blame them for anything, so there's nothing to apologize for. We were all tricked and betrayed, and while there are some wounds that might be slower to heal, I have no doubts that they *will* heal. Orion, Nihal, Castor, Alto, and Pollux are all that remain of the archangels, and although the Blade of Zodiacs has been returned to Samael's grave, we're all going to be far more careful moving forward.

Atlas kisses my forehead in farewell, then leaves my side so I can approach the lieutenants and my girls who surround the newlyweds and newly crowned king and queen.

"You look stiff in that suit, brother," teases Silas, wiggling his eyebrows at Gage while keeping Tally interlocked on his elbow, since the ex-genie has a habit of wandering off.

Gage growls, and a few humans nearby flinch and look on in fear. I laugh as I approach the group, especially since Gage now looks like a kicked puppy since he scared his new subjects.

"A little fear in regard to a new monarch is healthy, Gage," I tell him, then shrug a little. "It will take them some time to get used to you, but you'll outlive them all. They'll have no choice *but* to get used to you."

He sighs, dipping his chin. "I suppose you're right."

"I'm always right, wolf."

He laughs, sparing me a side-hug. "I'm gonna miss your daily quips, Rhesa."

I squeeze his waist, then pull away and flick his nose. "This isn't goodbye, Gage. It's just a prolonged *see you at dinner.*"

He chuckles again, grinning. "Yeah, I guess so." He glances up, and I follow his gaze as it falls onto Famine ahead of us, where he talks with the other Horsemen and the assassins. Dexter is by his side, dressed in Hellion leathers and bearing a shiny new rank of lieutenant.

"He's got big shoes to fill," drawls Malcolm, with a lavishly dressed Trix on his side.

Gage shakes his head, then smirks and shoves the demon's shoulder playfully. "I don't wear shoes. Paws, remember?"

And to showcase his point, he lifts a wolfish leg and wiggles his doggy toes. I snort.

Mal rolls his eyes. "You know what I mean, fucker."

Gage laughs. "Yeah. Try not to get him killed too soon."

"No promises, brother," muses Damian, and Fern giggles.

I smile at the group, then move closer to Althea and bump her hip with mine.

"You holding up okay?" I ask her softly. "It's nerve-wracking, I know."

She releases a breathy laugh, sparing me a gentle smile as she dips her chin. "I'm doing okay. I'm just trying to channel my inner Rhesa and play it cool like you."

I snicker. "Truth be told, I'm scared shitless the majority of the time." I jerk my chin at Gage, who's too busy bickering with his brothers to listen to our conversation. "That's why you have him. Lean on each other, communicate, and if you're scared, tell him. I'm certain that if he can't outright *murder* whatever you're afraid of, he'll still do his damn best to ease your worries."

She smiles. "I know." And then that smile fades. "Rhesa, I need to talk to you about something. Somewhere more private, if at all possible."

I tilt my head in question, then link my arm with hers and lead her through the crowd toward an empty hallway. Once we're sure we're alone, Althea leans back against a wall and takes a much-needed breath. I busy myself with observing the murals and portraits that decorate the walls until she's ready, letting her take her time.

"Rhesa, I know my history," she drawls, and I meet her kind gaze. "My parents were humble day traders, not royals. They died a boring death one winter due to sickness, and they're buried outside of Soulton. I have no other living relatives, at least none that I know of, and despite what everyone thinks, I'm no queen. I haven't the first clue of how to rule a kingdom, and while your court has been very accommodating and helpful, I fear I'm still at a loss."

I bow my head, then approach her and grasp her hands in mine.

"You're not a queen because you sit on a golden throne or because you wear the crown, Althea. You're a queen because you will do what is right by the people to ensure they prosper and are kept safe. You will grow into the role, and you will make a few mistakes along the way, but that's okay because you will learn. A woman in leadership is only as powerful as the title she *takes* for herself, and you claim queen, so you will act like nothing less. Don't allow doubt to corrupt what is now yours, Althea. No matter how you came to acquire the crown, it is now yours, and you will wear it well."

She inhales slowly. "You make it sound so eloquent and simple."

"It's everything but, Thea." I squeeze her hands. "You have friends in high places. You have powerful allies who would burn kingdoms for you. You are married and mated to a male who has commanded armies in war, a decorated soldier and hero of Hell, and a great friend of the Hellion court and its queen. In addition, you command not only a dire wolf but a *wyvern*. You are a Hellion wrangler, and while you may be new to the role of *queen*, I have no doubts that when it comes down to doing the right thing, you won't hesitate. You are this kingdom's queen because you are the right person for it. I don't doubt that for a second, so why are you trying to convince yourself otherwise?"

She lifts her shoulders, and tears gleam in her eyes. She releases my hands, then wraps her arms around my neck. I hug her back, melting into her warmth.

"I don't doubt it anymore," she says, then sniffles. "I think I just needed to hear it from someone I love and trust."

I squeeze her harder. "I've always got your back, Thea. Just like you've always had mine." I pull away, hands on her shoulders, so I can meet her eyes. "This kingdom and its people are a gift, Thea. Cherish it. Protect them. And you will be rewarded in ways you never thought possible. It won't always be gems and glory. Sometimes it will be as simple as a smile from a subject you thought for sure was frightened of you, or a child that offers you a flower crown."

She laughs, dabbing at her eyes. "Despite everything that has happened to you, you still manage to cheer others up first."

"Only those I consider a friend or family member. Everyone else can fuck off."

She giggles at that, and I cherish the sound.

"So," she drawls with a smile. "What does the next chapter look like for the queen of Hell?"

I lift my shoulders. "I think we're going to take a little break. Get away for a while."

"You certainly deserve one. Where will you go?"

I purse my lips. "I'm not sure yet . . . but just know, you ever need us, we'll be there."

"I have no doubts about that, Rhesa."

I offer her another smile, then jerk my chin back at the loud entryway that leads into the great hall, where the party still commences. "You better get back in there. Lots of hands to shake and babies to kiss."

She rolls her eyes with a smirk that must be modeled after one of mine. "As you wish, Your Majesty . . . Take care of yourself, Rhesa. I hope you find the peace you're looking for. You deserve it and more. The spheres owe you a great debt."

I shake my head. "Just make sure it doesn't go up in flames in my absence, and we can consider the debt paid."

"Sounds like a bargain, my queen."

Althea lays her hand over her heart, then takes her graceful leave.

I watch her go, then lean back into the shadows. Hands wrap around my waist, and Atticus nuzzles my cheek, being sure to avoid Ragnarök and his razor-like teeth.

"Are you ready to go?" he asks.

I hum, then turn in his embrace and wrap my arms around his neck.

"Let's get out of here," I say.

And I kiss him.

EPILOGUE
ALASTAIR

The starship Atticus created and assembled as a surprise for Rhesa is startlingly adept at pleasing in simple manners. The magic is nearly sentient and thrives off praise and attention, and Rhesa has an abundance of it to give. She loves reading to it, and it loves cooking for her when Atlas isn't. The ship stays warm for her despite the natural chill of the Starfall Sea, and the sails are never without wind nor the bow without a heading.

I'll give you this, brother. You know how to please our girl.

He and Atlas still snooze in luxury across the frigate's open floor plan, Embrace happily cuddling with Atticus on the cushioned floor while Ragnarök sleeps curled up in a little ball on top of Atlas's chest on the bed. I survey the two of them silently from the doorway, unable to look away for a moment.

Rhesa did this. Connected us and brought us back together after centuries apart, and I'll never be able to thank her enough for it.

I'll do my damn best to try though.

I leave my brothers where they are, as we're all still plenty sore and exhausted from taking turns with Rhesa for weeks on end. Stamina has never once been an issue before, but damn, I think that female has successfully milked me dry, a feat I never thought possible, but yet again, she has proven me wrong.

I step out onto the ship's main deck, making my way toward the bow, where Rhesa stands with a fluffy blanket clutched around her body, which I have no doubt is nude under there.

She says nothing as I get closer, and when I brush my bare chest against her back, she leans into me with a contented sigh. I nuzzle her hair, littering kisses across her neck before her breath hitches.

"Alastair, *look*."

I do, and I almost regret not waking my brothers up, for Atticus has spent all his life longing for a sight like this one.

Ahead of us, the mighty cetacean sing and roll through the starry waves, surrounded by luminescent starfish. The celestial whales flip and twirl slowly through the stars, kicking up stardust and the black water of this sea both above and below us. It is a strange magic here, and Rhesa grins at the sight of them. I'll admit they are beautiful, but admiring her in this light is even more rewarding.

While she watches the translucent, shadowed, starlit whales dance with one another and swim alongside the ship amongst schools of glowing bettas and angelfish, I watch as her hellfire eyes glitter with starlight. Her obsidian hair is down and curled around her shoulders, framing her face that is alight with wonder and *peace*, while her body is pressed against mine, safe and warm.

It hasn't been an easy feat to accomplish. She's been smiling, but she's also been quiet, and I think, like the rest of us, memories of long before we became what we are now in these bodies have slowly been resurfacing. Haunting us, enlightening us, but it's been overwhelming. There have already been countless nights on these starry seas that I or Rhesa and my brothers have awoken due to dreams or nightmares, and while we don't push each other on the matter until we feel the need to discuss it, I can tell that Rhesa has been taking all that has happened to us to heart.

My brothers and I do, too, of course. Because Atlas and I spent *years* in that fucking nightmare of a sphere, and Atticus thought us and Rhesa dead. An anguish I'm sure was not easy to deal with, because at least while I was isolated and alone, lost in the bloodshed of that sphere, somewhere deep down, I could still recall that Rhesa was still alive somewhere else.

But a great deal of this all started because a girl fell in love with a star. A son of a heartless and spiteful god, and despite what occurred afterward, I know Rhesa doesn't regret any of it. But even so . . . we've all forgotten so much of the lives we've already lived, and even though she denies it, I'm sure she wonders what if she hadn't threatened Astraeus?

What if she had never met him, and therefore us?

It's a place that I refuse to conjure up in my thoughts. That's for damn sure.

I squeeze her against me, needing her closer. Her body folds with mine in all the right places, and I mind her horns as I press a kiss to the top of her head.

"Is this what you wanted, little love?"

She grasps my hand and holds it over her heart. "Tell me this is real," she orders softly.

"*This is real*, Rhesamyre," I whisper.

Yes, they found peace. As did the rest of them.
Yes, centuries later, Alastair, Atlas, and Atticus each had a
child with her.
Their sons became warriors like their fathers before them.
While their daughter became the next queen of Hell.
And her king?
A once humble, ex-Mortal Sun named Dexter.

And yes, this story is over.

ACKNOWLEDGMENTS

Holy shit . . . just . . . wow.

I don't know how to begin to express my gratitude and thanks to everyone who has supported me throughout my writing career and publishing journey. It's been a hell of a ride, but I believe this story has come to an end. From January to December, all within the same year! I took 2025 by the horns, and I owe so much to so many people.

Mom and Dad, as always, I love you. Thank you for all you do for me and all the support and unconditional love you've given me. Without ya'll, none of this would've been possible.

Mel, you're literally my ride or die. Thank you for being my mentor and friend all these years. Horses have always been a big part of my life, and that's obvious throughout this series.

The artwork was once again done by the talented Barbara J Kennerly, and my editor did a great job finding all my stray commas. Jaime Ryter, thanks again, and I hope to continue working with you both on future projects.

To all my readers both local and from faraway lands, thank you all for sticking with the series until the very end. I wrote Rhesamyre's story to entertain myself and live out my own fantasy of being the queen of Hell, but I'm glad others have been able to enjoy the books, too, haha.

I will write more books, and I hope to share those with the world in the next few years, too.

In the meantime . . . Wyatt . . . wanna get married? :)

FOLLOW ME ON INSTAGRAM FOR NEWS AND UPDATES!

AUTHOR.ISABELLEGUERNICA